she if rea   long walk in the countryside. She can remember a time when she wasn't dreaming about handsome heroes and innocent heroines. Totally her mother's fault, of course—she gave Pippa her first romance to read at the age of seven! She is inconceivably happy that she gets to share those daydreams with you. Follow her on Twitter @PippaRoscoe.

Millie Adams has always loved books. She considers herself a mix of Anne Shirley—loquacious, but charming, and willing to break a slate over a boy's head if need be—and Charlotte Doyle—a lady at heart, but with the spirit to become a mutineer should the occasion arise. Millie lives in a small house on the edge of the woods, which she finds allows her to escape in the way she loves best: in the pages of a book. She loves intense alpha heroes and the women who dare to go toe-to-toe with them. Or break a slate over their heads.

DEMANDING HIS BILLION-DOLLAR HEIR

PIPPA ROSCOE

THE SCANDAL BEHIND THE ITALIAN'S WEDDING

MILLIE ADAMS

MILLS & BOON

First Published in Great Britain 2020
by Mills & Boon, an imprint of HarperCollins*Publishers*
1 London Bridge Street, London, SE1 9GF

Demanding His Billion-Dollar Heir © 2020 by Pippa Roscoe

The Scandal Behind the Italian's Wedding © 2020 by Millie Adams

ISBN: 978-0-263-27808-8

MIX
Paper from
responsible sources
FSC® C007454

This book is produced from independently certified FSC™ paper
to ensure responsible forest management.
For more information visit www.harpercollins.co.uk/green.

Printed and bound in Spain
by CPI, Barcelona

DEMANDING HIS BILLION-DOLLAR HEIR

PIPPA ROSCOE

For Jasmine Rowlandson,
whose incredible jewellery and sculptures
ignited a wonderful spark of inspiration that became Maria.

CHAPTER ONE

STUPID, STUPID, STUPID.

What on earth had she done? Maria had fled the opulent ballroom of the Hotel La Sereine after her argument with Theo—shaking and shivering at the devastation she'd seen in both his and his fiancée's eyes, the moment she'd accidentally revealed Theo's plans to leave Sofia at the altar. Theo Tersi—the man she thought she'd loved for nearly six years.

But, she hadn't. She'd realised it the moment she'd seen the horror and grief on the faces of the engaged couple. Nothing she'd ever felt for Theo had engendered that much…pain. Maria Rohan de Luen sucked in a huge lungful of air around the tears that were now freefalling from her cheeks. Tears for them, for herself. Because she *knew* that she'd destroyed something between them that she'd been looking for herself for so, so long. Knew that what she'd *thought* she'd felt for Theo was nothing more than the desperate need to…be loved?

She cursed herself for that weakness. Part of her desperately wanted to go back, to find Sofia and explain, to apologise to Theo…but truly she feared she'd do more harm than good and instead, after taking one step forward and one back, collapsed onto the soft grass banking the smooth, mirror-like surface of the lake stretching out beneath the night sky.

She resisted the urge to peek into the depths of the water, reluctant to see what would be reflected back at her. Her hand grasped the cool glass neck of the bottle of champagne she'd been blindly holding as she'd hurled words that threatened to sever the bond between two people who very clearly loved each other. She'd never much had a taste for the stuff, but if there was ever a time to get blind drunk, at twenty-two years old, Maria decided that surely now was it.

Part of her was conscious that she was on the verge of over-indulging in self-pity, and the other part wanted to punish, believing that she didn't even deserve that selfish act. Not after what she'd just done.

Theo, her older brother's best friend, had loomed-large in her life, ever since her sixteenth birthday. Sebastian and Theo had become almost instantly joined at the hip after a mutually beneficial business deal and there wasn't a family memory in the last six years that didn't have them both in it. Maria bit back a laugh at her inner thought's use of the word 'family'. She hadn't seen her father or stepmother in almost eighteen months. And she was fine with that. In some ways they factored so little in her day to day life that occasionally a random thought or memory would catch her by surprise and remind her of them.

She wondered what her father would think of her and what had just happened. He'd probably give her that gaze, the one that said he wasn't really seeing *her*, but another woman—one he had loved so all-consumingly that he'd not been able to recover from the loss of her. Then he'd almost start when Maria would speak because it only served to show that she wasn't her mother, no matter how similar they might have looked.

She had nothing else of her mother, no memories, no heirlooms—Valeria, her stepmother, had seen to that—save but one necklace. The one she wore, *always*, even though it served as both an anchor and a homage to a woman who had died giving her life.

So no, while exiled Duke Eduardo Rohan de Luen would have been as ineffectual as always on the subject of what had just happened, Valeria would have sniffed in contempt and been only gleeful whilst declaring that she'd always known *'that boy'*, Theo Tersi, would cause nothing but trouble.

And Theo's crime? Guilt by association. Valeria had never forgiven Sebastian for the drastic measures he'd had to take to save their family from complete and utter destruction. When Maria had been eight, Eduardo had doubled down on an incredibly risky oil investment in the Middle East and lost not only his own money, but a large portion belonging to other members of Spain's nobility. A shocking and shameful moment that had seen the Rohan de Luens exiled from Spain, yet allowed to keep their hereditary title.

The only thing that had kept them from bankruptcy had been Seb who, at eighteen, had taken control of the financial purse strings and done what was needed. This included selling off almost every single piece of property and valuable item that wasn't nailed down. And for a woman who had only married Eduardo for prestige and money, Valeria hadn't taken it well at all.

For Maria? It had meant leaving behind everything she'd ever known, moving to Italy from Spain, and starting all over again. But in her heart, she'd known that the damage was already done. Suddenly unsure about even the most seemingly permanent things in life, Maria had withdrawn from friends and education, choosing instead to lose herself in her art and sculpture.

Until London's Camberwell College of Arts had accepted her on a foundation course, and she'd fallen utterly in love with the place, the people and the freedom she'd found away from her family. The friends she'd made during her degree, the little flat-share she lived in… Now, sitting on the bank of the river, all she wanted was to be back there.

She groaned out loud into the night sky and pressed the heels of her palms into the orbs of her eyes.

Oh, God, what had she done?

'Is this seat taken?'

From the first moment Matthieu had seen the figure down by Lac Peridot, some strange sense of self-preservation told him to walk away. *Run.* From the empty veranda sweeping around the ballroom of the Iondorran hotel where a charity gala was being held, he'd seen the white lace dress worn by the dark-haired woman glowing in the moonlight. Tendrils of her long, gently curled hair had hung almost down to her hips and the sudden memory of his mother's favourite painting stole his breath. He'd not seen or thought of the painting for years and when the figure had turned, for just a moment, back to the ballroom, something in her features, as clearly picked out by the moonbeams as her dress, had called to him as if across the years.

Matthieu Montcour knew better than to approach a woman so clearly lost in her own private thoughts, but he couldn't help himself. There was something almost tragically beautiful about her. And Matthieu had had his fair share of tragedy. He knew how life could be one thing in one moment and an entirely new thing in another.

He'd been about to turn away from the figure and the direction of thoughts he rarely visited, when he saw her inexpertly take a swig from the champagne bottle, failing to account for the back flow of the bubbles, and nearly smiled as the froth rushed from the mouth of the bottle forcing the woman to lean out of the way as the alcohol funnelled onto the grass beside her. Nearly smiled, because smiling was something Matthieu did very little of. The figure gave up, indelicately wiping her mouth with the back of her wrist, placing the bottle in the nest of skirts she'd made between her legs and went back to studying the lake. The carelessness about her clothing spoke to her distraction. This was no skilled seductress, his usual preferred companion. There was an innocence about her, shining, glowing, and all the more reason for him to stay away. But something about her drew him in—even though he was the last person to play white knight. No. He was the beast that mothers warned their daughters about.

Yet for the first time in years, he simply couldn't deny himself the urge to take a closer look at the woman who had caught his eye and imagination. He'd stepped away from the veranda, leaving the sights and sounds of the ballroom behind him, and slowly padded his way over the soft grass, pulling up about a metre away from where she sat.

'Is this seat taken?'

She started, peering up at him from her seat on the grass, momentary shock painting her features that righted themselves back to neutral. He'd chosen English—it being the most widely used at the gala and, as such, he figured it a safe bet, given that it was highly unlikely she spoke Swiss French.

'Standing room only, I'm afraid.'

Her response surprised him, as much as her gentle European accent. Spanish perhaps? Maybe Italian? Taking his shock for persistence, she finally inclined her head.

'Pull up a pew,' she invited.

Frowning again, and confused instantly—which was untenable to Matthieu—he chose to comment. 'That's a very English turn of phrase for such a European accent.'

'That's a very round about way of asking me where I'm from.'

And whilst Matthieu decidedly didn't like confusion, he found the slightly circuitous bent of her conversation appealing. Too many women, once they knew who he was, decided upon a brute-force attack of the sensual kind, the only thing that he would respond to. But he didn't see that jolt of recognition in her eyes. When she'd finally turned to take him in, the woman seemed only to pass over his features as if gazing over a far horizon. And damn him if there wasn't a part of him that was pleased by that.

He took a seat beside her on the comfortable grass and felt a sigh of relief escape him. He was glad to be away from the ballroom. He hated this part of his role as CEO for Montcour Mining Industries. 'Schmoozing', Malcolm called it. Matthieu preferred to call it a waste of time. But he knew better than to argue with his Managing Director, oldest friend, and one-time legal guardian. The Iondorran Minister for Trade had decided that the charity gala would be a neutral arena to test the waters of a possible joint mining venture within the small European country. Matthieu was slightly on the fence about it—unsure as to whether Iondorra actually had the financial infrastructure to take on such an ambitious project. But he wasn't ready to shoot it out of the water completely. Not yet anyway. These days Matthieu was incredibly choosy about his ventures, simply because he could be.

He saw, from the corner of his eye, the woman beside him—young, he noticed now that he was closer—wipe discreetly at her cheek. A blade of grass, or a bubble of champagne from earlier? A tear perhaps?

The action had released a trail of perfume, wafting towards him on the warm night air, teasing his senses with tones of woody sage and something almost like the sea…salt, he realised. Inexplicably his mouth watered, desire creeping through his body.

'Would you like some?'

He shook his head at the bottle she nudged with her knee. Matthieu rarely drank, refusing to allow anything to dull his senses to such an extent. But in the back of his mind, he wondered if he was already part drunk on the woman and the situation he found himself in.

They sat for a while in silence as if neither felt forced to speak. It was a blessed relief after the hours he'd spent in the gala being solicited by the Minister of Trade. Being peppered with unwanted and intrusive questions that were almost ritualistic in any negotiation. *How are you finding Iondorra? What did you think of the capital Callier? Have you tried some unnameable food the small country hailed as their own pride and joy?* The man's offence that Matthieu had driven here from Switzerland, and intended to drive back without sampling any of this proud nation's delights, had been both clear and disapproving. Not that it mattered—Matthieu hadn't bothered with such things as niceties in a long while. He didn't have to. He was Europe's fourth richest man both in private income and net worth. People came to him.

But not this woman.

'Do you think that there are some things that are un-forgivable?' she asked into the night air, without glanc-ing his way.

In truth, he couldn't imagine anything done by a girl who couldn't even drink from a champagne bottle could be unforgivable. However he knew that yes, some things were beyond forgiveness. So he chose his words carefully. 'I think there are two sides to every story.'

She seemed to take this in, as if considering her reply just as carefully.

'I broke up an engagement tonight.'

'Really?' He couldn't help the surprised word that fell from his lips. 'Well, if that's the case, he either wasn't worthy of the engagement, or she wasn't constant in her feelings enough for it.'

'That simple?' she asked of his blunt declaration.

'It usually is, once you take emotions out of it.' He was good at that. He had to be. 'Do you love him?' he asked, genuinely curious.

'I thought I did.'

He knew that feeling too. 'Then he either lied to you, or her.'

'It's not what you think. He had his reasons.'

'They always do.'

'No, I mean…he never… I never…'

He frowned at her confusion, not quite sure what she was unable to put words to.

She turned to him then for the first time and he was struck full force by her beauty. 'What is it like to be kissed?'

He let out a breath he hadn't realised he'd been holding. 'You thought you loved him, but have never been kissed?' he asked, unable to hide the incredulity from his tone.

Perhaps I don't know what love is.

She hadn't said the words out loud in that rich accented tone of hers, but her face was so expressive he could almost read her thoughts. He was used to the practised masks of women hell-bent on seduction. But hers? So open, so revealing, it distracted him for a moment.

Her skin glowed as much as her white lace dress in the beams of the moon. Flawless. Her jaw was strong, angular almost, stubborn even, but drew the eye to perfect rosebud lips slicked with just a trace of something that glistened in the night. Dark brows above dark eyes, highlighted with just a trace of mascara and liner as to outline, rather than dominate the deep rich dark eyes that stared back at him with confusion and hope—and a request he was almost one hundred per cent sure she wasn't aware of.

What is it like to be kissed?

Maria was embarrassed. Should never have asked such a question. Especially not to a man like him. She might not have known who he was—which was partly why she'd felt able to speak her mind—but she didn't have to know his name to know that he *most definitely* knew what it was like to kiss, to touch...to... She yanked her mind back before she could give away her thoughts.

A blush rose almost painfully to her cheeks and she hoped that he might not see it beneath the cover of the night sky. She felt naïve and uncouth next to him. And small. Because...his body, his presence, it was huge. She'd seen the impressive width of his arms as he'd sat down and leaned his weight back on his hands behind him. Arms and muscles that looked too wide for her to encompass with both her hands. If it hadn't been for the champagne bottle, she would have pressed her thighs together against the feeling that was growing within her. She might have been innocent, but she knew the shocking arousal sparking within her was something she rarely felt, even with Theo.

She turned away, but even then, every single feature on his face glowed within her mind. Harsh cheekbones defined by the short beard that covered the strong line of his jaw, framing lips that were almost cruelly sensual. His eyebrows hung low above eyes that were a honey-green shade of hazel, so bright almost that she could have lost herself within their depths.

She thought he wouldn't answer and almost jolted when he did speak.

'There are lots of different types of kisses. Manipulative kisses, to get what you want. Cruel kisses to punish.' Later she would wonder that he chose those two descriptions first. 'Soft, gentle kisses a mother gives her child,' he said, his tone unfathomable and causing a sudden yearning in the pit of her heart. 'Passionate, mindless kisses that are all-consuming, thoughtless and more than a little selfish.'

She turned back to him, startled to find him looking so intently at her. As if trying to figure something out. As if...no. Surely it was only her wondering what it would be like to kiss this man.

'But your first kiss? Honestly? Probably messy and awkward.'

Maria felt a little sad at that. As if somehow he'd taken away the promise of something that would be...good?

'Perhaps I should just get it out of the way, then.'

He huffed out a gentle laugh—not at her, she realised. *With* her. There was a difference.

'Perhaps,' he said ruefully.

'Would you do me a kindness, then? Would you kiss me?'

He met her gaze then, this man whose name she did not even know. And she felt it. That low hum through her body, as if his penetrating stare could reach into the depths of her soul and figure her out, understand her. That was what she'd wanted, she realised. All this time, all these years. Someone to understand. And, having done so, choose to stay.

His eyes roamed her face, looking for what, she didn't know. The hairs on her arms lifted and goosebumps raised across her skin. She resisted the urge to shiver beneath his gaze, because she was scared. Not of him, but of what was happening to her. She'd never wanted something as much as she did his kiss. He frowned for a moment, as if fighting some inner battle she couldn't imagine. He reached out his hand and raised her chin with his finger, looking at her, inspecting her almost.

'Are you sure?'

She nodded, unable to speak. Wondering if he would walk away instead, or give into this strange web woven around them, separating them from the rest of the world.

He moved slowly, as if giving her the chance to turn away, to change her mind. She watched, wide-eyed and fascinated as he bent his head towards her, and…instead of pressing his lips to hers, he passed them, pressing his cheek to hers, stroking it almost, the heat warming her skin and heart, and she heard him breathe in, as if taking her into him, only to finally turn his head back towards her and almost brush a kiss across her lips. Once, then twice.

Her heart soared at the gentle yet firm feel of his lips against hers. Something within her rose to the surface of her skin, clamouring to reach out to him, to feel more than the simple contact of his finger beneath her chin and his lips against hers.

Desperate and fearful that he might pull away, that he might take this away from her, she reached up, inexpertly, to either side of his face, the soft hair of his beard against her palm, her fingers brushing the silky thick strands of his hair. Holding him gently, pulling him back towards her in case he turned away.

His lips hovered barely a centimetre away from hers, she felt his breath against hers, she drew it into her lungs and her stomach clenched as she wished so much that she knew what to do next. Instead, they hovered on this almost kiss, fire scorching through her veins, heart beating so wildly she thought she might never find equilibrium again. Then, as one, they moved, coming together—she opened to the tongue he'd pressed against the seam of her lips and she met it with her own, the first shocking feel of him against her, inside her, filling her and delighting her completely. She lost herself to the kiss, the dance of their bodies, the impossible almost dizzying feeling that consumed her.

She felt his hands in her hair, his fingers curling into the thick tendrils and tightening just a little in a way that strangely made her feel both safe and wanted at the same time. She stretched into the feeling, trying to hold on to each different strand of emotion and desire he was wringing from her with just a kiss.

She couldn't hold back the moan of pure pleasure that fell from her lips to his and regretted it instantly as he finally broke the kiss, his forehead resting against hers, breathing as harshly as she, as if as shocked as she.

'Is it…is it always like that?' she dared to ask.

'No,' he replied darkly. 'Never.'

He took her hand in his, gently pulling it down from the side of his face, his thumb pressing against the palm of her hand soothing a little of the hurt, until it tripped over the scar that stretched over her palm to the top of her wrist. She pulled her hand away, rubbing at the scar with her thumb, not from pain but from the tingles and sparks his touch had created there.

She huffed out a little laugh, disguising her shock from the pleasure he'd just given her.

'My stepmother hates them.'

'What?' he asked as if confused.

She shot a dark look his way. Surely he hadn't missed the callouses, the little scars and nicks around the pads of her fingers, and the larger burn scar that topped the oblique arch of her palm.

'My hands. The scars. She thinks that all well-born ladies should have delicate, unblemished, dainty hands and bathe in milk daily.'

'And sleep on rose petals, I'm sure.'

'And wrap themselves in cotton wool,' she replied, continuing their word game.

'And what do you think?' he asked quietly, as if more weighed on her answer than just her thoughts about herself.

Maria turned her hands over, inspecting them impartially for the first time in a very long time. Seeing them as more than a body part, but as the tools she used to create her jewellery, to meld and mould precious metals, to create beautiful things.

'I think they speak of hard work and sacrifice, hard-earned lessons, and I am proud of every single one of them.'

It was strange to hear her talk of the thing that had blighted so much of his life in a way that was full of pride and defiance rather than disgust or sick fascination. He had certainly met both those reactions. And then there was the other kind. The women who simply viewed what he could give them, in spite of the scars that covered almost half of his torso. The women who were more interested in his wealth or what pleasure he could give them.

'You wouldn't understand,' she said dismissively and he laughed. Properly then, out loud, from deep within him. She turned back to him, curiosity shining in her eyes.

He nodded once, quickly loosening his tie, releasing the button behind it and, moving his head to the side, he pulled slightly at the collar of his shirt. He knew that she would see the tendrils of scars that licked at his neck glinting in the moonlight. Then held out his arm, the same side of his body, and released the cufflink that held his shirt sleeves in place to reveal the edges of the scars that reached from his neck to his wrist.

'I'm sorry.'

As he secured the cufflink, forgoing the button at his neck, he reflected that he'd heard that phrase so many times. From the doctors and nurses who had originally treated him, even from Malcolm. And worse, from the women who decided they couldn't bear to be near him, to touch him. They'd all held *that* tone. Apologetic and, more often than not, disgusted. But this woman's voice held neither of those and for the first time he found himself asking, 'For what?'

'That you feel you have to hide them.'

A jolt passed through his body. No one had ever said that to him. No one had ever accepted his scars so simply and his mind went blank. Well. Almost blank. Because suddenly he was plunged back into the memory of their kiss. He'd not lied when he'd said that a kiss had never been like that for him.

Even now he felt the throb of desire coiled tight within him. His heart was still racing, which had probably accounted for why he had shown her his scars. Perhaps unconsciously he'd been trying to scare her away. Because she was threatening to undo him in a way he'd never experienced before.

'Passionate, mindless kisses that are all-consuming, thoughtless and more than a little selfish.'

His words came back to haunt him and he realised the truth of them. Because it had made him selfish. Her kiss had made him want more, a need rising within him, demanding to be heard and satisfied. *More.* He laughed at himself cynically. He didn't just want more, he wanted it all. Everything she could give him. Need fired his blood, throbbing thick and heavily through his veins. He desperately fought the urge to haul her into his lap and simply feast on her like the beast he was.

'They're from smelting,' she said, cutting through the raging desire he felt and pulling him back to the present. 'It's—'

'I know what smelting is.' His voice had come out harsher than he'd intended and she had noticed, if her look of confusion was anything to go by. 'Professional interest. Mining.'

She nodded as if that explained everything, including his seven-point-four-billion-dollar net worth that she clearly didn't know about. 'You don't like it though,' she stated.

'I don't like fire.'

'I can't work without it,' she replied, not dwelling on the probable cause of his injuries. She tapped the series of silver bracelets hanging loosely on her wrist. Jewellery. She must make jewellery.

He wished she hadn't said that. Because now there was an image of her taming molten silver, harnessing the power of fire and heat—his greatest foe—and bending it to her will. It would require a greater deal of strength than he'd thought her capable of only ten minutes before. But looking at her now, the pride and innate confidence about her work…her scars even, made her glorious to him.

'One of your own making?'

'Yes. My first piece,' she said lovingly of the simple silver band, not smooth like so many others, but beaten, textured, perfectly imperfect.

Matthieu hadn't realised how strong the cast of light was from the ballroom until it went out. The charity gala had ended and the staff of the hotel had clearly finished their clean up. A brief glance at his watch showed that it was nearly two a.m.

'What are you going to do now?' he asked, almost reluctantly.

She shook her head and shrugged a delicate shoulder. 'Not sure. I can't go back to the suites as my brother will be there and I'm not ready to…' Her rich accented voice trailed off.

'You can't stay out here all night.'

He might be a bastard, but he wasn't that much of a bastard. She had started to shiver as if the gentle light from the hotel behind them had offered both warmth and illumination. He shrugged out of his jacket and placed it around her shoulders, resisting the urge to smooth down the material that swamped her small frame. She smiled her thanks up at him and he cursed the innocence shining in her eyes. If only…

'The hotel is fully booked from the gala. You can have my suite.'

And for the first time that night it was as if his words had broken the spell. There, finally, was that hesitation, that sense of insecurity about his intentions, about him. It was only to be expected, from women who got in over their heads, women who weren't quite ready to 'bed the beast' as he'd heard one such descriptor of himself. She need not worry. He could never touch an innocent such as her.

'You will have it to yourself. Alone,' he concluded firmly.

'What about you?'

'I'll be fine,' he said, standing, firmly tucking his desires and wants for her away. He held out his hand to her. 'Come.'

CHAPTER TWO

MARIA FOLLOWED HIM through the dark halls of the hotel, still clutching the bottle of champagne she had snagged earlier in the evening, thankful that he had his wits about him when hers felt as if they'd fled. Because at first when he'd told her that she could have his suite, she'd been momentarily unsure. But when he had added that she'd have it to herself, alone, she'd been…disappointed.

Which was silly. Even she could recognise that. After all, she'd told him that she'd been in love with another man only hours ago. But Theo had never, *ever*, installed feelings that this man had conjured from her with his presence, his touch…his lips.

She knew she should be ashamed, but she couldn't quite bring the feeling to mind. His impressively broad shoulders took up almost the entire width of the hallway she followed him down, gentle night lighting casting him in shadows. He was huge in comparison to her. Maria didn't usually consider herself small at five foot four, but he must be well over a foot taller than her.

He drew up short at the last doorway at the end of the corridor. Turning to one side, he slid the slim black key card over the electronic plate beneath the handle, pushed the door open and gestured for her to enter.

She stepped past him, registering the oaky cologne

that made her think of autumnal woods, earth and something else…something musky and enticing. Her thoughts on that, it took her a moment to recognise the sheer opulence of the room she had entered and she nearly gasped.

Yes, her family might have once been well versed in luxury, but her little flat-share in South London had adjusted her expectations. And this? Plush cream carpets met floor-to-ceiling windows looking out at the stunning night panorama of Lac Peridot, her gaze instantly drawn to where the two opposing mountains met low in the distance.

From the corner of her eye she could make out almost obscenely expensive furnishings and a doorway that presumably led to a bedroom and en suite bathroom, perhaps. But she couldn't tear her eyes away from the view from the windows, just beyond which she could see a small wooden deck with a table and chairs.

She turned, expecting to find him right behind her, *wanting* to even, but instead, she was surprised to find him hovering at the threshold as if reluctant to enter.

'I don't even know your name,' she said, her words a whisper that pitched somewhere between humour and surprise.

'Do you need it?' he asked with a small answering smile curving his lips.

'I'd like to thank you properly.'

'Matthieu.'

She repeated his name, the word rolling off her tongue, shaped by her accent, and read sudden and shocking desire in his eyes as she did so. She felt it. Bound to it, to him. Firing in her a confidence she didn't know that she possessed.

'Thank you, Matthieu.'

He shook his head, dismissing her thanks, and made to turn, but she wasn't ready for him to go. Not yet.

'I—' she said, halting his departure, but also desperately searching for something to say, something to bring him into the suite, to her. 'I told you a secret. Before you go, would you share one with me?'

He frowned then, as if remembering her earlier confession, as if choosing whether to give into her request, and something passed over his features, something hard won.

'What? Like my favourite colour?' he asked, stalking towards her silently on the plush carpet.

'No,' she said, casting her head to one side, taking the entire breadth of him in her gaze. 'It's blue,' she asserted and then smiled when she caught the look of surprise. 'Your suit is deep blue, your watch straps are blue leather.' She shrugged her shoulder.

'That simple?'

'It usually is,' she replied, using his words from earlier that evening. He liked that, she could tell and it warmed her strangely, somewhere beneath her breast bone.

He had reached her and, now that they were standing so close, she had to crane her neck back to look at him. He really was breathtaking, his piercing eyes, a colour similar to rich honey, bearing down into hers.

'It's my birthday,' he said, his voice barely above a whisper, as if it really was a secret to be shared.

'Truly?' she asked as a wide smile pulled at her mouth.

'I don't…usually do celebrations,' he said somewhat distastefully.

She wanted to tell him then that she understood. That she hated her birthday too. But it felt…too personal, too intrusive. His birthday was about him. Not her. She pulled up the bottle of champagne she still clutched, and offered it to him, wondering whether he would take a sip this time.

He gently took the neck of the bottle in his large hands, put it to his lips, making sure there was enough air angled in the throat of the bottle not to funnel the bubbles over him.

But not once did he take his eyes from hers. After he'd taken a mouthful, he passed the bottle back to her and she placed her lips where his had been. The knowledge of it fired her blood once again, bringing a blush to her cheeks and the low v between her breasts. She followed his actions as she took a sip, faintly happy that she didn't end up with a face full of bubbles and look as naïve as she felt in that moment.

She didn't know what she was doing...how to do what she wanted to. And she really wished that weren't the case. Wished, suddenly, for experience to entice, to draw him to her. To know whether it was just her enthralled to this madness.

Matthieu could see it—what her body was asking for—and feared that she wasn't even aware of it. And God help anyone when she became aware of her power. The beauty of this woman could fell armies.

'You know my name,' he stated.

She smiled and nodded her head slowly, understanding the implied question, and delighting in teasing him for it. And surprisingly, he liked it. That teasing sense of her with no emotional undercurrent or ulterior motive. He watched as the teasing morphed into something else...something more primal yet serious.

'Maria. Maria Rohan de Luen.' It was said with a slightly Spanish flare and he mentally rolled it around his mind, liking the way it bounced within him. Unconsciously he mouthed the words, drawing her attention to his lips. The way she looked at his mouth caused that infernal beast within him to roar with pride and need and all the things he knew he should lock down tight. He should not be here. Not tonight, when this woman was threatening his cast-iron defences against things he had not thought of for years.

A timely reminder and one he needed to heed. He nodded once, to himself at his decision made, and then again at Maria, silently bidding her adieu. Because if he didn't leave here soon, he might not leave at all. And she was too pure, too innocent for that. Had never been kissed until this night.

He gave her an almost apologetic smile, the gesture unfamiliar on his lips, and turned to go. He had reached the door, his fingers around the handle before her words stopped him.

'Before you go, can I ask one more thing?'

He turned his head, not a single clue as to what she might ask for. But whatever had run through his mind, it hadn't been what she proceeded to say.

'Would you show me your scars?'

White noise was all he could hear in his mind and below that, somewhere deeper, a furious roar, snarling and gnashing as if some great wound had been reopened. It must have shown on his face, because Maria took a step back for which he felt instantly regretful. He didn't want her to be scared. But she would be if she saw them. They all were.

Instantly he was transported back to the first time he'd bared himself to a woman. At seventeen, he'd been naïve enough to think that Clara had cared for him. The swift fury that streaked through him at the memory of betrayal had him turning away from Maria.

But…

'I'm sorry.'

'For what?'

'That you feel you have to hide them.'

And why couldn't he show them to Maria? It wasn't as if he would ever see her again after this night, not once he left this room. She'd found strength and pride in her own scars, but what would she find in his?

'They're not pretty,' he warned.

'I don't care for pretty,' she responded defiantly, not once taking her eyes from his. There was that strength again. The steel that he recognised encased in soft perfection.

Gritting his teeth, he turned and stalked back to her, lifting his shirt from his trousers as he did so. One by one he undid the shirt buttons and still she didn't drop her gaze. The women he usually spent his time with either hungrily sought out the scars that had fuelled his reputation as a beast, or were barely interested in anything above his belt.

Having reached the last button, he took one last look at her before shrugging out of the white shirt and casting it aside, standing there before her unwavering gaze. Maria didn't break the connection between their eyes, not immediately and he gave her credit for that. But finally he closed his eyes, unwilling and unable to see those beautiful features puckered with disgust.

He felt her close the distance between them, the heat from her body pressing against his skin. The *undamaged* skin, because his nerves had been dulled by the injured tissue and skin grafts that covered nearly half of his torso. He felt her circle him, could have sworn he felt the weight of her gaze sparking a thousand starbursts across his body, even the damaged parts. He sensed when she had come back to face him and braced himself as he opened his eyes. But where he had expected revulsion and horror, even the morbid fascination he occasionally experienced, instead he saw wonder and something like awe.

Maria was enthralled. Utterly and completely. *I don't like fire*, that was what Matthieu had said. Yes, his torso had been badly disfigured from the scars that swept around his forearm and reached up to his neck, where she'd seen the silvery traces earlier in the evening. They covered almost half of his chest and, she had seen, wrapped around his flanks and up across his shoulder blades. The twists of tissue, strangely pale, nearly white against his tanned skin, and in some places shiny and criss-crossed from what she could only presume to be many, many skin grafts to help the full thickness burns she could see were from years ago.

The patterns she found on his chest were painfully beautiful to her and she couldn't even imagine the kind of agony he must have experienced for these to heal, nor the time it must have taken. His skin had reformed over the powerful muscles of his arms, just as large as she'd imagined, and the scars rippled over the muscles in his abdomen, the powerful outline of a six pack that spoke to a brutal physical training regime. Because that was what screamed at her most as he stood there, shirtless, his lower limbs encased in low-slung blue superfine trousers. Strength and raw power. Power that was almost straining at some kind of self-imposed leash.

'What do you see?' he asked. Demanded almost.

And she said the words that had come to her mind. 'Magnificence.' *Raw masculinity*, but she couldn't let herself say that last out loud. Because it spoke too much to her desire for him. It would have betrayed her.

She reached out a hand, but he caught it in the air between them. His large fingers wrapping easily, firmly but gently, around her slim wrist.

She threw her gaze to his, aware that her breath had hitched in her lungs. Aware that her skin was on fire as surely as his had once been. But hers was an invisible flame, one created by him and the need to feel his skin against the palm of her hand. Not from curiosity, but the desperation to make that connection. To feel that same incredible sensation she had experienced when they had kissed earlier. And then she realised to her shame how selfish that was. Just as he'd said earlier about passion. But it was more than that. She wanted to be with him, to soothe that ragged sense of...of...she couldn't put a name to what she saw in his eyes.

She pressed past her hand, still clasped in his, and closed the distance between their bodies. He held himself still, but she could see what an effort that took and she was torn...torn between recognising the stress he put himself under and the need to offer consolation. Instinct won out and she pressed a gentle kiss to his chest, on his pectoral muscle that had the twist and turn of a scar that had shaped itself in such a way that made her think of a great white oak tree, gnarled but majestic.

She traced the trail her lips covered across his chest with her free hand, delighting in the hitch in his breathing as cruel as it was. Because she wanted him with her in this. As utterly devastated and destroyed by the attraction that flamed between them. Though she was innocent, she could recognise the desire in his eyes, recognise it because she felt it within herself.

Pressing another kiss in the centre of his chest, she

felt oddly exposed, wanting his arms to wrap around her, hide her from the passion that was almost overwhelming her. He was so broad that she realised only lower around his waist would her arms meet were she to encircle him. But one hand was still captured by his, and the rapid rise and fall of Matthieu's chest was the only outward sign that he was not made of stone.

No. This man would never have been made of stone… pure silver, she thought, only just tempered, still seething with heat from the furnace, still malleable, but just as dangerous. A quiver of desire racked her body and only then did Matthieu finally release her hand. She looked up into eyes that were boring down into hers.

'Stop.'

'Why?'

'You don't know what you're doing. What you're asking for,' he stated, almost angrily.

'I may be naïve—'

'Maybe? You are an innocent, Maria. A true innocent.'

'Does that mean I don't know what I want?'

'It means you don't understand the *implications* of what you want.'

'Would anyone?' she asked.

'This is something that you should do with someone capable of staying with you.'

No one ever stays, her mind voiced, batting away each and every one of his arguments. She knew, deep down, that this was what she wanted with her entire being. She had never been more sure of anything, half fearful that if he walked away now she would have lost something that she had only dreamed of in the darkest of nights and the deepest of sleeps.

'I haven't asked for anything more than this night.'

* * *

Matthieu had been wrong. She *was* a seductress. A tempt-ress. Offering him something he could barely stand to walk away from. She was so beautiful, so pure…the light to his darkness and he would drag her down with him if he gave her what she wanted.

I haven't asked for anything more than this night.

He had never allowed himself to take anything so pure. His chosen bedfellows were ones who understood. Who knew the game. Pleasure to be given and received and nothing more. Because he had learned long ago that anything more was a foolish dream. And he refused to be the one to teach Maria that lesson.

But he couldn't help the thought that if he turned away now, if he left her alone, it might break something deep within him.

He shut that thought down as quickly as it had formed in a mental move practised over many years. What he was considering was madness. But then she pressed another kiss to his chest and everything in him was plunged into thick swathes of desire and need, and he felt the growl start at the back of his throat, desperate to stifle it before it escaped into the room.

'Please?' she asked between the infernal kisses she was drawing on his body, his skin, the places usually specifically avoided by others.

'Don't you see, Maria? You shouldn't have to beg for this.'

'I am not begging, I am asking. This is my choice. My request. Stay with me, just for this night. Please.'

And finally Matthieu lost the battle. The battle against being decent, walking away and leaving Maria un-touched. Because he could stand it no longer. He wanted to touch her, feel her smooth skin, so pale against his it seemed almost to glow. He wanted to tease pleasure from her so much that it was almost a physical ache within him. Finally he was about to live down to his reputation as a beast in the truest sense, because he felt the last vestige of restraint burn to dust beneath her lips.

This time he was unable to stifle the growl that rose in the back of his throat, as he wrapped his arms around her, drawing her to him and feasting on her lips as he'd wanted to from that very first moment.

This was no practised, gentle first kiss, this was desire, desperation even, as he plunged the depths of her mouth with his tongue, drawing little mewls of pleasure from her. Her hands, now free, swept into his hair, pulling him further down towards her. Not enough, he thought, it was nowhere near enough.

He lifted her up, so that her legs wrapped around his waist, and her lips met his, until finally he nudged her head aside and found the delicate, smooth arc of her neck and pressed open-mouthed kisses against her skin, lathing it with his tongue. Maria's head fell back, exposing the pale column of her neck and the v of her perfect breasts, accentuated by the silver necklace dipping between them.

He marvelled at how light she was. He could have held her there for an eternity. But her body shifted restlessly in his arms, wanting more, demanding it. She might have not known the words, but her body knew the moves, instinct driving them closer together in their need.

He carried her through to the bedroom, not once breaking the contact between his lips and her skin. As he placed her on the edge of the bed, he cursed. Her pupils so large her eyes were almost completely black, she was drunk on desire.

'Are you sure?'

'Never more so,' she said with a faint smile, faint only because the rest of her features were a mask of pure need and want.

'I need you to understand that you can stop this at any time. *Any* time.'

'You want me to give you a safe word?'

He barked a laugh at the mock coquettishness in her tone. 'No, I don't want a bloody safe word.' The sudden and surprising humour delighting him and, from the look in her eyes, Maria too. As if somehow she'd known they needed a moment, a brief respite from the all-consuming passion that had driven them this far. 'What do you know of safe words?' he queried.

'I may be innocent, but I'm not naïve.'

He dragged in a lungful of air, looking at her in the half light of the moon, cast through the large windows fronting the entire side of the room. Her white lace dress hanging low on her shoulders, exposing collarbones so enticing, he couldn't resist.

He leaned forward, Maria shifting her legs apart to give him room, and placed kisses there, his lips meeting the hard bone covered in soft skin and sucking gently. He pulled back only to place his forehead against hers.

'I want you to know that you can say "no", at any point. I want you to be *able* to say it.'

'I don't want you to stop, Matthieu. I want you to kiss me. To touch me, to—'

He couldn't take any more of her desires, he was battling enough of his own, so he stifled her words with a kiss. Her lips opened for him, offering him entry and damnation at the same time.

He gently pulled at the thin lace of the dress, exposing the smooth pale planes of her chest, the silver necklace she wore a guide line as he leaned her back against the soft bed and kissed his way towards her breasts. The rosy tips stark against the gleaming white skin. He took one in his mouth, his tongue sweeping over the stiff peak, drawing a moan of pleasure from her body and bringing her closer, pressing into his mouth instinctively.

In one hand he fisted the lacy material of her dress, drawing the material tight against her leg. She was glorious in her pleasure and he reached for her thigh, bringing it up on the bed, and feeling the length of her calf, the smoothness of her thigh, more. He wanted more.

Releasing his hold on the delicate lace he'd bunched around her waist, he pressed kisses against the plane of her skin where her hip dipped naturally, leading him to the flat stretch of her stomach, as he gently pressed her thigh to the side with one hand and drew her white panties down with the other to expose the dark curls between her legs.

He cradled her backside in one hand, gently pulling her body towards his, as he slipped the silky material down her thighs and away from her ankles. He ignored the slight tremor of his hands, the almost painful arousal pressing against the seam of his trousers, as he spread her before him and bent forward to taste, to delight in the secret heart of her. The taste of her sweet wet heat was almost too much for him to bear, but he would. He wanted to give her every pleasure she could experience.

Maria was shaking. Never before had she felt anything like this. Pleasure so acute and so extreme, she trembled, a thin sheen of sweat breaking out across the back of her neck. Her hips bucked against the exquisite torture his tongue was wringing from her body and she bit her hand to prevent the cry of sheer pleasure that wanted to escape from her lips. The other fisted the sheets of the bed, anchoring herself to something, anything, before her body threatened to drift away on a tide of pleasure so powerful she feared she might never return.

Rolling waves covered her body, as if desperately trying to reach the shore, but not quite, not yet. Again and again they bit at the edge of her body, threatening to drag her under. Then Matthieu threaded a finger deep within her, the pressure inside her coiling tight, her body unconsciously trying to hold him within her.

Her pleas became unintelligible demands, her breathing both desperate and stifled at the same time, her body on the brink of something she couldn't quite define, waves ebbing and flowing faster and faster until…

The orgasm he had wrung from her body plunged her deep beneath the surface of the water, the pounding waves now all she could hear as her body shook and shuddered, soothed only when she felt Matthieu's arms come around her, cocoon her in his embrace, keeping her safe and anchored to him while her soul soared towards the night sky.

As if on a string tied to him, her mind returned to the man surrounding her, caging her as if trying to keep out the night, the dark…the morning perhaps. Her arms reached around his trim waist, feeling along the powerful muscles bracketing his hips, and meeting the soft midnight-coloured material of his trousers. They were still clothed, she both marvelled and regretted. She wanted to feel him, all of him, against her skin, without barriers. Her hands sought out the fastening of his trousers and he shifted as if realising her intention.

Matthieu leaned back, almost regretting the loss of contact. For the first time ever he had found something like peace in her pleasure, in offering something of himself to another. But one look at the determined jut of her jaw, the challenge in her eyes daring him to ask her if she might want to stop, ironically only fuelled his need for her, as yet unquenched and unsatisfied.

Slowly he reached for the button of his trousers, gliding the zip down and loosening the stranglehold the material had on his crotch. His erection jutted free as he swept his trousers and underwear over his hips, down his legs, and kicked them away.

He watched and waited as she took in the sight of him, the unconscious way her tongue curved over her bottom lip and the teeth that plunged into the soft, wet pink flesh. He groaned again at the effect she had on him and his heart almost stopped as she reached for the hem of her white lace dress and pulled it up, over her thighs and hips, over her chest and head, casting it to some distant part of the room. She was glorious, her legs bent at the knee, sitting up, only her hands fisting the sheets of the bed giving expression to the barely leashed desire he felt meeting his own.

He reached into his wallet and retrieved the packet, tearing the foil with his teeth, not once taking his eyes from her. He watched her eyes grow wide with fascination as he rolled the condom over his length, her gaze glancing between his face and his erection, and if he'd had any doubts as to her certainty, the way she parted her legs, making room for him as he came down between them, burned them from his mind.

He leaned to support his weight on one elbow, the fingers of his free hand dipping and tripping over the skin from the centre of her collarbone, following the silver lines of her necklace down the irresistible v between her breasts, and over the gentle swell of her abdomen.

Maria's body gently shivered in the wake of his fingers and he couldn't help but press his lips to the centre of her chest. Her hands swept to either side of his face, fingers splaying in his hair and nails gently scraping against his scalp. He leant into her touch, kissing her wrist, and finally turned back to her watchful gaze.

A slight nod was all he needed from her as he gently pressed into her, forcing himself to go slowly despite how everything roared within him for instant completion. The damp wet heat of her surrounding him was so incredible it rendered him mindless, but not heedless, as he felt her stiffen beneath him, bringing an instant halt to his movements.

The hitch in her breath, the slight frown to her brows, through which he held his breath. If she wanted him to stop he'd do it. It might kill him, but he'd do it. But she didn't. She looked into his eyes, as if understanding the battle that waged within him, a small smile pulling at the curve of her lips. 'Please?'

'Please what, Maria? Because—'

'Don't stop. Please don't stop.'

Her hand swept around his neck and pulled him to her, into her kiss, into her more deeply and into an insatiable madness he didn't know he'd survive. Slowly he began to move, his hips gently driving into her depths, feeling her completely encase him, and he wondered somewhere if this was what he'd been missing his entire life. Her.

Maria's breaths became faster, her moans, full of pleasure and need, filled the air between them. Her hips raised against his, holding him within her, deeper and longer… The rhythm *she* was setting, *she* was dictating, one that only fired his blood and his arousal to a point where he didn't know whose heartbeat he could feel in his chest.

He reached beneath her and drew her closer to him, his chest pressed against hers, inhaling the sweet scent of her at the edge of her neck, the soft curls of her long hair tickling the skin on his chest. Soon thought became ephemeral, words intangible, and all he knew was her and the exquisite feeling of losing himself within her depths. Need and arousal became his oxygen and he inhaled it like a drowning man, intoxicated by her, lost to her.

As he felt her tighten around him, heard the way her breath hitched at its highest point, he knew they were both on the edge, on the brink, and one final thrust of his hips saw them cut their ties to the night and melt away.

Through the night hours, between sleep and waking, they reached for each other, finding pleasure, seeking more, and as the sun's early morning rays tripped into the room Maria spread her arm out behind her feeling only the cool silky sheets beneath her palm. Matthieu had done what he'd promised. Given her one night and then…left.

CHAPTER THREE

MARIA SHIFTED ON the seat to relieve the pins and needles that were creeping around the base of her spine. Her knee tapped an incessant rhythm, partly because after three and a half hours of sitting there, she really needed to go to the bathroom.

The foyer of the office building in Switzerland was immaculate—all concrete and steel—but faintly cold in the encroaching evening's darkness. The silver letters of Montcour Mining rose high above the reception desk she'd not been allowed to pass. Her knee bobbed away, which the blond haired male receptionist misunderstood and took as a sign of impatience.

She'd studied every inch of the two large canvasses bracketing the broad wooden-fronted desk. Rothko. In all probability real rather than reproduction. She deduced this not from the fine artistry, but more from the research she had done to discover Matthieu's last name and location.

It had been three months since she'd seen him. Two since she'd started to feel the waves of nausea that had completely taken her by surprise. One month since one little blue line had changed her life for ever, and only a few days since she'd had the first scan that truly confirmed that her life—*their* lives—had changed for ever.

Maria had thought she'd have to spend hours trawling through reams of pages on the Internet and had already considered reaching out to Princess Sofia, who had patronised the charity where Maria had met Matthieu for a list of attendees that night. Having reunited with Theo, Sofia had forgiven Maria for her indiscreet argument with Theo. It had been swept under the carpet with happiness and love that shined from the couple on their wedding day.

In the past, thinking of such a thing would have brought her the sharp agony of unrequited love—but that was before Matthieu and before... Her hand unconsciously swept over her abdomen. She avoided another glare from the frustrated receptionist, by focusing on the beautiful modern chandelier suspended from a ceiling that rose at least ten stories high. The lights fiercely illuminating the space, yet tempered and golden hued to soften the impact on the eye. The building screamed money. But then when a person was as wealthy as Matthieu Montcour it could be afforded.

She supposed that many would have considered themselves lucky to be tied to such a wealthy man. She was not one of those people and instead was more concerned about how *he* might feel being tied to *her*.

She had left his suite in Iondorra that morning and returned to find a furious Sebastian ready to read her the Riot Act for disappearing the night before. But he'd taken one look at her and when she had asked to go home, he'd relented and taken her back to her flat-share in South London.

For a month she had lost herself in days full of work, her jewellery making and her part-time coffee-shop job. But her nights? They were lost to dreams of Matthieu and the pleasure he'd wrung from her body.

In Camberwell, the daily reality of her life trudged on and he became something almost mythical to her, fantastical and almost imagined. She'd not said a word about him to Anita, or Evin, her two flatmates, who she'd met in the first week of her Foundation Course.

After the staunchness of her Italian schooling, Camberwell had been both a breath of fresh air and truly liberating. She fell hard for the heady mix of cultures, the strange juxtaposition of houses worth millions and council estates worth almost nothing. She felt as if it suited her life, having known both sides, extreme wealth and sudden shocking poverty after her father's near bankruptcy and subsequent exile from Spain.

She risked a glance at the imperious receptionist banging away on a keyboard as if it might make her disappear. But Maria wasn't going anywhere.

One month ago, after the third week of being unable to hold in her nausea, Anita had handed her a pregnancy test, given her a small smile, a pat on the arm, a cup of tea—so very English—and left her to it. Maria barely remembered the following two days. She had been numb with shock and battered by so many unanswered and unanswerable questions, and only one thought had remained constant. Remained true.

I'm keeping the baby.

She promised herself that once she reached three months, once she'd had her first scan, only then would she tell Matthieu.

The clipped sound of stiletto heels machine-gun-fired across the marble foyer, drawing Maria into the present. An obscenely glamorous woman in an ankle-length wool coat with a fur trim swept an about-turn to face a trio of sheepish-looking men in suits.

'That man is absolutely impossible. No wonder they

call him a beast.' The last word was hissed, as if to be conveyed in a whisper, but rang like a bell.

Maria had no doubt as of whom she was speaking. Not after her Internet search of Matthieu. She'd had two words. His name, and mining—his 'professional interest'. She hadn't held up much hope, but she'd been wrong. A second after she'd hit enter, the screen had filled with the image of his face—a stern headshot, his piercing golden eyes so intense she'd felt a blush rise to her cheeks as if he could see her searching for him.

'No wonder he's as rich as Croesus, when he's that tight-fisted with his business interests.'

Maria had discovered that too. Reportedly he was the fourth richest man in Europe. And it had shocked her. Clearly he had been wealthy, must have been to gain entry to the gala, but reports stated that his net worth was near eight billion. *Billion.*

But it had come at such a terrible cost. She'd gasped as she'd read descriptions of the fire that had not only consumed the estate where Matthieu had lived as a child, but also his entire family. The one that had caused the scars she'd felt beneath the soft palm of her hand, hard and twisted, but somehow also defiant and magnificent. The sheer number of articles on the years of treatments was surpassed only by the fascination with the shocking amount of the life insurance heaped upon an eleven-year-old boy, making him unimaginably wealthy independent of his family's business. Maria's heart had broken at the grainy images from years ago of the small boy accompanied by his, then, legal guardian following behind five coffins: his parents, two uncles and one aunt. She couldn't even conceive how devastating that must have been.

As the woman swirled back towards the exit, taking

the suits and the drama with her, Maria was dragged into the present and stifled a wave of nausea as the woman's sickly perfume reached her on the ruffled air.

The receptionist cleared his throat and stood, apparently having reached the end of his patience at housing the unwanted and uninvited guest in his domain.

'I'm afraid I'm going to have to ask you to—'

'Maria?'

Her head turned to the bank of elevators tucked off to the right of the reception desk to see Matthieu Montcour looking as shocked as she suddenly felt at seeing him in the flesh again after twelve weeks.

Matthieu watched her spring up from the sofa she'd been sitting on, a bundle of energy in the almost silent reception.

'Where's your bathroom?' she asked breathlessly, her tone betraying her desperation.

'It's—'

'I'm sorry, this isn't how I wanted this to go, it's just that I really...' she did a little dip as if to punctuate her need '...*really* need the bathroom. Please don't go anywhere, we need to talk, it's just that I need the—'

'Bathroom. Got it. Round the corner on the left,' he said, gesturing with his arm.

She ran, literally ran around the corner, skidding a little on her boot heels as she rushed through the doors.

And he couldn't help but laugh. A sound startling to his own ears, let alone his stiff receptionist.

He shook his head, trying to jolt himself free from the effect of her sudden and shocking appearance. It wasn't as if he hadn't thought of her in the last three months, thought of finding her, his fingers itching to type her name into the search engine on his computer. In truth, there hadn't been a day—or night—that he hadn't remembered her soft sighs, or the feel of her beneath him. The wrenching he'd felt that morning after, when he'd sneaked out of the room, leaving her asleep in the bed of his suite. Both hating himself and knowing that it was right.

But why was she here? What did she want?

Then a cold steel clamp choked his thoughts.

She knew. Who he was.

And just like so many women before him, Maria had come to cash in on his notoriety. Had thought to play on the vulnerabilities he'd accidentally exposed that night. The one night he'd offered her and no more.

Anger clenched his jaw. He had thought her different. He had thought her to be something…almost mythical in her purity. A purity that he had single-handedly taken that night. He should have known better. Had he not learned at seventeen what the female sex wanted from him?

The sound of her boots on the marble floor cut through his thoughts and he turned to find her looking up at him nervously, her hands twisting within each other, but valiantly bearing the weight of his scrutiny as he searched her expressive features for clues of her motivation for being here.

She was still breathtakingly beautiful. He'd half convinced himself that he'd imagined it. The shocking impact she'd had on him that night. The way that his pulse kicked up a notch, just being near her. The way his need rose within him to seize him by the throat.

'Hi,' she said simply.

He nodded, unable to trust himself to say more. To bring about the moment where she exposed her greed.

'Can we…?'

'Talk?'

She nodded, an almost sad smile on her features. And

for a moment he almost felt sorry for her. Because while she obviously knew who he was, she clearly did not realise just who she was up against.

'This way,' he said, his words as clipped as the sound of their shoes as he led them to the last elevator.

He swiped his key card over the electronic plate and the doors swished apart revealing the mirror-lined lift that led only to the top floor where his offices were housed.

She silently followed him into the confined space and when he inhaled he was swamped by that scent of hers. Sage and salt, something so unique to her and that night that he had to fight against the sudden wave of desire that rose up within him from being this close to her.

He studied her in the mirrors, Maria determinedly looking ahead and not making eye contact, offering him the chance to take in her appearance. The night they'd met, she had been dressed in white lace. Now, she wore tight grey denim jeans and a black leather waterfall jacket that covered a loose T-shirt in a burnt-pink colour.

Her hair, loose again, fell in waves over her shoulders and down her back, the slight curls twisting strands of dark browns and reds, making him want to reach out and touch. But he stifled the ridiculous urge.

The elevator drew to a stop and the doors opened, prompting him to gesture for her to go first, and then he realised how silly that was, when she pulled up short in the large area between three glass-fronted rooms. Two of which were meeting rooms, the third, his office.

He stepped around her and entered the latter. Immediately regretting not showing her to one of the large meeting rooms and ensuring that she would be ill at ease and more likely to reveal the truth about her intentions under such stark surroundings.

Instead, his office was completely different. Dark

brown leather sofas faced each other, with a corner chair bracketing the end nearest the side wall. A discreet unit fronted the rest of the wall on the other side of a hidden door in the panelling that led to a bathroom and shower unit. A fireplace was hidden by the large corner chair— one that he never used and tried as much as possible to ignore behind the smooth dark leather. His father had loved it when this office had been his and, as much as he'd wanted to brick it up, he couldn't seem to do so.

The opposite wall, in front of which was his desk, was covered head to toe in shelves full of books. Beautiful leather-spined tomes that gave the room an almost gothic feel, despite the sleek modern technology that covered the desk. Two large monitors fed into a discreet desktop hidden on a lower-level shelf just beneath the surface of the desk—a feature that had forced him to raise the desk a few inches in order to seat his long legs comfortably and without taking his kneecaps off every time he sat.

He turned to watch Maria take in the space.

'Would you care for a drink?' he asked, his hands un-accountably reaching for the bottle of whisky that had re-mained largely untouched for the three years it had been in his office's wet bar.

'Sparkling water, please.'

Where had the woman so full of words and even a bit of humour gone? Perhaps it was him. Was she picking up on his cynical reaction to her presence?

He poured sparkling water over ice, the cubes splin-tering and fracturing beneath the liquid in each glass. He passed Maria's drink to her and was about to say some pithy salutation when she blurted, 'I'm pregnant.'

The glass hovered before his lips, his fingers gripping it so hard, his knuckles turned white from his apparent shock. His eyes went from speculative to furious in a heartbeat and Maria inwardly cursed, wishing she'd had the courage to say it more gently, to warn him… Anything other than what she'd just thrown between them like an unexploded bomb. Only it wasn't unexploded. It had detonated three months earlier, though neither of them had known.

'Congratulations. Who is the lucky man?'

Maria frowned, both shocked and confused by his question.

'What do you mean?' she said, wondering why she was still holding the glass of water and he his, as if they were having a polite exchange rather than the fact he'd just implied that…that…

'Well, given that we used protection, *every single time*—'

'Wait, what?'

'You cannot really expect to turn up here a convenient three months after our…encounter, and lay claim to my being the father of this miraculous child?'

She was speechless. She had imagined this conversation so many times, but this? Not what she'd expected. Encounter? He'd called the night they shared an *encounter*? Now she was angry. Of all the feelings she'd experienced thus far, since discovering the fact she was to have a child, anger had not been one of them. Until now.

'You bastard.'

'I think the press prefer to call me a beast, but I suppose that will do just as well.'

'I shouldn't have come here,' she said, more to herself, rather than him. But it didn't stop him from answering.

'No, you probably shouldn't have,' he said, sighing as if she were an inconvenience rather than the mother of his child. 'Many others have tried to lay claim to such a thing, and believe me, Maria, they were much more skilled at deception than you. And ultimately, they were proved to be the lying, scheming serpents that they were. I must say, I'm quite disappointed. I had thought you different.'

Maria shook her head. Both at the shocking hostility in his tone and at the awfulness that there had been women who had apparently tried to trick him in the past. In a second, all the things she thought they'd shared, the beauty of that one night she'd clung to as her world had morphed and changed before her eyes, burned to dust. She didn't know this man. She was nothing to him. And she would never, *never*, force such a thing upon her child.

'Not as disappointed as I am. I hope that your conscience is kind to you when you realise just how wrong you are,' she stated, gathering her wits about her, and the scraps of her feelings from the floor. She placed the untouched glass down on the small coffee table, reaching into her bag to retrieve the black and white sonogram image of their, no *her*, child—the one thing that she could give him, the only thing, and, placing it beside the glass, she turned her back on him and stepped towards the door.

'Wait.'

'What for?' she asked without turning, her back still to him. 'For you to hurl even more insults at me? I don't think so.'

'Please.'

She turned then, not because his tone was pleading—which it wasn't—but because she would give him this chance. She needed to. She found him standing by the coffee table, one finger on the corner of the sonogram. He wasn't looking at her, but at it. The image of their child. She wondered what he saw in the grey shapes, the patches of darkness and the surprisingly detailed white figure of their baby. The head, the umbilical cord, arms and legs, all clearly visible.

Finally he looked up at her.

'Do not lie to me about this, Maria. Do not test me.'

She shook her head. 'I'm not. I'm pregnant. The baby is yours.'

'How?'

Again, shaking away the doubt and confusion she had felt when she'd first seen that thin blue line. 'Condoms aren't fail proof, I wasn't on any other kind of contraception. I…' She shrugged.

'You're pregnant. The baby is mine.'

Maria nodded and Matthieu's whole world shifted on its axis. He cast his eye back to the small black and white image on the coffee table. His child?

'I'm…' stunned, shocked…what? His mind was completely blank. Though the one thing he could recognise above the white noise roaring in his ears was that Maria deserved an apology.

'I'm sorry,' he said, the sea of confusion and chaotic thoughts making his tone dark, guttural almost. The instant refusal that had risen to his mind had been both cruel and devastating. He hadn't missed the way her already pale skin had turned almost bone white beneath his taunt. But it hadn't been that that had convinced him that she spoke the truth. No. It had been her ready departure. So different from the crocodile tears and insincere desperation he'd experienced in the past. Maria had been willing to walk away not just from him, but from what many others had tried to secure. His money. His ring.

A ring he'd once sworn never to put on a woman's finger. Never imagining for a second the need to do so. Never being so unfailingly irresponsible to sire a child that would, along with its mother, invade his carefully ordered life.

He gestured for her to sit and only after she had stiffly approached the sofa opposite where he stood, and sat, or rather collapsed slightly into the deeply upholstered leather, did he finally sit down too.

'What is it you want?' he asked, holding her gaze with the steel trap of his own, ruthlessly seeking out her intentions, almost willingly seeing hints of her avarice.

'Nothing,' she said, seemingly confused by his question. 'I just wanted to let you know. You…have that right.'

He bit back a cynical laugh. He doubted the truth of her words very much. She might not be after his money or his ring, but there must be something. There was always something.

'You waited three months?' he said, accusingly, not having to work hard to do the maths. He'd known every single one of the days since he'd last touched her, kissed her, brought them both to orgasm.

She nodded. 'The first three months are so…precarious,' she said, shaking her head and shoulders, as if she hadn't been alone to bear the weight of that knowledge, that fear that something could have happened, could have taken away their…their child.

The child he could see formed by light and dark in the small black and white sonogram on the table between them.

'Did you think that I would try to change your mind? Is that why you waited?' Not needing to work hard to find the fury at the possibility that she would think such a thing of him.

'It wouldn't have mattered. I'm keeping this baby, Matthieu, whether you want to be part of its life or not.'

'I would never—'

'How would I know that?' she demanded. 'I didn't even know your last name.'

'But you found out.' The unspoken question in his mind rang loud, beating in time with his heart.

'Only when I needed to.' Her assurance, the promise offered by her words that she had not sought him out until she'd had to, melted the ire edging his anger, transforming it, lessening it—but only slightly. 'Look, I respected what you said then about it only being one night,' she pressed on. 'I'm only here now to let you know, and to give you the chance to choose whether you would like to be in the baby's life or not. Nothing more, nothing less.'

'That simple?' he asked, unconsciously echoing the conversation from that night.

'I am beginning to see that where you are concerned, Matthieu, nothing is simple.'

He reached then for his water, not because he was thirsty, but to buy time. And he never had to buy time. He always knew what to say, how to react. Until now. Until her. He began to wonder if he ever had any choice in the matter at all. His body overriding all senses, all sensibilities.

Father.

He was going to be a father.

'We will marry.'

The look on her face would have been comical in any other circumstance. The horror and shock overriding the fierce neutrality that she had presented in the last few moments.

'No.'

That's different. So many had tried to coerce themselves into his life, but of course Maria was different. He briefly wondered if this might have been part of some larger game, some grander scheme, but he decided not.

There had been nothing about Maria then, or now, that indicated some ulterior motive. Wasn't that what had driven him to her in the first place? Her innocence?

'I don't think you understand—'

'No. It is you who doesn't understand,' Maria cut in. 'That's not why I came here. I have no intention of marrying you. I don't want that, or your money. My *only* interest is the level of your involvement in my child's—'

'Our child's,' he said, interrupting her.

'Our child's life.'

'And that is what I'm telling you, Maria. My interest will be deep, my level of involvement will be total.'

CHAPTER FOUR

MARIA FELT PULLED beneath a tide of emotion, some parts fear, some parts daunted, and all parts consuming. She hadn't lied to him. She hadn't come here to demand marriage, or anything more than maybe weekend visits. She hadn't imagined that he'd even want that if she was honest. Certainly not after reading the hundreds of articles on the 'notorious beast'. She hated herself for using that description even mentally. Because she knew why they had called him that. His scars had made him the subject of intense speculation, his wealth and almost cruel single-minded, driven success all the more so.

And now, to have all that focus pinned on her... She couldn't help but want to shrink back from it. But she couldn't. Not now that she had someone else to protect. Her unborn child. Her hands instinctively wrapped around her waist, his hawk-eyed gaze watching her every move.

'Why?' she couldn't help but ask. Everything about Matthieu screamed isolation. The way he did his business, the way he reportedly lived.

'I will protect my child,' he said, his determined voice sending a shiver down her back.

'Protect? Not love?' she demanded. Because in truth that was all that mattered to Maria right now. It was the only thing that mattered.

'Of course I will love my child,' he said dismissively. *But not the mother of his child.*

Maria pushed aside the sad thought. How had this happened to her? Just when she was on the brink of her freedom, her jewellery business beginning to find traction, her false feelings for Theo behind her, to discover who she was outside that, to find an independence that meant so much to her.

'We don't have to marry for you to…protect our child.'

He scoffed an almost cruel laugh. 'Are you that naïve, Maria? Do you have even an inkling of what will happen when the press find out?'

She hadn't thought of that. She simply hadn't thought of anything past the point of telling Matthieu about the baby. Unease began to grow within her at the sheer conviction in his tone.

'They will hound you, Maria. They will dig up every little thing they can find out about you. They will stalk your friends and family, they will offer money for any salacious story they could print, they will go through your rubbish and camp on your doorstep. They will follow you and anyone who knows you.'

Maria didn't have to work hard to imagine the awful things he was saying. Because she knew how the press worked. Had experienced a little of it first hand when her father had been exiled, when her brother had been forced to assume the purse strings and sell off nearly every single thing they had owned. Even now they still stalked Sebastian and every single woman he encountered. Some thought he courted it, but Maria knew he resented it, hated it. But he was happy as long as they'd left her alone.

Her brother. Her protector. Just as Matthieu wanted to protect their child. She didn't think for a minute that Seb could help her in this situation though. No. The Rohan de Luens were minor exiled nobility. Matthieu Montcour was a completely different level of notoriety and fame. She had seen that for herself within seconds of hitting enter on the search bar with his name in it.

His words had conjured exactly what he had intended. Fear. And more than that. His words had chipped away at her belief that she could still have her freedom, that she could still be in charge of her life the way she hadn't before now, and now never would.

'But *how* can we marry? I don't know anything about you,' she said, fighting back the rising tide of panic in her chest.

'You know my birthday and my favourite colour. That is more than most know.'

'You don't know anything about me,' she said, almost on a whisper as her last defences began to crumble. He waited until she met his gaze before speaking and his words were the final blow.

'I know that you make jewellery and that you do it in spite of your stepmother's objections. I know that you are kind and thoughtful or you wouldn't have been so upset at the idea of breaking someone's engagement, no matter how you thought you felt about the groom. I know that you are not after my money or this conversation would have been significantly different, and I know that you are strong, defiant and determined. And I *know* that you will do whatever you need to do to protect our child.'

I also know the feel of your skin beneath mine, the blush that rises to your cheeks when you can't fight your desires, and I know the sounds of your pleasure when you climax, Matthieu concluded silently, unwilling to speak his wayward thoughts out loud.

He watched as her eyes grew wide with surprise, a

faint blush—as if conjured by his very thoughts—rising to her cheeks.

'If we were to marry... *If*,' she repeated as if she hadn't already made her decision, which he very much believed that she had. 'What would that...be like? What would it look like to you?'

Terms. He was good at this. Securing contracts and finalising practicalities. He would have time later to consider the implications of impending fatherhood. Feelings had no place here, not now. The irony of that would have struck a more righteous man in the heart.

'You will live with me here in Switzerland. I can arrange for everything you could ever need to be available to you. As I'm sure you have already figured out, there are certainly benefits to marrying me. Especially for your business.'

'No. That's...that's not up for discussion. My business is mine and I don't want your involvement.'

He frowned. For many, that would have been enticement enough.

'I have contacts around the world and the resources to give you access to some of the finest materials—'

'I said no. I can source my own materials and any achievements I make professionally will be my own.'

Her words were fast and harsh, as dark as he'd ever heard her tone, both tonight and three months ago. Clearly her independence was important to her, but he resisted the urge to warn her not to let pride get in the way of success. Partly because he very much found pride in his own success. He knew what that meant and found that he respected her for it.

'Do you have a particular stipulation in mind?'

He also gave her credit for not flinching, though clearly she wanted to. It might have been distasteful to discuss the matter in such a way, but necessary to avoid future upset, misunderstandings…he couldn't say heartache, because he would never, *never*, allow himself such an indulgence.

'I…we…would stay married until our child is at least twenty.'

He almost laughed then, at her naivety, her innocence. 'Maria, hear this now. In the little time they were alive, my parents at least installed in me a sense of the sanctity of marriage. I may not be religious, but I do not believe in divorce.'

As if refusing to acknowledge his declaration, she looked at her hands.

'I'm not sure that I can just pack up my life and move in with you.'

'Really? I get the impression that you are more than capable of anything you put your mind to, Maria.'

Her gaze flew to his and her expressive face registered surprise, and something else…something warmer, serving only to heat his blood from within. He ruthlessly pushed that aside. It was absolutely vital that he got her agreement in this. He'd meant what he said. He would protect his child, and by extension her too. But he wouldn't lie to her. She had asked him of his expectations and it was important that he state his intentions now.

'My home is on the edges of Lake Lucerne, in the heart of this country. It is…certainly big enough for us, and our child.' He knew his words were modest. The large sprawling estate was an architectural marvel and he forced himself to stifle the discomfort at the idea of opening it up to another person, to Maria. But he would. He'd have to. The idea of Maria and his child being anywhere other than with him? Simply untenable.

'You will have access to anything you could want.

Truly. But I need you to understand one thing, Maria.'
Her eyes grew watchful, assessing, as if she realised that
this was the most important thing of all. 'Do not build
hopes and fantasies about me. I promise you now, that I
will love, care for and provide every single earthly want
for our child. But that is the extent of what I will offer.'

He was saying that he wouldn't, couldn't, love her. He
was refusing her the one thing she'd only just realised
she'd ever wanted. A wave of sorrow crashed over her
and she thought, *How funny. An engagement is supposed
to be a happy thing.*

She forced herself to focus on what he was offering
her. Her child would want for nothing. Her child would
grow up with the kind of security she had once taken for
granted, until it had been lost. Never would her child experience the shocking devastation she had. Because she
would protect their child. She, who had been protected all
her life, would become protector and that thought fired
her determination more than any other.

'One condition.'

'Anything.' His response, quick and sure.

'It will be a small wedding. No guests.' She didn't
want that day to be a public spectacle. Didn't want her
family there, her stepmother turning it into a farce. She
could already imagine the lascivious glint in Valeria's
gaze, the image of her mother in her father's eyes, and
the disappointment in her brother's.

'Just us and two witnesses?'

'Yes.'

'It will be so.'

He reached for her hand across the table, the heat of
his fingers searing as they wrapped around her cool skin.

A handshake, as if nothing more than a contract had been agreed to.

Tears threatened the backs of her eyelids, but she willed them away. Others might be full of joy and brimming with happiness, but she wasn't one of those soon-to-be brides. No. She was a soon-to-be mother and would do whatever it took to care for, protect and love her child in the way that she had not felt herself.

Matthieu might have wanted a quick wedding, but even he, with all his might and money, could not force Swiss bureaucracy to bend to his will. Once their marriage application had passed through the churning machine of legalities and regulations they had still needed to wait ten long days before the ceremony could take place. And Matthieu had used that time well. He might not have known much about Maria before, but, having collected the many required details for the application, he did now.

He was going to be a father.

He almost resented Maria the time she'd had to mentally prepare for impending parenthood. She'd had about a month on him before informing him, but he had been forced to absorb it all in a matter of an hour or two that night. But since then?

The vehemence of the connection he felt to his unborn child shocked him. The determination to protect, to claim, the yearning to meet this heir of his was utterly astounding. So long he had lived, ruthlessly avoiding any sense of commitment or connection to another… He had thought it would chafe, that he would wrangle against it defiantly. But he had been wrong.

As if in a single moment, the compass points of his life had changed, now pointing solely to his child and Maria. And as he looked at himself in the mirror, dark blue suit and a shirt of such pale blue it was almost white, for the first time in more years than he could count he wondered what his father would think. Matthieu searched his own features for traces of the father who had loved him so much he had searched a flame-ridden building to drag Matthieu out, unthinking and unheeding of the danger and damage to himself. Before he had gone back in for his wife.

A blade-sharp pain twisted in his chest before he closed the door on his thoughts.

'Ah, Matthieu.'

He turned to find Malcolm standing in the doorway of his office suite. The older man was nodding in approval. 'They would be so proud of you.'

Matthieu gritted his teeth against the sentiment. He doubted very much that his parents would be proud of his knocking up an innocent and forcing her into a marriage she had no desire for.

'Where is David?' he enquired of Malcolm's husband. The two had finally married once the bill allowing for same-sex marriage had passed in California. After almost eleven years of being together, Malcolm had felt that they didn't really need a piece of paper to certify their relationship, but the battle for legal recognition had been hard fought and hard won, and David and Malcolm had married for the world they wanted as much as the love they already had.

Goosebumps rose over Matthieu's skin, soothed only slightly by the soft cotton of his shirt. He didn't have to wonder if Maria had wanted that kind of love in her life. He knew she had, and for the first time since demanding that she wore his ring, he realised the cost to her, despite having paraded all that she would gain before her.

'David has gone to meet Maria at the hotel. He wanted to walk over to the register office with her.'

Matthieu bit back a curse. How had he not thought of that? Was he truly such a bastard that while he espoused the virtues of what his money could mean to her and their child, he had failed to even see to the first emotional requirement she might have on her wedding day? He would do better. He had to.

Maria stared at herself in the mirror, marvelling that it had almost been easier to pack up her entire life in Camberwell than to find a dress that would suit not only a civil ceremony but the burgeoning baby bump that still caught her by surprise.

Two days ago she had answered the door to an incredibly efficient removal team who had retrieved an almost miserably small stack of boxes containing her clothes, books, the few items of furniture she'd possessed to be sent on to Switzerland. But her equipment—her jewellery, the bits and bobs she'd gathered over the years—had been sent to her brother's estate in Italy. Those boxes must have looked as if they belonged to a very talented magpie: rich colours, sparkling, semi-precious stones, bursting from the seams. Her moulds, her tools and the series of bracelets, rings, earrings and necklaces she had already started to amass had been by far the greatest part of her belongings. For some reason, one she neither could nor would put a finger on, she hadn't wanted to take them to Switzerland.

She had bid a tearful farewell to Evin and Anita, and had allowed herself one last day in the small studio she had rented a space in, up near the Thames in Bermondsey. That was where she'd felt the pull greatest. That was where she had poured her hopes and dreams into the small projects that she had made for her first gallery showing only months earlier. That was where she had returned to after that fateful night with Matthieu and forged a new, determined and optimistic outlook for her future...until she had discovered her pregnancy and all her imaginings had disappeared in a puff of silver smoke.

And now when she thought of her future, one irrevocably bound to the father of her child, her future as his wife, she wondered at it. Would she be expected to be on his arm at business functions, the practically perfect wife? Or would he grow tired of her once she had his child and then package her off to some distant place? She had no idea what his home looked like, where she would be able to find space to create the pieces that were so important to her. Not once in the last two months had she been able to find that heady, almost meditative sense of creativity that would have, in the past, consumed and calmed her.

A knock on the door jolted her from her day dreams. She opened it to a tall, smiling, slightly rotund blond man, who seemed only to smile even more at her evident confusion.

'Maria? I'm David Antoinelli.'

'The witness?' Maria had remembered his name from one of Matthieu's emails.

'Yes,' he laughed easily. 'I did hope that you'd recognise my name. Didn't think you'd appreciate a *complete* stranger knocking on the door the morning of your wedding.'

She pulled the door open wide, gesturing for him to enter.

'I thought you might like someone to walk with you to the register office, given that...' He trailed off, clearly not wanting to point out that she was alone. But his rich, upper-class British accent was so wonderfully familiar, she instantly warmed to him.

'You're English.'

'Ha! Yes. I grew up in North London,' he said, leaning towards her conspiratorially.

'I live—*lived*—in Camberwell.'

'South of the river!' he exclaimed. 'I never really crossed the Thames much, but I did have some rather indecent nights in Vauxhall, but the less said about that to my husband, the better.'

Maria couldn't help the smile that grew on her lips, and the well of relief that bloomed in her chest. The thought of walking towards her wedding on her own...

'I must say,' he said, taking her in with a beam of approval, 'you look glorious.'

'Thank you,' she said, exhaling a breath of relief. The simple, knee-length dress had an empire waist cinching just above the beginning of her bump and a beautiful sweetheart neckline. The form-fitting cream satin was covered by beautifully detailed lace that rose up the material and covered her arms and décolletage. And even better, she'd been able to afford it with her meagre savings.

She had tamed her curls into braids either side of her head and pinned them up, leaving only a few strands of her dark hair free to frame her face.

David offered her his arm, and she held up a hand for one moment while she gathered the things she would need from the suite. The rest—her small bag of belongings—would, she had been told, be retrieved and sent on to Matthieu's house before they arrived there that evening. She stifled the blush that rose at thoughts of just how that evening would be spent. It was perhaps one of the only things that hadn't yet been negotiated and settled on.

She caught her shawl and the small bouquet of flowers

she had ventured out for earlier that morning. She had looked longingly at the sweet bundle of white peonies, sage and rosemary. She knew that a herb bouquet might be slightly unorthodox but she hadn't been able to resist them. With one last glance at herself in the mirror, one last look at herself as a single woman, she bid her adieu, took David's proffered arm and closed the door on her past life, ready to assume the role of Mrs Montcour.

Matthieu and Malcolm were waiting on the steps of the register office he'd deemed perfectly suitable for their needs until he caught sight of Maria. He felt the heated glare of disapproval from Malcolm beside him as his oldest friend looked from Maria and his husband to Matthieu and the building behind him.

Matthieu felt the instant denial on his lips. *I didn't know.* Because he hadn't. He hadn't known she would look so beautiful, almost ethereal. He hadn't expected to see the small, perfectly formed shape of the promise of their child beneath her dress. He hadn't realised that he would see her and think that he had absolutely got it wrong. They should have been in a church—the biggest one he could find, filled with everyone they knew to show off his stunning bride, with pride and adoration shining in his eyes. He just hadn't known that he would feel that way.

When they finally drew close, David pronounced in his usually enthusiastic way, 'If I wasn't an already happily married man, I'd be tempted to run away with the bride.'

'And now that I can see for myself exactly how lovely you are, Maria, I am tempted to do the same,' Malcolm replied, leaning forward to kiss her cheek.

Maria shone beneath the words of their encouragement, and only took a moment to seem slightly bemused at the contrast between his friends' open expressions and his utter silence. Because he was simply incapable of speech. The sight of her had robbed him of it.

The two men embraced leaving Maria and Matthieu to stare at each other, taking in each's appearance in silence, in weighted anticipation of what they were about to do.

'You look…beautiful,' he said, aware that his tone was guttural and hoping that it didn't sound begrudging. Because somewhere deep within, he did feel that way. Strangely resentful that he didn't deserve this. Deserve her. Deserve the child they carried. But Maria most definitely deserved more than he was able and willing to offer.

'Thank you,' she said, casting her eyes away from his as if she was embarrassed or flustered by his simple words.

He guided her into the building, Malcolm and David close behind them as they made their way towards the office where the registrar was waiting for them. Despite the almost ugly functional exterior of the building, the interior was a relief. The rich tones of whisky-coloured wood flooring soothed. Expensive, yet tasteful chairs filled the almost empty room, the focus of which was a beautiful mahogany table where the registrar and the officiant waited to greet them.

Matthieu felt oddly detached from proceedings he'd never thought he'd experience. In every one of his past encounters he'd ensured that the only thing that passed between the women who had shared his bed and himself was pleasure. Given and received—nothing more. Once they had left his life, he gave them little thought. Only that hadn't been true of Maria. There hadn't been an hour that had passed in between that night in Iondorra and the night she'd crashed back into his life with news that had changed everything, that he hadn't thought of her. From the very first moments leaving her bed, he'd tasted her on his tongue, felt her skin beneath his, the echoes of her sighs and gentle laughter, haunting his nights.

Now, he cast a look over to where Maria sat in the corner of the room with the celebrant, presumably going over the same questions that he was currently answering to the registrar. His mind working automatically to supply the requisite information as his heart picked itself up and reached for her.

'Are you ready?'

The question mocked him, but he nodded, swift and sure, knowing what must be done.

She deserved more.

He would give her everything he could, he promised. Not just because of their child. But because she deserved it. She had uprooted her entire life, placed it in his undeserving hands and no matter what the future brought them, he would make sure that she was protected.

'We are gathered here today...'

Maria let the words wash over her. She had wondered how she'd feel, ever since agreeing to Matthieu's outrageous proclamation that they would marry, and now that she was here, now that she stood before the registrar and officiant and they were saying the words that every young girl had dreamed of hearing as a child, she just didn't know. She didn't know how she felt. She had expected fear, but—she thought, resisting the urge to shake her head—that wasn't what she felt. Defiance? No, not that either. Hesitation? Oddly, no. Not even that. Numb, she decided. Numb as the words brought her closer and closer to the moment she would be bound to Matthieu for ever.

She suddenly felt as if she'd left something behind. That she'd forgotten something vital, but couldn't for the life of her think what it was. She frowned, then realised that the officiant had said something that required a response from her. Mistaking her lack of response for nerves, the officiant smiled and repeated the question.

'Will you, Maria, take Matthieu to be your lawful wedded husband?'

No words of love in this perfunctory service, then. No honouring above all else. But she wasn't doing this for herself. She was doing this for their child. There would be love, would be honouring above all else. There would be protection and security and…

'I will.'

'And will you, Matthieu, take Maria to be your lawful wedded wife?'

Finally Maria found the courage to look to Matthieu then, startled somewhat to find him gazing at her with an intensity that reminded her immediately of that night. In his eyes she saw the lake in Iondorra, she saw the stars that blanketed the night sky. She saw the deep pull of arousal in his eyes, hypnotic and unfathomable. And if her heart hurt, because for just a moment she saw how it could have been, she chided herself for wanting more.

'I will.'

'The rings?'

Rings. That was what she'd forgotten. She didn't know a single jewellery maker who hadn't spent hours pouring attention and passion into a creation that symbolised a couple's love for each other. She had once thought that she might make her own and her future husband's. There was a special part of her designs and sketches that, long ago, she'd thought she might use as the basis for what she would one day wear for the rest of her life. But the intensity of the last few weeks, the practicalities, had thrown that from her mind. And for a moment she was relieved. Because this was not what she'd wanted. Not really. While Matthieu reached to his pocket, she ran a hand over the lower part of her abdomen. The small, firm bump cradling her soon-to-be child.

She realised that Matthieu's eyes had snagged on the movement, and hesitated just a second before he produced something from his pocket. He reached for her hand and held the ring in his fingers in such a way that she couldn't see it until he had slipped it over her finger.

And she stared.

Stared and stared. Because in some impossible way it was perfect. As if he'd found what she wanted without her even knowing it. The silver band gave way to a circle of small diamonds encasing a beautifully cut shard of jet.

'This is how I see us, Maria,' he whispered to her. 'Joined together, surrounding our child with love and security, with protection.'

The sincerity and certainty shining in his eyes settled about her, her heart aching with the want of love, but appeased by the promise he was offering her. Not of fairy tales of happy-ever-afters, not with offers of obscene wealth that meant nothing to her, not with lies of unfelt emotions, but a promise of everything he could and would do for her and her child. Their child.

'I now declare you husband and wife.'

CHAPTER FIVE

MARIA BREATHED IN the cool scents of water and woods. She had been walking for twenty minutes towards Lake Lucerne, marvelling once again at the sheer breadth of acreage within Matthieu's estate.

She shook her head at the beauty of the sight before her. Water spreading out like a spool of molten silver, reflecting the blue of the cloudless sky and the stunning emerald greens of the trees bordering the banks of the lake.

Her fingers rubbed against each other, soothing the nipping bite of the cold against her skin, brushing gently the band of silver, diamond and jet that she had worn now for almost a month. Nothing had been as she'd imagined. Nothing she'd expected or dreamed of that moment he had slipped the ring over her finger had come to pass.

After their wedding ceremony, David and Malcolm and whisked them away to one of Bern's most renowned restaurants for an exquisite wedding breakfast, nothing of which she remembered tasting. If the jovial couple had noticed anything peculiar in the silence between the newly minted husband and wife, neither acknowledged it. Their happy, gentle, mocking banter had washed over her before the limousine had arrived to take her and Matthieu to his home, here on the edge of Lake Lucerne.

She remembered sitting beside Matthieu in the dark cocoon of the luxurious interior of the sleek machine that ferried them towards their wedding night, tension palpable and thrumming from where he held himself almost impossibly still and she practically vibrated with it. In clipped words he had told her about his home, the team of staff employed to service, clean and cook for them, the extensive gym and leisure equipment, including an infinity pool that overlooked Switzerland's famous lake. The walks that had been cleared throughout the estate, the woodlands and down to the shorefront.

'Anything is yours,' he'd said.

Apart from you, she'd noted silently.

As the limousine had eaten up the miles of smooth tarmac, winding closer and closer towards their destination, she had wondered why on earth he was talking. Reams of descriptions about the house, the architect, the way life would be, and all she could think was, *Yes, but what about now? What about tonight?* Because in truth she had been almost overcome by a maddening sense of him. Everything about the previous weeks had been about practicalities, packing up her home and life, getting to the register office, the exchanging of rings and signing of marriage certificates... But the moment it had happened, the moment that they had been declared husband and wife—she blushed now at the memory of it—all she had thought of was spending the night with her husband.

She had wanted to share his bed, to feel even just for a little the same kind of 'rightness' she had experienced the night they had conceived their child. To feel the heady sense of desire, the way that their bodies had somehow communicated beyond words or civilities but more with raw, intense and all-consuming passion. An equal passion—the one thing that they had most definitely shared.

It hadn't gone away, she'd marvelled as they'd drawn closer and closer to Matthieu's estate. She had seen her husband in the sweep of the passing road lights, illuminating the darkness that surrounded their journey. The soft dark swirls of his beard doing little to gentle the stark outline of his jaw. The thick dark brows almost startling atop eyes of pure molten honey that gleamed almost with traces of emerald. The width and breadth of him made her feel deliciously small, delicate but also strong—strong in her desire for him, the need to make that physical contact, any kind of contact with the man she had just married.

And when they had finally drawn to a halt at the top of a sweeping driveway beyond a set of stunning iron electronically controlled gates, she had thought, *This is it.* She had turned to him, just in front of the large wooden door to a building she had been unable to take in because of the sheer magnificence of her husband, her hand poised to raise to his jaw, her palms itching to feel the heat of him, the soft whorl of his beard against her skin, just as he'd pushed open the door, explained where her room was and stalked off to his 'office'.

He had left her standing in the foyer of an unknown home, alone, in her wedding dress, untouched and unwanted.

She had retreated to the room he had given some offhand directions to before the first tear had fallen. She had kicked off her shoes, before the second and third, she had collapsed onto the bed and pressed her face into the pillow before the sounds of her sobs could be heard. Because it was then that she'd realised what she had done. She had looked for love for her entire life and now she had consigned herself to a man who would never love her.

As she turned her back on the beautiful lake and made

her way back to the estate, Maria realised she had neither of the futures she'd envisioned for herself just before the wedding. She was not his perfect wife, nor the discarded wife. Instead, he had put her in this strange kind of half-life, and she feared that it was slowly choking her.

No matter what he did, Matthieu couldn't shake the stranglehold that had wrapped around his chest. Couldn't escape the realisation, sheer and shocking, that he had done something very wrong. It had started that first night they had come here. Before that even, in the limousine bringing them home. *Home.* He'd not really ever thought of this place as a home before. It was his sanctuary, yes, the place he hid away from the outside world. But a home?

In the limousine, he'd felt it. The sensual undercurrent ebbing and flowing between them. As it had done that first night in Iondorra, her expressive features, her body, it had called to him. Teased and tempted him. The thick band of arousal fierce and shocking, as everything in him roared to reach out and take what he wanted, to take *her*.

But he had meant the promise he'd made to himself, to Maria silently, the day of their wedding. He meant to protect her. Which meant that he needed to ensure that they started their marriage as it would continue. He would give her her every material need or desire. But he could not give her himself. Because if he lifted the tight leash he had on his control, if he did what he so desperately wanted, to sink into her soft warm heat, to give into the exquisite pleasure that she brought him, he wouldn't be able to hold himself back. And he couldn't shake the thought that doing so would unleash the thoughts and memories he felt biting at the edges of his consciousness.

So he *had* held himself back from her that night and

all the nights since. And if that meant he had to suffer this constant state of frustration, then so be it.

His legs pounded away on the treadmill of the sprawling gym housed on the floor beneath the living quarters and kitchen, and two floors beneath the bedrooms and infinity pool that stretched out towards the lake.

Sweat dripped down the sides of his head and he swiped at it with his arm. If he could exhaust himself, perhaps then he would find relief from this…thing. This feeling in him that felt like a ragged beast, tearing and snarling away in his chest.

Exercise had become something vital for him over the years. It had started with the rehabilitation after hours, days, weeks of surgeries in the years following the fire. He barely remembered those first few months. A pain so intense it had made him delirious with agony, which at times he'd actually been thankful for. Because it focused his mind on something other than the fact he had lost his entire family. Something other than the last look his father gave him, having hurled him from the living-room window before turning back for his mother.

His feet and legs compensated for the shiver that ran through his body, the heat and sweat turning icy cold beneath the memory of the screams from that night. Their screams, his screams, he couldn't tell. But neither his mother, his father, nor his uncles and aunt had escaped the inferno that had consumed the old estate.

Faulty electrics, a real Christmas tree, and a two-hundred-year-old estate. That was what the insurance investigation had decreed. An accident. An accident that had robbed him of everything.

He increased the treadmill's speed in an attempt to force his focus to shift back to nothing more than the movement of his feet and body. He never dwelled on thoughts of his family. He had become adept at avoiding them but as he picked up the pace, to run almost flat out, he couldn't shake the feeling that perhaps he was running from his past.

Because unaccountably since Maria had moved into his home, he'd felt it rising up around him. Memories of family meals, the echoes of childhood laughter at his parents' gentle mocking, or the warm love they offered, they all hovered around Maria like a promise of what could be, but what he would not allow himself.

So Matthieu had begun to avoid her, plunging himself into work, into new acquisitions. He'd even left her here while he'd travelled to one of the mines in Russia, hoping that the distance between them would cause things to settle back into what his life had been like before. But the moment he'd returned, he'd seen signs of her throughout the estate. Books left on side tables, a throw on the sofa that hadn't been there before. Having lived alone for more than ten years, he'd found it disconcerting. It had felt like an intrusion and, although he shouldn't, he found himself begrudging her for it. For presenting reminders, evidence of what she had done without him.

And soon it wouldn't just be evidence of his wife… it would be their child. Would he spend his future trying to avoid them both? *No*, he growled internally. Once again shocked by the possessiveness of his feelings towards his child.

A noise startled him and he nearly lost his footing. His hands flew to the bar in front of him to steady himself, as he mentally checked the ankle he'd nearly turned over, cursing loudly.

'Sorry! I didn't…'

'It's okay,' he said, between huge lungfuls of air, not having to look up again to know what had caused him to nearly fall from the speeding mill beneath him. He reached out and decreased the speed, waiting until it had slowed to a walk before casting a look up at the doorway.

He was already breathing hard when he took in the sight of her, thankful that he had a reason to disguise his body's natural reaction to her beauty, to her presence. She was simply glorious.

The long dark loose curls fell over her bare shoulders and hovered near her waist. Her leggings clung to shapely legs and he had a sudden and shocking urge to wrap his palm around the curve of her thigh. He drenched himself in memories of that night for just a moment before flinging the door closed on that train of thought. He was still staring at the way the vest clung to her breasts and to where it pulled tight across the increasing swell around her stomach. No. It was no longer a swell and had—in the last few weeks—most definitely formed into a bump. He marvelled at how her body had changed even in the weeks since their wedding, and couldn't help the word forming in his mind possessively and with no uncertain amount of finality…*mine*.

Maria had heard him curse and was startled that it echoed the exact same thought crashing through her mind. She hadn't expected to find him here having returned from her walk by the lake, convinced that he had left before dawn to head to his office, as he had done almost every single day since their wedding.

But he was here. And he looked…

Her mouth actually watered.

Seriously, she thought to herself, *am I that base?*

Yes. Yes, I most definitely am.

A pair of soft grey sweatpants hung low on lean hips, showing off the taut muscles dipping beneath its waistband. Because, naturally, he was shirtless, and all-consumingly magnificent. The breadth of his arms, the sheen of sweat covering his skin, her eyes ate up every inch of him. The scars becoming less something that she noted, but more something that highlighted the way his sculpted muscles shifted along with his body's movements.

She regretted the moment he reached for the T-shirt hanging from the bars of the treadmill, almost begged him not to cover up such sheer masculine beauty, and she very much hated that he felt he had to cover his body for her. He pulled it over his head, tugging it down over the breadth of his chest, and cut off the sight that had both shocked and enticed.

'I wanted to do some yoga and thought that...' She felt that she had to fill the silence, otherwise they might just continue to stare at each other, like combatants facing off against...what? Their desires? Their wants? Because she knew that he wanted her. She could see it in his eyes. And that made his almost continual absence from her presence so much harder to bear. She cut off thoughts that were beginning to feel a little too self-pitying and made her way over to the soft mat flooring by the floor-to-ceiling mirrors.

'Of course,' he said as he started to leave.

'I...' she started, and then stopped, as he looked confused as to why she might want to continue to talk to him. Might want him here. She cursed inwardly again. She couldn't go on like this. She couldn't live like this. Two separate people in one house, barely seeing or speaking to each other. 'I thought I'd take the car into town this morning.'

'You have an obstetrician appointment?' he asked, surprised, as if scanning his memory for some piece of missing information.

'No,' Maria replied, shaking her head, her curls cascading down the bare skin on her shoulders and back. That had been one of the last things they'd done together, met with the obstetrician—an efficient, kind Swiss national with gleaming offices and state-of-the-art equipment. They weren't due to visit Ms Klein for another three weeks. 'I wanted to go shopping.'

'What for?'

'A dress for the gala.'

'What gala?'

She shivered at his tone, which was cut through with shards of icicles. She frowned, wondering whether it was the purchase of the dress that bothered him or the attendance at the gala they'd received an invitation to.

It had been the first and only piece of correspondence sent to her—well, *them*—since her arrival at Matthieu's estate and the gentle scrolling swirl, *Mr and Mrs Montcour*, had caught her eye. She had been faintly surprised that she was acknowledged as his wife, not thinking that the news of their marriage had become public knowledge yet, but then had seen the silver insignia of Montcour Mining Industries in the bottom right-hand corner of the embossed invitation. Perhaps he had meant to tell her about the gala, presuming her to have a spare ball gown that would fit a burgeoning baby bump hanging in her closet. Either way, it didn't matter. She *was* Mrs Montcour and as such had absolutely every right to open a letter addressed to her.

'The one in Lausanne, this evening,' she said slowly and clearly, because surely he was feigning such a blank, strange reaction. 'I must say, I was a little surprised to find that you have a charity.'

'I have three goldmines, two diamond mines and a

multibillion-dollar business, why would it surprise you that I have a charity?'

'Please don't tell me it's just a tax write-off,' she bit back, resenting the dismissive list of his impressive assets. And suddenly she was angry. Angry that he seemed to think that she wouldn't want to attend a charity gala they had been invited to. Angry that he insisted on leaving her alone to roam this sprawling, yet luxurious estate. A place seemingly made entirely of concrete and steel, the cold greys serving only to remind her constantly of its aloof owner. Angry that she felt she had had to explain or justify her movements. Surely she wasn't trapped here and could come and go as she pleased?

'We won't be going,' he said, his tone almost a growl and his hand cutting through the air between them as if punctuating his decree.

'Why not?'

'I have business to attend to.'

'Well, I don't.' The thought of spending yet another night alone suddenly became impossible to her and everything in her wanted to escape. He looked at her then as if her wants and needs didn't matter. As if she had grown two heads and four extra arms and he simply couldn't understand her desire for more.

Enough. She'd had enough of tiptoeing around the father of her child.

'So I will be going,' she said, staring up at the stone effigy that her husband had become. 'You, however, don't have to. In fact, I'd rather you didn't. Because I find that I don't want you to spoil this evening for me, in the same way that you have spoiled almost every day since our wedding,' she said on a shaky breath, drawing strength from her new determination. 'I refuse to live like this, Matthieu. Yes, you might have offered me every material comfort within our marriage, but a person, a *human being*, cannot live in isolation and it's driving me crazy. I don't think that I've actually had a longer conversation with anyone beyond, "Hi, how are you?" "Fine, thanks, and you?" in over three and a half weeks! I know more about Tomas, your driver, than I do about you. He has three children, by the way—not sure if you know that— and he likes his coffee with a hint of caramel, though he doesn't like his wife to know as she's been after him to watch his calorie intake. Matthieu, tell me, how do you like your coffee?'

It was as if the dam had broken within her against the almost unending silence of the last few weeks and words—nonsensical words—had flowed forth like a flood. She was almost breathless from the speed with which she'd delivered her little speech, and now she held her breath, waiting to see how Matthieu would respond.

'How I like my coffee is irrelevant, Maria. We, you, I, or any combination thereof, will *not* be going to the gala. If you want to go out, Tomas will take you any-where you wish to go. But only if that somewhere has the very limited possibility of your outing being uncov-ered by the press. And as that will not be the case of the gala this evening, you will not be attending.'

She shouldn't have been surprised. He stalked from the room without a word and she felt even more furious than she had before. Press or no, she would not be a pris-oner here any longer.

Maria sat in the back of the limousine, the partition down between her and Tomas, who had kept a gentle running commentary since leaving Matthieu's estate in Lucerne, and she was thankful because if he hadn't the two-and-a-half-hour drive would have given Maria too much time to think. To wonder at what she was doing and how Matthieu would react when he realised she had defied his decree and sneaked out of his estate like a runaway child. This was the first time that she would have crossed him. But he didn't understand. She had needed to. She needed *this*.

Mrs Montcour.

Was she? Really? Given they hadn't consummated the marriage. Did something like consummation work retrospectively? And even if it did, who was this strange Mrs Montcour? Maria had been many things, the daughter of an exiled Duke, the sister of an international playboy, an art student, coffee-shop worker, jewellery maker. But now she was a wife, and would be a mother. And somewhere swirling amongst the discomfort in her belly was the fear that she didn't know how to be this person.

She had considered reaching out to her brother, but Sebastian had been unusually preoccupied recently, simply accepting her explanation that she had gone to stay with a friend in Switzerland for 'a while', rather than interrogating her over every minute detail as he usually did. As for her father, well, months could go by without speaking to him and she couldn't help but hide behind the familiar feeling that it was easier for her father not to see her and be reminded so painfully of his dead wife.

She had thought of reaching out to Anita and Evin, but what would she say? I tracked down the father of my child, happens to be a billionaire several times over, we married for the sake of the child and he whisked me off to his secluded lair?

The only person she had to tether her to her new role was Matthieu and he seemed hell-bent on leaving her alone and untouched.

'We're here, Mrs Montcour,' Tomas said, in his crisp Swiss-French accent.

It was then that she realised she hadn't really thought this through. She hadn't expected a red carpet, even pre-warned, she hadn't expected the sprawling mass of paparazzi lining the street to the entrance of the grand building where the gala was being held.

Maria stepped out of the limousine on autopilot. What had she been thinking? Would they even know who she was? Or would they think her some impostor trying to sneak into the gala? As far as she knew, no one had identified her, no one knew her as Mrs Montcour. She cursed as she drew to a halt, staring somewhat in horror at the huge sprawling mass of reporters and photographers quite possibly about to witness the ultimate humiliation of her being refused entry.

Tomas closed the door behind her and stood beside her as if ready to reopen the door and shove her unceremoniously back into the sleek black machine. Until a small, suited man holding a clipboard rushed up to meet her.

'Welcome…'

The query in his voice was so clear that it echoed within her chest. All her fears, all her questions, it was now down to her to own this new person she had come to be, whatever the consequence.

'Mrs Montcour,' she replied, hiding behind a steady voice.

The look on the man's face would have been comical under any other circumstances and she couldn't help the feeling that perhaps he wasn't going to believe her. Her fingers gripped the embossed invitation ready to thrust it towards him as if in evidence of her claim.

'Of course,' he said, shaking his head as if she might disappear at any moment. 'It is…*wonderful* to meet you.

We had not expected your attendance this evening, given that...' Whatever he might have been about to say was cut short as he stepped back slightly, his gaze drawn to the bump positioned almost between them. 'May I offer my congratulations, Mrs Montcour?' The pure beam of happiness shining from this small, suited stranger was oddly infectious, and she couldn't help but sweep a hand over her unborn child.

'Thank you,' she said, smiling, as the first flash of the bulb cut through their conversation, nearly blinding her. It was then that the shouts started and starburst-like strobe lighting covered her from head to toe. She vaguely saw the man gesture for her to follow him and, keeping her gaze down on the red carpet and away from the bright lights, she made her way into the gala, her heart pounding and irrationally slightly afraid.

Once up the stairs and through the grand entrance to the museum that had been co-opted for the gala, Maria blew out a shaky breath.

'My apologies for the scrum, Mrs Montcour, it is a necessary evil, but the notoriety brings much attention and finances for our charity.' The seemingly endless stream of dialogue coming from the small man was as much of a shock as the press had been. And suddenly Maria wasn't sure that she wanted to be here. Couldn't help herself longing for the quiet peaceful solitude of Matthieu's estate.

'Mr Montcour regrettably has been unable to attend our events in Lausanne for many years, the invitation is usually sent out as a courtesy, but we are truly honoured that you have come.' Maria found nothing but sincerity in the man's words, soothing some of her initial reluctance.

'That's very kind of you to say...'

'Benjamin Keant,' he supplied.

'Benjamin. It is lovely to meet you.'

'Charmed, Mrs Montcour. Simply charmed. Would you allow me to introduce you to some of the other patrons and guests? I can also tell you anything you'd like to know about our charity.'

Maria smiled, thankful that she could disguise her ignorance. 'Absolutely. And why don't you imagine that I know absolutely nothing about your charity and start from the very beginning?'

Already she had realised that she'd drawn the curious gazes of the many guests she could see in the large open foyer of the museum. It distracted her from the start of Benjamin's spiel, until she caught words that fired an alarm instantly within her mind and heart.

'And the money raised here is put back not only into the medical centres that deal with such devastating burn injuries, but rehabilitation, financial support for families who may struggle with the exorbitant costs of years-long, if not life-long, medical care, and emotional counselling and support for all affected.'

Burn injuries. Medical care. Emotional counselling.

A cold shiver passed over Maria's shoulder blades and down her spine as she realised exactly why Matthieu might not have wanted to be here. It had nothing to do with her whatsoever, and everything to do with him and what had happened to him all those years ago.

CHAPTER SIX

LONG BEFORE THE whirring blades of the helicopter slowed after touching down on the discreet helipad in the back of the museum's gardens, Matthieu's jaw had clenched in a vice-like grip. It had nothing to do with the hastily rescheduled phone meeting with the South African Ambassador about future mining prospects and everything to do with his runaway wife. He forced himself to loosen his jaw or risk losing a molar. Instead the tension travelled to his hands as he took long, powerful strides across the manicured pathways towards the gala, fisting and un-fisting fingers that topped white knuckles.

He did *not* want to be here. In fact, he had not attended the charity in nearly ten years, ever since that first time. Memories coursed through his veins, thickening the blood with anger and frustration, and something a little like scorn at his naivety back then. He'd had such great hopes of what the charity would become, but from the very first moment, the very first flash of a paparazzo's camera he'd realised that the vultures had descended not to support the charity but to feast on the wounds left by the loss of his family. To feast upon him. All of the resulting photographs and press had been so focused on the notorious Matthieu Montcour, with all but a few lines about the legacy he'd wanted to create. That night he'd

sworn never to attend again, never to detract from the
charity, to taint it with his own burgeoning reputation
as a beast. Instead he had left the running of the charity to the highly efficient man he had appointed almost
ten years ago. Not for a second did he regret founding
the charity—he just couldn't have anything to do with
it personally.

But Maria had no idea what she was walking into. The
press, the celebrities who attended his event feasted on
gossip and drama as much as water to live and breathe,
and the discovery that he had not only married but had
impregnated his wife would be irresistible fodder for tomorrow's headlines.

On the short flight over he had already fired off an
email to his secretary to handle the impending fallout
of the news. Security would be tightened not only at his
office, but at each of his properties, including the estate
in Lucerne. He hated living under a microscope, having done so both medically and publicly ever since the
deaths of his parents.

What did you think? an inner voice chided. *That you
could keep Maria to yourself? That you could keep her
and your child a secret for ever? Keep Maria to yourself?*

The words ran through his mind, almost like a direc-
tive, an order, a demand.

I refuse to live like this.

Maria's words from earlier that day in the gym had
cut through him like a knife and he cursed, wondering
for a moment if he had truly become a monster, locking
her away in his home, keeping her isolated from the rest
of the world.

But she didn't understand. She didn't know what it
was like.

Two black suited men stood either side of the small

white entrance to the back of the building, swirling white wires betraying the discreet earpieces indicating their business here. Noting his arrival, they cast an assessing gaze over him, almost in unison, their faces utterly impassive, before one pushed open the door allowing Matthieu entrance to the museum.

A small, blonde woman met him on the other side, simple make-up adding a professional sheen to her face in the absence of a smile. That was what he'd liked about Margery, the charity director's assistant. Unlike most, she didn't fawn, paw or even, like now, smile. Crisp, unemotional efficiency. The kind he'd always surrounded himself with...until Maria.

Margery explained in her no-nonsense way that Maria had arrived thirty minutes earlier, had been met by the charity's director, Mr Keant—never Benjamin, she never used his first name—but that the press had almost been rabid at the realisation of her identity. Keant had ushered his wife down the red carpet unharmed and was now introducing her to various guests. The keynote speech would start in five minutes, the dinner in thirty, and the quickest possible exit he could make without drawing undue attention would be after the dinner, which would conclude in ninety minutes.

He nodded as they came to another discreet door, accepting the information, digesting it, before he swiftly stepped through the door into the large foyer of the museum where the main reception was being held.

He saw her immediately, halting mid-stride at the sight of her. She was stunning. The midnight-blue dress had been drenched in a million tiny sequins, the material clinging to every curve, every inch of the perfect bump riding low on her abdomen, down over her thighs and reaching all the way to a pair of high heels that sparkled silver glints in the spot lighting high above them on the museum's domed interior. *Mine*. Everything in him roared with satisfaction, as if he'd found the one and only thing he'd wanted since he'd left the gym and retreated to his office earlier in the day, not even once imagining that she would defy him.

She was speaking to a couple, the woman holding a young baby, and the man holding the hand of a boy of about seven. She was laughing. That was what had struck him still. He hadn't seen her laugh since that night in Iondorra. Her hand was outstretched in front of her, where the baby was gripping her silver bangles and tugging on them, bringing more laughter from her peach-coloured lips.

His gaze searched the tableau, finally resting on the young boy, whose smile wasn't dimmed in the slightest by the slash of scar tissue reaching up from his neck and covering half of the child's face. There was no way for the boy to hide the damaged skin, not as Matthieu could.

He felt a sharp stab of pain in his chest, shocking and powerful as he took in the sight. All around him were patrons and guests of his charity, all ready and more than willing to donate to a more than worthy cause. And yes, there were a few glances his way, but most of the attendees were wrapped up in their present conversations. Here were people who had been affected, just like him, those who had fared both better and far worse than he.

Something harsh skittered over his skin, sending a shiver down his spine. All this time he had stayed away, telling himself that he hadn't wanted to take away attention from the charity, but for the first time, he wondered whether that was the true reason he had avoided the charity for so many years. Because the people who were here, the people who bore similar scars to him, rather than hiding away, stood proudly beneath the lights of the museum, bared themselves to the world and still smiled, still laughed.

In that moment, as if she had sensed his presence, Maria caught his gaze and a whole raft of emotions cried out loud and clear across the crowded room. Surprise, concern, apology and compassion. And all he wanted to see was flaming desire. The same sensation burning deep within him. He pushed away the sudden and shocking arousal, and stalked towards her in firm, quick strides.

'Matthieu…' she said, her voice slightly breathless. 'You came.'

'I did,' he managed to bite out beneath the swirls of resentment and shocking half-thought-out self-revelations.

'Thank you,' she replied, with a smile that soothed, and in that moment he caught just a glimpse of what kind of mother she would become. He'd told her that night at his office that she would be strong, defiant and determined. But now he could see that she would be kind, loving, supportive…all the things his own mother had been.

Suddenly he was plunged back into a memory—one from early in the evening of the fire. His mother was helping him with his tie for the meal they would share with their family. *You look so handsome. Just like your father.* She'd swept him up in an embrace that was tight—one he'd squirmed within—but was full of love and something a little like hope for what he would become. She'd kissed him on his forehead and taken his hand…

'Mr Montcour!' Benjamin Keant practically squealed, having discovered his arrival. 'It is so good to see you here.'

Matthieu shook off the shocking effect of a memory he had not delved into once since the night of the accident, simultaneously yearning for and strangely resenting the remembered feeling of his mother's embrace.

He ignored the varied ramblings of the director, but he couldn't shake the overly watchful gaze of his wife—the wife that saw far too much.

Maria had felt the pull from Matthieu almost as more of a physical tug than the hold the lovely little baby currently had on her bracelets. She had been talking to the couple and their children, finding relief in their easy open conversation more than the vacuous twitterings of the famous socialites or patrons attending the charity gala. Forging even more of a yearning to hold her own child one day.

But then she'd felt it. His gaze lifting the light hair on her arms, a tingling at the back of her neck. When she'd finally seen him, stalking towards her through the crowd, her breath had caught at the sight of him. Impossibly broad shoulders encased in a midnight-blue tux, the material pulled tight across the muscles on his arms, his dark tie pulled slightly at the neck of a startling white shirt as if he'd yanked at it in frustration. On many it would have looked disrespectful. On Matthieu it looked irresistible.

His dark brow and beard accentuated the severe look on features that softened momentarily when he took in the sight of her standing with the young family whose son, Edward, had been caught in a car accident that had swiftly turned life-threatening when the petrol tank had leaked and gone up in flames.

Though the charity director had released an almost unstoppable flow of words at her husband, apparently failing to discern the dark mood swirling about him, Matthieu had not once taken his eyes from her. She felt it almost as a physical touch, a caress, a brand across her skin. A promise of something she couldn't quite identify and once again she felt herself hurtling towards some kind of impending confrontation and welcomed it. She'd meant what she'd said to him earlier. She couldn't, *wouldn't*, live like this.

'I like your bracelets,' Edward said, reaching up to where his baby sister was still shaking them to produce a tinkling she took great joy in.

'Thank you, Edward,' Maria replied, unable to keep the beam of pride from her voice. 'I made them myself, so the fact you like them makes it extra special for me.'

'You make jewellery?' he asked. She thought of the boxes she had sent to Italy, initially unsure how to work her past into this new present—her marriage. But over the last weeks she had filled sketch pad upon sketch pad, ideas brimming from the stunning surroundings of the estate by Lake Lucerne. The beautiful natural structures of the woods, the trees, leaves and berries... The smooth, mirror-like surface of the water, the reflections to be found there, working with the solitude to fire her imagination. It had been strange to suddenly find this creativity—one that had been languishing, despite her faith and belief in her work, ever since she had left Iondorra. Ever since she had left his bed that first and only time.

'I do,' she decided, realising that it was as much part of her as the baby growing within her.

'And what will you do when you grow up?' Matthieu asked, a tone to his voice Maria didn't think she'd heard before.

Edward peered up at him, cast a quick glance to his parents as if to ask if it would be okay to speak to the stranger and, receiving encouraging smiles, answered, 'I am going to be a firefighter,' with no small amount of pride and determination.

'That would be a very exciting job—and a very important one too.'

'I know,' Edward said, almost dismissively, in that easy childlike way, of his scars.

Matthieu crouched down, bringing his huge frame to Edward's level. 'I do too,' he whispered conspiratorially, lifting back the shirt collar as he had once done with her. Maria held her breath as Edward's eyes grew wide and round, then narrowed in assessment. 'I had skin taken from my head and used in the graft on my face.'

'Wow,' Matthieu said, letting out a low whistle of awe that seemed to satisfy Edward greatly. 'Okay,' he said, making it clear that he was giving something deep consideration and bringing a surprising smile to Maria's lips. '*I* had *fake* skin used in my graft.'

'Split or full thickness?' Edward fired back challengingly.

Maria's skin vibrated with the rumble of laughter let loose by Matthieu and she couldn't help but feel it within her too as she watched her husband and the young boy compare and compete over their various conditions and treatments, seeing for the first time how he might be with their child. The bond she wanted and yearned for between them. 'Are you sure you don't want to be a doctor when you grow up, rather than a fireman?' Matthieu asked.

'I like the fire truck best.'

The group's responding laughter was cut short by the gala's welcoming speech. Benjamin spoke clearly, and surprisingly slowly, on how the money raised would be put to use, and introduced a few of the inspiring success stories from some of the guests present, leaving barely a dry eye in the room, before turning his final thanks and debts of gratitude to Matthieu himself.

Maria shivered from the effect of hundreds of pairs

of eyes on her and the powerful man beside her, who managed to hide the discomfort she imagined he must be feeling as he gracefully accepted the acknowledgement and thanks of the charity director. As the cheers from the crowd died down, and Edward and his family disappeared into the throng, Maria finally turned to her husband.

'Do you regret coming tonight?' she asked tentatively. She watched him choose his response carefully.

'Not yet, but the night is still young,' the ironic tone to his voice a fragile olive branch.

She smiled up at him then, reaching for his hand, slipping her fingers in between his, and marvelled at the jolt of electricity and happiness that shot through her as he squeezed gently, the light pressure saying so much more than his brief, carefully chosen words.

As Matthieu took her hand in his he looked about and saw the good that had been done by the charity he'd created from his family's insurance pay-outs. The help it had brought others. Both his uncles and his aunt had been younger than his parents with no children of their own and, as Matthieu was their next of kin, their wealth had all been funnelled his way. More money than he could ever imagine spending in a hundred lifetimes. On top of Montcour Mining Industries it would have seemed almost laughable, if it had not been tied to such a great loss.

Ever since that first gala almost ten years before, the intrusive press, the headlines of the 'haunted Montcour' taking precedence, he had vowed not to return. But in doing so, had he shut himself off from what the charity had achieved? Seeing the hundreds of people, if not more, that the charity was helping…it was as if his family had reached out to so many people in need and worked to help them when and however they needed it. It soothed an ache he'd thought buried too deep to reach.

He was about to turn to Maria when Margery appeared at their side.

'There is still a little time before dinner and Mr Keant thought you might like to see a private viewing of the exhibition the museum has put on display for the gala? They have been incredibly generous with their chosen pieces.'

'Can we?' Maria asked, hopefully. The excitement in her eyes shone as purely as ever and he couldn't refuse her in this.

'Lead the way,' he said, gesturing to Margery.

Once they were through the throng of guests, the quiet of the hallways felt oddly deafening, punctuated by the tapping of his companions' heels on the smooth stone flooring. Through dimly lit corridors they made their way towards a series of rooms closed off for the gala's exhibition.

'If you have any questions about the artists, please don't hesitate to ask,' Margery stated before unclipping the thick red twist of rope across the entrance to the first room. She hung back as Matthieu and Maria made their way into the surprisingly large space.

White walls gave way to incredible splashes of colour as the large paintings hung strategically on the walls led the viewer through and around the space, not chronologically or by subject matter from what he could tell, but more by shape or colour.

The quiet settled a kind of peace about them that washed over him, easing away what suddenly felt like years of tension. Maria walked between the paintings, searching for something he couldn't quite identify. He smiled, realising that she didn't waste time hanging back with undue reverence afforded to an artist based solely on fame, but instead drew up close to certain canvasses as if trying to work out how, rather than why, it was done.

While she studied the paintings, he seemed incapable of not studying her. Her reaction, delight, the slight scrunch of her nose when she found something distasteful, the way her eyes and body lit up with joy when she discovered a masterpiece she'd never thought to see in person. He marvelled again, not only at her beauty, but at his own ability to stay away from her these last few weeks.

They moved from room to room, Margery hanging back discreetly giving them a false feeling of isolation. But Matthieu rarely took his eyes from Maria, which was why it took him a moment to see it for himself. The painting. The one he'd never seen until now.

Maria was almost overwhelmed by the sheer beauty of the collection curated by the museum for the charity gala. Monet, Klee, Caillebotte, Duchamp, Renoir, Rothko, Freud—it was as if they'd gathered the greatest artists of the last two centuries. Everything from rural scenes, portraits, to sculpture and her eyes, heart and mind feasted on it. She felt overwhelmed by the beauty of these pieces, inspired to draw, to delve into her moulds, to melt down the materials to their base states and morph them into something even half as beautiful as what currently surrounded her.

They had come to the last room in the small, but exquisite exhibition and, although there was a huge Hockney taking up almost the entire length of one wall, she couldn't help but be drawn to a much smaller canvas, which depicted a couple and a young boy, all facing each other and laughing together. It wasn't the usual stiff, formal portrait, like others she had passed in the previous rooms. This was the kind that made you smile instantly, the artist somehow managing to include the viewer in a private joke, whilst also making them a voyeur to a family so engrossed in each other they were unaware of being watched. She frowned a little at the father, something about him snagged in her mind, and her gaze flicked to the small white placard, taking in the name of the artist and the family.

She felt as if she had been drenched in water from an ice bucket and couldn't have prevented her gasp of shock if she'd tried. Her hand flew to her mouth, trying a little too late to bring it back as her eyes flew back to take in the details of Matthieu's mother and father...and the young boy he had once been.

A wave of overwhelming sadness and grief covered her as she marvelled at the way the artist had managed to capture the love shining from Matthieu's father's eyes as he gazed at his wife and child. The way his mother only had eyes for young Matthieu, but still had her hand on his father's arm as if their connection was and would always be inviolate. But it was the joy that rocked her. The joy they had in each other...a joy that would be cut short within a year of the painting.

For a moment she didn't dare turn, didn't dare look at him. Matthieu was behind her and even through the distance between them she felt it. The shock, the grief, the anger, the pain... She soaked it up like a sponge, consuming it and letting that too wash over her.

An electronic sound of a picture being taken followed only moments behind the blinding flash and Maria flinched at both. Her eyes took a second to adjust, even though she had turned her face in the direction of the photographer only feet away.

Within seconds, several flashes stuttered into the room and Matthieu had stalked past her to thrust the man up against a white wall, their dark-suited figures stark in contrast. Angry incomprehensible words echoed within the empty gallery, security guards rushing in to drag the men apart.

Matthieu pulled away from the guard, speaking so quickly, Maria could barely translate. Not that she needed to. His tone was indication enough. From behind him, the photographer was pointing and yelling at her husband and, without sparing the man another glace, Matthieu turned on his heel and stalked from the room.

With his departure, the chain holding her still lifted and she practically ran after Matthieu, chasing the sounds of his fast footsteps as he left the exhibition. She passed Margery, barely registering the woman's distress, leaving her behind, and followed as Matthieu left the building through a discreet doorway and made his way out into the gardens of the museum, her heels plunging into the thick grass making her steps harder, as if even the ground were trying to hold her back from reaching him in that moment.

In very little time they reached a small helicopter and while the pilot frantically readied the aircraft, Matthieu held the door back to her with barely leashed emotion that had gripped his entire body in such a way that she dared not speak.

She climbed into the helicopter, quickly assuring herself that it was safe to fly at this stage of her pregnancy, and slid over to the far side to make room for Matthieu. But instead of joining her, he closed the door and slipped into the seat next to the now ready pilot.

Maria could have moved back into the middle but she didn't. Instead, she stayed in the far corner, clinging to the edge of the seat as the helicopter jerked up from the ground before sweeping up into the night sky.

Everything around her was dark, the mood, the light, the landscape beneath her. Shadows and little dots of lights punctured the thick, midnight blanket that had enveloped her, but did nothing to soothe the guilt that wracked her from head to toe. That the photographer had caught Matthieu at such a vulnerable moment, such an exposed, raw, heartbreaking moment... It had been the first time she had seen even a glimpse of the extent of her husband's pain.

Maria hadn't known her mother. She had died bringing her into this world, and Maria had inherited only memories from her brother and father to guide her in shaping an impression of the woman who had given birth to her. Maria's pain was more like that of a phantom limb, itching and aching in a way that was absent, rather than real. Yes, she had felt loss and anger and frustration, but in a slightly removed way, as if never really quite sure what she was missing.

But for Matthieu it was different. So very different.

It felt as if they had been flying for both an age and no time at all. Maria was pulled from her thoughts as the helicopter dropped gently on the helipad at the back of the estate in Lucerne she vaguely remembered seeing from one of her walks.

Although everything in her wanted to fling back the door and flee into the night, she wasn't sure of the safety protocol and only then did she realise she'd had her first flight in a helicopter, so lost had she been in her thoughts. Thoughts of him, thoughts of her.

The door slid back and Matthieu's shadowed, brooding form beckoned her forth. She picked up her skirts and hunched within the low interior, stepped out and followed his retreating form. As she followed him through the darkness, with the sounds of the helicopter's engine receding behind her, she heard the ping of Matthieu's phone. Once, twice. A brief pause between a third and fourth. But he ignored it in the same way that he was ignoring her.

And suddenly she was angry. Angry that he could not even bring himself to look at her, let alone speak to her. The closer and closer they got to the estate, the more furious she became, feeling a little as if she was being brought back to a prison.

A prison where her husband barely tolerated her presence. There were times in her childhood when she'd felt extreme loneliness—while her father, stepmother and brother argued about money behind closed doors, 'adult' business that didn't involve her. Decisions being made about their future, her future, ones she had no say in. She had once promised herself not to ever be in that position again. And the one time she had chosen something for herself, the one time she had followed her instincts, the consequences had seen her right back behind another set of closed doors, under the control of her husband.

He led them back into the house through the door from the garden and stalked into the open-plan kitchen and living room, but this time when Matthieu turned towards his office, the doorway she never breached, she couldn't take it any more. She knew he was angry, furious even, but she would not live in silence, she would not allow herself to avoid this any longer.

'Ask me why I went to the gala tonight,' she called out to him.

He halted, his hand outstretched towards the door handle. She could tell he was warring within himself, to push on forwards into the room he would close himself off in, or to turn and give into her demand. She only exhaled as she saw the tense outline of his shoulders turn and she finally locked eyes with her husband.

'Why did you go to the gala tonight, Maria?' His tone was droll and mechanical. Purposely so and it made her mad. Seething frustration and anger that she just couldn't get through to him. Couldn't get past the barriers he had built between them.

'I went because Mrs Montcour had been invited to a gala and I wanted to see her.'

He frowned. 'You're not making sense.'

She practically growled out loud, only just managing to resist the urge to stamp her foot. 'I went because I didn't know who I was as your wife. Maria Rohan de Luen? Yes, I was actually just getting to know her before this. She was just beginning to find her freedom. Just beginning to make her own decisions and choices,' she said, desperate to explain, to reach him, to make a connection. 'But Maria Montcour? She's new to me. I went to the gala because I wanted to see who she was, to see if she was different perhaps, more confident... more powerful even? And maybe, *just maybe*, going to a gala organised by a charity founded by my husband, whether he was present or not, would help me see a little more about who he is, what makes him tick, other than that he has a penchant for concrete!' She hadn't meant to shout, but that was where her little speech had ended. Her shouting at him. She didn't think she'd ever shouted at anyone before in her life.

For a moment, she thought that her words had no effect. None at all. He might as well have been made of the concrete he'd made his house from. His phone pinged another few times, cutting through the silence between them.

'Well, you certainly got to see that. And so did the

press,' he growled. 'Did you not think?' he demanded, spinning around to turn on her. 'About how tonight was everything I had wanted to avoid for nearly *ten years*? I tried to warn you about the press, about what vultures they are and how they would do anything to get even just a glimpse of the *beast* and the innocent now tied to him.'

Maria's heart broke just a little at his words. Was that truly how he saw them?

'The moment you stepped out on the red carpet the entire world knew that you were married to me and pregnant with my child.'

'I'll concede that perhaps I hadn't quite thought it through.'

'We don't have the luxury of not thinking it through. Not now.'

'Matthieu, the press were always going to find out,' she said gently but persistently.

'At a time of our choosing. Not one that would impact upon the charity!'

'Matthieu—' Yet another ping emitted from his phone, cutting through her words. 'Oh, for God's sake, what is wrong with your phone?' she demanded.

'Do you really have no idea?' he returned, seemingly incredulous. 'Here,' he said, sweeping a thumb across his phone before passing it to her. 'Take a look.'

As she held the phone in her hand, scrolling down through page after page of social media headlines about *the beast* showing his colours, the beast wedding an innocent, the beast's secret violence, some questioning if Maria was safe, the more ridiculous pondering whether she had been kidnapped, her fingers began to shake. Yes, there were a few positive ones, about how Matthieu Montcour had found his happy-ever-after, about the resounding success of the charity gala's event, the joy at the future heir to the Montcour dynasty, but her thumb stalled over the last image captured on his phone. The image of Matthieu standing behind Maria, her hand over her mouth in shock, the glistening of tears in her eyes as they both took in the painting of Matthieu and his parents. And the violation of that moment devastated her because in all her attempts of finding herself, she had brought the wolf directly to Matthieu's door.

CHAPTER SEVEN

MATTHIEU WAS FURIOUS. With the press, with Maria, with himself. For the first time in his life he couldn't blame someone else. He was the one who had truly lived up to his reputation as a beast the moment he had pushed the photographer up against the wall. It was his actions, his loss of control that had furthered the obscene attention-grabbing headlines.

Before the gala he had set his phone to notify him of any social media posts relating to him or Maria. And the phone gripped tight in Maria's slightly shaking hands was still pinging away.

Because he had lost control. Because that damn photographer had caught them, caught *him*, with his defences down and it had allowed all the anger and the violence out.

He closed his eyes, but the family portrait his father had commissioned months before the night of the fire was imprinted on his mind. He conceded that the artistry was perfect. Because the hours that must have gone into creating such a masterpiece had truly caught the truth of his family. The joy and love shining from their eyes, made so much more invaluable by the events that followed, had been too much. Too much and not enough. He'd barely remembered it being done because he rarely allowed memories of before to pass beyond the steel door he'd shut upon them once he'd left hospital. Because if he hadn't, he truly wasn't sure he'd have survived.

And now that he had seen it, now that memories were beginning to seep through the small gap that had been opened just a few hours ago, Matthieu slammed the vault door shut, hoping that it would be enough, hoping that he'd done so in time.

'Matthieu—'

'I warned you. I warned you what would happen but you went anyway!' He hated that he was shouting. Hated that he was still trying to wrestle his control back into place.

'I didn't… I'm sorry.'

'Your apology means nothing,' he bit out cruelly. 'I need you to understand. Understand that this is what it is like for me. Understand that this is what it is like to be married to me and what it is and will be like for you and for our child. That always the paparazzi will be stalking us, following our every move. Our every moment. They always have, ever since…'

He flinched the moment she laid a hand on his arm, trying to turn him to face her, and it took everything in him not to shake it off. Because she did need to understand. He needed to make her. That the world would never tire of the tragedy that was his past, never tire of the beast that was his present.

'After the funerals, I missed most of the press furore. Malcolm and the hospital managed to keep it away from me then. So I wasn't prepared for what happened. But I need you to be.'

'What happened, Matthieu?'

Matthieu blew out a breath. Resenting that he was about to open this wound for her, but knowing that it was better than the deeper hurt. Better than the hurt that he'd just locked behind the steel trap in his mind. 'Do you know how I first earned my reputation as a beast? The scars were one thing, but I was seventeen the first time they coined that phrase.' He turned then, because he needed her to see.

She was staring up at him, so small, so perfect, so fragile.

'Malcolm had wanted me to have something of a normal life,' he explained. A cynical huff of laughter escaped his lungs and bled hurt into the air between them. 'By seventeen I was finally well enough to attend school, but it was difficult. I'd been amongst adults, nurses, doctors, and private teachers for six years by that point. I had very little experience of being around people my age. Teenagers who had already formed friend groups and cliques. So I kept to myself. Head down, studied. Because of my private education I was put ahead a year and was already an oddity, and the scars? They proved more of a curiosity amongst the students than I had ever imagined. When one of the prettiest girls in the school asked me to help her with her studies, I…' He spared barely a sigh for the naïve young boy he'd been then. 'I had thought she might be different. When I realised that she was flirting with me, I was astounded, eager…desperate even.' He closed his eyes against the memories of those naïve fumblings, the sting of anger towards Clara never having gone away. Instead, turning into a lesson he revisited whenever he felt weak.

The self-recrimination, the *humiliation* of how innocent he had been was like a knife twisting in his gut. But he had to continue. Maria had to understand. 'In such a short time, she'd orchestrated my feelings like a maestro. I thought myself half in love and would have given her anything. She was very clear on what she wanted from me, and I knew no better. Until that point, no one had seen my scars. I had never done any sports, worn my school jumper even in the heights of summer. I should have known,' he said more to himself than to Maria. He turned away, casting his gaze into the night, but couldn't avoid the reflection of her face in the glass window. He could tell that she had a sense of what he was about to say. Could see, feel even, the sympathy, the concern, passing from herself to him. He shook it off and pressed on.

'She had a camera. I didn't know. She and her friends had been approached by an unscrupulous journalist who had offered them an obscene amount of money for a picture of me. But that wasn't enough for Clara. She arranged a greater pay-out for an accompanying article about how I had seduced her and tried to take advantage of her. About how I had grown angry when she wouldn't do what I wanted. A harsh irony because I had been the one to refuse to sleep with her, wanting to take things slowly. As if being rejected by a beast like me had burned her ego. Malcolm had an injunction taken out, the article didn't make publication, but it was too late. Rumours filled the school, reaching the parents, reaching the press…the damage had been done.'

Maria was shaking. With fury, with injustice… For the first time *she* felt like the beast, wanting to lash out and destroy. That such a thing had been done to him. That he had been so badly misused and betrayed, on top of the devastation that he had already experienced. Suddenly memories of their first night together crashed down upon her. It must have taken so much for him to give into her request It must have taken trust. A trust that she hadn't earned then, but wanted to now. She wanted him to see what she saw.

'I am truly sorry that happened to you.'

He shrugged his shoulder, as if dismissing her and the compassion she offered. But she wouldn't be dismissed. Not this time. She turned him around to face her and waited until he met her eyes.

'But you need to know that I did not and *do* not see you as a beast. And…' She paused, hoping that Matthieu would understand, would believe her next words. 'And I think you should also know that not all the posts on your phone, not all the press reports, do either.'

He scoffed and turned back away from her. She didn't need his phone to remember the other headlines.

Montcour Finds Happiness.

Montcour's Charity a Resounding Success.

Millions Raised by Montcour.

'Matthieu—did you ever think that the reason the press are so interested in you is not because of the scars, or your reputation, or the loss of your family, but because you survived? Because you turned something truly terrible into something amazing? A charity that gives back to those that need it?'

Disbelief and something painfully like hope shone in his eyes. It gave her the strength to carry on.

'That they aren't horrified, but amazed by how well you've done for yourself?'

He frowned and in that moment she wondered whether he had even seen those particular headlines amongst the dross that had spewed onto social media.

She could see him trying to assimilate what she had said into how he had spent years of his life viewing the negative headlines about him and what he'd achieved. She could almost feel the war within him as he tried to reframe the image of himself, not through the bitter lens of the desperate press, but as how she saw him, as how others might. But before she could tell what conclusion he had come to, he shut down. She could almost hear the door closing on his thoughts.

'I am going to bed.'

And he left her standing alone in the middle of the large open space, concrete and soft white leather, so stark in comparison to the way his entire being had become her sole focus, the large, heated breath of his body… She couldn't leave it like that. Couldn't just let him walk away. He was in pain, that she could see clearly. For a while she simply stood there, wanting to go to him, not sure if she had that right. But if she didn't, she saw how their future would be—two isolated and lonely people sharing the same space, the same love for a child, but not together. If she let him go this night, she suddenly felt that she would lose Matthieu for ever.

She followed the path he had taken up the stairs to the bedrooms, the one she had been allocated all the way at the other end of the house—as if as far away from him as possible. But she would not retreat, would not hide, would not abandon him tonight.

She pushed open the door to his room, the one she had never been in or seen. For a moment she was plunged back to the night they had spent in Iondorra. His room was just as large, almost big enough to contain the entire flat she had shared with Evin and Anita in Camberwell.

It was beautiful. The bed jutted out, as if floating inches above the floor, the frame and headboard made from reclaimed oak, warming the incredible breadth of the side wall that met floor-to-ceiling windows framed in black, making the most of the stunning view of Lake Lucerne, even in the night time. It must be incredible in

the morning, Maria thought. Either side of the inconceivably large bed hung a series of metal tubes, like huge
wind-chimes, glowing gently with discreet lighting. Behind her the entire wall was encased in antique mirror,
flooding her mind with shockingly sensual thoughts as
to what might be seen from the bed, bringing an almost
painful blush to her cheeks.

From the corner of the room was a corridor that must
have led immediately into the bathroom, because she
could hear the sounds of water streaming from a shower,
traces of steam tinged with the scent of lemon grass
reached where she stood.

She slipped off her shoes and made her way towards
the shower, swirls and twists in the steam beckoning her
forth. The long swathes of heavy silky material sweeping behind her bare feet made a gentle brushing sound
that barely reached her ears.

As she rounded the corner, the sight took her breath
away. Hidden lighting illuminated the space in long
strips, copper taps and accents warmed the grey tones
of the concrete, and the glass-fronted shower unit, large
enough for more people than Maria dared to imagine in
a shower, was only partially misted. Behind the glass she
could see Matthieu, his head bent under the powerful jets
of water, his arms outstretched against the wall as if he
was bracing himself against the emotions of that night.
For just a moment she allowed herself to watch as the
water cascaded over the stunning breadth of his shoulders, the way it twisted over his muscles, as if it clung
to his skin until it had traversed as much of the length
of him as possible. Her fingers itched to follow its path
across his skin, back and down to his legs and calves.
She had never been so enthralled by a man—not even her
naïve crush on Theo had been this devastating.

She fumbled with the fastening at the back of her dress but her fingers caught against the clasp and the urgency to go to him increased with each heartbeat to the point where she couldn't care less about the dress. Refusing to waste any time, she reached for the handle and swept aside the glass, catching his image in the reflection and noting that Matthieu's only reaction was a raised eyebrow, nothing else. Not even a turn of his head, not even the stiffening of his shoulders. Just a simple wry questioning gesture that barely acknowledged her presence.

But she would not be ignored. Not in this. Not now and not ever again.

She picked up her skirts, stepped over the threshold of the shower fully clothed, and ducked beneath one powerful arm, to bring herself in between them, facing him. He yanked his head back, finally unable to escape or deny her.

'What are you doing?' he demanded, but left his arms where they were, still braced against the wall, encasing her, as if perhaps teasing or testing himself, she couldn't tell.

The water soaked into the dress, making it impossibly heavy, but she didn't care. It turned her hair into thick ropes that broke free from the pins that had held them in place and fell around her shoulders and down her back. But all she wanted, all she could think of was his hands on her skin, the feel of him beneath her tongue, and touch. She reached up and cupped his jaw, running her thumb over the rich dark beard that was surprising in its softness. She gazed up at him as rivers of water poured over them both, each now breathing as hard as if they'd run a marathon.

'You need this. *I* need this,' she said before sweeping her hand around his neck and pulling him down to meet her lips, just as she said, '*We* need this.'

* * *

The moment his lips pressed against hers, Matthieu's mind and heart were consumed with need. She might have offered an alternative vision of how the press viewed him, but how he had viewed *her* had not once changed. She was irresistible. Her soft, wet slicked skin, the plumpness of her lips, he wanted it all. He braced himself against the cool concrete of the shower enclosure and devoured her, his tongue plunging deep, teeth gently scraping against the softness of her. Her hands were wrapped around his neck, clinging to him as much as he wanted to cling to her, her breasts moulded against his chest, bump against abdomen. He held himself back, bridged against the wall, yet consumed everything she could offer him with her mouth, her touch. He could have sworn he was shaking with the effort of fighting the need for restraint and the desire for more.

For an entire month he had avoided this, avoided her. Not because he hadn't wanted her. But because he had. Because he'd wanted her with such a raw need that it had threatened to undo him. But after tonight, after all the emotions dredged up from where he had kept them locked and hidden away, by both the press and the painting, he wasn't strong enough to deny him, *them*, this. And damn him, but he was going to take everything she had to give.

'The baby?' he said, the last barrier to lifting the leash on his desires completely.

'Will be absolutely fine,' she assured him, pressing another kiss to his lips. And it was the sweetest thing he thought he'd ever heard.

Leaning back and pulling one hand from the wall, he wrapped it around her back, bringing her closer to him, pressing her against the length of him, bringing a half laugh from deep within his chest. 'You're still wearing your dress.'

'What are you going to do about it?' she demanded, not full of coquettish intonation. More of a challenge— a challenge and a silent demand.

He wanted to growl and beat his chest, not like the beast she denied that he was, but the animal she was turning him into being. He wanted to tear it from her body. As the water cascaded down from above, he loosened his hold on the wall and reached down to fist the layers of material by her thigh. The soaking wet bundle leached more water, pooling over his hand and down his arm. He released his hold on the material and reached for what he really wanted. Her.

'Turn around,' he commanded and, casting him a look of sheer unwarranted trust, she did, turning her head to the side and exposing the long thin column of her neck to the hot sprays, causing her hair to dip and fall over one shoulder. Between her shoulder blades where each side of the dress gathered was the top of the zip. His fingers went to it and slowly, oh, so slowly, drew the tab down from the top, the weight of the waterlogged silks pulling the dress apart, exposing the length of her spine, the curve just beneath his fingertips so that he was unable to stop himself from tracing the progress with his thumb. She shivered beneath his touch and he wanted more. So he pressed open-mouthed kisses across the skin of her back, delighting and devouring in each inch that was revealed to him.

With one arm wrapped around her, covering her breasts, and the other drawing the zip down to the base of her spine, he felt as if he held the most precious thing in the world in his arms and that he was not, and never could be, worthy of such a thing.

She arched into his touch, as if desperate to feel more, and he could not deny her any longer. Slowly, he turned her in his arms, gazing into the dark brown orbs that studied him with an intensity he felt deep within him. He watched as she lifted a hand and brushed the material of the dress off her shoulders, fascinated as it poured from her skin, and she was left standing before him in nothing more than her panties, rivulets of water glistening trails of silver across creamy skin that he wanted to trace with his tongue.

She reached for his hands and pulled them gently around her belly and his thoughts splintered between the firmness of the slightly strange shapes beneath his palms and the fact that their child was within her, protected by her, loved by them both. He worried about his hands, so large, and Maria and their child so small. And she smiled up at him as if sharing the same thought.

'Surrounded by us both,' she whispered to him above the pounding of the water around them. Was it wrong to want such carnal things from his wife when she was pregnant with his child? he wondered. Ever since Clara, he'd always believed that intimacy needed to be emotionless, no expectation of hope or betrayal, desires simply and easily requested or refused—no judgement or pressure. But this? This sense of attachment to his wife was threatening to cut him off at the knees.

Because suddenly his needs and wants didn't matter—all that mattered was Maria and what she wanted and desired and how he could give them to her. When she had come into his shower, all he had wanted was to erase the night, to delve into sensual satisfaction that would rob him of thought and want, but now? Now he didn't care if he lived on a rack of his emotions for the next twenty years of his life. All he wanted was her to have every in-dulgence, every desire, want and need met and exceeded.

He hooked a thumb into the side of her panties, slowly drawing the material down over her hips and thighs, and pushing them to the floor. With one hand, he reached for her neck, pulling her into a kiss as he delved between her legs with the other, drawing a gasp from her lips, one that he immediately consumed, pulling her breath deep within him, wanting everything, her moans, her cries of pleasure. Almost instantly she bucked against his hand, quivering with unchecked arousal that matched his own. He felt the tremor run across her skin beneath the layer of slick water that poured down from above them. He cursed, so close she was to orgasm that he feared it would call forth his own. His hard erection jutted against the smooth firm curve of her abdomen, again and again as her moans grew sensually urgent and full with need.

Words, begging and pleading, fell from her lips and he wanted to give her everything. He dropped to his knees, supporting her with his hands around her backside, the glorious feel of it filling the palms of his hands, more exquisite than he could have imagined.

He followed the path of his thumb across her clitoris with his tongue and he preened beneath the stifled moan of pleasure that her hand blocked from leaving her mouth. Ruthlessly he drove her to the edge and back, over and over again, because he wanted, needed, her as lost in her passion as he was.

As her cries mounted, so did his need, but he held himself firmly in check, because it was no longer about him and his wants, but her. She came apart in his hands and mouth and he had never experienced anything more magnificent or beautiful in his life.

* * *

Maria was shaking and she didn't care, clinging to Matthieu's shoulders as if it were the only way she could remain standing. *Standing.* She had come to him for his needs and he had seen only to her own, but couldn't find it within herself to feel regret and instead focused on the soaring pleasure shimmering through her body.

She had thought that she'd imagined it, misremembered the dizzying heights Matthieu had taken her to that night almost five months ago now. But she hadn't. Instead, she wondered whether time had in fact dulled her memory because every touch, kiss, caress rang through her body like a song—the melody both familiar and yet strangely new and wonderful.

She let her head fall back as warm water cascaded over her. Matthieu rose and took her in his arms in a way she'd only dreamed of.

'You look like a mermaid,' he said, the honey-coloured glint in his eye highlighted by the surrounding emerald green.

'A large, round, pregnant mermaid?'

'You look incredible.'

'Smooth talker,' she said, gently slapping him on the shoulder, the wet of their skin making the sound louder than she'd expected.

'Hardly,' he admitted, his voice gravelly. He reached out a finger to loop beneath the silver necklace that hung between her bare breasts. 'You are always wearing this.'

'It is the only thing I have left of my mother,' she replied. 'She died bringing me into this world.'

Matthieu's breath left his chest on a *whoosh*, and he closed his eyes against her words. 'Maria... I am so sorry.'

And she gently smiled as if trying to ease his sympathetic ache. 'Had it not been for me, she would have lived. Sebastian would have had a mother and my father wouldn't have hidden his grief in apathy, a second wife who would rather spend money than love us, and risky business deals that almost destroyed us.' She placed a hand on his arm. 'I don't blame myself. I can't. I know that it's not my fault, that there was nothing I could have done, that I was a baby. She had a medical complication. But I do know something of loss, Matthieu.'

The words came unbidden to his lips.

'I am glad you have this. That you are able to have it with you. The only thing I have left...' He paused, the stab of pain stark and foreign yet somehow strangely familiar. 'The only thing I have that belonged to my parents is the present my mother gave to my father the night they died. It was their twelfth wedding anniversary, and she had given him the gift just before my bedtime.' His breathing became hard, as he remembered what had happened later, but forced himself back to the present. 'It's burned, mostly melted and deeply damaged by the fire.'

Maria frowned. 'Where is it?'

He shrugged his shoulder as if it were nothing, when it was everything. 'In my bedside cabinet.'

Matthieu looked at her then and saw what he had feared since the first moment he'd caught sight of her. Somehow he'd known, even then, that she would unearth his grief, his pain...understand it even. That she would be the one to break down the walls around his heart. Walls that he had relied on for the last twenty years. Walls that he didn't know how to live without. Because that would mean opening himself up...leaving himself vulnerable to the same kind of loss that nearly destroyed him once before.

She kissed him then, one of compassion, one of sympathy and understanding that he feared she might not want to have given when she discovered the truth about the present and what it had cost his entire family. Coward that he was, he lost himself in that kiss, deliberately stoking its fire, rousing the passion between them.

'Matthieu—' Her words cut off in a squeal as he picked her up entirely and took them both from the shower. Her cries turned into giggles as he set her on her feet and dried her in the most gloriously fluffy towel she'd ever touched.

'Maria Montcour, this is absolutely no laughing matter. I take my duties very seriously.'

At his half jokingly stern words, the laughter dimmed in her mind. 'I know,' she said, and couldn't help the vein of sadness running through her words. She knew he did and would. Because of who he was, because of what had happened to him, because that was the man he had become. But perhaps...not because of her.

She pushed aside the thought and reached to caress his jaw. This man who had offered her compassion and understanding for her own loss, when he seemed to hide from his own. She loved the feel of the firm proud line of it, covered by the soft swirls of the short beard he kept. Her heart leapt as he leant into her touch and placed a kiss on the palm of her hand. Then her wrist, and then down the inside of her forearm.

Surely it was wrong to want someone so much so soon after—

Her brain almost short-circuited as his thumb outlined the curve of her breast—her body so extremely sensitive and responsive since the pregnancy.

As he ran the pad of his thumb over her already taut nipple she fought the moan of pleasure that started deep within her. 'Bed. Now,' she commanded, wondering when she had become so empowered.

'As you wish,' he replied, sweeping her up off her feet and walking them to the bed where he gently laid her down and got in beside her.

Maria would remember that night for the rest of her life. Their lovemaking became just that. Loving, giving and receiving, pleasure almost indescribable as they each reached the heights of an impossible rapture. Neither were held back by doubts, or haunted by what was to come, both instead lost in pure unadulterated, endless unchecked bliss.

CHAPTER EIGHT

MARIA DIDN'T KNOW what she had expected following the night of the gala. Perhaps for her new life to go back to the strange untouched isolation that she had experienced after the wedding…but she couldn't have been more wrong.

On the first night she'd gone to her room only for Matthieu to stalk in, pick her up off the bed, carry her to his, gently lay her down on the bed and get in beside her. All without saying a word. It happened again on the second night and Maria was too confused to want to break the strange spell that had descended on them with questions or words.

On the third night, when the baby had been unsettled and sleep elusive, he had turned on the dim lighting, lain on his side facing her and asked her how she'd made her first piece of jewellery. He'd peppered her with questions about each and every step until she had fallen asleep in the middle of an explanation about the small forge that she had used in the studio in Camberwell.

Matthieu did it again on the fourth and fifth night until Maria was half convinced that he'd be able to make the perfect bracelet without ever once having touched the tools and materials he'd need.

He hadn't touched her, though. Hadn't recreated the

intimacies of the night of the gala and that was becoming pure torture for her. Days spent wondering, questioning, doubting... Had she imagined the connection she had felt forged the night of the gala? Had it just been what they'd needed in that moment? But if that was the case, then why would he bring her to his room each and every night...?

Each day, while he retreated to his office in Zürich, Maria walked the forests around the lake, losing herself in the beauty of the surrounding areas, the crunch of leaves beneath her feet, and the soft gentle heat of the departing summer. And each day she marvelled at the changes to her body and the child she carried. Her hands smoothed down the rounded shape hanging low within her, the weight and stretch catching her both by surprise and with something like awe. For the first time in her life, Maria had begun to wonder about her mother—as if her own pregnancy had soothed aside the hurt, and replaced it with a curious yearning ache for something she could never have, and never know.

But the tightening of clothes that had only been purchased a month before made Maria realise that she would need to return to the shops once more, her mind calculating what resources she had in her savings and hating the fact that she would either have to turn to her husband or brother for more money. Neither of which was a particularly pleasant option. For so long she had tried so hard to find her own independence, and now? She felt utterly trapped by a man who was so complicated, so tormented by his own past, yet also by a man she was beginning to see as something more than just the autocratic, albeit devastatingly attractive, isolated man she had married.

Though trapped was too simple a word to describe what her life had become. Because she did have her freedoms and, more, his focus. At night, they had begun to

talk less of jewellery and more of hopes and dreams...
names for the baby, plans for its future. All of which
painted a picture that Maria feared was more spellbound
than real, as if one wrong turn and it could vanish in the
air like a wisp of autumnal mist.

She reached a part of the woodland that broke over
the stunning view of Lake Lucerne towards the edge of
Matthieu's property and let out a weighted sigh, lost in
the way the horizon met the mirror-smooth lake, the par-
allel beauty of two shades of blue so close they seemed
two halves of the same whole. Something would break
the harmony she'd discovered in the last week, whether
it was her, Matthieu or someone else, she was sure of it.
The fragile détente they had found between them...it
just couldn't last.

She returned from her walk, her muscles pleasantly aching, the pressure from the too-small waistband not so
much. She reached for her phone, determined to find
some better-fitting clothes online, when she saw the
screen display fifteen missed calls from her brother. Fear
spiked through her mind, which panicked while she hit
the call button and waited to be connected to Sebastian.

Come on, come on, pick up.

When she heard his gruff voice answer she barrelled
questions at him in rapid fire.

'What's wrong? Has something happened? Are you
okay?'

'I don't know, sis. You tell me.'

'What?' Maria asked, dropping into the chair by the
table, relieved at least that he sounded okay.

'Well, I don't hear from you for a couple of months—
perhaps not so unusual given your tendency to get lost
in some project or other—'

Maria couldn't help but flinch at the way Seb dismissed her work.

'And then… Bam. There you are, front cover of over fifteen different magazines in several different languages, looking *decidedly* pregnant and apparently very much married? So you tell me if something "is wrong", if something "has happened", and by God, Maria, if you are okay!'

Maria knew on some level she had been blocking thoughts of Seb from her mind. Unable to find the words to explain. And she suddenly realised that she'd plunged her head in the sand and tried to ignore the reality of it all. Was this what was going to break the spell between her and Matthieu? Harsh reality?

'Seb, I—'

Her brother's exhale was harsh and loud in her ear. 'You said you were in Switzerland visiting "a friend",' he accused. 'Please, Maria, just tell me you're okay.'

'I am,' she assured him. 'Truly, I am.'

Over the next half an hour she lied to her brother—something she'd never done before—weaving a veil of fiction so thin over the way she had met and married Matthieu she could almost see the truth through it. But no matter what she said, it wasn't enough. Sebastian wanted to see her, to meet Matthieu, and Maria wasn't able to refuse the invitation, which was more of an ultimatum, to attend a dinner at his estate just outside Siena in a couple of days' time. And suddenly thoughts and fears cascaded through her mind on an endless loop.

By the time Matthieu pulled into the sweeping drive of his estate, he wasn't sure whether he wanted to swing the car round and drive away, or throw the car into park and rush towards the wife he couldn't quite figure out.

Ever since the night of the gala, he'd been unable—no, unwilling—to sleep in a bed without his wife. And he couldn't explain it. It had just felt…wrong. The moment he'd taken her to his bed, he'd felt something shift within him, something that soothed the raging beast in a way he'd never experienced. It wasn't her touch, her cries of pleasure. Unsettlingly it had nothing to do with the incredible heights of passion they'd shared. No, worse—it seemed that it was her mere presence that calmed him in a way nothing before ever had. Each night, when she couldn't sleep, he'd asked her questions…just to hear the sound of her voice. He'd lie awake at night, just watching the rise and fall of her chest, and their child that was to be. Because the night of the gala, the way she had brushed past the dark headlines and focused on the good ones, she had shown him something that he'd never seen before. *Survivor.* The word still rang round his head, making him wonder if that was how their child might see him, making him *want* it.

He stalked down the hallway, frowning as he heard Maria's steps taking her, what sounded like, back and forth. Matthieu was well versed in the patterns of pacing and was already frowning as he rounded the corner to find Maria turning on her heel, and twisting her hands round each other.

'What's wrong?'

She looked up, startled and almost guilty, then turned back to her pacing.

'Maria?'

She shrugged a shoulder, aiming for nonchalant, he presumed, and failing miserably. 'Oh, you know.'

'No… I don't, which is why I asked.'

She batted a hand in his direction without stopping her passage back and forth in the living area. If she didn't stop she was going to make him— Fear, sudden and crashing, carved a jagged wound in his heart. 'The baby—?'

'Oh, God, no. Fine, the baby is fine,' she said, stopping the movement of her feet and looking half appalled that he might have thought such a thing, before resuming her pacing.

His heart juddered and he took a few deep breaths to try and pull back the raging speed it had leapt to.

'It's just that…my brother… We have to go to Italy, and I'm not sure I'm ready for that. I don't even have the right clothes and—'

He couldn't help let out a laugh, now that he knew there was nothing wrong with their child, as he struggled to understand the chain of her thoughts.

'What do clothes have to do with Italy and your brother?'

'He knows, Matthieu. He saw a photo of us at the gala. A very pregnant, married "us".'

'You didn't tell him?'

'I…'

Matthieu felt his frown return. It wasn't as if they'd actually talked that much about her family. He knew she had a brother, that her father had remarried after the loss of his first wife in childbirth with Maria. Had he just assumed that she had told them? Perhaps he had assumed a little too much where his wife was concerned.

'What did he say?'

'He wants us to visit him in Siena. He wants…to meet you.'

Matthieu managed to resist the urge to laugh this time. Clearly this meant a lot to Maria. He'd never seen her like this before—all this buzzing energy and indecision. Casting his mind back, he was pretty sure that she'd been less panicked when telling him that she was pregnant.

'Then we'll go,' he said simply. And for the first time she stopped pacing.

'Really?'

'Yes, Maria. He's your family, it's important.' Good God, did she think he was a monster that would refuse to visit her brother? But rather than seem relieved, she turned a lighter shade of pale and Matthieu sensed that there was definitely something more going on.

'But I have nothing to wear,' she cried.

His eyebrows shot up—he was sure he could feel them disappearing into his hairline. When had Maria ever cared about clothing?

'Maria—'

'And shoes! My shoes don't even fit right now, because I'm just getting…fat. Everywhere. In places that aren't around my child. And don't,' she said, spinning back to him and pointing a stabbing finger in his direction, 'don't for one minute dare to even *think* that this is *hormones*,' she hissed.

'I didn't—'

'Because, yes, there are hormones, lots of them!' She was most definitely shouting now, and in that moment Matthieu was regretting the smooth planes of concrete he had loved so much and was yearning for soft furnishings to take the edge off the anger vibrating around the room. 'So many. Making me want to eat ice cream. All. The. Time. Surely that's what morning sickness is there for? To balance the scales. Why couldn't I just have morning sickness?'

'You want—'

'Of course I don't want to be sick, don't be ridiculous.'

Matthieu couldn't tell whether he wanted to laugh or cry, and sensed more than anything that Maria was also torn between the two. But he was now convinced that although there might be something to the hormones, it wasn't everything and if he didn't do something this conversation would end very badly indeed.

He stalked over to the freezer and hunted in the bottom drawer to find what he was looking for. He seized it with one hand and riffled in the cutlery drawer for a spoon. Returning to the small island that he strategically placed between him and his rather adorably flustered, but most definitely volatile wife, he took off the lid of the ice-cream pot.

'What are you doing?' she asked.

'Eating.' He plunged the spoon into the depths of the carton and retrieved a sizable amount and consumed the entire mouthful.

'Now? You're eating now? When I've just—'

'From now on,' he said, around a mouthful of the cold sweet dessert and swallowing, whilst digging around for another spoonful, 'I eat what you eat.' He stared at her with determination and watched her expressive features as they shifted focus from whatever crazy chain of thought she'd been on, to watching him eat spoonful after spoonful of ice cream. Only, he realised too late, he was about to get brain freeze. No matter. He'd eat the whole damn tub if it would make her feel better right now.

He waited until he was sure that he had her full attention. 'So we're going to Italy?'

'Sebastian has invited us for dinner at his in two days' time.'

'Okay, I'll clear my schedule. You're okay to fly?'

'Yes?'

'We'll take the jet,' he said, and although another mouthful of ice cream was the last thing he ever wanted to see again in his life, he pushed another spoonful in his mouth. He'd been deadly serious about his declaration.

'You…you don't mind?' she asked tentatively and Matthieu hated the thought that she was afraid to ask. Not just in this, but afraid to ask something that was so clearly important to her.

'Not at all. Not if you don't mind telling me what's really going on here,' he said as his stomach began to freeze from the inside out from all the ice cream. He nearly laughed as he watched her eyes lock onto the spoon he was about to put into his mouth. 'Would you like some?'

She clenched her jaw and seemingly tried to hold herself back, until he finally watched her give in. Her shoulders dropped and she closed the distance to the island counter.

'Yes.'

'Yes you mind? Yes you want some?'

'Yes to both?' she asked, not quite meeting his gaze.

Maria sighed. From the moment Matthieu had returned home, her mouth had run away with her and her mind was hurling everything and anything into her thoughts to prevent her from facing the one thing she didn't want to face, but in reality probably really needed to.

'When did you get so wise?' she asked Matthieu.

'Probably around the time my wife said, *"You need this. I need this. We need this."*'

In an instant she was plunged back into the sensations he had wrought to her body that night. The need, the passion…

'Mind out of the gutter, wife.'

'My hormones have a lot to answer for.'

'And I promise, when we've had this discussion, your hormones can feast on my body until they're sated,' he growled, the dark promise in his eyes almost too much to bear.

'Really?' she said uncertainly. 'Because you haven't…
we haven't…since that night.'

He sighed and she felt the gentle puff of air against
her skin, sweet with the taste of ice cream.

He placed the spoon down on the counter and she
reached for it, even though her stomach had finally re-
volted and given up any desire for food—or at least *that*
kind of feasting.

He ran his hands through his hair and finally leaned
on one elbow, resting his chin in his palm and looking
at her as if he'd given up some kind of internal fight.
'Honestly, I wasn't sure that was something you wanted.
I didn't want you to feel that because of that night, I automatically assumed that…'

'My husband could demand his nightly conjugal
rights?' she finished with a small sad smile. When had
things got so complicated that they couldn't simply act on
their desires, or feelings? Perhaps when they had rushed
into a wedding because of a child. 'Matthieu, no one has
a *right* to my body except me. But I have, and *do* willingly choose to share my body with you.'

'Your body, yes. Perhaps. But…*you*?'

She bit the inside of her cheek and nodded. He wanted
to know why she was so upset about seeing Sebastian.

The last time she had seen her brother was at Theo
and Sofia's wedding. In the short space of time since the
night of the charity gala in Iondorra and the wedding between Princess Sofia and Theo, Maria had realised quite
a number of things about herself, some of them harsh and
hard to bear, and others more…empowering. The determination to focus on herself had been in some ways both
wondrous and liberating. Until she had discovered she
was pregnant and suddenly the thought of facing Sebas-

tian with the consequences of her reckless actions had felt awfully like a betrayal.

'My brother has always looked out for me. Been there for me when…when it became clear that my father was not going to be.' Maria sighed, hating how the well of emotion catching at the back of her throat shuddered through her breath. 'After my mother died, my father just…he seemed to give up on everything. He went through the motions for a few years, marrying Valeria, seeking one failed business deal after another, but as I got older he seemed to look at me differently. Seeing not me, but my mother looking back at him. I could tell how painful it was for him, how it was tearing at him. I don't know which one of us started it first, but each in our own ways began to avoid each other, to ease the constant hurt that hovered between us when we met.'

Maria shivered at the memories from her childhood, hiding in various rooms within the house when she knew her father was home. She'd spent hours staring at the pictures in the family photo albums, obsessively consuming the images of the mother she had never known. Each time, Seb would come and find her. Take her out into the garden, try to distract her. Even then, all those years ago Seb had protected her.

'When my father lost nearly everything in one last investment deal, I was about eight years old. Seb was barely eighteen and was forced to act—or we would have been declared bankrupt. He took over the decision-making, finding ways to save what little was left of the family's finances. Everything was sold. Our home, estates, almost all the belongings in the houses, paintings, antiques and antiquities, all just enough to pay off the millions owed because of my father's stupidity and negligence.

The shame my father had brought on the Rohan de Luen name and title was enough to get us exiled from Spain.'

Across the years, Maria could hear the echoes of the arguments, the bitter accusations, Valeria's tears and recriminations, and through it all was the almost deadly determination of her brother. To be the man her father couldn't be, the protector, the decision-maker...

'What Seb did at the age of eighteen was incredible. He moved us to Italy, found a school for me, started a hotel business from the one property we had left in Europe, which managed to provide enough to keep Valeria and my father if not happy, then at least within some semblance of the life they were accustomed to. But they lived elsewhere. So it was just us. An eighteen-year-old looking after an eight-year-old.'

And only now that she was pregnant with her own child did Maria truly realise what a sacrifice her brother had made. She had known, previously, what he had given up for her. The decisions and sacrifices he had made had all revolved around her needs. And Maria had never really felt worthy of it. Any of it. She had, instead, felt more of a burden. And that ache in her heart had never really gone away.

'So your father was never really there?'

'For a while he tried. Seemed to make some kind of an effort, at least that's what I thought, until my sixteenth birthday.' Maria shivered. She hated thinking of that day, let alone actually talking of it. She had never shared that day, her feelings from it, with anyone. Fearful of the two possible reactions. That she would either be told to get over it, or they would understand...and the understanding? That would make it worse, because that would mean that the sadness, the anger, the pain...were justified. And that justification would be absolutely the worst. Because it meant that her father really didn't care…and that there was no hope for a future reconciliation.

'Seb had arranged everything. He would return from Rio where he was doing his latest business deal and for once, the family would come together. We would go to my favourite restaurant in Siena—right by the Palazzo Pubblico—long after the tourists had gone back to their hotels. I wanted to look grown up, to look beautiful… It was my sixteenth and I was about to become a woman and my family would be there to celebrate with me. Just for once it would be about me, not Valeria, not my father, not even my mother. But me.'

Goosebumps had risen on her arms as her memories took her back to that night. She almost smiled at the way she had got ready that evening. She'd forgotten how excited she'd been that night. How she had spent an hour tackling her eye make-up, getting her eyeliner *just right*. How she had admired herself in the mirror, the dress she had chosen especially for that day, the v neckline revealing the beautiful sliver threads of her mother's necklace, the way the waistline nipped in and then flared out at her hips. She felt…so grown up.

'What happened?' Matthieu asked gently, clearly aware that the ending to the tale was not a happy one.

Maria cast a glance to the night sky descending over the placid lake, the colours oddly reminiscent of the sky over Siena that evening.

'Seb had sent a car for me. It took me to the restaurant where I would meet everyone. When the chauffeur opened the car door for me, I felt like a movie star.' She laughed. 'Everyone was looking at the beautiful girl being escorted to a table in one of Siena's finest restaurants. And when I got to the table and saw that I was the first to arrive, that was okay. I could handle that. I was

a grown up that night,' Maria said with the same false
bravado she had felt in that instant. That even though her
heart had dropped, and fear had begun to creep in, she
had kept that smile on her face and even ordered a glass
of champagne. Because they would come. They would
be there, they just needed a little more time.

'People stopped staring after a few minutes, but as the
time dragged on, as ten minutes turned to twenty and
then thirty, curiosity won out and they resumed their
watchful gaze on the girl who sat alone at a table for
four. I hadn't really made many friends at school, so it
was supposed to be just us. My family.

'Almost an hour later—' she shook her head at the
memory, the first genuine smile gracing her mouth '—
he came.'

'Your father?'

'No.'

'Sebastian?'

'Nope,' she said again, shaking her head. 'Theo Tersi.
He explained that he was a friend of Seb's and that my
brother's flight had been delayed because of bad weather
and that he'd asked Theo to come and let me know as he'd
been in the area meeting with a local vintner. Theo must
have seen, must have realised in an instant that my father
wasn't coming, but said nothing. Instead, he sent all the
waiters in the restaurant into a panic as he demanded the
most exquisite, the most expensive things on the menu,
because—he announced loudly and proudly—it was "this
beautiful woman's birthday".'

Tears gathered even now at the memory of Theo's
kindness that night. She had never forgotten it and, in
turn, it had shaped so much of the following years of
her life.

'When I got home, Theo parked his car beside Seb's

and I rushed into the house to see him, so pleased that he was home. I heard him before I saw him. He was on the phone with our father.'

She had crept up to the office where Seb was, the light from the room dimly illuminating the corridor through the partially open door.

'What do you mean, you were busy? It's your daughter's birthday, for God's sake... I don't care about your excuses. Enough is enough. This will never happen again, do you hear me? Otherwise I will stop providing the finances for your and Valeria's lifestyle. I will cut ties. Do you understand?'

'My father was present the following year for my birthday, but not because he wanted to be there, but because my brother had threatened to stop his finances. After that...' Maria shrugged '... I didn't really like celebrating my birthday.'

Because what she couldn't tell him, what she could barely admit to herself, was the fact that on her sixteenth birthday it had felt like a rejection of her, of who she was becoming. And she had never wanted to put herself, her *sense* of self, on the line like that again.

Silence fell between them, a silence full of sorrow and ache, of compassion—which she could see shining in Matthieu's eyes—one that hurt almost as much as the memories of that night.

'I'm sorry that the two people who were most important to you couldn't have been there that night.'

Her heart juddered in her chest, as if both soothed and ripped open at the same time.

'After that Seb became almost consumed with being there for me. Being the father that our own could not. He looked out for me, paid for my education, my travels, anything I could ever want for. In some ways he stopped being my brother. And every gift, every penny he gave me, it felt…dutiful and tainted at the same time. As if it wasn't for me, but almost in spite of our father. And as such… I just wanted to be me. I wanted to be independent, to fund myself, to… I don't know. I could never repay my brother financially, but I wanted so much to show him that I was worthy of his investment, that I wasn't a screw-up.'

'Is that how you see yourself?'

'Pregnant and in a marriage for the sake of my child?' She smiled sadly. 'I just wanted not to need him, not rely on him in any way so that we could go back to just being brother and sister…'

So that I be loved by him because he can, not because he has to.

But looking deep into her husband's eyes, she wondered whether she was still thinking of her brother.

'Maria,' Matthieu said, taking her hand in his. 'I cannot make promises that I will always be there—'

'You're working a *force majeure* into a promise?'

Matthieu laughed, sudden and joyful, breaking some of the weight of the moment and bringing a smile to her lips.

'What does my wife know of contract clauses?'

'My brother is a leading international business figure. He calls it the Act of God clause, in case unforeseeable events prevent a contract being fulfilled.'

'Act of God. Okay, I can go with that,' Matthieu said, firming his grip on her hand.

'*Force majeure* aside, I will do everything in my power that you should never feel such a thing again.'

As Matthieu said the words, he felt them slip deep within him and take hold. He looked at the woman sitting across from him, the pain in her eyes almost too much to bear. His family might have been taken from him at a very young age, but he had never doubted their love for him. Not once. Yet here Maria sat, unsure of love from the two people that should have loved her the most. And he hoped upon hope that he had just made a promise that he could fulfil.

He understood her need for independence, that sense of self he'd admired from the first moment he'd met her and, even more so, when she'd brushed aside the accusations she was simply after his money when she had come to tell him about their child. He could see that she hated that she was now reliant on *him*.

'Maria, whether it's clothes, a lifestyle that you think is not yours, but provided for you by me, it's not. What is mine is yours. I meant that the day I said "I do". No matter what. That doesn't take away from you, who you are or what you've achieved. I'd like to think that you could see that it is only something that adds.'

She exhaled a long and low breath. One he wasn't sure how to interpret. Until her eyes narrowed and transformed, an impish light breaking the seriousness of the conversation. 'And now I'm hungry. And not for food. So, husband, are you going to make good on your promise and allow me my feast?'

He refused to withhold the smile he felt pulling at his lips. Refused to turn away from the warmth blooming within his chest. It was more than carnal desire, it was something like happiness. And if this was what it was like to live with the leash lifted ever so lightly, he wanted more. He wanted to know what life was lived like, not in the shadows of his grief, but in the light of Maria.

CHAPTER NINE

As Maria exited the car that had picked her and Matthieu up from the private airfield just outside Siena she clung to the words he had given her two nights before. Promises that she was not less than she had been for getting unexpectedly pregnant and marrying him, that he would be there for her. Always. *No matter what.*

She wasn't naïve enough to expect that her father might be here today, she wasn't really sure that he even knew that she was pregnant and married, and she couldn't quite bring herself to care. She had long ago given up on being concerned about his thoughts and feelings towards her. But Seb? Her brother? He had given her so much… and somehow she wanted to pay that back by being worthy…or by somehow being someone he could be proud of.

She pressed down the soft silks of the beautiful dress Matthieu had surprised her with yesterday as the wind blew about her and soothed both her nerves and her restless child.

'Are you okay?' Matthieu asked as he came around the car to stand beside her.

Maria nodded. 'I think our child is looking forward to meeting their uncle,' she said with a smile and another sweep of the now very much unavoidable bump she carried before her. 'Are *you* okay?' she said, thinking of the quiet that had almost consumed him throughout their journey.

He looked confused. 'Why would I not be?'

'Sebastian can be a little overprotective. He is, after all, my brother.'

He shrugged a shoulder. 'I have tackled multibillion-dollar deals with the world's toughest CEOs. Your brother will not be a problem.'

'If you say so,' Maria responded, a little sceptical at how dismissive Matthieu was of her concern. Perhaps she had misunderstood the reason for his brooding.

The door swung open and there he stood in the middle of three arched domes in the centre of the estate's façade. It was Sebastian's most cherished holding. It had been one of the first purchases he'd made once he had secured all the Rohan de Luens' finances. It was beautiful, perfectly formed. Not obscene as some of the estates Maria remembered from Spain, but large and nestled amongst a modest ten hectares of land, with some old and mostly untouched vineyards that Theo had always itched to get his hands on.

Seb had refused all of his entreaties, enjoying instead the wildness and untouched way it had sprawled beyond the broken, aged wooden confines and grew rampant and wild. In part, Maria liked to think that he kept it that way because it had inspired one of the first pieces of jewellery she had created.

Unconsciously she sought out Matthieu's hand and suddenly Maria was struck by how important it was for Seb to like her husband. Not the dark stranger she had met all those months ago, but the man she had come to know and like, the man that she was beginning to see he could be. Her inner voice scoffed at the soft word used to describe the complex emotion that had begun to form around her feelings for Matthieu.

But before her mind could follow that thought, Matthieu had started to walk forward and they were quickly face to face with Sebastian, whose eyes had rested on her very visible bump and had widened with something like…awe. And even he, though she could tell he was struggling to hold it back, couldn't prevent the smile from forming at his lips.

Any words in her mind were cut off as he dragged her into an embrace so powerful and consuming she felt a little as if she were coming home.

When he was done, instead of returning her to where she had stood, he placed her beside him, almost putting himself between her and Matthieu.

Her brother looked Matthieu up and down, and Maria was a little surprised that Matthieu let him, given the challenge that was locked into Sebastian's gaze. After a moment, as if Matthieu had allowed her brother his fill, he thrust out a hand and introduced himself. It was a beat before her brother accepted his hand. She rolled her eyes.

And so it begins.

'Come,' Seb said, apparently deciding that he needn't introduce himself in some form of alpha power play. 'The others are already here.'

'Others?' Maria hissed, trying to keep her voice away from Matthieu's keen hearing.

'Theo and Sofia were in the area,' he said, brushing her concern aside.

'You called in back up?' Maria demanded.

'Why would I need back up?' he replied.

Matthieu hadn't missed the way Sebastian had specifically positioned Maria out of his reach. Divide and conquer was a worthy route to take when being introduced to the husband of your sister, he supposed. He didn't have a sister, never had, but would like to think that he would be as ferociously protective of her as Seb appeared to be. He didn't have to like it, but he could most definitely respect it. Furthermore, while he *could* respect it, it didn't necessarily mean he would roll over and expose whatever soft belly Sebastian might be fool enough to think he had.

As he followed Maria and her brother down a corridor of terracotta Matthieu fought to shake off the tendrils of the nightmare he'd had the previous evening. The first one he'd had in years. He'd tried to dismiss it as mental foolishness, but it had sunk its claws into his heart and kept him almost silent on the way to Siena. He doubted very much it had anything to do with meeting Maria's brother, but couldn't shake the thought that it might have something to do with his feelings for his wife.

They rounded a corner and entered a large and surprisingly beautiful living area, bringing Matthieu back to the present. The soft cream and burnt-orange colours surprisingly soothing to a man who lived in monochrome. Instantly Matthieu eyed the presence of another man and his wife, who for a second were mid-conversation. The tall, dark-haired man Matthieu realised must have been Theo Tersi, and the woman, the Crown Princess of Iondorra.

For a second, Theo turned and cast him such a fierce look, Matthieu was impressed. Until the princess took one look at Maria and descended into squeals of pure delight and hand-wringing, which completely cut the tension in the room.

'Maria! Look at you,' the princess cried, rushing up from her seat and taking Maria in her arms, leaning back slightly as if not to crush the baby. 'Can I?' she asked, and, barely giving Maria a second to answer, her hands swept around the swell of their child. 'Oh, you are positively blooming.' And then she covered her hand with her mouth. 'Oh, that's such a trite thing to say, but you are!'

Maria laughed, the men in the room rolled their eyes, and the princess laughed again.

'Matthieu,' Maria said, turning to him, 'this is Princess Sofia de Loria of—'

'Please. No titles here. We're family.' The exquisite petite blonde woman turned to Matthieu and struck him with an aquamarine gaze.

Matthieu had met with more royals than he could shake a stick at and, no matter her pleas for familiarity, still bowed his head ceremoniously.

'Your Highness.'

Sofia laughingly sighed. 'Okay, but it's Sofia from here on out.' She turned to Maria. 'Now, we're just going to let the men do their thing and once they've got their chest-beating out of their system, we can eat,' and the princess drew Maria from the room, while his wife cast worried looks at each of the three men.

For a moment, they watched the retreating forms of the two women, and then returned their attention to each other. Finally deciding to get this over with, Matthieu gestured for them to continue, to which Sebastian simply raised an eyebrow and Theo simply sighed.

'So, Montcour—'

'It's perhaps a little late to be asking about my intentions,' Matthieu cut in. He might be respectful of Sebastian's position, but that didn't change a lifetime of being in control and in charge.

'And there I was, going to ask you if you wanted a drink. But that's fine,' Sebastian replied with an insincere shoulder shrug. 'We can get straight to business. Your reputation, whilst discreet, is colourful.'

'And yours, while quite shockingly public, is perhaps a little obvious,' Matthieu shot back. Before coming here, he had most definitely done his research.

'Obvious?' Seb said, as if outraged.

Theo made a face to suggest that there might have been something in what Matthieu was implying.

Seb must have caught it. 'I don't know what you're so smug about, *TT*.'

Theo simply grinned back at his friend.

'I think we can all agree that our reputations *before* have little bearing on *now*,' Matthieu said.

'Absolutely not. You have married my sister!'

'Yes.'

'And she's pregnant!'

'Yes,' Matthieu said again, his tone almost bored. 'These are undeniable facts.'

Sebastian scowled. 'I take it there wasn't a pre-nup, given the hastiness of the wedding that ensured Maria's family and friends would not attend.'

'That was Maria's decision,' he replied, refusing to allow the sting of guilt and the righteousness of Sebastian's ire to penetrate his thoughts.

'The pre-nup or the wedding guests?'

Sidestepping the answer, Matthieu pressed on. 'Maria is entitled to everything I have.'

'Everything?' Theo queried.

Matthieu shrugged. 'All seven point four billion dollars of it, should she want it.'

Even Sebastian looked begrudgingly impressed.

'Is it in writing?' he demanded.

'It is with my lawyers.'

Seb glanced at Theo, who shrugged.

'For Maria, it's not about money.'

'Yes,' Matthieu agreed. 'I've realised that.'

'Her life, her childhood, it wasn't easy.' Sebastian bit out the words through a jaw so clenched Matthieu feared for his dentist. 'I… I tried to provide what her—our—father was unable to. Montcour—she is exclusively the *only* thing in this world I care for. And if you hurt her, I swear to God—'

'You will be entitled to take whatever form of revenge you deem fit,' Matthieu said easily and sincerely. 'Truly.'

Sebastian narrowed his eyes as if trying to work out what Matthieu's game was.

'I mean it.'

He cocked his head to one side. 'Maria may come across as spirited and independent, but there is a softness to her that people like us can so easily crush.' Matthieu frowned at the description, an action that Seb caught. 'You disagree?'

'When I think of Maria I don't see softness, I see strength. Determination. She is fierce when challenged and quick with her laughter and her generosity. She is truly unique and very much a credit to the Rohan de Luen name.'

'Don't think to win me over with compliments, Montcour.'

'I have neither the inclination nor the desire to do so,' Matthieu pressed on. 'No offence, but you matter very little to me. All that does is Maria. She clearly wants the two—*three*,' he said acknowledging the importance of Theo in her family unit, 'of us to get on. I'm sure that we can manage to be civil.'

'There will be nothing civil about me if you break her heart,' Sebastian warned.

'As I said. That I understand and respect. I'd expect nothing less from my wife's brother.'

A gentle knock interrupted the conversation. Sofia stepped over the threshold.

'Lunch will be about twenty minutes, and, Matthieu, you can find Maria in the room on the second floor, third door on the left. I believe that you've all had enough *man-ticulating* for now. If not, then perhaps it could resume after dessert?'

Matthieu couldn't help but smile at the sweetly intoned speech Sofia had just delivered and, casting a last look at Sebastian and Theo, went in search of Maria.

Maria was in the room she stayed in when visiting with Sebastian. The last time she'd been here was nearly a year ago celebrating the end of her degree, which…now felt like a lifetime ago. So much had happened since then, she couldn't help but think as she smoothed a hand over a belly that contained a child. *Their* child.

The room was large, soft and warm, but oddly she found herself comparing it to the stark but beautiful estate on the edge of Lake Lucerne. Maria had lived in many places over the years, always reluctant to see any of them as a home, after their exile from Spain, but that was exactly how she'd begun to see Matthieu's estate. *Her home.*

Over by the far wall were the ten boxes she'd shipped here before she went to marry Matthieu. And oddly she found herself half hesitant, half urgent, to riffle through her jewellery equipment and materials.

She was just about to cross the room when she heard a knock on the door. Turning, she called for Matthieu to enter. She knew it was him, felt it on her skin, in the air, as if somehow she had become so attuned to his presence, she just…knew.

'Hi,' he said as he stepped into the room, taking it all in with one expansive gaze, before finally settling back on her. It gave her the time to assess for any physical damage.

'So it didn't descend into fisticuffs, then?' she asked, half afraid of the answer.

'Why would it have? I *can* be charming, you know.'

'It wasn't you I was worried about.'

'They are both perfectly intact, I assure you.'

Maria couldn't help but smile, only to follow the return of his gaze to the boxes lining the far wall. She turned back to look at them too. The sum total of her life in London.

'What are in those boxes?'

'Mostly equipment and materials.'

'You sent them here?'

Rather than bring them with you?

The implied question rang in the air like the vibrations of a bell tolled.

She walked over to one of the boxes and peeked into the depths where the tape had come away. She couldn't help but smile as she peeled back the tape a little more and slipped her hand inside to retrieve the spool of silver threading. She ran her hand over it, caressing it like a long-lost friend. Only now did she realise how much she had missed her time in the studio space she had rented in Bermondsey. The busy hum of others as they worked around her, each person lost in their own imagination, bent on creating reality from dreams.

'I didn't want to look as if I was moving in and taking over,' she replied, the lie falling heavily even to her own ears.

She felt Matthieu move across the room behind her, the heat from his body warming the cool that had descended over her. Using that heat, feeding off it, she went to the small lock box of finished pieces that she had packed shortly after returning to London after their first meeting in Switzerland when she had told him about their baby.

Opening it, she removed one of the pieces from the clear plastic bag and unwrapped the soft tissue paper carefully protecting it. It was a ring—the last piece she had made before discovering she was pregnant. This was the first piece she had made since the exhibition that wasn't a commission. That wasn't for someone else. This one had been for her.

'It's beautiful,' Matthieu said quietly and with some reverence.

'Thank you.' Pride gently shimmered through her words. A small pearl sat within a swirl of beaten gold, sweeping up around the orb like a wave, as if on the brink of concealing the beautiful natural formation. She had always been fascinated by the concentric layering of pearls... How something so stunning was formed through layers and layers of calcium carbonate surrounding what was once an irritant to the small mollusc that created it. This pearl hadn't been considered perfect enough to be classed as a gemstone, but it was no less precious to her.

'Do you miss it?'

'Yes and no,' she replied honestly. 'Coming home from Iondorra, after... Theo and Sofia, after you... I was determined to forge a "new me",' she said slightly ironically. 'To put aside the childish fantasies I had hidden behind for years. That night...it was so much for me,' she said, turning back to Matthieu. 'I realised so many things. Like how I'd been hiding behind an infatuation with an idea of someone, when in truth the reality of you

was so…overwhelming. And how much I had allowed
my brother to protect me from the harsh realities of life.
And while that was fine, it felt as if I'd also been protected from other experiences.

'Before I discovered I was pregnant, I threw myself
into a lot of commissioned work—many of which had
come from my first exhibition. I was almost feverish in
the determination to make this "work" pay, to provide
security for myself, to become independent from Sebastian, from anyone really.'

She paused, now thinking of the way her imagination
had unfurled in the last few months. The way that her
self-imposed hiatus from jewellery had, in a way, fed her
starved creativity, which had diminished since she'd accepted more commissions after her show.

'Thinking of it now, I was running before I could
walk. I was overwhelmed by how wonderful it was that
people wanted my work, but somehow sacrificed some of
my *self* in the process. I think I lost a little of that—was
certainly at risk of morphing into the extreme of what I
had always wanted.'

'And what was that?'

'I just wanted enough. Enough to get by and allow
me the time and finances to pursue the pieces that I *really* wanted to make. And if people, customers, wanted
those pieces, all the better. But I never wanted to lose the
love of it—I never wanted to destroy the one thing that
had given me so much pleasure and so much…company
during my childhood.'

'Company?'

'Sorry, that sounds strange. But even as a child, I
would spend hours lost in my imagination, designing
pieces in my mind, trying to work out how it could be
done, what materials would be best…'

'You were lonely?'

'A little perhaps. Seb was forced to work all hours to ensure that the family didn't lose *everything*. My father and Valeria were rarely there, either locked away in a different part of Italy, or still desperately trying to cling to a lifestyle they no longer had. Meanwhile I had been thrust into a new school with a new language, which didn't exactly form the best basis for deep and lasting friendships.'

Matthieu seemed to take that in before turning back to the ring. 'May I?'

Maria gently pressed it into his open hand.

'So without commissions, this is what you like to create?'

'Yes.' The smile returning to her lips warmed the word, warmed her deep within.

'There is space in Lucerne for a studio if you—'

'No,' Maria interrupted. 'No, that is a kind offer, but… I prefer to be around others when I work. There's a strange but wonderful feeling when you are lost in your own world, yet surrounded by others. It feels…'

'Less lonely?'

Matthieu silently cursed. He couldn't help but think that he had somehow taken this bright and beautiful woman and hidden her away from the world. Dragged her back to his lair, and for a moment he feared that he might actually be harming her. Keeping her locked away from the sunlight and from the things that she needed most.

He cursed the nightmare that had somehow lifted the lid on memories he had not confronted for years. Because he knew so well, too well, how lonely a child could be. All those days, weeks and months spent in a hospital room, checked on by nurses and visited by Malcolm, but when he was alone, the silence had wrapped around him and become deafening.

A silence that had carried on in his life until… Until Maria.

Matthieu bit back another curse. Even as Maria spoke of the need for company, to be surrounded by people and life, all he wanted to do was take her back to Lucerne and surround her with himself. To protect her, hide her away from the world where she only knew him. The beast began to stir in his breast again, roaring *mine*. As if his heart had recognised her as his and only his, the world outside be damned.

And that, above all things, scared him the most. Because he had worked so hard, for so many years, to ensure that he was never bound in such a way to another person. And now that he was…

Matthieu pushed aside the thought that had grown thorns and threatened to bloom into his mind. He looked at Maria, lost in her own thoughts as she caressed the spun silver in her hands, and purposefully unfurled his clenched hand to reveal the ring she had made before she had come to live with him.

'It doesn't have to be that way any more, Maria,' he said, no longer sure if he was talking about her loneliness or his past.

'It doesn't feel as if it is,' she said, her hand once again sweeping over the outline of their child. Her eyes held a ring of truth, shining within them, offering, rather than asking for, assurance. An assurance he suddenly wanted to turn from. Because his wife was upsetting everything he thought about his life. Every natural instinct to turn around and retreat, to close himself off from the world just as he was beginning to hope. To hope for something more than the constraints he'd put on his heart the night of the fire.

* * *

'You can stay, Maria, if you need—or want,' Sebastian said, sweeping her up in his arms to say goodbye even as his words contradicted his actions. She smiled, relishing the comfort and more that her brother offered.

The meal had been delicious—Matthieu keeping to his promise to eat everything she chose for herself, making her smile and the men at the table sceptical. Although the conversation had been a little slow to start, Sofia and Maria making the most of it, both her husband and her brother had soon relaxed into the gentle, teasing tone that had descended. And it had felt glorious to Maria, who had been so worried at the thought of any kind of confrontation. She had been so grateful to Sofia, who had completely put aside her faux pas from the night of the gala in Iondorra, and now when Maria looked at Theo she marvelled at how deeply wrongly she had interpreted not only their relationship but her own feelings for him. Joy rose within her chest as she thought now of how they had found happiness together...the same kind of happiness she had found with Matthieu perhaps? She couldn't help but cast her mind into a future where she and her husband surrounded a beautiful child, with dark wayward curls and devastating honey-green eyes, with love and happiness. Some long-distant sunlit future, the thought of which filled her with inescapable joy.

'That's okay. I'm good, really, Seb. I am.' And she felt it too. Somehow talking to Matthieu, sharing something of herself with him had forged a connection deep within her. Unaccountably she felt overwhelmed by emotion. As if being reunited with her things had triggered something—and not just the idea that had sparked in her mind the moment she'd seen her equipment and materials. The urge to create something for Matthieu, something that would potentially mean so much to him. She couldn't shake the feeling that she wanted to give something back to him. Because in a way, that was what he had done for her. Bringing her here, to see her brother, to stand beside her. She had shrugged into the safety he had offered her. The future.

One where she realised that now she *could* make the jewellery that she wanted to. Not dependent on commissions, not dependent on her meagre pay cheque from the café. And she wondered at how different it felt. Accepting the financial security he offered, when everything in her had railed against the same from her brother.

Trust. She felt it unfurl within her. She was beginning to trust him. Trust that he would be there for her and her child. And it began to fill her, consume her and make her feel… Excited for what was to come? Hopeful?

Seb released her from his hold, casting a glance over her shoulder to where Matthieu was arranging for all the boxes from her room to be sent on to the private jet waiting to take them back to Switzerland. *'Mi amor,'* he said and sighed. 'I am pleased for you. And for this little one,' he said, his eyes crinkling and his hand warm on her belly. 'And I suppose Montcour is acceptable,' he begrudgingly admitted. 'But… I do know of his childhood. I know what happened to him, and that kind of damage, that kind of baggage… Anyone would have to be blind not to see how closely he guards his heart. I just fear that those walls might be a little too high even for you to climb.'

'We all have baggage, Sebastian.'

'Perhaps, but I just want you to take care.'

As Maria and Matthieu were whisked away from Seb's estate in Siena and towards the small private airfield, she tucked away her brother's warning. Put it into a box and buried it deep. Because for the first time in what felt like for ever, she wanted to hold onto this feeling. To keep it within her and let it warm her from the inside out. Let it nurture both her and her child. Because this feeling, Maria realised, was love.

CHAPTER TEN

A SILENT SCREAM tore from Matthieu's mouth as he bolted
up from the bed. He was covered in that kind of cold un-
natural sweat that came from a night terror. The kind that
he'd experienced three times already in the weeks since
returning from Siena with Maria.

Heart pounding in his chest and shivering, he turned to
where Maria lay on her side in the bed, the only balm to
his soul that she hadn't been woken by his nightmare. He
rubbed a hand over his face to try and erase the memories
of the haunting dream. The way his father had looked
at him from the window of their home, flames licking
around the edges of the wooden frame, the crackling,
screaming sound that filled his ears as the fire consumed
everything in its path.

Even now his gut churned, his heart twisted just like
the flames in his imagination…because it wasn't a dream.
It was a memory. Or had been until he'd seen Maria over
his father's shoulders, looking down at him as she caressed her heavily pregnant bump, seemingly unaware
of the danger she was in. She had looked at him with
trust, with complete acceptance, as if she truly believed
that he, in the body of an eleven-year-old, would find a
way to save her.

In the dream he had screamed until his throat was raw

and, now awake, it felt scratched, thick with an ache that wouldn't quit. Casting one last look at his wife, serene in her peaceful sleep, he peeled back the damp sheets and padded from the room, each step rippling beneath the icicles that covered his back and chest.

He turned on the shower, not seeing past the images that had haunted his nights and even sometimes during his days, during moments of weakness that he had come to hate as much as his memories. It had been fifteen years since he'd last had these dreams, since he'd built up his mental and emotional defences to protect himself from them.

And now they were back. Because of Maria. Because of his wife.

Because on the brink of fatherhood himself, he could no longer understand the actions of his father. Or worse... because for the first time in his life, he actually did. He did understand why his father chose to seek out his wife that night, rather than finding his own freedom, rather than choosing his son. He understood the sheer magnitude of what tied his father to his mother, and him to Maria.

Matthieu's legs buckled in the shower, as if he'd been sucker punched low in his belly and every single thing in him hurt, ached, cried out for...the devil knew what. He stifled the cry that raged and thrashed within his chest, furious for release, desperate to be heard. He thrust his fisted hand, white knuckled, into his mouth and bit down to prevent its escape.

Nausea swirled in his stomach and he tried to suck in lungsful of air around the streaming water, around the hand in his mouth. He hadn't had a panic attack for years and he knew what he should do, but was helpless against the thick clogging fear that had descended over his mind.

The sound of his heartbeat mixed with the pounding of the water's jets from the shower head and all he wanted to do was curl up on the smooth white flooring beneath him. But something, somewhere deep within him, prevented it. A sign of weakness that even in his darkest moment he refused to succumb to.

He had no idea of how long he had stayed like that but finally, and only when the pain in his muscles cut through his lost thoughts, he reached up to turn off the water. As he towelled himself off, choosing not to return to his bed, *their* bed, he stalked the corridors of his home and sought out the gym, even though every instinct in him wanted to go back to Maria. Instead he turned to the treadmill, exhausting himself further until he might eventually fall back into a dreamless sleep where nothing and no one could reach him.

Maria stretched an arm out to Matthieu's side of the bed and frowned at once again finding it empty. She had tried to ask him about it after the first night, but he had brushed aside her concerns and insisted that he was fine. That he was distracted by an issue with one of the mining companies. The next time his absence was explained by a midnight international phone call. And Maria honestly couldn't remember the following reasons.

In the deep reaches of her heart, she knew he was pulling away. Could feel him almost imperceptibly slipping through her fingers, even as her love for him made her grip tighter, hold on as hard as she could. As if it was the only thing that would keep him with her. So she half believed his excuses and instead focused on making the spark of an idea she'd had back in Siena a reality.

She had sought out a studio in Lucerne, not too far from their home, and the moment Matthieu left for work, she would leave herself. She would share a conspiratorial smile with the driver she had sworn to secrecy and pass the ride to the studio with images of Matthieu's happy surprise when she presented her gift to him. She was sure, so sure, that he would be filled with joy when he saw what she had created for him.

Days before she had sneaked into his bedroom and retrieved the small box hidden in a drawer of the side cabinet. Opening the badly burned box had revealed a thick, broad silver ring, blackened by fire and partially melted. Her heart had ached for the small boy who had lost everything but this. Ached for the man who felt that he had to hide it away, rarely to be looked at or acknowledged. Remembering how happy he had been for her that she had her mother's necklace, something she could have with her every day, had given her the confidence that she was right in her plans for him to have the same. She had taken it from its allotted space and wrapped it as carefully as she imagined she would one day swaddle their child. From that moment in her room in Siena she had been consumed with need to give Matthieu something of his past that he could keep with him at all times. Something that he could cherish. The moment she laid eyes on it, she saw how she could clean the dirt and damage from the precious metal and had seen what she could do with it. How she could reforge the symbol of his grief into something new. She would use the silver of the ring to form the basis of a new piece, a new creation, from both past and present that he could carry with him into his future.

Still a little concerned about the impact of the fumes on her unborn child, she had instead focused on the mould for the piece she wanted to create. For hours she would lose herself in the design, carefully choosing how much additional silver would be needed to create the bracelet she wanted to give him, where to place it in order to retain the purity of precious metal belonging to the ring and how to join the two representations of the past and present. For hours she would lose herself in the shaping of the mould, pouring her love for Matthieu, for their unborn child, layering every single ounce of it she had, into the work that became almost her sole focus. Because even though she would deny it to herself, deep down she couldn't help but feel that time was running out for her. For them.

She had met with Georges Sennate and had immediately found a kindred spirit. The owner of the small studio was perhaps nearing seventy, even though his eyes twinkled like those of a teenager. She had come to relish his owl-like stare as he'd opened his space to her, shared the excitement of the piece she was creating for her husband. And had been touched as he'd offered his thoughts and knowledge of his own silverwork with her. And Maria had been so thankful that she had met someone that she could entrust such an important part of the process to. She could tell from the way that he showed as much care to her work as his own that he was the right person to melt the silver for her. Heat it to the point where the dark smoke stains could be swept aside, cleansed in the same way she had come to realise Matthieu had cleansed her, her childhood hurts slipping away with the hours she spent creating her gift to him.

She watched Georges's form bent over the forge, pouring the silver into the moulds below a large air vent from about three metres away. The heated silver glowing in the darkness like a living thing. It would set and then she'd be able to go to work. She knew that soldering would be okay, if she wore a mask to protect her, and her fingers itched to get to work on the piece she wanted to present to him at dinner in just four days' time.

She had only told Matthieu that it was a special occasion. Some strange inclination had her withholding the fact that it was her birthday. Because she didn't want that night to have the burden of history. Maria wanted to start that celebration anew with Matthieu. The new beginning she had never known she'd wanted.

Matthieu sat in his leather chair staring out of the window of his office in Zurich almost obsessively counting the minutes passing the hour he should have met Maria in the restaurant. But he couldn't move. In the last few days, Maria's simple acceptance of his withdrawal had become somehow worse than any kind of argument or demand. The beast within him wanted to rage, wanted to snarl and gnash its teeth and, although he wouldn't want to unleash that onto Maria, the fact that she accepted his behaviour caused it only to increase. He felt as if he were building to some impossible point where he would explode and his head pounded with the need of it. A combination of lack of sleep, the nightmares and his wife was almost too much to bear.

All his assurances that he would never treat her like her father, that he would be there for her, came back to haunt him as he struggled almost by the second with what he wanted and what he feared the most. Because in the last few days, his nightmare had morphed and changed into something new, something far more terrifying. He was no longer the small boy looking up at his father in the window. Now he had assumed the role of the father, looking down at his child and being torn between his wife and his son. It had played out in each and every conceivable way. Sometimes he went to his child, sometimes he went to Maria…but each and every time it hurt, sliced open his heart as he was only ever able to save one without the other.

He rubbed a hand over his face, all the while watching the minute hand jerk across the clock face and, even knowing the pain he would be causing Maria, he simply couldn't move. Instinctively, he knew. He knew that by failing to show up that evening, he would force her hand, he would hurt her so greatly that she would have to walk away. He hated himself for it, but knew that it was the only option he had…for his own sanity but, more importantly, for Maria. Because he could not tie her to this life, to him. Not without destroying the very thing that he loved about her.

Maria sat in the restaurant in Lucerne, her back straight and her head high. She could see them. The stares, the supposedly surreptitious glances her way. She could feel the curiosity from the other diners in the restaurant washing over her in waves.

The waiter approached and asked if he could get her anything and she smiled, a barely audible 'no' falling from her lips. She steeled her hand, hiding the tremors at her fingers, as she reached for the water glass and hoped that she would be able to swallow it past the clogged ache in her throat.

As she placed the glass back on the table, her gaze was drawn to the small black box she had placed on the plate opposite her. She had wanted it to be one of the first things Matthieu would see. She had wanted to watch the curiosity from his face turn to delight and, even deeper, to recognition of what she had done for him. The revelation that she had understood his pain and transformed it into something new.

Instead, in the space of his absence, the fear of a different reaction had begun to invade her imagination. One of anger, one of horror as he raged at how she should never have done such a thing, how she had no right, how she had trespassed on a hurt she had no possible way of understanding.

As the minutes had ticked across the hour, her thoughts had turned from the gift to herself, as her heart lurched between him and her. Stuck between the past and the present, what she could see around her had shimmered before her eyes and instinctively she knew that there would be no rescuer tonight. Her mind battered and bargained with itself. Just five more minutes… Just another one. He might have been caught in traffic. In a meeting. In an accident. Anything that would excuse the four unanswered calls to his mobile phone. And although she would never wish that upon him, she was desperate, reaching for an excuse. Because the reality was so much more painful to bear.

She wanted to laugh even as tears threatened to fall from her eyes. Whether he had known it was her birthday or not, he could never have been naïve enough to deny that leaving her here, in a restaurant, wearing a dress she had bought just for him, would hurt her deeply. So he knew. But he had chosen to do it anyway.

Through a haze of barely formed tears, she watched the head waiter slip through the tables discreetly, making his way towards her. She almost wanted to throw up her hand, prevent him from telling her what she already knew. But was instead stuck still. Frozen. On the brink of a precipice as if his decree as to whether Matthieu had simply been delayed, or was unable to come, would draw her back to safety or…

'Mrs Montcour, I'm terribly sorry but your husband

has sent word that he has been unavoidably detained and won't be…'

Maria didn't hear the rest of the sentence over the roaring in her ears. Unaccountably the man seemed to be waiting for some response from her, and she stared up at him in confusion. Surely Matthieu couldn't really have done this to her. Surely the man she loved wouldn't inflict such pain upon her in this way.

'I just need a minute,' she said to the head waiter, who slipped back past the tables of people staring at her like their favourite TV show.

Her hand flew to her stomach when her baby kicked out as if in sympathy with her, him, or defiance, she couldn't tell. All she knew was that she could not stand for it. Could not, would not, live like this again. Not for her child, and not for herself.

It was as if the spell that had stuck her body still had been lifted and she jerked up from the seat. The noise of the chair screeched across the subdued lull of the restaurant, drawing everyone's attention. She stood there for a moment, the barest of ones, permitting their curiosity, their pity, and silently promised herself that this would never, *never*, happen again.

She reached for the small black box from across the table and, with more poise and elegance than a queen, left the restaurant even as tears rolled down her cheeks.

When Matthieu finally arrived home that night, he was exhausted. From the lack of sleep, from the emotional warring within him as he had struggled almost violently with the need to go to her in the restaurant and the desperation to stay away from her. In a last-minute moment of blind-eyed panic, he had rushed to the restaurant—realising far too late that he had been wrong. That he shouldn't, couldn't push her away. But she had already left.

He threw his keys on the side table and stalked through the estate, desperate to find her, to beg for forgiveness. The desolation, guilt and devastation he had felt had cut him off at his knees. Entering the large living area, he stared at the three suitcases by the front door. Stared at them as if he couldn't tell whether they were real or part of his twisted imagination. Couldn't tell whether he was relieved or plunged swiftly into the deepest despair he'd ever felt.

He listened for sounds of her within the house, but it was silent. The lights were off, the whole house cold and dark, as if forecasting his future without her, without his child.

The thought ignited a primal cry within him, full of pain and anger.

A breeze reached him and he looked to the French windows that led out to the decking, seeing that they were open, and finally spying Maria's silhouetted form out there beneath the night sky. Her skin, glowing beneath the light of the moon, her glorious long dark hair flowing around her shoulders, and instantly he was plunged back to that first night. The way that her entire being had called to him like a siren.

Just the way it was doing now. And for a moment, he wished he could take it all back. He wished that, instead of hiding in his office like a coward, he'd got to the restaurant in time. That he'd met her, held her, and told her how much she meant to him. But he couldn't. Instead of going backwards, he went forwards. His feet taking him through the opening in the French windows and out onto the decking, just behind her.

The slight hitch in her breathing letting him know that she knew he was there.

Neither said a word. The silence between them vibrating with unspoken hurts and needs, as if the stars alone bore witness to a great tragedy.

'Maria, I'm so—'

'Don't. Don't you dare apologise.'

She turned then and he wished she hadn't. He could see the tear tracks on her skin, the slight redness that screamed against the shocking pallor of her cheeks. Maria was not hiding her pain as he did. No. She claimed it. Owned it, was even glorious in it. He bit back a thousand curses that would send him to hell and keep him there.

'Do you know what today is?' she asked as if she wasn't flipping the switch on the detonator for a bomb he knew, *knew*, was about to change everything. He could feel it in the air, taste it on his tongue and he desperately wanted to stop the words from falling from her lips.

Instead, he bit down and shook his head, fearing her answer as much as needing to hear it.

'It's my birthday.'

Curses rose in his mind so loud until they were screaming at him. If he had known…would he have done things differently? He was so torn, so confused, in so much pain he couldn't tell any more. All this time his nightmares had shown him losing her in the most violent painful way, and now he was making it happen in reality. Pushing her away to protect himself and he knew that made him the worst kind of beast.

A small sad smile painted her beautiful features. 'Perhaps it is fitting that we met on yours and part on mine.'

'Maria—'

'And I was the one who had a present for *you*,' she said through a half-laugh, full of sadness and loss.

It was then that he saw the small box being turned over in her small hands, the paleness of her skin in contrast to the black velvet case. He frowned, trying to make sense of the shiver of apprehension that streaked through his body. But all he wanted, all he could think of was trying to make her stay.

'I was wrong, Maria. I never should have left you in that restaurant.'

'You were. And you shouldn't have. You knew what it would do to me and you did it anyway. For the first time since I met you, you truly lived up to the reputation you have clung to.'

The knife twisted in his gut, even as she thrust out her hands to give him the gift he did not deserve, had never deserved. Without taking his eyes from her, he retrieved the box and held it. 'Maria, please—'

'Open it.'

'Don't you think we have more important things to discuss right now?'

'No,' she said, shaking her head. 'Because I think that somewhere in that gift is the heart of exactly what is going on right now.'

Frowning, he pulled back the lid of the box and everything in him stopped. It was as if the sight of the contents had not only stalled his breath, but the thoughts in his mind, the blood in his veins. It took him a moment to compute what he was seeing—what he knew he should have been seeing and instead what was actually there.

The three beaten, hand-moulded, textured strands had been woven in a plait that seemed to have no beginning and no end, and though he didn't want to, though he desperately tried to hide from what Maria had created, he could sense how she had wanted each strand to represent his mother, father and himself, and then shift and morph into her, him and their child… And it might have. If it hadn't represented something to him already. Something dark and dangerous and devastating.

'You shouldn't have done this.' Matthieu barely recognised his own voice, unable to even bring himself to look at her.

'I… I thought that this would be something beautiful for you. A way to keep something of your family with you at all times.'

He could hear the confusion, the hurt, in her voice. Perhaps even a trace of fear.

'You have no idea—'

'Of course I don't, Matthieu. Because you don't talk to me! Don't tell me what you're thinking or what you're feeling.'

'You don't want to know what I'm feeling right now,' he warned her.

'But I do, Matthieu. I do. I don't just want the bits of you you deem fit for me to see. I want everything. Not the beast, not the carefully contained husband. I want *you*.'

'You want to know *me*? You want to know what I'm feeling? What I'm feeling right now is sheer horror. Horror that you would take something so personal from me and change it into something completely different. That you would take the very reason my parents are dead—' He cut himself off mid-sentence, desperately warring with himself to grip the fine strands of silver in his hands, or hurl it from him as far as he could. And it was her fault. He never would have been standing here, sharing this with her, had she not pushed, not demanded, not *wanted*.

'Matthieu, I—'

'The way my father looked at my mother when she gave him his present that night…so full of love, so full of life. They sent me to bed before I was able to get a good look at it, promising that I could see it in the morning, but...'

He shook his head at the memories. The childish frustration that he'd been sent to bed, the desperation to see more clearly what his mother had given his father.

'I was too impatient. I sneaked from my room and found it downstairs in the dining room. My parents wasted precious time searching my room, the whole of the first floor, time that they could have used to leave the burning building had it not been for me. Had it not been for this—' He held up the bracelet to punctuate his point.

'—Or what this once was, my father could have made it out. He could have leapt from the window he pushed me out of. I remember the moment he looked at me and made his decision to go back for my mother. I remember the tears I saw in his eyes, how desperate he was to be with me and desperate he was to find her. I saw him there in the window, the words of love he sent me drowned out by the sounds of the fire raging through our home.'

'I'm sorry!' his father had yelled, the words barely reaching Matthieu staring up at him with horror and fear and pain.

'Do you know what it's like to feel responsible for your parents' deaths? To wish your father had chosen you over your mother? Can you conceive of the guilt? That you would rather your mother have died alone than be alone yourself? Or, better yet, not have rescued me at all, but taken me with them?'

His voice broke on the last word. He'd never admitted that to anyone. He'd never even said it out loud.

The silence around them vibrated with thick emotion. Her warmth was the first indication he had that she had come up behind him. That she stood so close, he could feel it.

'The fire was not your fault, Matthieu,' she said, her voice breaking over the words, as if she hurt just as much as he did just then. 'Their loss was not your fault.'

'Really? You believe that? That I'm innocent of that loss, that I'm not the beast I proved to be tonight when I left you in the restaurant *on purpose*?' he bit out, hating that his fear, that his pain was making him just as cruel as she accused him of being, but simply unable to stop. Because pushing her away was safer, for her and for him.

'Don't—'

'Don't what? Lift the veil of whatever fantasy you've woven around us? The same fantasy you wove around you and Tersi? The man you thought you loved *the day we met*.'

It was as if he had struck her. The flinch yanking her head back and the colour draining from already pale features.

'I don't know what you're talking about.'

Confusion and pain fell from her eyes like tears, each one landing hard and fast on his heart.

'Yes, you do. You *do* know. You find people in your life to weave impossible relationships around, because that's easier for you than to face up to the reality that not everything can be a fairy tale, not everyone can be as perfect as you really want them to be. Not your father, not your brother and damn sure not me.' And even as he said the words, he half believed them, half hoped that he was speaking the truth, because the pain he was causing her, causing himself would be somehow less, and damn him if that didn't make him a bastard. 'And what is the reason for that, Maria? You once told me you wanted to know who Maria Montcour was, but, in truth, whether you're a wife, or a mother, a sister or a daughter, you don't seem to know who *you* are. And without that, we will all be playing roles in your fantasies. Ones we never have any hope of living up to. You demand love from us, but how could we if you don't even know yourself?'

Maria let his accusation lie within her. She almost felt herself shrugging into it as if rearranging a piece of clothing over her skin. The horrifying realisation that he might be right robbing her momentarily of thought. Suddenly it was as if something within her snapped into place. As if he had thrown a mirror up to a person she vaguely knew but hardly recognised. Because he was right. It was easier to play a role within these desperately fantasised relationships. Because any rejection she experienced wasn't a denial of *her*, it was the role that she had assigned herself, one she could discard and move on from.

Had she really done that? All these years…she recognised the truth of it in what her feelings had once been for Theo. But no matter what Matthieu said, she knew that she did love him. She could see him almost mentally scrabbling around for anything that would push her away, that would defend himself against his own feelings for her. And if he was going to tear strips from her heart to reveal some inner truth, then she would do the same for him. If this was the last time she would ever be able to meet him with honesty then she would.

'Oh, how righteous you are, accusing me of not knowing myself, of hiding in roles, but what about you, Matthieu? What are you hiding from each time you leave my bed?'

'I have to. I have nightmares, and they are…'

'Just dreams, Matthieu.'

'No, they're not. They are real, they are memories for me! Each night I see my father, my mother and my house all burn. Sometimes you are there. You and our child. And I can't—'

She could see the pain rippling across his shoulders and down his spine. Even in the warm night air, he looked frozen, cold to the touch even as his words were heated and blistered with pain. Her heart broke at the sight of it. Hating that he had hidden this from her.

'Why didn't you tell me? Why didn't you talk it through with me? We could have faced it together, but instead you bottled it up and kept it to yourself.'

'I'm not like you. You have your brother, you have family. I am alone in this, and have been for more years than I have not been. Of course I didn't tell you. I don't tell anyone anything.'

'But I'm not just anyone,' she couldn't help but cry. 'I'm your wife. A role more real than any other. And as much as you might fight it, try to deny it and palm it off as fantasy, I love you. I do. It's overwhelming, incredible and wondrous and you won't let me share that with you, which is unspeakably sad.' The words were a call to action in her heart, rippling out through her body. She hoped above all that even now, even as she knew she must walk away, he would change his mind. Change his heart.

'But you won't let that happen for yourself,' she pressed on. 'Instead you hide your pain, hoarding it as if it's precious, as if it's the only thing your parents left you with. Ignoring the fact that they gave you the building blocks to become the amazing man you could be, if you just let yourself.' She could see the way he flinched at her words as they struck home, as they knocked aside the lies he had built around his heart to protect himself. 'When I first told you about our child, you asked me what it is that I wanted. Now I'm asking you. What is it you want?'

'I don't know!' The shout left his mouth and crashed against her in the most painful way. Because she wanted to give him the benefit of the doubt, desperately wanted to help him find his way to the truth. But she couldn't.

'That's not good enough.'

'It was at the beginning. I told you that I would be there for the child. I told you that you could have whatever material thing you could ever want or need. And I told you that I could not give you more than that. You're changing the terms of our agreement.'

'Yes,' she said defiantly. 'I am changing the terms. Because you've shown me that you are capable of more than you pretended to be. And you made me want that person, you made me want more.'

Matthieu couldn't even deny it. Because he had changed. From the first moment that he saw her by the lake in Iondorra, he had known it would happen. It had started long before the nightmares that plunged him back into memories that he had long ago buried, never wanting to feel the pain, the devastation, the loss—the loss he feared he would experience if she or their child ever... He couldn't even bring himself to think it. She *had* made him want more, want to be more. But it was too much. And the beast within him ached, snarling, biting, growling and gnashing its teeth.

'And until you are ready to be the man I know you can be, I don't want to see you. I don't want you near me. You will have access to our child any time you like. I would not deny our child or you that right. But know this. When it comes to our child, there is no *force majeure*. You will be there at every birthday, every Christmas, every celebration whether it be a music exam, a school exam, or a driving test.'

Maria was painting a picture of the future he would deny himself. The future he was almost forcing through his hands like sand and it was eviscerating him.

'No *force majeure* and no three strikes. Miss one, and you are out of their life for ever. Do you understand? Because what I have learned from my childhood and my time with you is that I will not inflict any kind of physical or emotional absence upon my child.'

My child. She was removing him from her life just as he had wanted before he had returned to the house, and after she had given him the present. At first it had been because he thought they would be better off without him. Now? He simply couldn't imagine how he could live with them. Them and the constant fear that he could lose them at any moment. So yes, he needed her to go.

'My child will grow up knowing they are loved, they are supported by their family. That no matter what, they come first. And they will know that because I will lead by example. So no matter how much I love you—and I do, Matthieu, so, so much—I am putting myself and my child first. But, Matthieu, for you? You have to face this. You cannot live in the shadow of the reputation you have lived down to as beast. You cannot let it rule your life.'

She walked past him, then, head held high, so beautiful it made his heart ache. But he knew it was for the best that Maria Rohan de Luen, the woman he loved too much to bear, left his life.

CHAPTER ELEVEN

YOU CANNOT LET it rule your life.

Maria's parting words had echoed within the walls of his estate, had roamed around his mind for hours and even days after she had left.

His phone calls and emails had gone unanswered. He had not been back to the office since that night. Because in truth, her words had come to consume him. In the years following the fire he had thought, in his own way, that he had dealt with the events of that night. But now Maria had shone a light on his darkest, deepest hurts and the door that she had unlocked now swung open, fully flooding him with everything.

At first he had been cowed by the loss, a loss as fresh as it had been all those years ago. But once the first flush of memories from that night passed through him, other memories emerged. A holiday they had spent in Antigua, the way his mother always dressed in bright colours, pinks, turquoises, purples and bright oranges. The way his father would gently tease his mother for her choice in unusual earrings. And it hurt. The realisation that he had pushed down all the things that had made the two of them unique, loving, sometimes even like bickering schoolchildren. And it made him want more.

A week after Maria had left, he'd called Malcolm,

who had arrived at the house within hours. The concern and shared pain on his familiar features almost a balm to Matthieu's wounds. He had peppered his oldest friend with questions about how his parents had met, what they had been like, things that perhaps he would have learned in time, had they had the luxury of it. For hours they had talked, Matthieu relishing everything he had never wanted, never been able to bear, before.

Until finally Matthieu had talked about that night. Opening up his grief for someone other than Maria to see. To own his shame and guilt over his actions that night.

'I never knew,' Malcolm had said. 'If I had… Matthieu, why didn't you tell me you felt that way?'

'Admit that it was my fault?'

'But it wasn't,' Malcolm had said, pressing a hand on the wooden table as if to hold himself back from a stronger physical act. 'Matthieu, do you remember how the fire started?'

He'd frowned, knowing by heart the fire marshal's incident report he had once scoured as if it held answers. 'Faulty electrics.'

'Where?' Malcolm had prompted.

'What do you mean?'

'Where did the fire start?'

'On the second floor.'

'And where were you?'

'Downstairs in the living…'

Malcolm had levelled him with a heavy gaze. 'The fire wasn't your fault, Matthieu, and if you'd been in bed that night, and not further down in the house, then… Then you might have been one of the first casualties of that night. Your father didn't waste precious time, and even if he had, he would have done so because he loved you and wanted you to live. If he went back into the fire for your mother it was because he wanted the same for her. Your father might have survived, but the man I was lucky enough to call my closest friend in the world wouldn't have forgiven himself if he had not tried.'

He wanted you to live. He wouldn't have forgiven himself if he had not tried.

Long after Malcolm had left, Matthieu had sat gazing, unseeing, at Lake Lucerne. He had been shocked by the realisation that he had not been living. That he had not been trying. Maria had been right. He had hoarded his pain, hoarded the precious, sometimes painful, but more often incredible loving memories of his parents as if they had a portion of allotted time before running out, before disappearing from his mind. But the more he thought, the more he remembered. And the more he realised that he had made a terrible mistake forcing Maria from his life.

Nearly a month later, Matthieu stepped out of the limousine parked outside an estate in Siena, and knocked on the door, bracing himself for what was to happen.

It swung open and Sebastian Rohan de Luen took one look at him and swung. In truth, Matthieu had seen the punch coming from a mile away, but took the hit, feeling it was pretty much deserved at this point.

He cupped his jaw, rubbing at the small sting at the corner of his mouth with his thumb.

'A friend would tell you to use your words,' he said to Seb.

'Yeah? Well. I'm more about actions. I warned you. Dammit, I bloody told you—'

'I know. You were right. I deserved it and much more.'

Seb looked at him long and hard before stepping back and letting him pass through the door and into the dark living room of the estate Matthieu had last visited with

Maria. That was when Matthieu noticed the glass of half-drunk whisky and empty bottle on the table. Seb had come to a halt in the middle of the room and was staring at a painting propped up on the mantelpiece above a large fireplace. It was only then that Matthieu really looked at the painting.

'Wait…is that a—?'

'Yes.'

Matthieu was struck by the image of the woman staring out at him, from one of Europe's most famous and expensive painters.

'Jesus, is that—?'

'Our mother. The resemblance is remarkable, don't you think?'

Matthieu chose not to answer, suddenly realising just how hard it must have been for Maria's father to see the face of his wife in his child. Suddenly realising how difficult it must have been for Maria. 'That painting must be worth at least one hundred million.'

'You aren't the only billionaire in the room, Montcour.'

'Did you *buy* this?'

A pregnant pause filled the air before Sebastian reluctantly admitted that it was a long story. Matthieu looked sideways at Sebastian. 'Are you okay?' he asked, genuinely concerned.

'I don't think you're here to talk about me and my feelings, are you, Montcour?'

'No, but—'

'Don't,' Seb interrupted, slashing his hand through the air to cut off the direction of the conversation, and resumed his watchful stance over the painting.

Matthieu sighed. 'Do you know where she is?'

'Yes.'

'Are you going to tell me?'

'Only if you give me a good enough reason to,' he replied, finally turning that powerful, predatory gaze on him.

'I love her,' Matthieu said simply. He let the truth shine from his words and fill the darkness in the room. In the last few weeks he'd spent hours thinking through his feelings, his fears and the darkest parts of him. Regretting almost every second that he'd not allowed Maria to help him in this way, but knowing that in reality it was better, healthier for him to have forged this realisation himself.

'You might do. I might even believe that you do. But that doesn't mean I will give you what you want.'

Matthieu couldn't fault him for that. It took him nearly an hour to convince Sebastian to reveal where Maria was. As he returned to his car, he pulled out his phone and got his assistant to track down the telephone number for Theo Tersi. The conversation was brief and to the point and Matthieu put all thoughts of Maria's brother aside the moment Theo promised to come to Siena as soon as humanly possible. Then, with his sole focus on Maria, he put the key in the car's ignition and hit the gas.

Maria pulled into the driveway of the house she had rented in Umbria, both physically and mentally exhausted. She had visited with her father and Valeria and it had been...she shook her head at the direction of her thoughts. Difficult? Yes. Painful? A little. But better? Perhaps.

It had taken a good few weeks of soul-searching just to find the courage to face Eduardo. To be truly honest with herself. She had allowed her father's withdrawal to dictate far too much of her life. She had allowed him to see her mother in her, not having the courage to stand and be *Maria*. And in the same way, she had sought only the idealised relationship she had dreamed of, not the father she *did* have. But it didn't have to continue on that way, and it didn't mean that there couldn't be a relationship there. He might never have really been able to say it or show it, but deep down, despite his faults, she knew that he did love her. And for the first time in what felt like for ever, she had met with her father not beneath the blanket of pain at what he wasn't capable of, or who she was not, but with the comfort of hope as to what he might be and who she was. And no matter how much devastation her argument with Matthieu had wrought that night, if this was the one good thing she could take away from it—she would take it.

She stepped out of the small rental car feeling both emotionally exposed from her visit, but also oddly stronger and more resilient, and walked towards the front door of the beautiful property she had found nearly a month ago. Using the money that Seb had set aside for her—the account she'd once sworn never to touch—she had fallen in love with it almost the moment she had seen it and leased it for at least one year. Settled in between sunflower fields and tobacco fields, the one-storey structure was everything Matthieu's estate beside Lake Lucerne was not. Warm terracotta tiles sloped over the gentle roof topping ancient stone walls. Beautiful shutters held off the penetrating sun when it became too much and in the afternoon, as the sun passed overhead, a stunning pergola almost buckling under the weight of sprawling tendrils of clematis and honeysuckle provided shade for an outdoor courtyard that she had taken up almost daily residence in.

The villa was just under two hours from Sebastian, three from her father, and what felt like a lifetime away from Matthieu. She had thought at first that she would fall into a pattern of numb, exhausted moping—but she didn't have the luxury to do that. Not to herself, not to her child. Instead of being drained by her separation from Matthieu, from the hurtful accusations they had thrown at each other that night, she had somehow been ignited by them, driven and determined in a way she had never encountered before. Driven, beyond all else, to discover who she truly was.

She had sat down with her accounts, with her wants and needs for both herself and her child, and made plans. And while it hurt that those plans were made in Matthieu's absence, they formed a future that was created, not from fantasies and falsities, but the conversations they had once shared through nights where neither had been able to sleep. It was a future that honoured the desires of both parents.

But in the plans she was beginning to make for her own future, how she hoped to juggle parenthood with her jewellery making, for once not seeing the finances from Matthieu as a tie, but a gift that would allow her to explore both sides of who she was and what and how she wanted to be, she had found that inner sense of self, that sense of accomplishment she had felt had been missing.

For the first time in what felt like for ever, her future had a shape, had a solid direction that she had created for herself. And in that, she began to know herself. Her recent appointment with her new doctor had gone well, both her and her child flourishing here. She had even started to look at schools—which was a way off—and had bought a crib for her child. Yes, she had once imagined doing that with Matthieu and the thought of putting it up herself without his involvement did hurt, but she would do it.

As for her thoughts of Matthieu, she didn't seem able

to touch them. To access them. They were sealed beneath the same closed door that she had accused him of shutting over his memories of the past. But now, she understood. Understood just a little of what and why he had been forced to do that. In time, she hoped that she'd have the courage to deal with them, as she had encouraged him to deal with his hurts. But this kindness she gave herself, because that door she had slammed shut was locked with a hope she barely dared acknowledge. Hope that he would come for her.

She had just poured herself a cup of lemon and ginger tea when the sound of a vehicle on the gravel driveway drew her attention back to the present with a little jolt of excitement. That would be the crib. She had spent far too much money on it, but for the first time she didn't mind. Money didn't have strings, or checks or balances that tied to a heart. Her brother had set her up with the fund out of love, not obligation, and she would embrace it for both herself and her child.

She put down the cup and made her way to the front doors of the villa, too busy pinning them back against the wall to see the form of the man standing in the middle of the entrance, blocking out all the light as if it was his right.

'If you could just—'

Her words caught in her throat as she took in the sight of Matthieu, her quick, hungry eyes almost tripping over the features she'd gone to sleep imagining every night since she'd left Switzerland. The dark furrow of his brow, the strong jaw line, the impossible breadth of his shoulders and arms. All of it. She wanted it all.

Her gaze flew back to his eyes, shining a heady combination of hope, sadness and something she dared not put name to.

* * *

Matthieu felt the breath whoosh from his lungs with a sense of peace the moment his eyes finally rested on his wife. He knew, as sure as he knew anything, that he still had a mountain to climb, but allowed himself this one moment, because in all the days, nights and weeks since he had last seen her, he'd known only that a vital piece of him was missing. Something integral to his existence.

'May I come in?' he asked, promising that if she said no, he'd respect it. But also knowing that he'd come back every single day until she did let him in. Because he knew that he had hurt her. He knew that he didn't even deserve a second chance, but he desperately hoped for one.

She looked at him for the longest time and just when he thought she was about to refuse him, she frowned.

'What happened to your mouth?' she asked, shocked.

He put his thumb to the corner of his mouth where Seb had caught him and smiled ruefully. 'Nothing I didn't deserve.'

'My *brother* did that to you?' she demanded furiously before disappearing into the dark hallway of the villa, muttering curses and dire promises of punishment.

'Maria?' he asked as he rounded the corner to find her stabbing at her phone in fury.

'Hold on.'

He frowned in confusion. This wasn't exactly how he'd planned this to be.

'Maria…'

Her name on his lips felt like a balm and if she gave him the chance, he'd say it a million times a day.

'What?' she said, as he stalked over and gently prised the phone from her hands.

'I don't want to talk about Sebastian or anything else right now. I came here to…'

She cocked her head to one side, looking, for just a moment, the way she had that first night in Iondorra. But somehow even more. She just looked and felt so much more he wasn't sure that he wouldn't explode from it. But she was still distracted by the phone, by Seb, clearly searching for anything that would buy her time, or postpone it, he couldn't tell. This wasn't what he'd wanted at all. He turned and stalked back down the corridor.

'Where are you—?' her voice came from behind him.

He bent to unhook the front shutters from where she had pinned them back and pulled one closed, before stepping out into the sunshine.

'We're starting this again. Because it's important. I'm going to get this right,' he said determinedly, pulling the second shutter too and taking a deep breath. He waited, took another. Composed himself and knocked on the door again.

When she pulled open the shutters there was an odd look on her face, part humour, part sadness and a large part confusion.

'May I come in, Maria?'

This time she seemed to take the time to consider it. And in that moment, his heart nearly stopped in his chest. Because in the long shadows pouring from either side of the hallway, he could see how much bigger their baby had become. And everything in him wanted to drop to his feet, place his hands and head on her bump and beg and plead for her forgiveness.

She moved aside before he had the chance to actually do it and gestured for him to come in.

This time he followed her down the hallway, uncaring of the villa around them, and back out into the sunlight of the most glorious courtyard he'd ever seen. Huge swathes of white and purple flowers created a canopy hanging low above their heads and the sweet smell of honeysuckle rained down upon his senses. He marvelled because this was uniquely Maria. Warm, colourful, sweet…perfect. It was everything that he'd missed the moment he had thrust her from his life.

And he shook his head at the sea of thoughts crashing against his mind. He didn't know where to start—and feared that it might all come out in a jumbled mess. He had thought this through. Had tried and tested the words over in his mind on his way here. But now, with Maria standing before him…

'Pull up a pew?' she asked. It was an olive branch and it was a chance. To start over. To get things right. But that would mean ignoring everything that had happened between them. Everything that she'd helped him see about himself, all that he'd been forced to realise was wrong within himself.

'I'll stand, but thank you.' He let out a sigh, his gaze for a moment on the stunning riotous fields of sunflowers surrounding them, while he picked his words. 'Maria, I cannot ask you to forgive me for that night. Leaving you at the restaurant was unforgivable.' Finally finding the courage, he sneaked a glance back at Maria—terrified of seeing her agreement, not even thinking for a moment he would receive clemency for it. Instead, he saw patience— a patience he did not deserve, but would take with open arms. 'You were right. About everything. I had not told you about the nightmares, or the fire, because, in truth, I didn't want you to help me see through them. Because that would have meant that I would have had to face the fact that…the fact that you had become so precious to me that I could lose you and, having lost my family, knowing the very real pain of that, I honestly didn't think that I would survive losing you or our child. And instead, I pushed you away, and lost you, all the while promising myself it would hurt less now, rather than more later.

'And it was my fear of that, the genuine terror of just how much you mean to me, just how much I have come to love you, that made me cruel. On your birthday, I took your love for me and turned it against you and that is unforgivable. So no matter what happens after today, I want you to know that no amount of time apart will change the way I feel about you. If you choose never to see me again, that is absolutely your decision. But I will always love you. You brought light to a life I didn't realise was dark. You brought truth to my soul when I didn't realise it was shrouded in secrets and guilt. And love to my empty heart. I love that I can now accept and embrace and that… that will go to you and our child always.

'The pain of the past is still there, but it is somehow… less. Honouring that pain, remembering it hasn't taken away what happened, but bringing it into the light has allowed both the hurt and the joy, the love to become a part of me, not separate or isolated, but present, and it has made me realise how much more I am with love in my life.'

This time, when he looked at his wife, he could see tears in her eyes, the slow roll down her cheek, that made him reach up and brush one away.

Maria's gaze snagged on the glint of silver that had caught her eye when he reached for her cheek. He was wearing the bracelet that had meant so much to her when she had made it. And when her gaze turned from that to her husband, all she could see was the man she loved staring back at her, glorious and proud, exulting in his feelings, and it was a marvel.

'When you first gave me this,' he said, 'all I could see was the past, was the pain, the guilt and shame that this represented to me. But, talking to Malcolm, remembering that night myself, allowing myself to remember more… You've given me back a part of me I thought long since gone and I am awed by it, by the incredible generosity of such a thing, and the beauty of what you brought me. And now I can have this with me every single day, wherever I go.

'I can see now, that it not only represented my connection to the past, with my parents, and my future with you and our child, but more than that, it represents how the present could come from a past once thought damaged and burned by pain and loss, and be not only strong, and beautiful now, but hopeful and wondrous in the future.'

Tears fell freely from her eyes now. She was overwhelmed by his understanding of what she had tried to imbue into the gift, the sense of connection between them somehow even more powerful now. But she knew that she needed to speak, needed to say the words crying in her heart. She covered her hands with his.

'I want… I need you to know that I heard you too.' He tried to shake off her words, as if the memory of that night was hurtful and shameful. 'No, don't. I know that our words were angry and dark, but just as you found goodness because of them, I did too. I realised that much of what you were saying was right. I was so afraid of being rejected, of being unloved myself, that instead I wove fantasies around relationships, casting myself in roles that I could shake off, move on from if those relationships failed. And it wasn't fair, to anyone, my father, brother, you or myself. I went to see my father,' she confessed, with a small smile. 'And, no…he's not going to suddenly change, but reframing our relationship, not with what I *wanted* it to be, but how it *was* and could be…it was healing, and generous, and kind and hopefully one day loving. And I wouldn't have had that without you or what you said that night.

'But more than that, because of that night, I forced myself to truly take a look at who I am, who I want to be. I'm beginning to learn about "just Maria" and,' she said with a much larger smile, 'I like her.' Then she frowned. '*Me*. I like me. I like discovering who I am and, more than anything, I truly want you to come on that journey of discovery with me. I am so thankful for that night in Iondorra. I honestly believe I fell in love with you that first night, when in some ways we were each more ourselves than we have been since then. And I would very much like to spend the rest of my life being that way with you and our child.'

'Can you say that again?' he demanded on a shaky exhale.

'The whole thing?' Maria demanded, a little worried that she'd not be able to do it.

'No, just the most important bit.'

She smiled, instantly understanding what he was looking for.

'I love you, Matthieu Montcour.'

'I will never tire of hearing that, Maria. And I will never tire of saying it myself. I love you so, so much.'

Her hand reached out to caress his jaw, to reach for him and pull him to her in a kiss that was just as much joy and love and acceptance as it was passion and desire and need. Her heart soared as he swept her up from where she was sitting and into his arms, entwined beneath the clematis and honeysuckle as if they were weaving themselves together for ever.

Matthieu would wear the bracelet every single day for the rest of his life, through the birth of their first child— a beautiful baby girl, boisterous and full of laughter and as naughty as she could get away with—and their second, a gorgeous baby boy, sometimes serious, but always loving and considered and kind. He would wear it when he renewed his vows with his wife in the wedding he wanted to finally give her, surrounded by family and friends full of laughter, love and joy. And he would wear it as they weathered the storms that came through loss or hurt, but he would always wear it with the love that filled his heart completely for his wife, their children, his parents and himself. And he would never not be thankful that his beautiful wife had opened his heart to love and shown him that he was not the beast he had spent so long thinking himself, but someone worthy of the queen of his heart.

* * * * *

THE SCANDAL BEHIND THE ITALIAN'S WEDDING

MILLIE ADAMS

For the book girls.
Keep dreaming.
Keep reading.

CHAPTER ONE

It was rumored that Dante Fiori could condemn a man to any level of hell he chose with the mere lift of his brow.

Powerful. Ruthless. Determined.

Dante was not a man to be trifled with or tested. He'd raised himself up from the slums with the aid of his mentor, Robert King, but then not only had he gone on to exceed the man's expectations, he'd increased his fortune, as well.

Dante was a force in the world. A man all other men looked to—save his best friend, Maximus King, who found him overrated in the extreme and was the only person who had the nerve to say so. A man all women wanted to be with.

A king in whichever kingdom he chose to rule, whether he was a King by blood or not.

So it was shocking, then, when the world turned on its axis right in the middle of the King family's grand living room.

Dante was in town, and he'd been invited over, as he often was, to join the family for their rather loud and raucous get-togethers. They were celebrating the launch of their oldest daughter Violet's new makeup line, in a live video being broadcast from a nearby San Diego beach, to millions of viewers on her various media platforms.

Robert was lounging in his oversize chair, his wife, Elizabeth, sitting on the arm. Maximus was sitting back on the couch, one leg flung out in front of him, phone in one hand, a scotch in the other.

There was one family member missing. Two, actually. Minerva King, the youngest daughter and constant irritant, and her baby.

Dante had difficulty accepting the existence of the newest, smallest member of the King clan.

Min was nothing like Maximus or Violet. Maximus was a brilliant PR mind. A handler to the most difficult clients in the world. He did everything with a smile that the untrained eye might not be able to see was shot through with steel.

Violet was stunning. Keen and ambitious, she'd transformed her beauty into a multimillion-dollar enterprise. She was the driving force and face of her brand.

Then there was Min.

A little brown mouse who scurried about the grounds, always trailing about the place with animals dripping from her arms and a skinned knee. Her cheeks were always red, her hair always in a state.

And she talked. Constantly. About nothing.

She'd gone abroad to study nearly one year ago, and when she'd returned, it had been with a baby who was barely a month old. While initially shocked, over the past four months her family had accepted the existence of the little girl easily enough. The Kings weren't old-fashioned.

The shock hadn't come from the fact their daughter had broken with tradition and had a child out of wedlock—presumably with a foreign stranger—but that it had been Minerva and not Violet.

Dante did not feel accepting of it at all. He felt a strange burning in his chest when he looked at Min with the baby. This untamable, wild thing now tied down to earth by a child. By motherhood. She should be…out climbing trees. No matter that she was twenty-one, he couldn't wrap his mind around the fact that she was a woman now.

A *mother*.

The other urge he had was to find the man who had done it to her and send him back to dust.

Send him straight down to the ninth level where he could sit next to Lucifer himself.

It infuriated him perhaps because Minerva always seemed so hapless. Running around like a windmill, and falling down, often undented. Though she had been badly dented once at an event of her father's, and he remembered it well.

Some boy she liked publicly humiliating her on the dance floor.

Robert King had nearly had a stroke, and his anger had only embarrassed Min all the more.

She'd been seventeen or so. Dante had danced with her because she'd needed a partner.

Don't let them see you cry.

He'd said it sternly. More than he'd meant, but it had done the trick.

The idea that someone had harmed her now enraged him all over again.

He wasn't in the habit of questioning himself. He simply acted when he felt action needed to occur. And perhaps that was the issue here. There was no action to be taken.

It didn't matter. Minerva didn't matter. Neither did her current situation.

All eyes were on Violet and would be for the next fifteen minutes while she unveiled her next series of products. And then it would be time for Dante to speak to Robert about the joining of the two companies again.

He had been trying to tell Robert it was the best thing for everyone. And, of course, some of it was that Dante felt entitled to King Industries as he had helped to build it. He had gone off and made his own fortune, but his ultimate goal was a merger between the two.

Of course, Robert had feelings about keeping it all in the family.

But Maximus had no interest at all. Maximus was a billionaire, and his business methods were unorthodox. He had no interest in manufacturing.

Violet was much the same, and while she used King Industries to help make her products, she developed them on her own, and used her father's business simply for the manufacturing end, containing development and distribution within her own brand.

Only Minerva remained to take over the family business, and he knew that Minerva would have no interest in such a thing.

She was not… Ambitious.

Minerva was not brave.

If she were here now, it would be as if she weren't. She would simply be sitting in a corner, clutching her baby and looking around.

Unless she began to chatter.

But typically, she was quiet as her father commanded during times such as these.

Violet's beautiful, perfectly made-up face appeared on the screen, and the whole family paid heed. Dante looked up, sparing the screen only a glance before looking back down at his own phone.

But then, a moment later it wasn't Violet's voice he heard.

"I know you're watching to hear about my sister's products, and not to hear family gossip. But, as her new makeup line is called Rumors, I thought that I would put some rumors about me to rest."

He looked up and saw his brown mouse.

There was Minerva, her dark hair hanging loose and unstyled past her shoulders, not straight, not curled, somewhere in between. She was holding the baby, gripped tightly against her body.

"There has been much discussion in regards to the paternity of my baby girl. I'm used to being the King that no one has any interest in. And yet, the interest surrounding Isabella's birth has been unprecedented for me. Well, it's time for the secret come out." Brilliant green eyes met the camera, Min's only stunning feature. And they were glowing now. "The father of my baby is Dante Fiori."

Whatever else was happening on the screen, not a single person in the family was watching now.

All eyes had turned to him.

He looked into his friend's eyes. And he saw only murder there.

She had done it. In a panic, she had done it, and Violet had been more than happy to allow her to step up and make the announcement because Violet loved nothing more than a spectacle.

Well, Min had promised her spectacle. She had delivered.

And now, in the limo, after the announcement was done, Violet had exploded.

"Dante?"

"Yes," Minerva said, lying through her teeth and feeling more and more terrified by the moment.

"Dante? Dante slept with you?"

She couldn't work out if Violet was shocked because Minerva was not the sort of woman Dante typically went for, or if Violet was angry that Dante had touched her, or if Violet was angry because she was... Well, maybe a little bit jealous.

Violet was the great beauty in the family, there was no questioning that. Minerva wasn't much at all. She never had been.

Until she had returned from a trip overseas with a baby. And then speculation about her had begun to swirl. She should have known there would be no avoiding rumors. She should have known that avoiding the press would be impossible. She should have known that every jerk with a smartphone would try to take her and Isabella's picture, and that those pictures would be posted everywhere, for anyone in the world to see. And that Carlo would see them. And he would suspect.

And once she had gotten the threatening text, she knew that she had to act.

She was in danger. Isabella was in danger.

She didn't believe that Katie's overdose had been purely accidental, and she never would. Carlo was the kind of man who had access to all sorts of things, and her friend had been terrified during those last days of her life. Because he had found them.

It had been so simple for a while, to stay under the radar in Europe. Minerva wasn't a particularly famous face, in spite of her connection to the King family, and outside the United States nobody ever gave her a second glance. If she had been with Violet, everyone would have recognized them.

But on her own, she was just a university student. The same with her friend and roommate.

But clearly, Carlo had figured out who she was, and where she was.

And worse, where Isabella was.

She had no choice but to tell this lie. To throw him off the scent.

Because this baby could not be Carlo's baby. Not if it was hers. Not if it was Dante's.

There was a reason the deception about Isabella had been so paramount when she had first come home. That she insisted the child was hers.

Everyone had believed it. And she had thought it would be enough. It was one reason she hadn't worried over much when photographs of herself and Isabella had begun circulating.

She had never slept with Carlo. Therefore, any child of hers could not be a child of his. And besides, she was used to her superpower. Invisibility.

A wren among a gaggle of peacocks, Minerva was simply accustomed to being forgotten. She didn't imagine for a moment that Carlo would remember her face. He had only seen her a handful of times during the time she'd spent studying in Rome. And he had been entirely focused on Katie.

But clearly, he had begun to piece things together.

And so…

And so.

She had promised her sister a show. She had delivered. But she did *not* seem pleased.

"Dad is going to *kill him*," Violet said.

"Do you think so?" Her father had responded to her return with a baby in an extremely sanguine manner. As far as Robert King was concerned, as long as none of his children were crack addicts he had done fine enough.

She had asked him if it bothered him. That she had a child without a partner.

He'd said: "Why would I mind? You're not a teenager, and you have the money to take care of her. It's not like the house isn't big enough."

And that had been the end of it.

She couldn't imagine he would be angry simply because the baby was Dante's.

Dante, on the other hand…

She could only hope that he was somewhere far afield. On the East Coast. In his New York office. Perhaps he would be in Frankfurt or Milan.

Just so long as he wasn't…

The limo pulled up to the front of the King family mansion, and all of Minerva's hopes and dreams were dashed when she saw him standing there.

Her heart nearly lurched up her throat and out of her mouth.

She had forgotten.

How imposing he was. How large.

How utterly, devastatingly handsome.

Which was ridiculous, because she had seen him only a month earlier.

She could still remember the awkward, horrible dance at one of her father's parties. Her biggest crush ever had only agreed to be her date for a dare. To see the inside of the infamous King mansion and to report back to friends at school.

Dante had taken hold of her after Bradley had embarrassed her, and held her close, shielding her from curious eyes. He'd been so strong and solid, and all the anguish and shame inside her had caught fire and burned hot. It had been so embarrassing but she'd also been unable to pull away from him.

But he'd been pity dancing with her. He'd added to the confusion of…everything.

And compared to Bradley's bony shoulders, Dante's had felt so broad and solid.

It had all been weird.

Even with that she could forget.

But she didn't think that the impact of a man like Dante Fiori could live in its genuine state inside a woman, or anyone. You would die of it.

It became clear only in person.

He had always made her feel small. Rattled.

She had the tendency to run at the mouth whenever he was around. He made her stomach feel like it was quivering.

She disliked it intensely. And yet, she had always felt drawn to him like he was a magnet. She had always felt compelled to get a response out of him. To go to him. And she could no more understand any of those tendencies then she could understand quantum physics.

Which was to say: not at all.

"He is unhappy," Violet said softly.

"Well… He'll just have to deal with it."

Minerva lifted her chin, affecting a posture of determination she did not feel. Her brother appeared behind Dante, and behind him was her father.

Everybody *did* look remarkably unhappy.

Min was not accustomed to being the source of people's unhappiness. She was used to being ignored, and when she'd shown up with her parents' first grandchild, they'd been happy.

No one looked happy now.

The car stopped, and Dante didn't wait. He marched over to the car and jerked the door open.

And she found herself face-to-face with his stormy black gaze.

It was fathomless. As if she could look all the way down into the depths of his soul. Into the depths of hell itself.

She knew the things they said about him. That when her father had encountered him in Rome when he was a boy, Dante had been attempting to rob Robert King at gunpoint. That something about the boy had made Robert pause. That he had given him his watch, but also his card, and told him that if he wanted to change his life, rather than just live to commit another robbery, he should contact him.

And that shockingly, Dante had.

But that he had been a man who had committed a great many atrocities prior to his salvation and education that had been financed by Robert King.

She had never believed the stories.

Mostly because her father loved a story, and it was one he did not tell. Which forced her to believe that the truth of it must be less dramatic, and far less interesting.

Now she wondered, though.

Because she felt like she was staring down the very devil.

"We have a lot to discuss, don't you think?"

Dante took hold of her hand, and lifted her from the limo, depositing her gently onto her feet. She looked past his shoulder, at Maximus and her father.

"And when you're done speaking to her," Maximus said, "I think you and I need to have a talk."

"I'm sure this will give you time to rally the firing squad," Dante said, his tone dry.

He was still holding her hand.

She could recall, with perfect ease, another time Dante had touched her hand. Not the dance, but earlier.

She had been a girl. All of twelve, and she had fallen out of a tree in the backyard.

Dante had found her lying pitifully on the ground, pondering her fate, and he had been afraid that she had broken her neck. He had yelled as much at her as he had lifted her up. His touch, hot and strong, had started to quiver low in her body.

She hadn't liked it. She had pulled away from him, then bent down to wipe the blood from her knee. "I'm fine."

"You are a menace," he'd said back.

She could imagine the exchange happening just that way now.

"I have to get Isabella," she protested.

"Go," he said.

She did, stumbling as she went. With shaking fingers, she undid the seat belt and lifted her baby girl up from the seat.

The thing was, it didn't matter who'd given birth to Isabella.

Minerva was her mother.

She'd cared for her from the time she was born while Katie shrank away in increasing fear, self-medicating away the terror of the possibility of Carlo finding them.

Min was not brave by nature. But she'd known someone had to be brave for Isabella. And since Katie couldn't, it had to be her.

They walked past her brother, who was looking at Dante as though he wanted to flay him alive, and her father, who looked stoic. Into the house. Up the stairs.

Totally silent.

Minerva clung to Isabella, thinking of her in some

ways as a shield. Surely not even Dante would yell at her while she was holding a baby.

He opened up the door to her father's study, and ushered her inside, slamming it behind them. "Explain this, Minerva, because you and I both know that I am not the father of your baby."

Well, she was disappointed on that score. Dante was clearly fine yelling around an infant.

She cupped the back of Isabella's downy little head. "Did you tell them?"

"No, I didn't tell them. You're going to have to tell them, because if I tell them they're not going to believe me. In the hour it took you to get home from the press conference, I had to tell your brother about ten reasons he shouldn't kill me where I sat. And the leading one was that I might be the father of your child, and that you might need me in some capacity."

"I *do* need you," she said.

Silence settled between them as he waited for her to explain.

"I'm sorry," she said finally. "I panicked."

"Why did you panic? What is happening?"

"You were the only name I could think of. The only name that was big enough. I had to protect myself, Dante. I had to protect Isabella! And I thought seeing as you are so close with my family, it was believable enough that you and I…that we…"

"Yes, well. The problem is, *child*, that the idea I would touch you in that way is laughable in the extreme."

Minerva had never felt so small, or quite so dull.

Standing next to the brilliant Dante Fiori made her feel as plain and inadequate as she was.

He was right. The idea that he would touch her was laughable, though it seemed as if Maximus and her father were more than willing to believe it. So why wouldn't the rest of the world?

She knew he'd only ever danced with her four years ago because he'd pitied her. Everyone knew it.

Still, she held her head high.

"Men are renowned for touching women that don't make sense. It is common knowledge that the secret sexual fantasies of men are *unknowable*." She leaned in and did her best to seem confident when she was very much not.

"Is it?" he asked. "Well, mine are fairly knowable. Often plastered on the front page of newspapers here and there. *You* are plainly not my fantasy."

She thought of all the women he'd been seen with over the years. Sleek, polished and curvy. Brunette, blonde, pale or brown, didn't seem to matter to him, but there was a sophistication to the women he enjoyed.

Quite like her sister, and not at all like her.

"Well, that is good to know," she said.

"Why did you do it, Minerva?"

"I am sorry. I really didn't do it to cause you trouble. But I'm being threatened, and so is Isabella, and in order to protect us both I needed to come up with an alternative paternity story."

"An *alternative* paternity story?"

She winced. "Yes. Her father is after her."

He eyed her with great skepticism. "I didn't think you knew who her father was."

She didn't know whether to be shocked, offended or pleased that he thought her capable of having an anonymous interlude.

For heaven's sake, she'd only ever been kissed one time in her life. A regrettable evening out with Katie in Rome where she'd tried to enjoy the pulsing music in the club, but had instead felt overheated and on the verge of a seizure.

She'd danced with a man in a shiny shirt—and she even knew his name because she wouldn't even dance with a man without an introduction—and he'd kissed her on the dance floor. It had been wet and he'd tasted of liquor and she'd feigned a headache after and taken a cab back to the hostel they'd been staying in.

The idea of hooking up with someone, in a circumstance like that, made her want to peel her own skin off.

"Of course I know who he is. Unfortunately... The full implications of who he is did not become clear until later."

"What does that mean?"

She could tell him the truth now, but something stopped her. Maybe it was admitting Isabella wasn't her daughter, which always caught her in the chest and made her feel small. Like she'd stolen her and like what they had was potentially fragile, temporary and shaky.

Or maybe it was trust. Dante was a good man. Going off the fact he had rescued her from a fall, and helped her up when her knee was skinned, and bailed her out after her terrible humiliation in high school.

But to trust him with the truth was something she simply wasn't brave enough to do.

Her life, Isabella's life, was at risk, and she'd lied on livestream in front of the world.

Her bravery was tapped out.

"Her father is part of an organized crime family. Obviously something unknown to me at the time of her... you know. And he's after her. He's after *us*."

"Are you telling me that you're in actual danger?"

"Yes. And really, the only hope I have is convincing him that he isn't actually the father."

"And you think that will work?"

"It's the only choice I have. I need your protection."

He regarded her with dark, fathomless eyes, and yet again, she felt like he was peering at her as though she were a girl, and not a woman at all. A naughty child, in point of fact. Then something in his expression shifted.

It shamed her a little that this was so like when he'd come to her rescue at the party. That she was manipulating his pity for her. Her own pathetic nature being what called to him, yet again.

But she would lay down any and all pride for Isabella and she'd do it willingly.

"If she were in fact my child, then we would be family."

"I… I suppose," she said.

"There will need to be photographs of us together, as I would not be a neglectful father."

"No indeed."

"Of course, you know that if Isabella were really my child there would be only one thing for us to do."

"Do I?"

"Yes." He began to pace, like a caged tiger trying to find a weak spot in his cage. And suddenly he stopped, and she had the terrible feeling that the tiger had found what he'd been looking for. "Yes. Of course, there is only one option."

"And that is?"

"You have to marry me."

CHAPTER TWO

TWO THINGS HAD become clear to Dante as he'd stared down into Min's green eyes.

The first was that if Minerva and Isabella were in real danger then he would have to protect them. There was no choice.

He could not uncover her lies, because no matter how convoluted it might be, his protection was perhaps the only thing standing between her and this man she claimed wanted to do her harm. Dante was not so foolish as to think he could simply involve law enforcement and make an issue like a man connected to a crime family go away.

But he had resources. Men at his disposal. And more important, he had money. If her plan didn't work, he had other methods of being able to protect them.

And then, there was the second thing that occurred to him. Which was that if he wanted a stake in Robert King's company, then marrying his daughter, and being the father of his granddaughter, was likely the best way to accomplish that.

Dante had always known he would marry. It was a given. He had no plans to love his wife, as indeed he had no plans to love, much less the ability. But he had always thought that he might want a son. Someone to carry on what he had started.

He was a man from nothing. Nothing had been given to him. And he had much that he could pass on to an heir.

So yes, he had often thought that he would marry. Why not Minerva? Why not when it would benefit them so?

No, he would never be attracted to the skinny, dull little hen, but it didn't matter. They already had a child between them, as far as the world was concerned. And genetics meant nothing to Dante. The man who had fathered him had gone off God knows where and hadn't given a damn about him. While his mother…

She had cared the best she could. But she had been an old, tired whore—in a literal sense, not a euphemistic or insulting one—and in the end, the comfort of drugs was much more enticing than the grind of impoverished motherhood.

She had given up taking care of Dante when he was about eight years old. And she had given up living when he was ten.

He had been on his own ever since.

And while he was not sentimental, not really, on that score, he felt some measure of passion over the idea of protecting Isabella.

He did not need to become emotionally entangled in order to do this. It required legal paperwork and public trappings, and it was all the sort of thing he could engineer easily without needing to change diapers or rock her to sleep in private.

He also felt some grudging admiration for Minerva.

Minerva was protecting her child. She had come up with the solution that had seemed best to her in a moment of panic.

And he had the means to protect a child. He would not leave Isabella exposed. Not as he had been.

After all, he had been dependent upon the good graces of a man who had not been his father. Robert King was, in many ways, the closest thing he had to a father.

No, genetics were not required to make a family. Genetics, however, had been required for him to gain access to Robert King's company. And now…well. Now he'd have a link there, as well.

"Marriage?" She recoiled. "You have to be kidding me."

"I'm not."

Where did she get off looking horrified by the prospect of marrying him? He was the one who would be saddled to this plain little creature from now until eternity. *He* was the one who ought to be concerned.

"Yes, Min, marriage."

"You're *old*," she said.

He barked a laugh. "And you're a child. But you wanted my protection, and I am willing to give it. But you have to give me something in return."

"Marriage."

"Yes."

"What are your motives? Because I know it isn't to gain access to my bed."

"Indeed it is not. But what I would like is for your father to consider merging his company and mine, and barring a family connection, he is not interested." Her green eyes were jewel-bright and full of rage.

"So you're willing to help me, but only as it benefits you in a business sense?"

"Please, Minerva," he responded. "I don't need this. Make no mistake. Had I needed a family connection I would have pursued it on my own terms long ago. With Violet. Not you."

Her cheeks flooded with color. "Oh, really?"

"She is much more in keeping with my image."

"Your image!"

"Though, to be perfectly frank, little one, I could have seduced you at any point over the years if I'd wanted to. I did not need your little scheme. Had I wanted to marry you, I'd have done so."

She looked a second away from howling. "You could not seduce me, Dante Fiori," she spat. "I don't even like you. I never have."

"Oh, is that why you used to follow me around like a puppy?"

He did not know why he felt the urge to prod at her, only that he did. She was the one who had walked them into this situation, and now she was going to put up a fight because he had found a way to make it tenable for him. Well. He would not have it.

This little sprite did not own him, and she was not in charge here.

If it weren't for the fact that he was not quite the monster that the press made him out to be, he could destroy her farce easily. All it would take was a simple paternity test.

"You are using me to clean up for your bad choices, Minerva. All the better for you if you'd been seduced by me. Because at least I would have offered marriage, and I would have posed you no threat."

"You are a threat," she said darkly.

"A threat to what?"

"Common human decency."

The door to the study opened, and Robert King filled the space. "I think we need to have a talk," he said.

"Whatever you have to say to Dante you can say in front of me," Minerva said.

"I don't think that's true, Min," her father responded.

"It is," she said stubbornly.

"Fine," Robert responded. He slammed the door behind him. "How dare you use my hospitality so poorly. She's a child compared to you."

"You weren't angry when I came home with the baby!" she protested. "But now you're mad?"

"Why rail at you for your decisions?" Robert asked. "You were out in the world on your own, and you did not consult me on your choices. You came home and presented them, and what was the point in holding a postmortem on it? I'm not angry at you. I'm angry at him."

"That doesn't make sense," Minerva shouted.

But Dante knew that it did. Because Robert knew exactly where Dante was from. Not only that, he was thirteen years Minerva's senior. A man who had seen more and done more than Minerva ever would.

She had been cloistered, sheltered by her family connections, and Robert had extended the same to him.

Robert had always counted on Dante to take care of Minerva.

Oh, yes, the fact that he was treating it as a betrayal made perfect sense to Dante.

And it spoke volumes about Minerva's actual inexperience and age that she did not.

"Just tell me that you never took advantage of her when she was younger," Robert said, his voice like iron. *"Tell me."*

"I would not," Dante said, keeping his voice even. "I swear to you, I would never abuse what you gave to me."

"And yet," Robert said, "here is the evidence that you have."

"I seduced *him*," Minerva proclaimed.

Both of them turned to look at her. Dante wanted to

laugh. There she was, looking as she ever did, a university student in a sweater that was overlarge and a slouchy pair of jeans.

He couldn't imagine her seducing a trembling virgin. Let alone a man of his vast experience and particular appetites.

"It was the night of my going-away party. Before I went to study overseas." She gave her father a conspiratorial look and lowered her voice. "He was very drunk."

Madre de Dios...

Dante remembered that night well. He was not drunk, and had in fact been in the company of a lush heiress who was much more age-appropriate to him.

"I've *always* had a crush on him," she continued as the color rose in her face. "Yes. You see, I've always wanted him, and I thought that before I left I would get what I wanted. So I crept into his room and I... Well, I'm afraid I took advantage of him."

"Min," he bit out. "Stop helping."

"It's true! You were reduced. Your senses. I apologize for my predatory behavior. And I was ashamed. That's why I didn't... That's why when I found out I was pregnant I hid it."

"And why did you decide to announce it on TV today?" Robert asked.

"Well," Minerva said, clearly hunting around for an excuse.

And if Dante weren't so irritated he would be entertained watching her scrabble around for a reason why she'd chosen to reveal all today. And in public. She squinted. "I had been trying to talk to him. But he hasn't been returning my calls. I assumed because he was embarrassed."

"I was embarrassed?" Dante asked.

"Well, you were quite drunk," Minerva explained, like he was a child. "I don't know that you were up to your usual standards."

He could strangle her. Cheerfully. If she weren't holding a baby he might.

Her father, for his part, looked badly like he wanted to exit the conversation, and at least on that score he could give Minerva some points. She had successfully turned an uncomfortable situation into a horrific one, and Robert no longer looked angry so much as he looked utterly and completely appalled.

"You will, of course, do the right thing," Robert said, directing that at Dante.

"Of course," Dante returned.

"What's the right thing?" Minerva asked.

"Obviously he's going to marry you," Robert said.

"In fact, I informed her of this only a moment before you came in," Dante said. "She's being stubborn. She has no concept of the consequences of her actions."

"Well, then it will be up to you to ensure she does."

"Dad," Minerva said, her tone scolding, "stop playing the part of tyrant. It doesn't suit you."

"It does, however, suit me, *cara mia*," Dante said.

She shot him a fearsome look.

He would never have ascribed a word like *fearsome* to Minerva before. She had always seemed timid to him. But standing there, cradling her baby as she was, her posture defiant and defensive, he found that *fierce* and *fearsome* were words that described her extremely well.

As irritating as he found the situation he was in, he could only admire it.

That she was a woman willing to do whatever it took to protect her child.

Along with that came the discomforting thought of

her being touched by a man who was involved in organized crime.

What had happened? Had the man seduced Minerva? Had she seduced him? Was it a piece of truth buried in the outrageous story she had made up about taking advantage of Dante while he was drunk?

Minerva was twenty-one, but he couldn't imagine that she had a very long or intense history with men. For as long as he'd known her she'd been unattached, and she had never seemed overly interested in that kind of thing.

He was basing that off her total lack of efforts when it came to making herself up. Her sister was a makeup mogul. If Min wanted to improve herself she could have easily done it.

But then, the fact that she had come back with a child, the fact that she had claimed for all the world that he was the child's father, and the fact that he had never guessed she would do any of those things made him acutely aware of the fact that he didn't actually know her that well at all.

"Your mother will want to speak with you," her father said.

"I imagine Maximus will want to speak with me," Dante said.

Robert gave him a long look. "Yes. I imagine. Though as you are marrying her…" He appraised him slowly. "You do know, I suppose, that this will put King Industries in your hands."

"It had occurred to me." There was no point pretending it hadn't. Robert knew him too well.

"Had the timing been different, I would've suspected you of nefarious behavior, but you never inquired about the child, or made any effort to see if it was yours."

"It didn't occur to me the child could be mine," Dante said. "And no, I didn't plot this."

"No," Robert agreed. "A plot of yours would've been much neater."

Dante grinned ruefully. "Well, at least we both agree on that."

"I will leave you for the time being. But Dante, the wedding must be planned sooner rather than later. Now that it is revealed, you will move to make an honest woman of her. I do not want speculation to go on. Our official statement will be that fearing you wouldn't be receptive, Minerva kept it from you, and the moment you found out…"

"It's not a story," Dante said. "It's the truth."

Then Robert turned and walked out of the study, leaving the two of them alone again.

"You're a fool, Minerva. Did you not think that me marrying you was inevitable?"

"It never occurred to me that my father would force the issue. He was so… Lackadaisical about me being a single mother. About me returning with a stranger's baby."

"Yes, because he cannot force a man he's never met to act with honor and integrity. But he would expect it for me. Surely you must have known…"

"I didn't think about it," she snapped. "When Carlo texted me, I panicked. I did the only thing I could think to do. I jumped in front of the cameras. I don't regret it. Even now."

"Good. I'm glad to hear that you have committed to lying in the bed you've made."

"How long do you suppose we'll have to stay married? It seems to me that we should be able to have Carlo dealt with in a timely fashion, and even if we don't… Well, if we can keep up the facade for a long enough amount of time, then surely he'll fade into the background eventually."

He regarded her closely. "*Cara*, I'm Catholic. Divorce is out of the question."

CHAPTER THREE

MINERVA HAD BEEN stewing on his sudden devoutness to his latent Catholicism for two weeks.

He couldn't be serious. He absolutely *couldn't* be serious.

Their marriage would have to have a term limit. She couldn't stay married to him *forever*. She wouldn't *need* to. And the idea of being shackled to Dante for her entire life…

It made her feel like her skin was too small.

She was the last woman on earth whom he wanted to marry, and surely at some point in her life Minerva deserved to be something other than last.

She didn't regret taking Isabella on. She could have allowed the police to take her into custody when she'd come home with Isabella and found out the news about Katie.

She hadn't had to claim that Isabella was hers.

She could have come home with her and found her another home here in the United States, where she would maybe even be safer from Carlo.

But she… She felt like Isabella was her child.

She'd cared for her during Katie's depression.

Her stewing was productive ultimately. Because by the time the evening of their engagement party rolled around, she had realized the perfect solution.

He was *Catholic*.

Which meant that while divorce was complicated, there were ways around those complications. They would only need an annulment. Provided, of course, that the marriage wasn't consummated. And she was well aware that that would cause some slight issues with their ruse, but by the time they separated they wouldn't need it anyway. And neither she nor Dante was in any danger of temptation to consummate.

She was feeling borderline triumphant by the time she met with her sister to get her hair, makeup and wardrobe done for the event that she didn't even want.

But her family was under the impression that this was a real marriage, and not only was it a big deal because she was getting married, it was a big deal because Dante was getting married. The fact that they were getting married to each other was making it a whole King family spectacle.

"You need gold," Violet said authoritatively. "Gold eye shadow, gold bronzer, a gold dress."

"I'm going to look like an award," Minerva pointed out.

She was feeling out of sorts because she did not have Isabella with her. Her mother had Isabella for the time being, and then for the party itself she would be up in her room with a nanny attending.

"Well, that is exactly how you should look," Violet said. "Like a prize that Dante has won, right?"

She looked at her sister's sullen face. "Except, you think that *I've* won the award," Minerva said. "The award being Dante."

Violet's eyes locked with Minerva's. "I don't really. It's fine. I had a slight crush on him for a while, but I'm over it."

"I'm sorry," Minerva said. "I really didn't know."

"Mom said that you had a crush on him for years."

"*Honestly*, the rumor mill in this family."

"She said you had a crush on him for all your life."
Minerva felt doubly guilty, because not only was she
marrying the man that her sister had feelings for, her
own feelings were a fabrication.

"Yes," Minerva said, her throat going dry. "It's why I
always followed him around."

He was the one who had brought that up.

That was not why she'd followed him around. She
had felt compelled to interact with him. To be near him.
Like a person might stare at a big cat through the bars
of a zoo cage.

He was wild and compelling, and it had never failed
to call to something inside her. Though, she didn't know
what to call that thing.

Maybe it was because nothing in Minerva was wild
or compelling at all.

She was bookish, and she was a tomboy, and she was
ever injuring herself while running around outside imagining she was various literary characters that she found
between the pages of her books.

She'd been called a dreamer more than once. Someone
who didn't connect well with the harshness of reality.

And so there was something about the darkness sim-
mering beneath the surface of Dante's skin that she had
always found wickedly interesting.

Like he was a dragon in folklore.

And that was down to her rather dreamy nature, as
well.

It had nothing to do with him. And it certainly had
nothing to do with feelings of any kind.

If she had any sort of feelings for him, it was that

sharp, tangled-up gratitude over his helping mitigate the shame of her being rejected in front of an audience and then, of course, the way he was helping her now.

"It doesn't matter," Violet said. "I haven't really fancied him for ages. But he is handsome. You have to admit."

Minerva felt her face getting hot, and she wasn't sure why.

Violet shook her head and rolled her eyes. "Of course you already know. You've seen him naked."

The temperature in her face increased. She had not seen Dante naked. And she would not.

But surely her sister knew all about these things. Violet was so lovely and smooth. She did so well at parties, mingling with important, high-powered people everywhere she went. Her ability to harness her image and control a brand was renowned.

She imagined her sister was much more sophisticated when it came to men than Minerva was.

Then, the average sixteen-year-old was slightly more sophisticated when it came to men.

Of course, no one could *ever* know that.

"Let's get you fixed up," Violet said.

And true to her word, Violet did fix Minerva up. Quite well, in point of fact.

And she had been right about the gold. It took her mousy brown hair and made it something else. It surprised Minerva that she had left her hair mostly unstyled. Letting it fall in waves down her back, though it seemed much glossier after her sister had sprayed something on it, and the gold leaf headband that she had woven into her hair made it all look very intentional, rather than that Minerva's hair sat somewhere between curled and straight, and she didn't know what to do with it.

The dress she was wearing made the most of her slight curves, and the plunging neckline looked elegant, and not trashy. A gift, Minerva supposed, of having a very small chest. If her more voluptuous sister had worn the dress, she would've looked stunning, but the effect would have been different.

"I love it," Minerva said, but her stomach felt hollowed out, and her body felt unsteady. She lifted her hand to touch her hair and her sister caught it, examining her bare fingers.

"I do hope that Dante is planning on giving you a ring," Violet said.

"Oh," Minerva responded. "I hadn't even thought of it."

"You do want to marry him, don't you?"

"I need to," Minerva said. "Desperately."

"Good," Violet said.

Well, it hadn't been a lie, she did need to marry him. It just wasn't because of her emotions or anything like that.

Her sister had been kind to her, and rather than putting her in heels had chosen a pair of sparkling, pointed-toe flats that were actually quite pretty. They were also very comfortable. And made Minerva feel like less of a gangly, awkward deer than she might have if she had been up on stilts.

She left her sister's bedroom, nearly ready to go down to the party, when she ran into her mom coming up the stairs.

"I was just coming to fetch you," she said.

Elizabeth King was a stunningly beautiful woman, more along the lines of Violet and Maximus than Minerva.

They all looked a lot alike and there was no question of the fact that they were siblings, but there was something about the way her parents' features had rearranged themselves on both Violet and Maximus to be an even more pleasing configuration. And somehow, on Minerva it had always seemed wrong.

Her nose was similar to her mother's, but it was longer, more like her father's.

Her mother had a full upper lip, slightly more so than her lower, which gave her the brilliant look of a rather exquisite doll.

Minerva's was yet more imbalanced, her cheeks somehow looking round, rather than sculpted, in spite of the fact that Minerva didn't have an ounce of extra fat on her body, nor curves to speak of.

What was commanding height on Maximus was gangly on her.

Her mother's hair could be called a brilliant toffee, while Minerva's was more mouse-ish.

"I'm here," Minerva said.

"You look lovely," her mom said. "Are you ready?"

"Yes," Minerva said, suddenly feeling horrendously insecure. "Don't I look ready?"

"Of course you do," Elizabeth responded. "That isn't what I meant. I meant… You want this, don't you, Minerva? Because I will tell your father to call the whole thing off if you don't. I know that he got angry and he insisted that Dante do the right thing, but if you don't love Dante then this isn't the right thing."

Bless her mother, who only wanted her happiness, but of course this wasn't for Minerva. It wasn't about Minerva.

It was all right, she was used to that. Nothing in her life had ever truly been about her.

Every member of her family was a brilliant gem that shone brightly in their own right. Her mother was a former model and beauty queen. Violet modeled herself, and additionally was a business tycoon. Maximus had taken his share of their father's fortune and multiplied it exponentially. His face was famous, his business acumen renowned.

And her father...

California King had been the headline of business pages for years, along with the requisite mattress jokes. But Robert King was not a joke. He was one of the most highly successful manufacturers the world over. Managing to be both savvy and profitable, while maintaining a strict standard of treatment for workers.

Only Minerva was *nothing*.

And she had been content to be, in many ways. *Privileged* to be.

Because there had been no pressure for her to go out and make something of herself in order to survive.

Her survival had always been a given. Because no King would be tossed out onto the streets if they failed to make a living for themselves.

Her survival had always been a given until Isabella. Until Carlo.

The one good thing about all of this was that at the very least she had discovered that when things were difficult she did possess the mettle to get through it.

"You don't have anything to worry about," she said to her mom. "I know what I'm doing."

Really, for the first time in her life she felt like she knew what she was doing. At least with a grander and broader purpose than simply trying to stay unnoticed.

And everything would be fine in the end. Because this would buy her time, it would keep her safe, and then she and Dante could be free of each other.

Her mother escorted her down the stairs, to the exquisitely decorated backyard.

Their home and the large courtyard overlooked the beach and the ocean. The family had private access, and the whole stretch of sand belonged to them.

There was a bonfire already going there, and the sun had set, casting an orange glow that faded to purple in the sky, silhouetting the palm trees that lined the shore.

So many people had come, and she didn't know any of them.

She had friends from school, but most of them were out of the country still.

And, of course, poor Katie was gone.

Oddly, the fact that the place was littered with strangers, and faces that she only knew because she had seen them plastered on television screens and newspapers, hit home the point that she was doing the right thing.

That what she did she did for Isabella, and it was important.

Certainly of more significance than the rest of her life.

But it was the sight of Dante that unraveled something inside of her.

He was wearing a white shirt, the sleeves rolled up, and a pair of dark slacks that somehow made her very aware of the fact that his thighs were powerful.

Which she thought had to be the oddest observation in the history of observations.

"Glad you could join us, *cara mia*," he said.

"Of course you knew that Violet wouldn't allow me to show up until at least an hour after the party had started," she stated.

"Of course," he responded. "That seems an incredibly Violet perspective on things."

"One has to make an entrance. One cannot do that if they arrive early."

"Well, I had no idea I've been doing entrances wrong this entire time."

She studied him, his sculpted jaw, his imposing height and his broad shoulders. "Honestly, Dante, I imagine whatever time you arrive you create a spectacle."

"Thank you," he said, inclining his dark head.

"That was *not* a compliment," she said.

"I took it as one. Anyway, you must look happier to see me, Minerva," he said. "As you *are* madly in love with me. So madly in love with me that you decided to seduce me in an inebriated state, taking terrible advantage of me and my agency."

She rolled her eyes at his ridiculousness. "I had to say *something*. Otherwise my father was going to skin you alive."

"I believe the offer of marriage was sufficient. Though I appreciate your efforts to protect me." He said the last part so drily she could tell that he didn't mean it at all.

"Well, you're of no use to me if you're dead. You can't protect me then."

"I don't know. If Carlo believed that your dad killed me because I had fathered your child…"

"Well, I don't want you dead," she said. "Not at the moment. Though—" she held a finger up "—I have arrived on a solution to your issue of divorce."

He narrowed dark eyes. "Have you?"

"Yes," she said brightly. "Obviously we'll get an annulment."

His dark eyes flicked up and down. "An annulment?"

"Yes! Because we won't consummate."

The look he treated her to could only be described

as pitying. "Minerva, on what planet would anyone believe that?"

"You said yourself that you are not…attracted to women like me. I'm not offended by that. I'm not attracted to men like you." She patted his forearm, then removed her hand quickly when she found him disturbingly hot and firm. She cleared her throat. "Your tastes are public. So, no one will be surprised."

"Except the public, and your family for that matter, think that we had a child together."

"A fluke. And we will claim that there was no spark left once we married. And at that point Carlo won't be an issue. So it will be a mere blip in the headlines."

"Minerva, it would be a blip in the headlines if it were only you. But sadly, I am included in this, and I am more than a blip in any headline."

Minerva sighed heavily. His ego was such a massive yoke over his shoulders it was a miracle they were so straight and broad. They should be sagging beneath the weight.

Sadly, nothing on the man sagged.

"It *will* work," she insisted.

"So you think that your father will blithely allow me to leave you?"

"If we explain."

"Explain?"

"Once…" She looked around. "Once Carlo is no longer an issue we can explain everything to my family. And at that point he'll be so grateful he will likely allow you to continue on with your efforts in the company."

He looked at her as though she were a child, his expression nearly pitying. "It is not something we need to concern ourselves with."

"We simply need to concern ourselves with *not* consummating."

He looked at her for a long moment. "I will try to control myself."

The arid reply left her feeling scraped raw, and she trailed after him at the party rather angrily thereafter.

But of course she couldn't *look* angry.

She had to look pleasant.

It was very strange, acting the part of accessory to someone. She had never done it. And here she was, keeping position next to him, moving as he did, trying to mirror his body language, and facial expressions, so that they seemed as if they were in one accord, whether they were not.

By the time they had made their rounds, Minerva was famished, which was only adding to her mood.

Then Dante swept her aside, taking both of them out of the glow of the string of lights that went overhead.

"It's time to put on a show, *cara*."

"Show?"

"Yes," he said. "I have a ring for you."

"Oh," she replied.

"Look surprised," he instructed as he grabbed her hand and dragged her back beneath the lights.

"Of course I'll look surprised," she whispered. "I *am* surprised."

"Try to look *happy* too," he said.

She had no time to respond to that before he had turned toward their guests and, somehow, by his very motion commanded the attention of the crowd.

Minerva stretched her lips into a wide smile that she had a feeling fell flat around the corners.

"As this has come together very quickly, there is one aspect of our courtship that I have neglected. We have done a great many things out of order, Minerva and I."

This elicited light laughter from the crowd.

Of course, in the rather sophisticated culture of the rich and famous in Southern California, having a baby before marriage—or without marriage at all—was not considered out of order.

But no doubt the chuckles were in deference to the presumably more conservative culture Dante came from.

"And in all the activity I have neglected to give Minerva her ring. I will do so now."

He pulled a ring box out of his pocket, and he did not drop down to one knee. "I've made the request already, I think," he said, opening the box and presenting it to her. It was huge. A statement piece if ever there was one, and she herself was so very not a statement piece that it seemed shocking, and nearly vulgar.

But he didn't ask her, and instead was sliding the monumental rock onto her finger.

As if...

As if something so magnificent, something so glorious, should be there. On her thin, fine-boned hand that was not manicured or elegant or anything of the sort.

She recalled her school friends had once likened her hands to *claws*.

And there was Dante Fiori's ring.

On one of her *claws*.

Min swallowed hard, and when she looked up at him, he was gazing at her with sharp intent. It pierced her, made her feel like she couldn't breathe. And before she could do anything, say anything or decide how she might react, he was moving in toward her.

All that sharp intensity was focused on her, and somehow she could feel it gathering in her stomach, nearly painful.

He was so close they were breathing the same air.

And then, his mouth was on hers.

His mouth.

This, *she knew*, was not kissing.

It couldn't be.

She had been kissed before by that stranger in the club, and that hadn't been kissing either. Because it had been unpleasant and cold, and it made her want to run, rather than embrace the man giving it.

But this…

It was not romantic.

It was not gauzy and sweet, wrapped in warm summer breezes and crashing waves. Blooming flowers and other grand literary euphemisms.

It made something in her stomach twist hard. Made her feel like some creature was biting down on her windpipe. The feel of his lips against hers was so *real*. So very physical. They were warm, and firm, and as he took command of all things, he took command of her mouth.

Shifting her slightly so that she was fitted more firmly against him.

All in all, the kiss was not terribly long, and it was not terribly intimate, but when it was done she felt like she had been hollowed out, her hands shaking, her whole body shaking.

And he looked… As unreadable as ever. Utterly infuriating, that man. He was like a block of obsidian that could not and would not be disturbed, not by anything. Least of all by her.

He had just handed her a ring, and then he had pressed his mouth to hers and tilted her entire world on its axis.

And there he was. Like a guardian of the underworld, completely unbothered by the whole thing.

The audacity of the man.

He had just kissed her. And he hadn't had permission. She would badger him about it, but she had the distinct impression that he wouldn't care.

"Shall we go mingle, *cara mia*?"

He whispered that question in her ear, and he made it look as though there was an intimacy between them that there just wasn't.

That is the entire point of all of this. Keep it together.

But she was having difficulty keeping it together. Because he was very large and hard beside her, and because she had always liked the idea of creating an effect in him. When she had followed him about and pestered him when she was a girl, part of it was that she had enjoyed seeing if she could get a reaction.

But right now it was clear that he would always have the upper hand. She would never, ever be the one to get a superior reaction out of him. He would always be the one to create havoc in her.

Because that was what it was, wasn't it? Her chasing after him. He was affecting her. She had always imagined herself leading the charge in those interactions. But it wasn't true.

It was him. It always had been.

Even in this, even in her scheme, he had somehow managed to take charge.

It was demoralizing. Dispiriting.

In front of all these people, downright humiliating.

She felt red and sore and exposed somehow, and she couldn't pinpoint why.

"Smile," he whispered, bending down, his lips nearly touching her ear, a shiver winding down her spine.

And so she did.

She had to remember that this was for Isabella. It wasn't for her.

And her own discomfort had nothing to do with it.

For Isabella, she could do this. For Isabella she could do anything.

It wouldn't be forever.

She stared at his patrician profile. No. Whatever he said it would not be forever.

Dante Fiori might be used to running a business. He might be used to commanding women, manipulating them with his good looks and power. And maybe in the past he had had an effect on her behavior, as well.

But she knew now. Was unbearably conscious of it.

Minerva King might be the least famous of her family. The least successful. And the least powerful.

But she was also stronger than anyone knew.

And in the end, that strength was going to carry her through.

CHAPTER FOUR

IT WAS HIS wedding day. His secretary had informed him firmly on Friday that this was to be the happiest day of his life.

He'd done his best not to laugh at her. Because she was sincere and just because he didn't possess the ability to see the world in such a pure fashion didn't mean he had to destroy the illusions of others.

Dante had never been under the impression that this would be a joyous day for him. Rather, he had always known that it would be a calculated move that benefited him in some way.

But this… This was not what he'd envisioned.

They had put the wedding together very quickly, and Min had been lying low in the meantime, rarely leaving her parents' house, at his express command.

Though she had told him with great umbrage that she didn't need him to command a single thing because she was completely happy to hide until they had made things legal between them.

Security. That was all. Just added layers of security.

Dante was not a man who believed in taking unnecessary chances.

He was standing in the back room of a cathedral sanctuary with his future father-in-law and his future brother-in-law standing on either side of him.

He had not imagined that Robert and Maximus would be in that position. Had it been another scenario, he would have imagined they were offering support. As it was, he had a feeling they were making sure he didn't run away.

It was all a bit close and familial for his taste.

He would always appreciate what Robert King had done for him, and if he had a friend, Maximus King was the best one he possessed.

But the way that they were with each other, the ease that the family had with one another, had always made his skin itch.

He was not familiar with these sorts of dynamics. Not privy to the way families typically acted with one another. He didn't understand. He hadn't grown up with it.

If he had siblings, then he didn't know any of them. His father had never been part of his life, and his mother had died early, and even before then she hadn't exactly been the model of maternal care.

He wasn't angry about those things. It was simply life.

Life, in his estimation, was not fair, from conception.

You could be born into a family like the Kings, or you could be born into the streets of Rome as he had been.

You could have a father like Robert King, or a father like Isabella's who was threatening the life of her mother and trying to drag her into a criminal underworld that was no place for anyone, let alone a child.

These things were accidents of fate and there was no point railing against them.

There was only making decisions about what you would do with the things you were given.

Dante believed that firmly.

He had made the most of what he'd been given. He had been given a hand up, and he had taken hold of it.

But that didn't mean that he felt completely comfortable with his situation, or his position.

In some ways, he would have imagined that Maximus would be with him on his wedding day in this capacity. He just hadn't imagined he would also be related to the bride. And that was where the connections became uncomfortable.

"If you hurt my sister," Maximus said, smiling and clapping his large hand on Dante's shoulder, "I'll kill you myself."

There weren't many men who stood at eye level with Dante, but Maximus was one of them. With ice-blue eyes and blond hair, he was a Viking counterpart to Dante's fallen angel.

He would never have thought of something so fanciful, but when they had gone out together in the past, women had made such comments.

Which gave Maximus's threat a lot more weight. After all, Maximus had seen up close Dante's appetite for beautiful women, and he imagined that his friend's believing that such an appetite had spilled over onto his younger sister was something that was never going to sit easy with him.

In fact, Dante imagined the only reason that he wasn't dead was that he had fathered a child—supposedly— with Minerva.

Had they simply been caught in a compromising position, he imagined that Maximus would have simply dispatched him on the spot.

"I believe it," Dante said, because he knew that was better than any empty promises that Maximus would have discarded.

And he *did* believe it.

They were friends, it was true, but they were not blood. The King family was connected by blood.

Dante had no such connections. And it was fine by him.

"You have always been like a son to me," Robert said.

And Dante knew that the old man *thought* he meant it. But Maximus had never had to worry about whether or not he could have access to sharing his father's company.

Dante wasn't bitter about that. It was just a difference. One that he was ever aware of, even if Robert was not.

"I suppose we had better get things started," Dante said.

"Nothing will start on time," Robert responded, looking at his watch. "I believe Violet is in charge of hair and makeup?"

"Yes," Dante said. "I imagine she's also in charge of entrances."

"What?" Robert asked.

"Never mind."

They filed in from the back, and all of them took their places. Robert made his way back to where the bride was.

It hit Dante then that whatever differences between himself and Maximus, Robert was seeing to the double duty of being father of the groom and bride.

Had Dante been capable of feeling warmth over such a gesture, he would have, he was sure.

The crowd that filled the sanctuary, Dante knew, was not enthralled by any love story between himself and Minerva. No, they were hoping to gain the attention of either himself, Maximus, Robert or Violet.

It hit him that no one would be here for Minerva.

It was a strange thing to be bothered by. He had rarely

given consideration to Minerva beyond cursory. But Minerva didn't possess anything that anyone might want.

He was under no illusions that anyone was here because they cared about Robert or Maximus or Violet.

They cared about what any of the aforementioned people might be able to do for them.

He wondered if that was how Minerva had been vulnerable to a man like Isabella's father. If she had been left vulnerable because of her position in the family.

As he had been thinking earlier, life was very much what you fashioned from what you were given. Minerva could have created anything.

As it was, she had created a baby with a dangerous man. And that had been her decision.

But not Isabella's.

And if he was being magnanimous in any way, then it was on her behalf, because he knew what it was to be a child hamstrung by his parents' poor decisions.

And yes, there was the matter of getting to have possession of King. That did matter to him.

What he had not expected was for Minerva to look quite so lovely last night. And for the kiss to send a jolt of electricity through his body.

The very strange thing was that Minerva's reaction was...unreadable.

She had been angry with him at some point during the evening.

She had not gone pliant, she had not melted against him, she had not responded at all.

Quite the opposite, she had been stiff. She had been still against his mouth, behaving like a woman who didn't know what to do.

He had done his best to seize control of it, to change the tenor of things, but she had not allowed it.

And he could not for the life of him figure out if it had been inexperience or disgust that caused her to react in such a way.

Mostly because he had never kissed a woman who found him *disgusting*.

But then, he had never kissed a woman for show.

What made him most irritated was the fact that he was not disgusted by her.

Minerva wasn't *beautiful*.

There was a prettiness to her. It was simply that she was also a bit plain, and he preferred something a bit gaudier. He had been raised, after all, with a prostitute for a mother. For the years when she'd been well, she'd been all hair, perfume and jewels, and it had been the same with her friends who had passed through their run-down apartment. His concept of beauty was a bit more bedecked.

She was also young. The younger sister of his friends, and because of that she'd been firmly off-limits from moment one.

The fact that she had the power to effect a response was irritating in the extreme.

The bridal party began to come down the aisle, though it was a simple bridal party. Violet walking arm in arm with Maximus, who came to stand next to Dante. He flashed his friend a smile.

"I will kill you," he whispered, never breaking that smile. "I did mean it."

Dante said nothing. But a grin tugged at the corner of his mouth as he turned to face the doorway of the cathedral.

And suddenly there she was.

Her hair had been twisted and gathered up into a complicated style that was loose and sparkling, thanks to jewelry of some kind that had been woven in.

The dress itself was simple, soft, flowing fabric that seemed only barely there. It rested over her curves like a fine mist. With each step she took, the long billowing lilac fabric swirled around her.

Something had been applied to her cheeks that made them glow in the candlelight, her lips, pale and shimmering.

She had been made up, but it was still very much her. Even more so than it had been the night of their engagement party. And somehow it was as if it had uncovered the essential beauty that Minerva possessed. A beauty he had never seen before.

She was ethereal. Like a creature of the earth transformed into one of the sky.

A treasure that had been hiding only to be brought out and polished now.

When she looked up at him, her green eyes shone bright, and he could see that it was her. And suddenly, the Minerva that he knew every day blended with this one, and he knew that he would never be able to unsee the beauty, even if she were to revert back to the way she'd been before.

When they joined hands, a sly smile crossed her face. Anyone watching would be forgiven for mistaking it for intimacy.

"I'm glad you decided to follow through," she whispered.

"I would not abandon you," he said, offended by the assessment he might.

"No," she said, frowning. "Of course you wouldn't."

The priest began his solemn intonations and there was something about the way Minerva held herself, about the strange expression on her face that caused a response in the vicinity of Dante's heart.

He had to wonder if for Minerva, this was somewhat conflicting.

He should not feel sorry for her at all, given the fact that she was the one who had gotten them into this position in the first place.

She was the one who caused this, and if she didn't like the end result, that was her problem.

But he couldn't overlook the fact that she was softer than he was. That for her, marriage was never intended to be a cynical meeting of people who wanted to firm up business deals.

No, for Minerva it was never supposed to be that at all.

That she had gotten herself into this mess, and the fact that he had twisted it to suit him as well, wasn't something he was going to waste time feeling guilty about. He didn't waste time feeling guilty in general. It was a fruitless exercise. Just like wishing that a pauper had been born a prince.

Or that a street urchin from Rome had been born a King.

It did nothing to solve one's problems.

For him the vows were easy. But she hesitated over each promise she made, possibly because she was afraid of what would happen when she didn't keep them.

It hadn't been nice of him to make fun of her about not being able to divorce.

He had done a great many things the church wouldn't approve of. He was hardly going to start worrying over much about his eternal soul now.

At the end he could go to confession, take his penance and spend the last bit of his life atoning.

He was far too busy to atone now.

But, the question of the permanence of the marriage was a tricky one considering that it would impact his portion of ownership with King Corporation. He had a feeling that Robert King would take an even dimmer view of Dante divorcing his daughter than he did to Dante marrying her in the first place.

That was a considerable issue.

Though, she did have a point. If when it was all said and done, they were able to explain everything, then Dante would possibly be considered a hero when she told the tale. Something he wouldn't have asked for, but a possibility.

It wasn't as if he wanted to stay married to Minerva forever.

When it was finished, it was time for them to kiss again, and she shrunk away from him.

One thing was certain: he could not stay married to a woman who shrunk away from his touch.

He wrapped his arms around her and she gasped slightly.

He didn't give her time to react. Because if he did, he feared that she was going to cause difficulty.

He crashed his lips down onto hers. Swallowing her gasp and parting her lips with his tongue.

He didn't know why, but he felt compelled to affect her. Perhaps because she had affected him, and it didn't seem right that she'd had nothing but a negative response to him. An unreadable response.

A nonresponse.

He had a kick in his gut the moment he related that desire to instigate a response from her with the way that she had followed him around when she was a young girl.

The way that she had always been trying to gain a response from him.

It was petty. And it was childish.

But he allowed his tongue to delve between her lips anyway.

And she tasted… Like sunshine. Spring. Something that was indefinably Minerva.

Still, she was frozen beneath him. Her hands clutched at his shoulders, but they were motionless. Not impassioned in any way.

And when they parted, it was like yet another veil had been ripped from his eyes.

He could no longer see a girl.

But a woman.

That hint of fearsomeness that he had seen when she had defended Isabella shone through those green eyes now.

Not a hen. Not a mouse.

A tigress defending her cub.

He had misjudged her.

And for a man like Dante Fiori, this was a terrible sin. He was never a man to misjudge or underestimate an enemy, an adversary or a potential partner.

But he had misjudged Minerva.

He had looked at her, and he had seen all that she had shown the world, which was only a facet of what she was.

He wondered what Isabella's father had seen of her.

He couldn't help it. Was she a tigress for him?

He despised the other man.

They were presented to the guests, but he was not conscious of what was being said, or what was happening.

There was a ringing in his ears.

They charged down the aisle and into the waiting room where he assumed that Minerva had been before.

She went over to her purse, and diaper bag, and began to root around inside, pulling out her phone.

"Eager to check your social media?" he asked drily.

"No," she said. "I'm worried. Because our wedding is today, and I'm concerned that…" She went pale. "He texted me."

She handed the phone to Dante.

I feel that I should come to the reception so that I can have a look at the child and see if she is indeed mine.

"Well, he's not getting near you, or Isabella," Dante said. "And at this point, I think we should inform the police that you have been receiving unwanted attention from a stalker. Nothing more."

"Do you think?"

"He's organized crime, and he's not from here. But if he does set foot in the country, he will face legal recourse from the law here. That's important. We must make sure that we put barriers in his way. And in the meantime, you and I are going on our honeymoon early."

"We are?"

"Yes. We are. Somewhere where he won't find us."

"Where is that? Because he found me, and he found her."

"No offense, *cara*, but your family is quite conspicuous, and you are known to live here. Plus, he clearly has your mobile number."

"I didn't give it to him," she said. "I got a new phone the moment I set foot onto American soil again. I changed my number."

Dante swore. "Well, it's no matter. I own an island, but it is not in my name, and it's hidden by a shell company. No one knows about it, and he won't know where to look. There will be no way for him to discover our whereabouts, and I will be using private investigators to make sure I find ways to remove him as a danger to your safety."

Her eyes went round. "In what way will you remove him?"

Dante waved a hand. "That is not your concern."

"Dante... I don't want you to do anything illegal."

He chuckled, low and dark. "That ship has sailed, I'm afraid. Or do you not know how I met your father?"

Her shoulders narrowed. "I thought that was just... A story."

"It is a story that has been greatly watered down."

He saw himself then, a boy of fourteen, holding a handgun extended toward an older man, pressing it to his forehead.

His hands were shaking. He was sweating.

One of his mother's boyfriends had told him that if you were going to do this kind of thing, you couldn't flinch. You couldn't shake. And you certainly couldn't sweat.

Above all else you had to be willing to pull the trigger.

And as Dante looked into the calm, kind face of the man that he was about to rob, he knew that he could not pull the trigger.

"Lower the gun, son," the man said in soft, clumsy Italian.

It was the kindness that immobilized Dante, for he had never known anyone to look at him with anything other than resentment, disgust or pity.

Until Robert King.

"You really held my father up at gunpoint?"

"I did," he said. "Believe me, I have no concern for what might happen to a mafioso. Men like him... Well, they bring ruin everywhere they go. They most particularly have brought ruin to my country, my streets. To women like my mother. They are part of a system that operates on fear and oppression. He is doing it to you in this personal capacity, but I guarantee you he has done it to many in a broader sense. I will not have it. I will not." He reached out and touched her face, and he suddenly meant those words more than he had ever meant anything in his life. "Nothing bad will happen to you or to Isabella. I swear it."

He took her hand, and led her out of the vestibule, and they nearly ran into Elizabeth, who was cradling Isabella, and Robert.

"There has been a change of plans," Dante said. "It seems that Isabella has picked up a stalker from her time overseas. She is being threatened."

"By who?" Robert asked.

"A man called Carlo Falcone. He's from a crime family in Rome. Whatever he says, don't listen to him. He's insane, and he will use anything he can to try to manipulate you and the situation. We must notify the police that he intends to show up at the reception."

Robert's lip curled up into a sneer. "I'm more than able to handle him by myself."

"Can you handle the retribution that will come if you dispatch him? It isn't the law I worry about, but the rest of the family."

That seemed to calm some of Robert's readiness for a shootout. "I don't want anyone in my family targeted by this man."

"No. So we're going to call for police presence at the reception, but I also want you to make sure that it gets out that Minerva and I have left. That we are not there. Have Violet post it to one of her social media accounts. I believe that he's tracking our movements this way. And also, if she would be so kind as to indicate we've gone on a honeymoon in Italy, that would be brilliant."

"But you won't be," Robert said.

"No. He will not be able to find us where we are going. I will be able to keep her and Isabella safe. You can trust me."

"I do," Robert said. "And that is not a statement I made lightly, Dante, and it is not a statement I would make to most men."

"You saved my life," Dante said. "With all that I am I will protect hers."

Robert nodded, and he took Minerva's hand, then he used one arm to scoop Isabella from Elizabeth's arms. He had never held the child before. He was surprised by the way that she felt. Warm, and like a feather.

A small little thing he could have cradled in the crook of his forearm.

"I will keep them both safe."

CHAPTER FIVE

MINERVA'S HEAD WAS spinning and she couldn't breathe. Didn't breathe in fact until Dante's private jet had lifted into the air. Only then did she believe that they might be safe.

Isabella was laid in a plush bassinet, and Minerva had no idea how Dante had managed to acquire it so quickly.

And in the time she spent wondering about that she found time to worry about photographs from the wedding. It was stupid.

But the headlines after their engagement party had been…

They hadn't been outright cruel, but they had included a photograph of her from four years ago.

Seventeen, with her face streaked by tears, and him so much taller and broader and outlandishly beautiful than she could ever hope to be.

She imagined that the implication of the photo was he'd been involved with her even when she'd been scandalously young, but looking at it she knew no one would ever take that seriously.

He was Dante Fiori. She was… Minerva the Mouse.

The girl who was worth a date only so her class could get a look at her house. And she'd heard later he'd wanted to get a look up her sister's dress, as well.

Violet had laughed herself hoarse after hearing that and then had gotten a deadly look in her eye. And Minerva had known if she'd ever seen Bradley after that Violet would unman him with the sharp end of her tweezers.

But that was the thing.

Violet was the hero in that story. The object of beauty and the one so above the idiocy she could laugh and make threats.

Dante was the hero in the story.

Willing to dance with her in spite of the fact she was gangly and unattractive and sad.

She was the object of pity.

And she feared when her wedding photos were splashed across the media it would be the same story.

Sad, pitiable Minerva snags a man due to a faulty condom.

Just thinking about *Dante* and *condoms* made her get hot to the roots of her hair.

"There will be supplies for her already on the island, as well," he said casually as he poured himself a drink and settled back into the plush leather sofa.

Minerva curled more deeply into the chair she was seated on, leaning over Isabella and adjusting her blanket unnecessarily. "How?"

"There are people that work for the shell company. They will be gone by the time we get there. None of them will ever know who gave the instructions. Who actually owns the house. They won't see us."

"Why do you have something like this?"

"I bought it quite a while ago as a precaution. Because one never knows when one might need to escape."

"Dante, you're not involved in anything illegal *now*, are you?"

"No," he said. "But when a man comes from a background such as mine he learns to be paranoid."

"I suppose. And I never did learn to be paranoid enough. Not until now."

Everything in her felt jumbled up.

She would love to think more about the kiss that he had given her at the altar. One that had turned so…intimate. But she hadn't had time to think about it or parse the way that it had made her feel, not in the face of the threatening text that she had received from Carlo so soon after.

"It is only a small island," he said. "The only building on it is my home, and the rest is unspoiled white sand and jungle. I think you'll like it."

"At this point, I like anywhere I'll feel safe."

For the moment, they felt united.

For the moment.

Dante busied himself with work during the journey, and Minerva slept when Isabella did, and woke when she was fitful. She marked the hours in feedings and diaper changings.

Until finally, the plane began to descend.

There was a small runway on the island, clearly.

"Your pilot knows where we are," she said.

Dante acknowledged this with a nod of his head. "I do trust him."

"*How much* do you trust him?" she pressed.

He lifted a dark brow. "Enough to allow him to fly me fifty thousand feet over the ocean?"

"Yes, but in that case his fate is tied to yours."

"Oh, believe me, Minerva, his fate will always be tied to mine. Because should anyone betray us—and in this case, the only option would be him as he is the only person on earth who knows we are here—his fate would be in a precarious position indeed."

"You're filled with death threats of late."

"Well, as is your life. Therefore, I find the situation merits more of them than I would typically be meting out."

Minerva pondered this as they got their things together and disembarked. She suddenly found him to be something of a stranger.

She had always known that he was hard, but she had also felt safe goading him. Now he had kissed her, and that made him feel unpredictable. And wholly different from what she had imagined he was.

Then there was his willingness to threaten someone's personal safety.

He did so with ease and without compunction. And it made her wonder what kind of man he was on a day-to-day basis.

She knew whom he was when he was interacting with her family, but she was beginning to think that wasn't the measure of him.

And given that he had actually robbed her father at gunpoint, she did wonder if Robert and Maximus had a better idea of who he was than she did.

Or Violet. Or Elizabeth.

She wondered if the women in the family were entirely ignorant of that side of him.

"You're thinking so hard I can see smoke coming out of your ears, Min," he said.

She tapped her chin. "I'm just thinking about your ruthlessness."

He lifted a shoulder. "People often do."

"Well, I didn't know that. You always seemed like

somewhat of a stern older brother to me." She wrinkled her nose. "Stern. Not dangerous."

"Ah," he said. "An easy mistake to make, I suppose. Though, I don't think anyone else in the world has ever made it."

"Well, they don't know you like I do." She frowned. "Like I *did*."

They got off the plane and there was a car parked just there, waiting for them. It was fitted with a base for Isabella's car seat, and as soon as she was safely secured they were on their way.

The landscape was beautiful, and desolate as he had said. Dense forestation on one side, and brilliant white sand on the other. And there, built into the craggy hillside overlooking the sea, was an intensely modern, modular home, white squares to match the sand with glass all around.

"Home," he said. "For a while yet."

"It's very wild," she said.

He chuckled. "Wild?"

"Do you know what it reminds me of? *Swiss Family Robinson.* More the film from the 1960s than the book, I suppose. But it's a very modern house sort of up in the trees in the jungle."

He nodded slowly. "I thought of that, as well."

She turned to look at him, feeling surprised. "Did you?"

"Yes. I quite liked that movie when I was young."

"Did you?"

"For a while I went to a free community day care center, and they had a few old films on VHS. *Swiss Family Robinson* was one of them. I always thought that would be a good life. Off on a remote island where no one could reach you. Where you didn't have to answer to anyone.

And you could build whatever you wanted for yourself. Make whatever you desired. Resources from the land. Provided you weren't attacked by pirates, of course."

"I thought the same thing," she said. "But then, I also thought that I wanted to live on a farm on Prince Edward Island. And that I might want to live in Atlanta in a grand mansion." She sighed. "I've been so many places because of books. My college travels were supposed to be… They were supposed to be my big adventure where I could be the heroine instead of simply reading about heroines."

"And you brought back an enemy."

"I did," she said mutely. "I wanted adventure, but not quite like this."

"Well, you can have an adventure here. I promise you it will be safe."

Something about that promise settled heavy and hot over her skin, and she tried to ignore it. It was very disconcerting, the way his words had the power to affect her. They shouldn't. Things should be the same between them. Their mouths touching a couple of times shouldn't have profoundly shifted the balance between them any more than vows that had no honesty behind them.

"You've gotten very quiet again," he said.

"I should think you would like me to be quiet."

"I find it unsettling. Because it's not normal."

"I've never been accused of being normal, Dante. You of all people should know that."

Their eyes met for a moment, and she had the vague sense he could see something inside her she couldn't even see clearly herself.

"What possible attraction did a man like this have to you?" When he asked, the question was so rough and fierce it caught her off guard.

"What do you mean?"

"You don't seem like the kind of woman to be taken in easily, Min."

She sniffed loudly. "Who says it was easy?"

His expression tightened, even as he kept his gaze on the road. "He didn't force himself on you."

"No!" The denial came swift and fierce. She knew enough about Katie's story, and about what had attracted her to Carlo, that she could easily repeat it to Dante, but she found that she couldn't. She didn't want to talk about being seduced, not when she hadn't been. Nor would she take a trauma on herself that she hadn't experienced. So she thought it best just to change the subject. Deflect as best she could.

"It is impossible for me to say what the attraction to a man like him is." She placed each word carefully, as if it were a footstep in a minefield. "Once you know everything about his character, whatever might have been charming is lost. He's not a good man."

That much was true.

"And he is dangerous," she said, thinking of Katie again.

They drove up the house, and Minerva—who was used to a certain amount of grandeur—was utterly enthralled. Her family's opulence was like a mix of Tuscany and California. Ornate and lavish.

This was incredibly sleek and spare, but each detail was perfect. Everything about it looked solid, like the best version of itself.

It was—she thought—exquisitely Dante.

He was that sort of man. Not a spare ounce of body fat on him, muscular, honed. His suits cut to tailored perfection, sleek, dangerous lines. Nothing overshadowed him. Rather it became a part of him. Absorbed into his orbit.

This house was no different.

He moved to the back seat of the car and retrieved Isabella's car seat, his movements as casual as if he had been doing it for the past three months.

"You're very good at that," she said.

"Thank you," he returned, and she couldn't tell if he was genuinely thanking her, or if he was making fun of her. She could never tell with him.

He made quick work of showing her the rooms about the place, and when he showed her to the beautifully appointed nursery she nearly collapsed.

It was an oasis. And Isabella would be safe.

Her daughter would be safe.

Whether Isabella had come from her body or not was irrelevant.

Carlo was her father, and he had blood ties to her, and it didn't mean that he cared. It meant nothing.

What mattered was love.

Isabella had given Minerva a sense of purpose she'd never experienced before. And yes, it had come with extreme exhaustion, uncertainty and a niggling feeling that she might be doing something wrong.

But mostly it was…purpose that she hadn't found before.

She'd left home to study in Rome because at home she'd always felt lost. She hadn't had a clear sense of what she wanted to study and she'd switched classes around at an alarming rate. History. Art. Art history. Business— which she'd quit immediately because it had depressed her since she had felt she would have to compete with Violet of Maximus to make it relevant.

But with Isabella she felt focused. She felt…fulfilled.

She gave Isabella a bottle, changed her diaper, and yet again, the little girl was ready to nap. Minerva took the opportunity to explore the rest of the house. Her bedroom was beautiful. Stark white walls, a white marble floor with the plush marble throw over it. The bedding was also white and soft, with large windows overlooking the sea. And she found that when pushed, they slid open, and were actually doors that gave way and led to a path outside. As far as she could tell that path led to the beach, and she had every intention of exploring it later.

For now, she needed a bath.

She slipped into the en suite and found a large tub that was also white, and looked like a freestanding bowl. It appealed to the romance in her spirit, and she began to fill it as she went back into the bedroom and began to rummage around for clothes.

It was then she realized that none of these were her own.

But of course they weren't.

Dante had procured a wardrobe for her. As she looked at the pieces, she couldn't imagine which woman he had been dressing when he had selected them.

Of course, Dante hadn't had anything to do with it.

But for a moment it was… Interesting. To entertain the idea that he looked at her and thought that she was the sort of woman who should wander around a place like this in a brief crop top, flowing pants and a sheer caftan. That she was the sort of woman who should wear many dresses in various bright colors and… A white bikini.

She hated wearing swimsuits, and she definitely didn't gravitate toward bikinis. Not when her sister often wore them in her signature purple, showing off her brilliant curves.

Minerva's curves were so slight she doubted she could even roll a penny down the slope of her breast.

She imagined herself in the swimsuit. If it got wet it might be somewhat see-through. She wondered what Dante would think of that.

The idea sent a sip of something forbidden through her body and she immediately turned away from it. She went back into the bathroom with the crop top, pants and caftan and stripped her clothes off, settling herself into the warm water. It was only there that she allowed herself to reflect on everything that had happened. The kiss…

She was submerged in warm water, and yet she felt her nipples pebble when she replayed it in her mind.

No. She wasn't going to think of it. It was shocking. She should be angry at him, because he had kissed her in a way that no one would expect a man to do in a church.

Then she began replaying what he'd said about *Swiss Family Robinson*.

And that had an even deeper effect on her. Something that turned deep inside her and made her feel something in her chest.

She liked that even less.

The kiss was safer.

She got out of the tub hastily, wrapping herself in a towel and exiting into the bedroom. It was then she realized that Isabella was crying. Panic slammed against her, and she began moving around frantically looking for her clothing, but before she could, the bedroom door swung open and Dante appeared, cradling her in his arms.

Min just stood there, clutching the towel to her chest. "I was on my way," she said.

"I don't know what to do with the baby," he said, his tone accusing. "Take her."

She wasn't thinking clearly, and she reached out, taking Isabella into her arms, in spite of the fact that she was only barely wrapped in a towel. "I should've gotten dressed first," she said.

Dante paused, and looked at her, his dark eyes seeming to slowly register the scene in front of him.

"Neither thing is my problem. Handle it."

And with that he turned and walked out of the room, and she wondered where the caring man had gone who had told her about *Swiss Family Robinson*. Even the man who had issued death threats to the one who had indicated he might cause her harm was better than this one.

She didn't know why he was angry with her.

It was like he wasn't capable of holding a baby for a moment.

She sighed heavily and went over to the diaper bag in the corner of the room, hunting around for a pacifier. She popped one in Isabella's mouth, then took a blanket and spread it out as best she could with one free hand before setting her on the floor.

"I'm just going to get dressed," she said, keeping one eye on her the entire time. After that she saw her safely soothed, but she found that she could not soothe herself.

She was going to be stuck here with Dante for the foreseeable future. And she truly didn't know how she was going to survive.

She might be physically safe with him, but she didn't know what was happening inside her.

Didn't know what was happening inside him.

And like it or not, something about the vows that they had spoken had affected her. Had changed something in her.

What was a person to do when she found herself angrily married to her older brother's best friend and stranded on his private island?

You know what one of your heroines would do...

Minerva blinked, and pushed that thought aside.

It didn't matter what one of her heroines would do.

No matter what her dreams had been, she wasn't one of them. She never had been. And she never could be.

CHAPTER SIX

ALREADY THINGS WERE not going according to Dante's plan. And Dante had very little experience of things not going according to his plans. He was not a man who often had to deal with defiance, whether it came from another person, or life. Not a man who had been put in a position where another human being might come into his sphere and create disorder.

Chaos.

His life had been utter and complete chaos when he was a child. From the time he was born until he had been swept off the streets, half-feral, and put into a private school by Robert King.

Dante had been in possession of some concerns about Robert. Mostly, he had been convinced that a man who offered such things to a boy must have nefarious intent for him.

Dante had done a lot of thinking about whether or not he cared.

Because the streets had visited vast amounts of atrocities onto him. And when you were lean, and hungry, you tended to have a very flexible idea of what you might be willing to do for your next meal.

With that in mind, he had decided to take Robert's deal, and he had come to the conclusion that depending on what the man might ask of him, he would either comply and take the education, take the money for the time being, or he would follow through with what he had originally intended to do. Robert had given the gun back, after all.

All of those thoughts seemed so wildly removed from who he was now, and the kind of life he lived.

But it all came back when the baby had been wailing wildly, and he hadn't known what to do.

And then, he had gone looking for Minerva, only to find her standing there in a towel.

Her shoulders were enticing.

Her hair had been up, falling damply around her face, and he had found it disconcerting in the extreme. And resentment had burned in his chest. For what he and Minerva both new was that Isabella was not his child.

And if she cried, she was not his responsibility. The responsibility was Minerva's.

And he would also like to speak to her about her responsibility when it came to not being an enticement.

Of course, he had no desire to admit to her that she was an enticement.

He ate dinner, and found himself at loose ends.

There was little work to be done, simply because he was not a man who was ever behind.

He took on work. More than he could handle, many would say, but he always managed to get it finished. And he was constantly being lectured on the fact that he should find a way to have more leisure time.

But for what?

He could never figure it out.

He went out when he felt like it. Oftentimes, there were business reasons to go out, connections to be made when he did. And then, if he managed to meet a woman in whose company he wished to spend the night, it was a pleasant diversion. But he didn't need more recreation time for that.

Often, words like that were spoken by those who didn't know what it meant to be hungry.

Who had never once had to entertain the idea that it might be preferable to endure the physical abuse of an older man in order to feed oneself.

No, in Dante's world, work and money were king.

It was a wall that he was building between himself and what he had come from so high and so thick that nothing would ever be able to cross it.

Safety.

He suddenly heard a soft voice, and the sound of a baby, and he turned and saw Minerva, wearing pants and a top that showed her stomach, coming down the stairs. "I'm starving," she said. "What's for dinner?"

"I ate," he said.

The look of thunderous fury that crossed her delicate features would have been amusing if it hadn't been quite so dark. "You ate? Without me?"

"I was not under the impression that we were required to eat in tandem."

"But what am I supposed to do?" she asked in a fury. "I would have thought that you would eat with me. *On our wedding night.*"

He cast her a flat stare. "Minerva," he said. "Don't tell me you were hoping for a more traditional wedding night."

Her mouth dropped open, then she shut it again. "Of course not. We mustn't consummate. Remember? Your Catholicism."

He huffed a laugh. "Thank you, for your dedicated concern to my Catholicism, but I promise you I have not forgotten it."

"Well."

"I wear it like a hair shirt every day."

"Fine," she said, her eyes green like beetles, and just as mean.

"Let's find you some food," he said. "I wouldn't want to get on the wrong end of you when you're hungry."

She followed him into the kitchen, and he opened up the fridge. He already knew that there was an elaborate charcuterie board in there, and some meals to be reheated. That was one of the issues with having staff off-site.

He did know how to cook for himself, but his skills were a bit crude, owing to the time in his life when he had to provide for himself.

Spaghetti with tomato sauce was all well and good for an eighteen-year-old going to university, but he had moved past that.

"You can start with cheese," he said, taking the platter and setting it out on the white marble countertop.

Minerva, clutching Isabella to her chest like she was a tiny shield, went over to the board and began picking at the offerings. She picked up a date, bit into it and closed her eyes, an obscene moan escaping her lips.

He gritted his teeth and turned away from that. "Fish or steak?"

"Steak," Minerva said. "Always steak. I haven't the use for fish."

"Well. I suppose that means you'll be consuming all the steak during our stay."

"I could give you a bite," she said.

"Oh, don't flatter me by offering me your castoffs, Minerva."

He took one of the meals out and began to heat the steak and vegetables in a pan for her.

She sat there, holding the baby with one arm and eating cheese with another.

"This really is very nice," she said.

"Oh, now your anger has subsided?"

"I don't know very many people who can stay angry while eating cheese," she said.

"You seem like someone who could," he said.

"I find that very flattering."

He had the distinct impression that she meant it.

He finished heating the food and set it out in front of her. He noted she was very comfortable being served.

She looked around. "Can you hold her?"

Several thoughts went through his mind all at once, careening around like a runaway train.

And he wondered for the first time—not just since this started, but in years—if he had miscalculated. He had assumed he could make a delineation between the public and private. Not have to handle anything to do with the child in private.

Clearly, Min thought different.

He had no experience with babies. He wanted no experience with babies. And, also, there was no way that he, Dante Fiori, could allow himself to be defeated by an infant.

Practicality dictated that Minerva needed both hands to eat. And that meant that he should hold the child while she did so.

"Give her to me," he said.

"You might want to work on your tone," she said, rising up from her seat and bringing Isabella over to him, depositing her into his arms. Then, she went and sat back down in front of her plate. The child was so light. She was barely a weight in his arms, and yet she was warm. She leaned against him, so trusting. So very… Fragile.

Minerva was busy eating, and he was pondering this. The baby's fragility.

How could adults leave small things such as this to fend for themselves? How could they ever put them in danger?

"I'll kill him," Dante said, his hand resting on the back of her downy head. "I will kill him for what he's put you through."

"Well, that's not something I expected," Minerva said, looking up from her plate.

"It is true, though. It is wrong, what he's done to you. And her. But mostly her."

"Well, thank you very much."

"We are adults, Minerva, and we must answer for our actions. A child like her has done nothing except be born into a broken world. She is helpless. She is dependent on the people around her to make decisions for her survival, her safety."

"I know," Minerva said. "And that's why I was willing to do whatever it took to keep her safe."

He nodded. "Of course. You would understand that."

"I do understand it. There was nothing to be done. I had to… Whatever the cost, Dante, I had to make sure that she would be protected."

Minerva ate in silence for a while, and then he shifted his hold on Isabella, who promptly made a sound like a very juicy hiccup and cast up her accounts on his shirt.

"Oh!" Minerva jumped up from her seat. "I'm sorry."

She reached out and grabbed hold of Isabella. And he looked down at his damp shirt. He gripped the hem and tugged it over his head. "I'll leave this for the staff when they come pick up the laundry."

"Staff?"

But her eyes were not on his face. Rather, they were resting in the center of his chest.

"Yes," he said. "We will make sure that we are not about when they come, but we will need to have supplies brought here, laundry dealt with, food replenished."

"Yes," she said, her eyes darting up, down and back and forth, but never going higher than his shoulders.

"Minerva," he said. "My eyes are up here."

And then she did look stunned. Her cheeks turning red.

Minerva was not unaffected by him. She was just very, very good at playing games.

He was shocked by this realization. But, now that he had his shirt off, he seemed to have reduced her mouthiness by 20 percent or so.

"I know where your eyes are," she snapped. "I believe your shirts are upstairs, if you want to find one."

"I'm perfectly comfortable. Aren't you comfortable?"

"I'm not," she said, growing edgy and pink. "But that's because it's a little bit warm in here. And… I might walk down to the beach."

He arched a brow. "Might you?"

"I might."

He wouldn't have imagined that a woman—a grown woman with a child—could be made so uncomfortable at the sight of him without a shirt.

He knew that women found his looks impacting. It was something he'd enjoyed the effects of for the past twenty years. But he was used to purring, coquettish glances. Touching. Flirting. Not…fear.

"There's cake," he said.

Min tilted her head. "At the beach?"

"Here," he clarified. "Chocolate cake, if you would like to stay for some. However, if you're indisposed…"

She sat, holding Isabella. "I will accept cake."

He chuckled, and went over to the other side of the kitchen, procuring a slice of cake and setting it on a plate.

He liked this reversal of fortune.

Because it had been bothering him that Minerva had had an effect on him, and now the tables had turned.

For a brief moment he saw his own actions, his own satisfaction, clearly.

He was delighting in some kind of sensual victory over Maximus's little sister. A woman who had been—until a few days ago—as a child to him.

But hell, they were going to be stuck here in this place for God knew how long. He supposed he had to take his victories where he could get them. He held the plate out to her, and with great effort, she looked up at his eyes.

CHAPTER SEVEN

SHE DIDN'T KNOW what was happening to her. She felt warm and flushed all over and she couldn't seem to do anything but stare at his chest.

She was trying to remember if she had ever seen Dante without a shirt before. She must have. At least when she was younger, and they went to the beach.

She was around shirtless men all the time. She lived in California. They had beachfront property.

She didn't know why this felt different, why it made her insides shiver, and why she felt overheated.

It had been strange to watch him hold Isabella, the way his powerful hands gripped her delicate body.

It made her so unbearably conscious of his strength, and the control that he utilized in unleashing it. And now he was offering her cake.

And the image he made, shirtless and extending that decadent treat to her, his muscles shifting and bunching…

He had hair on his body. Not enough to conceal his muscles, but just enough to make her unbearably aware of his testosterone.

And that prickling in her skin was back. That racing in her heart, that unbearable, unsettling feeling that made her feel as if she had to do something. Anything. To get his attention. To get him to notice her.

And with a sudden horror, she realized what that feeling was.

And it was a feeling she had for a very long time. For Dante.

No. No. *No.* She wouldn't acknowledge it. She couldn't. She could not... Would not...

She had never.

And suddenly, she realized the little lie that she had told her father, her mother, her sister, might not have been such a lie after all.

Had she had feelings for Dante all this time?

That something in her simply refused to make them into the shape of what they truly were?

It was as if in that glorious chest of his she could see clearly. The most absurd thought she ever had in her life, but it was true.

Years of following after him, trying to climb trees in his sphere so that he might say something about her daring, talking and talking and talking at him even though he was so patently disinterested.

But she had never allowed herself to call it what it was, because he was far too old, far too beautiful, and if he was going to choose a woman from her family...

It would have been Violet.

It never would have been her.

Ever.

But maybe that was the real reason why the kiss in the club in Rome had felt so disappointing.

Because the man wasn't Dante.

And maybe that was why she had shut down completely the two times Dante had kissed her.

Because it wasn't real.

Because it was all a farce that she had set up, and if she really did feel this way, if the burning intensity of that bright something in her chest really did mean that she… That she had a crush on him, then perhaps using his name, using him as a solution, the fact that he was the father of Isabella, as a solution to her problem was…

The very idea made her squirm. Surely her subconscious hadn't done that.

But then, her subconscious was apparently a straight-up hussy for Dante, and she had kept her actual conscious from acknowledging that somehow.

And now, shirtless and with cake, she couldn't ignore it. Couldn't deny it.

Couldn't help but identify the sharp, reckless heat that had cut through her seventeen-year-old body the moment he'd taken her up into his arms to shield her from censure, to shield her from the world, had been…

Desire.

She snatched the cake from his hand and then looked down at it resolutely.

"Something wrong, Minerva?"

"Nothing is wrong," she said.

He approached her, and tilted her face up. "Nothing is wrong?"

He had touched her before. He had touched her many times, and this time it burned. Because this time she knew. Knew that that little prickling sensation he left all over her skin when his fingers made contact with her wouldn't happen with any man. Knew that it wasn't static electricity or something else that she could easily dismiss.

It was Dante.

But more than that, it was her feelings for him.

"I'm fine," she repeated.

But he was far too close to her.

"Good to know."

And then he moved away from her, and she realized, with stunning humiliation, that he was playing with her.

That he had known that she had been powerless in the face—or rather, the chest—of his magnetism.

She gritted her teeth and dug into the cake with ferocity. "I am fine. And I don't need you to eat dinner with me. After all, you ate already. You clearly didn't want to share a meal with me, so why hang around pretending? Go wash your shirt."

But he didn't obey. Rather, he stood there, watching her eat cake. And she refused to get up. Refused to let him win. So she ate every last bite, and then cleaned up each remaining crumb. Then defiantly rose, carrying Isabella in one arm, and the plate in the other hand, and deposited it in the sink before going back up the stairs. "I think I will get Isabella and me set up to have a date on the beach tomorrow. I know that you're very busy and have lots of work to see to. But it's fine. We will be just fine without you."

She was grateful that her hands didn't start shaking until she got back to the bedroom and closed the door firmly behind her.

Because she didn't want him to see just what he did to her.

It was beyond a cruel joke.

Because as Dante had said more than once, she was not the kind of woman who would ever turn the head of a man like him.

She was much happier when her brain had understood that, and buried her feelings for him, sparing her from any disappointment.

Now she just felt deflated and frightened and uncertain of how she was going to get through the next chunk of time.

CHAPTER EIGHT

THERE WAS A crackling fire burning beneath his skin, and he found it unconscionable.

True to her word, Minerva had been scarce the entire day.

When he peeked into the nursery, he saw that a great many of Isabella's items were gone, and he thought that it might be true that she had tramped off to the beach intent on staying there for the day.

Which meant that he would simply stay in the house and work. As she had said.

Dante had never had difficulty burying himself in work. No, quite the contrary, he had always found it to be a great solace. Another brick in the wall. But today he was restless, and today he found he would rather be outdoors.

Not a thought he often had, considering there had been a time in his life when he had been forced to be outdoors twenty-four hours a day, for lack of home.

Not that he didn't enjoy the beach on occasion, but he had been rather fond of temperature control since his first experience of it.

Before he could think much about it, he had stripped his T-shirt and jeans off, and gone on the hunt for swim shorts. Once he had acquired those, he took hold of a light T-shirt and put it on before making his way down the path that led to the private beach.

The sight of Minerva and Isabella did something strange to his chest. It tangled things up in there. And he didn't like it.

Minerva was wearing a white bikini, and he had never seen so much of her skin. She also had on a wide-brimmed sunhat, and she and Isabella were beneath a cabana, staying out of the sun.

Minerva's skin was that golden California-girl tone, courtesy of a lifetime spent at the beach. She had no makeup on today, her hair a riotous tangle beneath the hat, and he was sure that she had been out in the waves at some point. Her curves were slight, but they were delectable, her midsection slim but strong, muscles visible in her stomach.

Her arms were the same, slim but toned, as were her legs.

Her breasts were small, but round and high. His hands would eclipse them completely.

The thought sent a slug of desire straight through him.

What a strange moment. Standing there, looking at her as though she were…an object of desire.

Minerva.

Min.

When she looked over at him, her eyes widened, and the corners of her mouth turned down. "What are you doing here?"

"I came to check on you. Because you've been gone all day."

"I told you we would be," Minerva said. "I could think of nothing better to do while feeling safe than come to the beach."

That made him feel slightly guilty for terrorizing her last night.

"Have you been afraid of him all this time?"

"I… Yes," she said. "I had hoped that escaping would make him feel further away, but I was just waiting. Waiting for him to figure it out."

"Figure what out?"

She blinked. "Nothing."

"I know what it's like. To feel afraid all the time."

His mind was cast back to whom he'd been. That boy on the streets.

That boy who had held a gun to Robert King's head.

"It's terrible," she said softly.

"It is," he agreed.

He felt unkind that he had given her a false sense of what would happen in their marriage in the future. And now that he recognized she was so pleasing physically, there really was no question of them getting an annulment.

"Minerva, I know what it is to be afraid. I lived my life without security on the streets of Rome."

"I've been to Rome, and I can honestly say that now that statement means a lot more to me," she said.

"I'm sure it does. It is a terrifying thing to have no control. Whether that be because of a lack of money, or because a person has decided to dismantle that. And when you figure out how to have power, you'll never go back. Not ever."

"I don't suppose."

"Then you will understand why there is no question of the two of us divorcing."

"What?"

"I'm solidifying this business deal with your father, the best way that I can. And if I were to divorce you it would cause problems."

"We talked about this. About… You helping me. And how he surely won't be angry with you if he knows that what you did you simply did to keep me safe."

"To a certain point. It is about consolidating power, Minerva. In my life I have always imagined that I'm building a wall between myself now and my past. Whenever I can build it stronger, build it higher, I will. This is such an opportunity, and I will take it."

He was not asking her for anything untoward, not in his mind.

It wasn't as if she were an innocent. She had a child.

"I will give Isabella my name," he said. "She will be my daughter. I can adopt her, legally. All of this can be accomplished once we are certain you're safe. Everything I own will be hers someday. And I will be her father."

The words sent a strange surge through his chest. "There are many things about family I don't understand. And I won't. I have been in yours for a great many years, and still… The foundation that is built beneath us during our earliest years matters a great deal. And I know that more than most. I can't promise I'll be the best father, but I will be better than the one that biology gave her. And I will be better than my own."

She picked Isabella up, in a move he now absolutely recognized. "And what about as a husband?"

"I will be good to you. Have I ever not been?"

"But will you ever love me?"

"You said yourself, Minerva, you don't even like me very much. What do you care if I love you? You won't love me."

She bit her bottom lip. "Well, that's a pretty sad start to a marriage, don't you think?"

"No," he said. "I don't. The mutual interest of protect-

ing your daughter, a desire to unite our family names…
And you don't dislike me. Admit it."

"I will do no such thing," she sniffed. "You're old."

"Yes. I know. When I was a child I had to walk to the
soup kitchen, in the snow, uphill both ways."

"Stop it," she said.

"I'm offering you security," he said. "I can offer you
nothing that means more to me than that. Security is what
I have built my entire new life on. And I will give it to
you. You must understand what value that has to me. And
with that I give you the greatest thing in my possession.
It is better than love. Love is fickle and it breaks. Love
destroys the moment that it malfunctions. I have seen it.
My mother loved my father, and what did that get her?
Years on the streets. Prostitution. She loved many men,
and all they did was take from her. And that love that she
felt for them gave them that power. It is a folly to love.
Did you love Isabella's father?"

Her face took on a strange pallor. "No," she said. "I
didn't."

"Well, then. I suppose there is no comparison for you
to be had there. But by God, Minerva, you must know
that what I would give you, what I would give her, is better than the potential of someday finding a relationship
that could give you what? Will a man claim Isabella so
wholly as his own? Or will he always make her feel second? Will he care so much about the interests of your
family? As much as I do? Will he be able to keep you
safe in the way that I have done?"

"And you'll do this… All for a business?"

There was something in her look that was beseeching,
and he knew that she wanted another answer.

He had one. Much to his surprise.

"I see myself in Isabella. A vulnerable child. There

is little outright good I have done in the world, but if I can spare her the realities of life, that harshness, until she must absolutely face it, then I will. I will be her wall against all that is behind her, all that would seek to harm her, and the brilliant future that she can have. I will be a man she can call father safely. I will not harm her."

Minerva's green eyes were glistening now. He knew that he had said the right thing.

"All right," she said, setting Isabella down on a blanket beneath the shade. "I agree. I'll be your wife. Really."

What shocked him most was the roaring in his ears. It took him a moment to realize that it wasn't the waves. That it was some kind of hot flood of triumph that was rallying through him like a river. He closed the distance between them, and pulled her into his arms, and then, he claimed her mouth for real.

Not because of their farce.

Not because there was an audience.

Because she was his wife.

And she was his.

CHAPTER NINE

MINERVA FELT LIKE she had come down with a terrible fever. She was hot all over, shaking, and her stomach felt like it was tossing and turning.

He was kissing her.

And it was different than the kiss that had happened at the engagement party. Different than the kiss at their wedding.

It was different than anything.

And she feared that she might be too. That somehow, between the revelations of last night, and this moment when his mouth had met hers, and all the in-between—those moments when he had made such a rational case for her being his wife permanently, and she had created a web of justification inside herself and pulled each gossamer strand tight, hoping that it would act as a safety net when she inevitably fell.

And fall she was doing.

Hard. Fast.

Into this deep, dark sensual kiss that kicked against her and made a mockery of what she had thought the day of their engagement party.

That she had thought it was in a kiss. Not a real kiss. For, a real kiss was supposed to make her feel light and airy, was supposed to fill her with joy.

But the feelings that she had for Dante were so much more complicated than that. A series of complications, in fact. That could never be so simple as a fantasy realized. Would that they could be. No, it was nothing like she had imagined because, of course, she hadn't taken into account that kissing involved another person.

Which meant that the movements were not all hers. Which meant that she wasn't in charge of how firm it was, of how deep it was.

And because there was another person involved, it was physical.

He was in a misty vapor of her fantasies the way that it all materialized in her head when she was reading about a handsome heroic character that she might want to dream about.

Because Dante was real. Mortal. A man in the flesh, with hot skin and a pounding heart. With hard muscles and hard...

He pressed his hand to her lower back and drew her up against him. Hard.

Yes. All of him was hard.

He desired her. Whether or not it was because he was a man and he could desire whatever he chose at a given moment, or because he desired her specifically, she didn't know. But he did.

And that was... Intense and heady and frightening.

She also wanted to lean into it as much as she wanted to run from it. More than anything in the entire world. Why was nothing about this simple? Why wasn't it easy? Why did it feel world-ending and wonderful all at once?

When they parted, she knew.

She looked into his dark gaze and she knew that it was him.

Dante.

And she had no idea how she had come to be the one kissing him.

She, Minerva, who was nothing.

Not by comparison of her exceptional family. And certainly not in comparison with him.

She had done one vaguely heroic thing in her life, and that was take care of Isabella.

But then, she had to wonder if it was heroic at all, or if she had just been reacting.

Because what could you do when there was a little girl vulnerable and alone in the world, her mother was dead and the police were declining to investigate.

She could have allowed Isabella to go into foster care in Italy, but that would have only made her vulnerable to Carlo.

She would've bounced around and…

And Minerva would never have seen her again.

So Minerva had told the police that Isabella was her daughter.

And that was how it had continued.

Dante thought that she was at least interesting enough to have engaged in an affair with a mobster.

But she wasn't.

She had just been a witness to it, and that made her all the more bland.

She suddenly felt small and weak and trembling, and she hated herself for it.

"What's the matter?" He lifted his hand and dragged his thumb along her lower lip.

"Nothing," she said.

She lied because there was nothing else to do. She lied because all of this was a lie, so she might as well be one too.

"I think we had quite enough of the beach, don't you?"

"Have we?"

"Yes. You're my wife. And it's time to make that real."

"Oh… Well, it is real, in that it's legal."

"You know," he said, his voice lowering to a growl. "There were days when a marriage wasn't considered a marriage until it had been consummated."

"Right," she said. "Wasn't there some barbarous practice of hanging bloody sheets out the window to alert the nation of the purity of the bride?"

He chuckled. "Luckily," he said, "neither of us have to worry about your purity."

Her stomach fell.

"Luckily."

He bent down and picked up Isabella. With shaking hands, Minerva began to gather her things.

"Leave it," he said. "It will be dealt with later."

Min was half out of her mind by the time they tromped back up to the house, by the time Dante laid Isabella down in her crib and closed the door to the nursery behind him.

"Will she sleep?"

"She doesn't run on a schedule. She does what she does."

"But she is…due to sleep?" he asked.

If there was one thing that made Dante seem a little bit flummoxed, it was Isabella. Babies in general. And truly, she had managed to destroy some of his composure with her impromptu announcement about his being the father of her baby. She supposed that on some level she should be triumphant in that.

She might be relatively boring, but she had caused Dante Fiori a moment's concern. Had made that patrician brow crease for but a few seconds before he had taken control of the entire endeavor.

So she was several steps ahead of the rest of the world.

Maybe that made her not so boring.

But then, he thought that she was not a virgin. Thought that she might know something about how to please a man, and on that score he was going to be very disappointed.

"Do you really want me?" Her voice was small, and she despised it.

"Minerva," he said, his voice rough and hard. "Of all the things to come out of this ridiculous ruse of yours, the most disturbing is that I cannot look at you as I once did. I was content to leave you in the category of child. My friend's younger sister, the daughter of my mentor, but you insist on making yourself unique and singular. A woman who belongs only to yourself, and now, to me. I don't have a choice."

"You don't have a choice in what?"

"Wanting you. It is damned inconvenient, and I was content to stay immune to you. How… How have you made it so that I'm not? It makes no sense."

"Because I'm not your type," she said, feeling breathless.

"Not at all," he said, advancing on her. "I like women with dramatic curves, who wear makeup and style their hair." He reached out and took a lock of her own hair between his thumb and forefinger, rubbing it absently.

"I like women who respond to my touch with enthusiasm and not trepidation. I definitely don't like women who tell the world I have fathered their children and force me into a fait accompli. And yet somehow… Here we are."

He wrapped his arm around her waist and pulled her against his chest.

And they were right back where they'd been on the beach.

He wasn't just kissing her, he was consuming her. And she didn't know where she began and he ended. Didn't know what she wanted from all of this. Except that all she wanted was for it to keep going. For it to never stop.

No, kissing wasn't what she had imagined it might be. It was more. It was everything. It was physical. It consumed her. It made her doubt everything she had ever believed about herself and gave birth to entirely new ideas there on the spot.

It was magic. Dark, chaotic magic that she didn't know how to contend with. His hands didn't stay still. They roamed over her body, exploring dips and hollows in her spine, her waist, beneath her breasts.

He wasn't touching her anywhere outrageously intimate, and yet it almost seemed more scandalous for it.

She had been held in a man's embrace only one other time. And he had gone straight for the obvious places, his hand beginning to move to her breast even as his other hand had already moved down to grab her bottom.

She knew all about those obvious things, and she had found them so base and obvious they had contributed to the utter turnoff of the entire situation.

But Dante managed to take something base and elevate it. To make it feel like high art rather than simple pornography. It bewitched her. Mesmerized her. Made her into something she didn't recognize. But maybe that was a good thing.

Because she had never been all that entranced by what she did recognize inside herself. But he made her feel new.

He made her feel beautiful. And perhaps this would make it so.

He continued to kiss her, continued to explore her in that innocuous way that didn't feel innocuous at all.

She breathed in deep, inhaling the scent of him, the sensation of him as his mouth continued to move over hers.

Were they really going to have sex?

Was she really going to lose her virginity to Dante Fiori?

Her husband.

For a moment she was convinced that she had escaped the real world and slipped in between the pages of a book.

Because this was something that would happen to one of her heroines, but not something that would happen to her. This deep, rich, exciting experience that was all tongue and teeth and glory.

The hands of the man whom she cherished most, no matter that she had tried to pretend she didn't.

The kiss was all fraught, endless glory, and she reveled in it.

Then, he picked her up, cradling her against him as he carried her past her bedroom and toward his.

She hadn't set foot in Dante's bedroom.

No, quite the contrary, she had avoided it.

Hadn't wanted anything to do with that.

But she could see now that it was because she did want something to do with it that she had avoided it quite so studiously.

These revelations about herself were coming too fast and on the heels of physical sensations that were far too new for her to fully understand them.

Why did she avoid the things she wanted most? Why did she bury them?

Why did she think she couldn't have these things?

She didn't know. Except that everyone had been so shocked by the fact that Dante was the father of her baby, that he wanted to marry her, that she knew on some level they all thought it too. That it was an accepted truth about Minerva to an extent.

Even though they loved her. Even though they supported her.

She was not now, nor had she ever been, considered a great and wonderful beauty.

And she had decided that meant she couldn't have things.

Had decided it meant she shouldn't try.

Even the way that she had been made up for the engagement party and the wedding had made her uncomfortable because she knew that people would compare her with Violet. She didn't want it.

But Dante wanted her. He was spreading her out on his large bed, and staring down at her with dark, keen eyes.

Then he stood back and stripped his shirt off, as he'd done the day before.

But the day before she hadn't been about to touch him. Hadn't been about to...

"Now you don't have to pretend that you aren't looking," he said.

"I would never pretend," Minerva said. "I don't have the kind of capacity to play games that many do. I'm honest."

But that was a lie. She wasn't honest. Of course Dante believed that she had experience with men. And she didn't.

But she wasn't about to tell him. It made the whole situation that much more precarious, made her connection to Isabella so much more tenuous.

"Well, then let me return your honesty with the same," he said.

He leaned over, grabbed the hem of her top and jerked it up over her head. Her nipples beaded in the cool air, a blush warming her against the chill. No man had ever seen her like this, and that this perfect specimen of one was staring at her now was more than a little bit embarrassing. But he looked… Well, he looked as entranced as she felt. And it made her feel… Something. Something so deep and intense, it made her want to cry. Made her want to turn away from him and turn toward him all at the same time.

She began to shake as he lowered himself down onto the bed, stretching his body over her.

His lips were a whisper away from hers, and all she wanted was for him to taste her again.

Because when his mouth was on hers, she couldn't think quite so well. And not being able to think was a gift.

She wanted to be carried away in the fantasy. She craved a little bit more gauze, a little bit of protection from this hard, physical reality. But she didn't know if she was going to be able to get any.

Not with him. Not with him so hard and real and large above her. Not with her heart threatening to pound out of her chest.

With her breath eluding her lungs.

A smile tilted up the corner of his mouth. That smile was… Wicked.

And she realized that she had never seen Dante like this before.

She had always found him beautiful. Formidable.

A tiger safely contained in an enclosure. She knew that he would never turn that focus, all that brilliant, amber glory, on to her. Knew that his fangs would be reserved for other quarry.

He had only ever protected her. But in doing that he'd concealed the most powerful parts of himself. Had hidden the true danger from her.

Except, now it was all focused on her. Deeply. Intensely.

Now, the tiger was looking at her as if she was going to be his next meal.

And here she was, lying down wantonly to be consumed.

He pushed the shorts he was wearing, discarding them quickly, and her mouth dried. She had never seen a naked, aroused man.

And the very first thing she wanted to say was that there was no way he would fit. On the heels of that came the hysterical urge to laugh. Because of course he thought she had given birth. In which case the size of a man's penis would be the smallest of concerns to her.

Though, his penis could never be called a small concern.

Yet again, she had to fight back the hysterical urge to laugh. Because it was either that or cry.

Either that or give in to the fear that was gripping her chest. No, it wasn't fear. Because she didn't want to run away. It was something deeper than that. Something that scraped at a raw edge in her heart. That call to deep emotion inside her that she didn't want to deal with or acknowledge.

That she wanted him to look at her and see beautiful.

That she wanted to be wrapped in his arms and held close, close to his body, and more than that to his heart.

That for her, this would never be a simple business deal, nor would it ever be a defense against the terrifying things out in the world. That for her, this was about feeling.

That for her, this would always be about her connection to him.

Because she couldn't have chosen another man.

She wouldn't have been able to imagine herself with another man.

She never would have been able to say the things she did to another man.

Just like she didn't want to kiss another man on that dance floor in Rome.

Because it was Dante. It always had been. And it always would be.

And that made her want to hide.

First of all because she was sure that he would see that shining out from her eyes. But second of all because she was absolutely convinced that she was reaching the highest, most brilliant peak of her life at the age of twenty-one. That she would never be able to have more or better than this moment.

Because at the end of it they would have to contend with reality. With what remained.

And perhaps he would be able to tell she'd never done this before, and perhaps he wouldn't. Maybe the farce would be over, and maybe it would not.

But whether or not she would be able to keep it up was another question entirely. Because once he had joined his body to hers…

Well. She would be new. She would be different. And she didn't know what would be waiting on the other side.

He grabbed hold of the waistband of her swimsuit bottoms and dragged them down her legs, leaving her exposed to his hungry gaze.

Yet again, he moved his hands to a place she didn't expect.

He pressed them against her hips, slid them upward, and then finally did he move his thumbs over her nipples. Back and forth. Stoking the heat in her body. Stoking desire in her soul.

He kissed her neck as he teased her there, kissed his way down her chest, pulling one beaded nipple into his mouth and sucking hard. And it was as if her universe now originated from there. As if she was nothing beyond that bright, white-hot point of sensation where his mouth met her body. He kissed her ribs, her belly button. Continued down her body until he grabbed hold of her thighs, wrapping his arms around her and tugging her down toward his mouth. And yet again he defied her expectations. He didn't ease her in with the touch of his fingers. No. Instead, his first contact with her most intimate area was with his tongue, sliding across her slick folds. Then he took that sensitized bud between her legs and sucked it between his lips, teasing and tormenting her with the tip of his tongue. She gasped, her bottom bowing up off the bed, and he took advantage of that to move his hands around to cup her there.

And then he held her up in place as he continued to torment her. As he continued to lavish pleasure on her until she couldn't breathe.

Until she didn't know herself. He had transformed her into a begging, weeping creature of need.

And this was what she had always feared. Truly, deep in her heart, she had feared this. That she would be debased before him. That she wanted him so much would be revealed and so easily.

She wanted him. No woman twisting and sobbing in the arms of a man, on the verge of orgasm from a few strokes of his tongue over her most intimate flesh, could pretend that she didn't have feelings for him.

No woman could pretend that she was dispassionate when she wasn't horrified by such an act, but craved more. Reveled in the intimacy of it. In the intensity. And then, he added a finger to his pleasuring. Pressed one digit deep inside her before adding another.

She felt herself begin to stretch. She felt like she was going to fly apart. Like it was too much. Like this was too much. How would she ever be able to accommodate the rest of him if two fingers pushed the edges of reason for her body?

Except all she knew was that she wanted more. Whether or not she was convinced she could handle more.

She wanted him. She wanted him even if it made no sense. She wanted him even if she would cry. Even if it would cause her pain.

What a strange thing. That a woman must want a man so much the first time that she would willingly submit herself to that pain. That invasion.

That a woman must have a physical marker of her virginity in a physical cost for losing it.

But she was willing. She was willing to pay the cost.

And when he made his way back up her body, as she was spent from her first climax and his mouth met hers, treating her to absolute evidence of her own need for him. Of the intensity of it.

And yet, she wasn't ashamed. To the contrary, she was spurred on.

Because she did want him. She couldn't pretend she didn't. And maybe that was the key.

Minerva had little to offer him. But she had herself. All the desire in the world. And the purity of her need for him was real.

She could give him that. And perhaps that was something he had never gotten from those practiced, beautiful socialites whom he was accustomed to.

An authenticity of need.

Maybe...

Maybe there was a gift in her innocence. In all that she was. Maybe that she had no skills or tricks or trinkets to offer him was a gift in and of itself.

"I'll go slow," he said, his voice rough.

And she realized that he intended to go slow because he thought she was only three months out from having given birth.

Not that she was a virgin.

But perhaps that would help.

When the thick, blunt head of him probed her untried flesh, she winced, and when he began to inch inside her she cried out. Gritting her teeth as he met the resistance that she knew signaled her inexperience.

And then, he had breached her. It hurt. Terribly.

And there was no way she could pretend it didn't. She cried out, and cursed herself as ten times the fool that she had ever thought for believing that she could hide this from him.

He began to withdraw and she panicked, grabbing hold of his rear end urging him back in.

"No," she said. "We have to. I need you."

He began to ease forward again, the effort it was taking him to go slow visible in the way the cords stood out on his neck.

"Please," she beseeched him.

And on a growl he thrust all the way home.

She had not been prepared. For the intensity of this. For the invasion of this.

For his rampant masculinity in the way that it would utterly and completely demolish her softness.

Her femininity.

For the fact that it was like a conquering.

But one she had surrendered to. Willingly. Joyously.

His dark eyes met hers, his expression that of a fierce warrior. His mouth moved, as though he was about to speak, and she stretched up, capturing the words with her lips, swallowing them. Because she didn't want to talk about anything right now. She didn't want to inhabit reality.

All she wanted was this.

For him to inhabit her. For him to take her and remake her, so that she was new. And maybe, maybe parts of him would become new too. Maybe they could do that for each other. Maybe.

He growled against her mouth, but he didn't try to speak to her again. Instead, he began to move.

Hard and fast, establishing a rhythm that left her breathless.

That carried them both up to the stars.

And when she shattered there up among the heavenly bodies, she finally felt like she belonged.

Like she was beautiful.

Beautiful in his arms. Beautiful for him.

Crying out her pleasure with no shame at all.

And when he tipped over the edge, a roar of pleasure coming from deep inside him, she held him. While he shook. While he poured himself out inside her.

She had never felt so female. She had never felt so powerful. Wrapped around this hard, muscular body that might have been carved out of rock were it not for the heat that radiated off him.

Were it not for the way he breathed. Hard and jagged as though something had been broken inside him.

When it was finished, he rolled away, and looked at her. His eyes were unreadable. Unfathomable.

And she couldn't guess what he would say next.

But she also couldn't contain the lie inside her anymore.

Whether he had guessed or not.

Based on the expression there, she had a feeling that he didn't know what he might have guessed or not.

But she wouldn't make him guess. She wouldn't make him speculate. There was no place for that with them.

"I didn't give birth to Isabella," she said.

And by the way the mountain moved, she could tell that he hadn't been close to guessing that at all.

CHAPTER TEN

DANTE WAS STILL reeling from the ecstasy that he had found in Minerva's arms. He had been ready to lecture her on allowing him to hurt her while her body was still tender, and then she had dropped that bombshell on him. And it made him go back in time. Every moment, every kiss, every touch since they had embarked on this farce.

The moment that he had first entered her body and she had flinched.

It was impossible.

It couldn't be.

That she was not an innocent was one of the only reasons that he could have justified demanding that she become his wife in body as well as in name.

He had been certain that she had known exactly what he was demanding of her.

But she did not.

And while he didn't hold to medieval ideas about virginity, and he was certainly not going to go hang a sheet out the window, it was about his age. His experience. The fact that he had swept her off the beach and taken her practically straight to bed without...

She had wanted it. He was certain of that.

But how could he be sure that she knew what she had wanted?

And how dare she lie to him?

Because he had been embroiled in this entire situation against his will, and apparently, Isabella was not her daughter.

Which begged the question… Who was the child?

And whom was Minerva actually hiding her from?

"Dammit," he said, moving to a sitting position. "Have you stolen this child?"

"No!" Minerva scrambled to a sitting position, clutching the sheets to her breasts. The entire left side of her body was still completely bare, and his eyes were drawn to that golden skin that he knew now was softer than he could have anticipated.

And he had no reason to be staring at her now. Not when he was looking at a traitor.

She had lied to him.

"Then explain this," he said. "Explain this entire thing. She's not your child?"

"Not biologically," Minerva said. "I said I didn't give birth to her. I didn't say I wasn't her mother."

"You adopted her?" he pressed.

"Not exactly. I lied. And everything… Everything to do with her birth was a disaster." She pressed her hands to her temples. "I have to start at the beginning."

"You had better."

"You know when I left for school I was planning on doing a new country each year, a new university. Right. Well, when I went to Rome I was rooming with a woman named Katie. She was also from the States. We didn't know each other before, but we became friends. She was very different from me."

Minerva clasped her hands in front of her and made a study of them. "I liked her. I was fascinated by her. Mostly because I'd never known anyone like her. I know everyone thinks that Maximus and Violet are wild because they go to parties all the time. But nobody as successful as they are isn't working most of the time."

Minerva lifted a shoulder. "I was studying, mostly. And Katie was in and out at all hours. Finally, I agreed to go out with her one night. We went to a club down in Rome. We met men."

A dark anger welled up in his chest. "But you didn't. You didn't have sex with him. You were a virgin."

He didn't know why now he felt the need to confirm that. And why the idea that this other man might have done something with her angered him.

"He kissed me once," Minerva said. "I didn't like it. I told him I wanted to leave. But Katie didn't want to leave, because she had met someone and she wanted to go home with him. I went back to our dorm by myself. The next morning, she came home, and she was in a good mood. She liked Carlo. She wanted to keep seeing him."

"And then what?"

"She started realizing he wasn't a good man. She tried to pull away. And it seemed to work. He seemed to lose interest. Then she changed. She started seeming more depressed than wild. That was when she told me she was pregnant. And we had to hide it from him. She said he was dangerous, and that was why she had left him. But like I said, it seemed as if he had lost interest in her. But he came to visit one day months later, and he saw that she was pregnant, and he said he wanted the baby. She told him no. We called the police. But…"

"Connections within crime families extend far. I know."

"We hoped that we were safe. After she had Isabella, she slid into a depression. Only two weeks after Isabella was born she started using drugs. I mean, she had always used them, but when she went out for the night. Not at home, and not during her pregnancy. But she was paranoid, and she was anxious, and she needed something to calm her down. I quit going to class too." She looked down at her hands. "I was so worried about her. I was so worried about Isabella."

She took a breath and forged on. "I took care of her, like she was my baby. It just…happened one day. I decided I couldn't do half. And since Katie couldn't do it at all, I just did. I fed her, clothed her, rocked her to sleep." She blinked hard. "One day I went out shopping with Isabella, and when I came back there were police at our apartment. Katie was… Her body was gone already. They said that she had died of a drug overdose. But I was afraid that wasn't true."

Min's eyes met his, and the green fire there was intense. "I will always be afraid that isn't true. That he wanted the baby. I told the police Isabella was mine. And then the very next day I packed up and I left Italy. I came back home with her. And then he found me. I wanted him to believe that Isabella was my baby. I wanted to… Cast doubt on it. Because I'm sure that he never paid enough attention to me to know whether or not I might have been pregnant. In fact, I doubt he ever would have recognized me no matter how many times he saw me. I'm plain, after all. But I think he found out who was rooming with her, and he began a search. I think he can't be certain that Isabella is his, and I'm counting on that. I was counting on you standing with me. Because I never slept with him either. So if… If I have a baby. If I have one with you…"

Helpless rage coursed through him, because what could he say? He had been lied to. But Minerva had been doing the very best she could.

There had been nothing else.

And he would never have suggested another plan. There was nothing else. She was correct in that. Claiming the child for her own was brilliant, and using him was brilliant in ways he hadn't understood.

"He doesn't believe you, though," he said.

"He doesn't know, though," she said. "I'm sure of that. He's not completely certain. I don't think he ever saw Isabella. I don't think he can be sure if Katie had the baby. Only that there was a baby in our apartment."

"But you know he wants her anyway."

"Yes. And if he does any test then he'll know for sure that she's his. I fear that if he did a test and found out she wasn't he would have simply..."

"He doesn't care for anyone or anything," Dante said. "Men like that don't. Men who don't value life don't value life of any sort."

"She's in danger. And so am I." Min swallowed hard. "I think he had her killed, Dante. I do. I can't prove it, and maybe the police covered it up. But what would he do to her? What would he expose her to? And me? Well, he'd just get rid of me, wouldn't he?"

"You didn't make that clear enough," Dante said. "I'm going to make sure he's dealt with."

"Please," Minerva said. "Please don't..."

"I'm not going to have them killed. But I am going to finance operations to destroy that crime family. And I think I have the connections in Rome to do it. It will all have to be done at once, and it will require money they likely don't possess. The problem is you have to get everyone within law enforcement on his payroll at the same time."

She nodded slowly. "Right and that... That's difficult."

He shook his head. "Difficult is coming up from the streets of Rome. Starting out the son of a prostitute and becoming a billionaire. That is difficult. This just takes the right moves at the right time, and the right amount of money. And it will be done."

He stared down at her, at his wife. He had made her his wife in truth, and he could never go back on it. Minerva was his wife, and her protection was his responsibility.

He had grown up on the streets among men like Carlo.

He knew that his father was likely a man quite like him.

And this was his opportunity to do more than simply build another brick in the wall of his own security.

But to knock down the wall that separated an organized crime family from justice.

And he would do it.

For Minerva. For Isabella.

For the boy whom he'd once been.

This was all he could do. At the end of the day, it was the only thing.

He would be a father who protected Isabella. A husband to protect Minerva.

God knew he didn't have anything else to offer.

CHAPTER ELEVEN

TIME SEEMED TO move differently on the island. It went in a haze, long leisurely days, gourmet food and sunshine. And then at night Dante made love to her.

She had the sense that he was angry with her for the deception, but he also hadn't turned away from her. She half expected him to. After the revelation that she'd been a virgin, she had expected that he might find her... She didn't know.

But time and time again he showed her that he didn't find her to be a problem. That he was attracted to her. That he wanted her.

And she wondered why that still didn't feel like enough.

She had never imagined that a man like him would find her compelling in the first place. And he did. Shouldn't she be happy with that? Shouldn't she, the less attractive sister, be happy with the crumbs that she was being handed?

Well, it didn't really matter. Because what they had was what they had.

And on the island it was only the two of them anyway. And whatever insecurity she felt about taking this into the real world...

She didn't doubt Dante's commitment. Not in the least.

He was a man who would keep his word, she was certain of that.

But what she was less certain of was his feelings. Those… Those were unknowable. Utterly and completely. Today, she had talked him out of simply working in the office and had badgered him down to the beach. Often, she and Isabella spent their time there alone. Dante was a workaholic, though she was exposed to enough billionaires to know that you didn't build empires without being married primarily to your job. But still, she felt lonely.

And then she had to wonder if she was being selfish. Because wasn't she with her dream man? How could she want anything more?

Isabella began to fuss where she was lying on the towel, and she turned to Dante. "Can you pick her up?"

He looked stiff.

"She's our daughter now," she said. "Yours as much as mine."

"Meaning not?" he asked, his tone hard.

She looked at him for a long moment, trying to gauge that statement. What it meant to him.

"No," she said, slowly. "Meaning she very much is."

"Blood matters," he said.

She narrowed her eyes and studied him. "Why do you think that?"

If he noticed her careful appraisal, he didn't acknowledge it. "Because."

"You think that blood is more important than caring for a child. That blood trumps love?"

"No. I don't suppose I thought of it that way."

"But you think it matters."

"Of course it does," he said. "After all, your father didn't offer the company to me, not until I was engaged to marry you."

"Did you expect him to?"

"He always says that I'm like a son to him," Dante said. "But it's not the same."

"It very much is," Minerva said. "He loves you."

"And I'm a brother to you?"

Her cheeks heated. "Of course you're not the same as my brother. But that's the problem. You never have been. Not to me. You too... Well, I hear tell that my brother's beautiful, and I suppose that I'm proud of him in that way that a sister is. But I don't see his beauty, not in that way. Yours I could never unsee."

"Did you really have a crush on me when you were young?"

"I'm still young," she sniffed. "And you're changing the subject."

"What, you want to turn the subject back to something that's upsetting you? I don't know very much about marriage, Minerva, but I know enough to know that I shouldn't aim to upset my wife."

"I was willing to put my life at risk for her," Minerva said. "I am willing to do that. I was willing to uproot my entire life for her. Tell me, do you think that that needs blood to be more intense? Is there anything more intense? I would fix everything in her life if I could. I would vanquish all of her enemies. All of them. I hate that she's been exposed to threats. I hate that someone would harm her. Please, tell me, Dante, if you think her biological father loves her more than I do."

"Enough," he said. "This is a useless fight. The concept of family... It's good she has you. That you're willing to do that. For my part, I offer what I can."

"They say blood is thicker than water," she said. "I know they say that. But in my opinion blood can be dangerous. Blood can stain. It is not about the blood in your veins. The heart pumps the blood, after all. Isn't the heart the most important thing?"

"No," he said. "The heart is not most important. It is your brain that will serve you well, Minerva. It is your brain that you need."

"Your brain?"

"Your brain is capable of great compassion. Of rationalizing what the safest and best thing is to do. Your brain was fully engaged, your sense of duty when it comes to humanity. To tell you the truth, I don't believe even blood creates a family."

"What holds my family together, then?" she asked.

He made an exasperated sound. "Your father has a strong sense of civic duty. Something that I will now employ, something I will pay back with Isabella."

"You think *civic duty* is what holds society together?" she asked incredulously. "That is the most depressing thing I have ever heard."

"Yes," he said. "I do."

"You think… Swiss Family Robinson survived and built a house on an island because of civic duty? Or did they… Did they put their hearts into it?"

"That's more than a clumsy metaphor and *Swiss Family Robinson* is fictional."

"We learn from fiction, don't we? To see ourselves? The world? Our hearts?"

"Our hearts want things that are bad for us, Minerva. Witness your friend and Carlo. Carlo is another prime example of people who have corrupt hearts. Tell me, what can we count on to guide us with evidence such as this?"

"Love," she said. And it was clear, simple and concise to her. That love was what separated these things. That love was what made people choose someone else over themselves. Time and time again.

"Love," he said, the word a sneer. "Do you know what my mother loved?" he said. "Drugs."

"I thought that your mother… I thought that she was a prostitute to help support you."

"She was a prostitute to help support her cocaine habit."

He looked out at the horizon. And there was something so bleak and desolate in his dark eyes that she felt wounded by it.

"Dante, I'm sure that she loved you."

He shook his head, his lip curling up into a sneer. "Do you want to know one of my most vivid memories of my mother?"

"Yes," she said, knowing for sure that she didn't, because she could sense that there was nothing but pain in his next words.

"One of my very first memories of my mother was on her last birthday. I was eight years old. But I already knew how to cook for myself. I already knew how to cook for us. I had taken the money that she kept in our cookie jar, and I took it to market. With that I bought all of this, and I bought cheese. I bought bread. Pasta. I bought a feast, because I wanted to celebrate her birthday. There was cake. We never had cake. But it was for her, so I felt that it was okay. And when she got home, do you know what she said to me?"

He looked at her, his dark gaze unwavering. "She said, *'You stupid boy.'* And then she slapped me across my face."

Minerva clutched at her chest, her heart nearly folding in on itself. "No," she whispered.

"Yes. She said that she was going to have to go out and earn more money on her back to buy what she really needed for her birthday. It wasn't dinner with me, just so you know. It was more of her drug. She loved that more than she ever loved me. She took care of me out of a sense of obligation, and this is where I come back to duty, because thank God she did. Otherwise, she might have left me somewhere to die. Instead…"

He cut off his words.

"Dante," she said. "I'm sorry. But you must know that's not… That's not how it's supposed to be. Not in a healthy family."

"Really? And tell me, Minerva, in your healthy family, how is your sense of who you are? How is your sense of self when compared to everyone else?"

"I can't help it I was born into a family of overachievers," she said.

"I suppose not. But I'm just saying. Your family is among the most loving I've ever known, and can you honestly tell me they haven't given you issues of some kind? Love doesn't erase all of the issues out there in the world."

"I never said it did," she said.

"No, but on some level I think you believe it might."

"Wouldn't it be a nice thing to believe?"

"I'm not sure where that would leave my life."

She nodded slowly. Then she rose up from where she was sitting and crossed to him, pressing her hand to his bare chest and stretching up on her toes, kissing him slowly. Usually when they came together, there was an urgency to it. He was extremely conscious of her inexperience, and it had taken her a while to figure out how she felt about that.

Because the first time he had been considerate, but he had treated her like she knew what she was doing.

He had a tendency now to treat her like glass.

But still, they didn't linger over these sorts of kisses. He braced his hand against her hip and held her as they did, and she felt warmth flood her body. An ache. A need that went beyond sexual. And when they parted she looked into his eyes, and she tried to see something. Anything. Caring. A connection.

She couldn't read it. She couldn't read him.

"Dante, you can have whatever life you want. You're a billionaire."

A small smile touched his lips and he brushed his thumb over her cheekbone. "Do you get all your ideas from books, Minerva? Or have you lived any of your own life at all?"

The words were said softly enough, but they were designed to pierce her chest.

They were designed to reinforce the fact that she was younger. That whatever she thought or felt, it would never be right, not in his eyes, because he knew more, had experienced more.

It wasn't fair.

And he knew it.

She turned away from him and went back and picked Isabella up. "It's fine," she said. "And yes, Dante, I have experienced things in life. You know, the death threats. Making the choice to be a mother to Isabella. And when I made that choice, by the way, I didn't make it thinking that it would be temporary. Thinking that all he would do was offer her base protection over her life. I knew that I was giving myself to her. To this. Maybe I understand more things than you think."

It was only when she had reached the relative safety and sanity of the house that she realized he had succeeded in derailing the conversation, even if she was the one who had left it on a good parting shot.

He was uncomfortable talking about family.

And given what his mother had done to him, she did

understand. But it had nothing to do with her or Isabella. And none of it did anything to soothe the longing inside her. For this to be real. He'd said that she was going to be his wife in truth, but he didn't mean it. Not in the way that she recognized it. He meant sex.

And the sex was lovely, she wouldn't pretend that it wasn't. But for her all it had done was open up a deeper desire inside her. It satisfied nothing.

Because there was only one aspect of them that was engaged in it. Or rather, one aspect of him. His body. Not his heart.

And she wanted…

She wanted it. His heart.

She was perilously close to being in love with her husband.

He saw her. Whether clothed or naked, on the beach or in the kitchen, their bedroom, he saw her. And she had spent a lifetime feeling very unseen.

He wanted her.

And most of all, he had pledged to protect her, and to protect Isabella.

He had been protecting her for years.

Picking her up when she scraped her knees. Rescuing her from humiliation on a dance floor.

Oh, yes, there was a lot to love about that man.

The realization made her gasp. Because she could think of nothing lonelier. Nothing sadder than a life spent loving someone passionately, pouring out your desire, your body, to them and getting a hollow facsimile in return.

She would love Isabella. And Isabella would love her back. And Dante would be her father.

He was right… He was right that with him she would

have something much better than Carlo. She wasn't being robbed of anything there.

And Dante could not withhold his heart from his daughter. Whatever he said, Minerva knew that. Isabella was a baby, and babies existed to be loved by those who cared for them. Those who were not violent criminals anyway. Which Dante was not.

She was another matter.

But she was always another matter.

And she had Isabella to consider, which meant she would have to remain another matter altogether.

And she would have to find a way to be fine with it.

Three mornings later Dante was informed that Carlo had been killed in a shootout with police. The members of his crime family, including the top boss, had all been taken into custody, as had three members of the police department who were on the payroll.

It was the largest such operation to be completed in years. Dante and his money were largely seen as being responsible.

But all Dante saw was an opportunity to get back to his real life. To get back to the real world.

And it was time.

He was tempted to forget himself here on this island with Minerva. Tempted to get lulled into a sense that life began and ended here. The white sand to the line of the crystal blue ocean.

The longer they were here, away from life, the easier it was to forget who he was. The easier it was to let Min fill his vision and forget that there was reality waiting for them both.

But he had work back in New York, and he had to see to those things. Had to remember who he was.

Minerva was in her room. It was strange to him that she had opted to keep her own bedroom, especially considering she slept in his bed every night. But her things were still in the white room by Isabella's. And she was holed up in there reading a book. He startled her when he pushed the door open. "Carlo is dead."

"He is?" She sat up, eyes wide, and there was a kind of glittering triumph in her expression. Then it softened. "You didn't..."

"I didn't. It happened when the police tried to take him into custody. There was nothing for it. But either way. You're safe."

"Does that mean we're going home?"

"Yes," he said. "We're going home." She let out a whoop, which surprised him, and leaped across the space, into his arms.

He stood there, unmoving for a moment, and then wrapped his arms around her.

He never knew quite what to do with her.

"I thought you liked it here," he said.

She separated from him. "I do," she said, her cheeks turning pink. "But..."

"Yes. It's rather isolated."

"Yes. It's just... As beautiful as it's been, I miss normal life. Isabella deserves normal."

"Well, you did marry a billionaire. Normal may not exactly be in the cards."

She laughed and shook her head. "Fine. I'll take your normal."

She smiled, and it tugged something in his chest. "We'll leave immediately."

"I guess I should get packed..."

"No need. Everything will be waiting for us when

we get to our home. And anything you need here will be sent."

"Oh."

"The pilot is already on his way."

They were in the sky only an hour later.

Minerva was beginning to seem agitated.

"Why are you picking at your fingernails?"

"I'm not," she said, pulling at her finger.

"You are." He put his hand over hers. "What are you doing?"

She stopped then. "Nothing."

"Something."

"We didn't discuss… Dante, I know that you have a terrible reputation for being a womanizer. And you… You treat me like I'm fragile. You treat me like you might break me when we're in bed."

He was taken aback by her frankness, but he let her go on.

"I don't know any kind of bedroom tricks. There are always magazine saying there are one hundred sex tips in there. I don't even think I know two." She wrinkled her nose. "Well, no. I do. I might know three. But even then, they're not very well developed. And it was one thing when we were on the island and there were no other women. But are you going to… Are you going to get tired of me?"

"We said vows," he said. "I will not violate them."

She wrinkled her nose. "That isn't answering my question."

"Didn't you want to know if I was going to be faithful?"

"Well, yes. But I also want to know if you're going to be *bored*."

"I can have the same concern, Minerva. You've only

been with one man. How do I know that you won't get resentful of that fact? That you won't want to try someone different. To experience variety."

"I won't," she said.

"Very confident. All the confidence of the inexperienced."

"No," she said. "It's that I had opportunity in my life, and I didn't take it. It took me all this time to realize it was because of you. Because of how I felt about you. That I... That I was attracted to you."

"Right. But now you know what it is to be with me. Perhaps the mystery is gone."

"It was never about mystery," she said.

"How about we simply both promise each other fidelity."

"Okay," she said softly.

And he could tell that he had done something wrong, but he wasn't certain what.

It was clear he had done another thing wrong when the plane began to touch down several hours later and Minerva let out a gasp. "Where are we?"

"I told you, we are going home."

"This is not home. This is... Manhattan."

"I live in Manhattan," he said.

"I don't," she said. "I live in San Diego."

"Not anymore," he said, feeling irritated now.

"You just assume that home would be your home."

"And you assume that home would be yours."

"Well... Well..."

"And I am the one with the private jet, so really, I was the only one that wasn't making assumptions, but had charted a course. If I were you, I would have checked if I was uncertain."

"I was not uncertain!"

"Well, clearly you should have been."

She huffed inelegantly. "Dante, this isn't going to work if you just think you can run around making all the decisions for me."

"I didn't make a decision for you. You didn't ask what decision was being made."

"You're infuriating. Somehow, I forgot that on the island. It was all the kissing."

"Well. I am good at kissing, even though I am infuriating."

"I miss my *family*," she said.

He didn't know why, but that word family caught him in his chest just then.

But of course she did. She missed Robert and Maximus, Violet and Elizabeth.

They were her family.

They were her blood.

"We will go and visit," he said. "And I promise you I will look into buying a home there. But my business is largely conducted out of Manhattan, and that is where we will be."

"And when you join with my father?"

"I imagine it won't change. As long as he is running things on the West Coast, I will be of more use to him here."

"I don't want to live in New York," she said, frowning deeply.

"You have something against it?" He looked out the window at the gray. Gray sea. Gray skyline.

"Please," she said. "It snows here."

"It's not like snow is imminent," he said.

"It's so busy."

"Wait to pass judgment until you've seen our home."

She kept her peace, at his request, and she only stared

wide-eyed out the car window as they drove through the streets of Manhattan heading toward his penthouse apartment.

Then, she continued to be silent as they migrated to the building and went up in the gold elevator that carried them to the very top of the high-rise.

"This does not seem like a very good place to raise a child," she said.

"We are not in the penthouse yet," he said.

"We're in the elevator. It's adjacent."

"You must reserve your opinion until you see it."

"I mustn't *do anything*," she said, sounding crabby.

"You know, *cara*," he said, "many people are afraid of me."

"I suppose those people don't have any experience of you dancing with them to spare you humiliation at a party."

"Your father clearly expected it."

She bared her teeth, and he would have been amused by her show of anger if he weren't...compelled. And he didn't know what he felt compelled to do or why. She reached into places inside of him and...did that thing that Min did.

She couldn't leave well enough alone, not ever.

"Fine, then," she said. "I suppose those people also don't have experience of them marrying them so that you can protect a baby."

"That isn't the only reason I married you."

"It isn't?"

"No. I did want a share in your father's business."

He knew that that was unkind. He knew that it was the worst thing to say to her, and yet he'd said it anyway. Her entire frame sagged. But then, the doors to the elevator slid open and it revealed the grand penthouse. Dark, marble floors and a grand view of Central Park.

"Those windows don't open, do they?"

"No," he said.

"It's very strange being so high up."

"You act like a country mouse. You were raised in California."

"Yes. And San Diego is the city. But not like this. This is *The City*."

"Yes. That's why I like it." Perhaps *like* was a strong word, but he appreciated the way that New York effectively drowned out his thoughts and memories. It was like a comforting white noise that followed you everywhere you went. So busy, so consumed with its own self, that it left you little time to reflect.

"I won't like it," she said resolutely.

"You've been here many times, and you do like New York."

"To visit," she said. "I love to see the Christmas tree in Rockefeller Center. And I love tea. Everywhere. I love the museums. But I've never wanted to live here."

"Isn't it a shame, then," he said, drawing the words out, "that you married me?"

Furious eyes met his. "I'm beginning to think so."

A muscle in his cheek ticked. "Do you wish to keep your own room here?"

"Yes," she returned.

He gritted his teeth. "Fine. You will find it is the second door on the left, and I believe clothes have been moved in for you."

"You knew that I wanted my own room."

"You kept one on the island."

A strange wave passed between them, a question that she didn't ask, and one that he didn't press.

"I'm going into my office."

"Where is that? Which room?"

"Not an office here. I must go into the office. We were gone for so long, and before that I was already in San Diego. Everything has been handled in my absence, but I need to make an appearance."

"You just got here."

"Yes. But you are in New York. I'm sure that you can find something to occupy yourself."

The man he'd been on the island wasn't the man he was in truth, and the sooner Minerva learned that the better.

There was no place for tenderness or pity inside him. No place for hope.

He knew that those things only brought about destruction. And he would never allow himself to be destroyed again.

And without a backward glance, Dante walked back out of the penthouse, leaving Isabella and Minerva behind him.

CHAPTER TWELVE

THEY WERE IN a strange standoff that Minerva couldn't quite decode. She had slept in her bedroom for the last three nights, and he hadn't come to her. On the island sex was how they'd communicated. And maybe that wasn't healthy, but it had provided some sort of closeness at least.

This confirmed that her decision to ambush him about the sex on the plane was valid. She'd had the sense if she didn't say it there, she wouldn't have the chance.

Almost as if she knew that once they were in this great gray city it would all be changed.

It was.

And she was oppressed by the gray. Emotionally and all around them. Even the view of Central Park felt gray.

And maybe out of sheer stubbornness she had not gone out of the apartment to explore the city. He was right, it was New York and there were endless things to do. But Isabella was still small, and Minerva was conscious of the various illnesses that lurked out there on every park bench, handrail and shopping cart.

At least, that was what she told herself.

And she did not allow herself to think that maybe she was just being stubborn.

That she was refusing to accept her new life out of sheer spite. Because she didn't want to be in this.

And why? She wasn't entirely sure.

It wasn't like she hadn't left home before. She had. On her grand adventure to Rome—which had ended up containing a little bit of disaster.

She swallowed hard.

Mostly, she was a little bit grateful for this strange coolness between them.

It had allowed her some time to regroup.

On the island she had been convinced that she was in love with him. Or at least, mostly in love with him. Here, she could see that it had been a combination of sun and sex. Here, she could see that she was inexperienced, and was responding to him in that way.

That she had been afraid of leaving the island in part because she had known that it would affect a change in their relationship.

That losing the cocoon of intimacy that had surrounded them there would thrust them back into the real world, and she would have to contend with the fact that marriage vows neither of them had particularly meant would not create an unbreakable bond.

Neither would they create feelings where they didn't exist. At least, not on his hand.

But it was fine. Because her feelings had been magnified.

She had to accept that she had a crush on Dante, and now that she was working it out she had a bit of clarity.

When he returned home that night, his expression was stern. "Three dresses are being sent, and the nanny will be here shortly."

"Nanny?"

"Yes. The nanny that you were using back in San

Diego is on a plane on her way here. We have an engagement to go to tonight."

"We do?"

"Yes. A gala. As I didn't know if I would be back in the city I hadn't committed to it, but as it is, it's a connection that your father would very much like me to make. It is in the interest of King, and given that, it is important that you come with me."

"So, my father has been in touch with you? He hasn't been in touch with me." She could have easily been in touch with her family. But she was in high avoidance mode. Feeling fragile and not wanting to deal with the realities of her family, now that she married and slept with Dante, and she didn't want to hear anything about the news reports on them either.

She wanted to hide in this apartment. And she wanted to be home.

She didn't make any sense even to herself.

And she was far too wrung out to care.

"We had business to discuss."

"Well. I'm glad to know business is so important." She felt wholly shunted off to the side, which wasn't fair at all. She didn't care.

"Minerva," he said. "Being my wife is a role. I apologize if you didn't realize that, but you took the vows. You needed me to fulfill my end of the brief, and I have done it. Additionally, I am acting as Isabella's father."

"You're not acting as her father. You are her father."

For the first time she was starting to worry he might not bond with her. She'd taken his reluctance as a typical reaction from a man who had no experience with babies. Now she was a bit concerned about the distance. Which was beginning to seem resolute.

"Fine," he said. "According to the paperwork that we will soon process, I am her father."

The distance in those words kicked against Minerva's heart. "Yes," she said drily.

"And you are my wife. What I need from a wife is someone to come to events on my arm and look appropriately adoring at me. I need you to help enhance my image. I most particularly need you to do this as I act on behalf of King. It would not do for me to be seeing to this business and having you looking dour beside me. You know what people would say."

"The truth? That it's a marriage of convenience?"

"It is a decidedly inconvenient marriage," he said. "And I would like it to be more convenient."

"It didn't seem so inconvenient to you when you had sex on tap."

"Who turned the tap off?"

"I was under the impression it was mutual."

She sniffed off to her room in a huff and fed Isabella. Then, when the dresses arrived, so did the nanny, and she was overjoyed to be reunited with the baby.

Minerva felt slightly annoyed by it, but she was happy that Isabella would be with someone familiar.

The dresses were beautiful. Far too beautiful for her. There was a note pinned to one of them. From Violet.

Minerva nearly burst into tears, and she picked up her phone and dialed her sister's number. "The dresses are wonderful," she said.

She couldn't put on a front, not now. She didn't have the strength to. Violet had breached her hiding place, and she couldn't be angry. She wanted to connect to someone too badly.

"What's wrong?" Violet asked.

"It's a disaster," Minerva said. "We're at each other's throats. He's not speaking to me hardly at all and he's not… Well, he's not anything and I miss him and I shouldn't. It's not fair! I didn't ask for this part of it!"

"I don't understand…"

The whole story came pouring out of Minerva. She didn't want secrets between herself and her sister. She desperately needed an ally, and whatever issues she had with Violet were her own. Her own smallness. Her own feelings of inadequacy.

"Wow," Violet said. "I mean… Minerva," she said. "That is the bravest thing I've ever heard of."

She sniffed, sitting on the edge of the bed, feeling worn down. Brave was the last thing she felt. "I don't know if I was very brave."

"Yes, you were. Why do you have such a hard time taking credit for the good things that you do?"

She picked at the velvet fabric on the duvet cover. "Because they're nothing. Nothing compared to the kind of things that you and Maximus do."

"I manufacture makeup," Violet said drily. "And I sell it very effectively. But I've never saved anyone's life." Minerva was distinctly uncomfortable with that statement.

"You're amazing," Minerva said. "Don't minimize it."

"We are talking about *you*," Violet said. "And you can't even handle a compliment when you're the topic of conversation."

"Vi," Minerva said. "You shouldn't have to talk yourself down to try and make me feel better."

"I'm not," Violet said. "Trust me, Minerva, my sense of self is pretty well developed. But you're clearly lacking in perspective."

"I just…" Min fell onto her back and gazed up at the ceiling. Even from this perspective the light seemed gray.

"He doesn't love me. He never even slept with me. I mean…before all this started."

"You have now." It was more of a confirmation request than a question.

"Yes," Minerva admitted. "I did have feelings for him. I mean, like a crush. You remember what he did for me at Dad's party."

"Yes. When that snot-nosed Bradley called you an ugly duckling on the dance floor?"

"Yes. I… He rescued me. And I think in my head it became something. I hid it, deep down, but not far enough and when I needed help he was the one I thought of. I know that moment didn't make him…want me. But since then… We've been married, you know? I thought maybe he had some kind of attachment to me but I don't know if he has an attachment to anyone or anything."

"What about you?" Violet asked.

"What about me?"

"Do you feel something for him? I mean, more than your crush."

"Well… Who wouldn't?"

"A lot of people. He's quite difficult. That's why even though I also had a crush on him at one point I let it go a long time ago. I prefer men who are a little bit less… *hard.*"

"He is hard. But I think he's good. He had a hard life, but he wants to do the right thing, in spite of the fact that I don't think anyone has ever shown him what the right thing is. Well, anyone except Dad. But he's convinced that he's not… Really a part of our family."

"Well, he is now. By marriage at the very least."

"That might be the only thing he really likes about me."

"I don't think so."

Unspoken between them was the truth that if he really wanted that, he would have married Violet. Not just because she was more beautiful, but she was older. It made more sense. In just about every way.

"Well. It's an asset. He really only agreed to the marriage because he wanted to help me. And now… We're married. So he's making the most of it. At least from a business standpoint."

"And you love him?" Violet pressed.

"No," she said, the denial kicking hard against her chest. "I'm not that silly. I'm not. I know that he's not ever going to feel that way about me. I think we can have a partnership, but I just have to figure it out…"

"You're not cut out for halfway, Minerva. That's your problem. You keep hiding yourself because you're afraid that you can't measure up to Maximus and me, but nobody ever asked you to. I'm not like Maximus. It would be easy for me to say that what I do is superficial. He bails people out of pretty terrible situations. And I'm sure that he would tell you sometimes he feels guilty about the people that he rehabilitates images for, since they oftentimes don't deserve it. But we do what we do, and we are who we are. Whoever you're destined to be… That's you. And you were never meant to live in shadows or to be quiet. And that's why you just… Shrink in on yourself altogether. Because if you speak out, you know it's going to be loud. And if you love, you know it's going to be big. That's good. It's not a bad thing."

Sure, it was easy for Violet to say. Minerva would be the one left with a fatally broken heart.

"You should wear the red dress," Violet said.

"Red?" Minerva questioned. "But I'll be so… Conspicuous."

"Be conspicuous, Min. You've been hiding in books,

in the garden, behind that horrible mean-kid stuff that happened to you in high school. They don't get to decide who you are, you do. Isn't it time that you took center stage?"

"I have done that multiple times over the last few weeks," Minerva pointed out. "First of all at your product launch. Second of all at the engagement party, then at the wedding…"

"And you did it for Isabella. Do something for yourself. Is that so wrong?"

"Yes," Minerva said. "Because I'm not… I'm just me."

"Yes, you're just you. And you is pretty amazing. Be kinder to her."

"I am being kind to her. I'm hiding away from the potential broken heart."

"No. You're hiding away from life. You let all that stuff get in your head. You let yourself think that you were less than we are."

"I'm not as pretty."

"That's a lie. It's all about how you present yourself. And there's nothing wrong with being you. There's nothing wrong with not being flashy. I can't be anything else. I have to wander around with a pound of my product on my face all the time."

"I would look silly that way."

"Yes. You would. Not because you aren't beautiful, but because it isn't you. Different is fine. Different is good. But don't accept less."

"So what should I do? Put on the red dress and demand that he love me?" The very idea made her skin crawl.

She'd cared about a boy once, and she'd thought he'd cared too. Instead he'd humiliated her on a dance floor.

"Yes. Have you ever considered demanding that he

love you? Because it might not be the worst thing in the world."

"Or it might be," Minerva said darkly.

"Or it might not be."

"I don't even know if I love him." But she was beginning to accept that that was a lie.

"Then I guess the question is… Are you going to stay with him even if you don't love him?" Violet asked.

"He can be Isabella's father…"

"So what? Set her aside for a second. Or, don't even set her aside. Would it be good for her to watch you live with someone you're miserable with? And who cares about Dad and Dante and their business thing? They can work that out on their own. It's not up to you, Minerva. If you love him, then you should demand more. If you don't love him, then you should demand more too."

"When did you become an expert on love?"

"I'm not." Violet's denial was vehement. "This isn't about knowing anything about love. But I do know a little bit about life. I know that if you are successful people are going to come after you, and it's easy to get caught up in trying to please everyone. No matter how independent and strong someone seems. You're caught up in this idea that you're not special, and I think because of that you work too hard to please everyone around you. And you don't work hard enough at pleasing yourself."

"The red dress?"

"Whatever makes you happy. Not what you think will make him happy, or even me happy. And not what you think you should wear. What do you want to wear?"

She got off the phone with her sister and she looked at the dresses again.

The red one.

She really did want to wear the red one. And why

wasn't she wearing it? Because a boy had embarrassed her four years ago? Because she'd let the kids at school make her feel like she was ugly, like her family was the only interesting thing about her?

Because she'd chosen to get lost in the quiet nooks and crannies of her home when she was a child, lived in books, lived in her head, and then wondered why she felt left behind sometimes?

She wasn't like everyone else. But did that mean there was something wrong with her? Or did it just mean she was her?

Slowly, and with great care, she took the dress out of the bag and took it off the hanger.

She slid the glorious fabric over her body. It was slinky and perfect, molding to the curves that she had, making the most of her figure.

She worked on her hair, and her makeup, employing tips from videos that Violet had posted online.

She didn't do them quite like Violet. She did them like herself. And when she was finished, she felt…beautiful.

She felt like she was stepping out into the spotlight. Into something new and frightening. And she didn't know why it should seem that way. Because it wasn't as if any of this centered on her. Not really.

Except it felt like it did.

When she emerged in the living room, Dante was standing there looking beautiful in a suit, a crisp white shirt and a black jacket that conformed perfectly to his masculine physique. His dark eyes were unreadable, and passive as they took her in. "Are you ready?"

Her kneejerk response was to ask if she looked ready. To ask him why that was even a question. If there was something wrong with what she had chosen. But she knew that she looked amazing, and she didn't need to be insecure. She didn't need to question anything.

She lifted her head and squared her shoulders. "Yes," she said. "I'm ready."

CHAPTER THIRTEEN

Dante couldn't keep his eyes off Minerva. She was stunning in red. Her lips were the same crimson color to match, her eyeliner dark and winged. Her green eyes seemed like emeralds tonight. Had he ever thought that she was anything less than stunning? Had he ever thought that she was somehow the less beautiful King?

He couldn't even think of her as one of them, not now. She was set apart.

Glorious and otherworldly, because it all seemed transcendent of here and now. It wasn't just beauty for the eyes. He could breathe it in. Taste it. Feel it settle over his bones.

And yet, there was something about this beauty that felt like a challenge. It made him hesitant to touch her, and Dante was never hesitant.

But when they got out of the limo in front of the museum where the gala was being held, he pressed his hand against her lower back, a show of possession before the two of them walked up the stairs and made their way into the venue.

He didn't need to check in at the door, because everyone recognized him by face alone. At first, he thought Minerva might shrink against his side, but instead she stood proud. And when he introduced her as his wife, the mother of his child, she smiled and shook hands with each person with extreme confidence.

He didn't know what had possessed her this evening, but it was doing a very fine job.

After a time, music began to play and the guests filtered out onto a dance floor. Minerva saw this, and her eyes went wide, then she blinked rapidly. He knew just what she was thinking of.

That night four years ago.

He had seen the whole thing. And he had lied to her when he'd said that her father put him up to anything.

He had watched that boy take her out onto the dance floor, lean in and whisper something in her ear. And then he had watched as she crumpled.

And he had taken pictures. Wrapped his arm around her shoulder, taken a selfie with a tear-streaked Minerva and himself.

And that was when Dante had stepped in.

"I have been waiting to dance with you all evening, Ms. King."

And though he knew Minerva hadn't seen it, the boy had paled. And he had looked... Perhaps like he thought he had made a grave mistake.

She had felt slight and bony to him as he held her. Her body had changed quite a bit since then.

He had felt... Protective of her at that time. Like when he had helped her up off the ground when she had been much younger, her knee skinned.

He had always wanted to protect Minerva.

And now she had come into his sphere as his wife, and the fact of the matter was there was no way for him to protect her from himself.

But they were here.

And she was beautiful.

So they might as well dance.

"Would you like to dance with me? And no, before you ask, I have no designs to humiliate you."

A small smile touched her lips. "Okay. If you really want to."

He smiled in return, because he couldn't help himself, and he took her out to the center of the dance floor, holding her close and spinning her. Then he drew her back to his chest. She looked up at him, the smile on her face brilliant.

It was a strange thing, to be with Minerva apart from the baby. Without her present as a clear and obvious reason why the two of them were together. Yes, they had spent time alone together, but it had all been in service of Isabella.

It had nothing to do with a farce. There was no reason for a farce anymore.

He could let them go. They would be safe.

For some reason, the idea filled him with a hollow kind of terror, and he couldn't account for why.

He drew her close, leaned in and whispered in her ear. "What did he say to you? That night at your father's party."

Her eyes went misty. "Do we have to talk about that?"

It still bothered her. It was hard for him to imagine that. He'd lived through poverty. Loss and pain. And it wasn't so much that he didn't think people like her—people who lived in comfort and relative ease—didn't also feel pain for the things in their lives. It was simply that of all the things he'd ever cared about, the good opinion of others wasn't often one of them.

Robert, he cared about his opinion because the man had changed his life.

But in general, he'd never… He'd been thrust into private school with boys who had been privileged and cosseted all their lives. They'd either found Dante to be a source of fascination, or something quite beneath them.

He hadn't care for either. But he hadn't cared about it, either.

He'd had trouble connecting. The only person who had ever mattered to him was Maximus. Their friendship had been unsteady at first, Maximus clearly not understanding why his father had ever cared much about the Roman urchin he'd pulled off the streets.

Eventually, slowly, rooming together at boarding school had brought them closer together. Dante had told Maximus about holding his father at gunpoint and he knew then it would either break their bond or solidify it forever.

Maximus had nodded and said: "You do what you have to, I guess."

And so, solidified their bond had been.

Whatever anyone else thought hadn't mattered. Minerva, though, was still clearly haunted by her humiliation.

Witnessing that had enraged him, and it bothered him she was still hurt.

That no man had stepped in to heal that wound.

You're her husband. The only one she'll have.

It was a profoundly depressing realization.

For *her*.

Another man might have eased this pain already, but he had not. Suddenly he found that he did want it. More than anything.

"I want to know," he said.

"He… He just said that I was stupid if I thought he really wanted to be here with me. He just wanted to be at the party. Wanted to see the house. Being my date was a dare. What he really wanted was a chance to see my sister."

"I see," Dante said. "What is more beautiful? A ruby or an emerald?"

"I don't understand."

"What's more beautiful, a tropical island or a desolate mountain?"

"They're both beautiful," she said. "Just different."

He nodded slowly. "Exactly. There are some things you cannot compare, Minerva, because they are not alike. One is not less. You cannot compare yourself to Violet. She's beautiful. She's successful. I don't want her. I do want you," he said, his voice rough. "Because the truth of the matter is, whether an emerald or ruby are equal in beauty, or a tropical island or a mountain-top are both perfect in their natural splendor, there is always one that a man prefers. And it has nothing to do with how it looks, not really. But what calls to his soul. And in this case, to my body. That's you. I cannot explain it. But it is."

"You don't sound very happy about it."

"I'm not. I was very happy to go through my life never having been bewitched, Minerva, and finding myself held in thrall by a woman that I have known for more than half my life is a very strange thing. I am not sure how it happened. This is not the first time we danced, but it is not the same as that first time."

"But still, when the pictures get published in the paper I imagine the headlines will be the same."

"I don't think so," he said. "But even then, what do you believe about yourself? What you know to be true, or what a bunch of strangers say about you?"

"I don't know," she said. "But... I do like what you said about me. I suppose, even if I can't win with strangers, I can content myself to have nice things said by you. Does this mean that we are going to be... Nicer to each other again?"

"I hope I was never unkind to you."

"I felt lonely."

"I don't know how to be a husband," he said.

"You were doing a pretty good job a minute ago."

"The last thing I want in this world is to hurt you, Minerva. I have done my best to protect you when I could. I owe a great debt to your father for all that he did for me. I would never want to harm what was most precious to him."

"Is that the only reason you don't want to hurt me?"

"No," he confirmed. "But that doesn't mean I won't. You have to be careful with men like me."

"You keep saying that. But the man that you are for the rest of the world... He's not the man that I've seen."

"You have such faith in me, Min, and I fear it is misplaced."

"I don't think so," she said, smoothing her hand up his chest.

His body reacted. Violently.

He pushed her back, the motion reflexive. Like he'd been burned.

"Sorry," he said. "I see David Carmichael back there." Thankfully, that was true. "Your father wished for me to speak with him before we leave."

"Oh...okay."

He took her hand and led her from the dance floor and was summarily stopped by a floppy-haired blond man in a suit that looked intentionally askew. It took him a moment, but he recognized him.

Chad Rothschild. A spoiled asshole he knew from his years in boarding school. Someone who had been friends with Maximus until Dante. Then he'd made an ass of himself pretty routinely all the years since.

"Dante," he said. "What a surprise to see you here."

To see he wasn't back in the gutter, Dante imagined. Though Chad had to know he was not, as his reputation was legend. Chad's, on the other hand, consisted of many instances where he'd had to say, *But my father's a lawyer.*

"I don't see why it should be," Dante said. "This is, after all, where I do business. I am not sure what it is you do."

"Investments." A code for nothing. Chad's eyes flickered over Minerva. "Well, your ugly duckling certainly cleans up well."

"Excuse me?" Dante asked.

He felt Minerva begin to tremble then. "I'm teasing. But surely you've seen that old picture of the two of you. I have to hand it to you, you seemed quite chummy with Maximus in school. I had no idea you were messing with his sister."

Dante's lip curled. "I was not."

"If I were going to do that it would have been the other one."

"I'm sorry," Dante said. "Am I having a stroke? Are we back in boarding school?"

Chad kept on as if he hadn't heard the warning buried in each of the words Dante had just spoken. "She's not exactly the fabled beauty of the King clan, but I suppose if you have access to Robert King's millions and influence you're going to take what you can get. Though I thought that your own wealth exceeded that."

"My wealth is not in question. Neither is the beauty of my wife. I think it's apparent to all here that she is the most beautiful woman in the room."

"Undoubtedly, she is compelling," Chad said. "But I'm surprised you didn't marry her sister instead."

Dante saw red. And not just the red of Minerva's dress. A red haze of rage covered his vision. But Minerva's gentle hand on his arm stopped him.

"I appreciate that money is the only reason you can think that someone might marry you," Minerva said. "But that isn't the way it is for everyone. I care about Dante. We have a child together. I care about him more than anyone will likely care for you unless you do something to fix your repellent personality. Undoubtedly, someone will marry you for your money. But if I were you I would aim for more. It's quite sad."

And with her head held high, Minerva released her hold on Dante, and began to walk away. Dante went after her.

"What he said…"

"It's what people think," Minerva said.

"It doesn't matter what anyone thinks."

"No," she said. "It doesn't. Not really. It matters what I think. And the problem is that I believed the same thing for far too long."

He grabbed her arm and dragged her into a courtyard, away from the crowd. Away from prying eyes. And then he pinned her against the wall, his hand on her neck. "You incite me to madness," he growled. "No one else ever has. What he said… There is no reason for it. And he is wrong."

She touched his face. "But you didn't choose to marry me."

"Does that matter?"

"It always will to some people."

He arched his hips forward, letting her feel the effect that she had on him. "Does this feel like a choice to you?"

"No," she said. "I think even that you feel somewhat angrily."

He released his hold on her. Because she wasn't wrong. He hadn't chosen to feel what he did for her. It rearranged things inside him, and he didn't like it. He couldn't find where he had put his resolve, his reserve. He couldn't find himself at all. And he found it nearly unbearable. But it was no more unbearable than spending nights in separate rooms.

That he could truly no longer endure.

"We should leave," Dante said.

"Don't you have a business deal to make?"

"I will make it later. And I will make it without using you as a pawn. I will not subject you to more censure and speculation."

"Dante…"

"Your father will understand. And if he doesn't… Well. That's hardly my problem."

He had to get out of here. Before he did something they would both regret. Either to Chad or to her.

He felt… At the end of himself. And he didn't know what Minerva had done to him to make him feel this way.

He had no way to correct course, because he couldn't understand where the wrong turn had come. Heart pounding, he grabbed her hand and made his way toward the exit. He sent his driver a text, and the limo met them outside.

"Drive around the block until I tell you to stop," Dante said.

When they tumbled into the back of the cab, he grabbed her, kissing her, hard and deep, pouring all of his anger, his frustration and confusion into the kiss.

He didn't do fear.

He didn't do confusion. He was above it. Beyond it. He had ascended in life, and he refused to be dragged back there. Certainly not at the delicate hands of Minerva.

He didn't need anyone.

He didn't need anything. He had learned long ago that he had to depend only on himself to survive. That he could not expect anything from anyone. Simply because he had received kindness from Robert King didn't mean that he could come to expect it from anyone else.

He didn't even take it for granted from Robert.

And then there was Minerva. For whom everything was so simple. Isabella had needed her, and so she had made herself available.

She claimed that she knew she didn't want another man, ever, in spite of the fact that she had no other experience of sex, and couldn't possibly understand what she might truly want in a few years.

No, for her everything was so straightforward. So simple.

And he wanted to…punish her for that. Something in him did.

So he kissed her. And it wasn't a kind kiss. Wasn't a nice kiss. Wasn't infused with the kind of gentleness that he had tried to inject into all the lovemaking on the island after he had discovered that she'd been a virgin their first time together.

Her dress was exquisite, beautiful. Off the shoulder and clinging to her curves just so. He tore it down, revealing her breasts, their gorgeous, rosy tips, to his inspection.

She was perfection, was Minerva, and that man who had dared to make commentary on her beauty deserved no thought from her.

Even in his anger, anger that was unwieldy and reserved for any target in his path right now, he could not deny her beauty.

Her beauty was the only thing that made sense.

Because nothing else did.

Nothing else felt like him.

On the heels of that thought came another one, far more disturbing.

That he wasn't sure exactly what him was.

A boy who had tried to throw a birthday party for his mother. A boy who had found her dead the next morning of an overdose and had held her body and cried for hours. Afraid to leave her. Afraid that if he didn't no one would ever come.

The boy who had held the gun to Robert King's head.

The one who had taken his education and transformed it into a billion-dollar industry.

The one who was here now in the back of the limousine with Minerva, kissing her as though she were oxygen and he would die without her.

None of it felt real.

Except her hands. Her mouth. The physical sensation of touching her, holding her.

That was real.

He wondered which piece of her was real.

The little girl who had run around on the estate and fallen out of trees, skinning her knees and terrifying her mother.

The dreamy teenager with her nose stuck in a book.

The brave tigress who had demanded marriage to protect her cub.

The woman in his arms now.

Were they all every piece of those things?

And how did they bring them together?

Was it even wise to do so?

All those questions burned away in his consciousness as Minerva kissed him back. As her hands went to his tie, loosening it and undoing the buttons there. He batted those hands away.

He leaned down, taking one pert nipple between his lips and sucking it in deep.

She gasped, arching against him. But she wouldn't hold still, and her hands were skimming over him. He grabbed hold of her arms and pinned them to her sides, holding her still as he continued to lavish attention on her breasts.

He had to have the control here. She couldn't.

"Dante… Your driver can't…"

"Soundproof," he said.

"You told him to drive until you asked him not to."

"Undoubtedly he knows," Dante said. "But why should I be ashamed? Why should I be ashamed that I can't keep my hands off you? That I need to have you now. That I cannot wait until we are safely ensconced in the penthouse."

He was asking himself that question as much as he was asking her.

"Why should I be ashamed of you?" he said, their eyes meeting. He pulled her dress down as far as he could, until he met resistance at her hips. Then he moved down her body, grabbing hold of the hem of her skirt and pushing it upward. He exposed her legs, grabbed the center of her panties and swept them aside, exposing the heart of her. "How could I ever be ashamed of you?"

He pressed his fingers down against her, spreading her wide, then leaning in to taste her. Deep and lavish and long.

She tasted like Minerva. Amazing how distinct that had become to him. Unmistakable. This woman.

This woman.

One who had known more versions of him than any other woman he had ever taken as a lover.

But she was more than a lover.

More than his friend's sister, that was for damn sure. She was his *wife*.

He growled, his ministrations on her body intensifying, surging forward, his hands joining in with his mouth as he pleasured her. As he pushed her to new heights. As he kept at her until she cried out. Until she pulsed with pleasure, her orgasm crashing over her, causing her to shake and shudder out his name.

After that, he couldn't wait anymore. Couldn't wait to join himself to her. He needed her. And he didn't want to admit to need. It was anathema to him. This feeling in his chest. The sense that he no longer belonged to himself.

That somewhere along the line he had lost some of himself in her.

But he couldn't stop himself either.

No. All he could do was take control.

"Up here, sweetheart," he said, lifting her and then turning her so that she was facing away from him, her face to the window, to the cars that were passing them by.

"Dante…"

"No one can see," he said. "The windows are tinted."

"Oh," she said. And he wondered if that was what she was even asking him about. Or if there was something about this that bothered her.

It wasn't up to her.

"I'm going to take you like this," he said, his voice rough.

He undid the closure on his pants and freed himself, pressing the blunt head of his arousal to the entrance of her body. Sliding into her was like coming home. She was perfect. In this, they were perfect. This was right, it was good. Because she needed him. This wasn't simply his wild need. No, she was right there with him. And that made him feel powerful. That reminded him that he was the one in control. Not her.

He plunged into her, and she gasped, arching against him. And he gripped her hips, slamming her back against him. She whimpered, her face pressed against the window.

"Dante," she whispered.

Over and over she said his name as he drove himself home. Until she was sobbing his name. Until she couldn't control herself at all.

Until he felt like he had fixed some of what had gone wrong inside him.

He knew this. And he knew who he was.

This was only sex. That was all.

She was beautiful, so of course she appealed to him. But that was all. It was all.

He repeated that himself, over and over again. She might have been any beautiful woman.

But then she looked back over her shoulder and the light from the neon that flashed on the buildings outside illuminated her face. Those green eyes.

And he knew it could only be her. Minerva.

She began to shake. Her climax taking her over.

"Dante," she said, whispering his name one more time.

He clenched his teeth shut to keep from saying hers.

But his orgasm consumed him, grabbed him by the throat and shook him.

Minerva.

Her name echoed inside him, but he refused to give it voice. He refused. But the deep, physical need came for him all the same, and he was spent, destroyed in the aftermath of his release. Splintered.

Except he was coming to realize that the splinter wasn't new.

Something had broken in him indefinably when he was young. And he had no earthly idea what could be done about it. He had the feeling that the answer was contained somewhere in her. He rejected that. And he pulled away.

He was Dante Fiori. And whatever he wanted, he could have. Whatever he needed was contained inside himself. He did not need anyone else. Least of all his friend's little sister.

He straightened in the limo. "Fix your clothes," he said.

She looked at him with wide eyes, but she complied. Then he lowered the window between himself and the driver. "You can take us home now."

He felt very much like he had broken something. But he could not quite put his finger on what.

And he could not give a reason for why it bothered him at all.

CHAPTER FOURTEEN

MINERVA HAD TAKEN herself to her bed and cried herself to sleep after she and Dante had gotten home.

She hadn't wanted him to be quite so careful with her sexually as he had begun to be, but she hadn't wanted that either.

It had been physically wonderful. It had left her feeling emotionally hollow.

He had used that position to distance her from him. And when she had looked behind her and established a connection with him, he had been very apparently angry.

She wrapped her arms around herself and looked out at Central Park. It was so cold outside.

She didn't actually know if it was cold. She hadn't checked. She hadn't been outside and she hadn't looked at anything to see what the temperature actually was.

But she assumed that it was. Because of all that gray.

Maybe the gray was inside her. Because if she stopped staring at it all like one big chunk, she could see the grass, she could see the trees.

But somehow, she couldn't feel them.

She was upset. And she supposed she didn't have anyone to blame but herself.

Last night had been a perfect opportunity for her to tell Dante how she felt.

After all, she hadn't hesitated to tell Chad how she felt.

But then, even though she had stood up for herself in the moment, she had also felt small when he had said those things. Because they echoed inside her.

Because they played at certain insecurities that she had no matter that she had put on a red dress. When it came to mothering Isabella, her confidence had grown.

When it came to other areas of herself… She was still a work in progress.

She sighed heavily, and went to check on Isabella, who was kicking happily in her crib.

She picked her up, and set her in a swing out in the living room so she could gaze out at the park too.

She had a feeling that Isabella didn't particularly care.

She should be happier. There was no threat on Isabella's life. The paperwork for the adoption was very nearly finished. Everything was easier because of Dante's money.

Her father had money, so it wasn't as though she didn't know that things were easier when you had it. It was just that Dante wielded his with authority and power, and even when it came to the workings of the upper class, Dante seemed to command a greater amount of attention than those around him.

He was one of those men. Legendary. Whispered about in every room he entered.

And she had been around him all her life.

He had a great impact on her, even with all that familiarity.

She almost felt sorry for women who hadn't had such long exposure to him.

He was devastating even with it.

Of course, it was more than just physical devastation that she experienced when she looked at him.

She was in the grips of soul-deep devastation. She had no idea what to do with it.

She sighed heavily and turned to the laptop that was sitting on the marble island that separated the kitchen from the living room. She pulled up a homepage, and much to her surprise saw her face staring back at her from the society pages.

She had a triumphant smirk on her face, and she was standing in front of Dante, who was left slightly blurred.

Fiori's New Wife Unleashes Fury at Gala

She read on, and saw that the article described in great detail the way that she had flayed that ridiculous man the night before. The article concluded that she had been wrongly overlooked all this time, because she was clearly much more interesting than anyone had given her credit for.

She stared at the woman there in that picture. She looked strong. She looked confident.

Her phone buzzed and she looked down at it.

You wore the red.

Her sister Violet's text of triumph made something resonate in her chest.

She had.

And she had come out on top.

Except…

Still not with Dante.

Well. She was the only person that could fix that.

Minerva King had allowed herself to be leased for far too long.

It was finally time for her to do something for herself.

* * *

She made sure that Isabella was taken care of for the evening by her nanny, and she prepared dinner. Now all she had to do was wait for him to come home. She really hoped that he did.

It wasn't like he had ever not come home, but he sometimes did come home late.

She could have texted him, but she didn't want to.

Because she didn't want to…

Oh, there was no point trying to play it cool.

She had never done it, not once in her life. There was no point starting now.

She picked her phone up.

I made you dinner.

She waited. And waited for a response. Five interminable minutes went by without a response.

You didn't have to do that.

Obviously. Since I don't normally.

I'll be a little while yet.

Come home soon.

I have to finish some things.

Come home now.

She didn't get a response after that, and she paced around waiting.

Ten minutes later, the door to the penthouse opened. "I don't take orders."

She smiled and smoothed her hands over the tight, emerald green dress she was wearing. "Except, clearly you do take orders. Because here you are."

"A coincidence. I managed to finish everything on time. Why did you make dinner?"

"Because I wanted to… On our wedding night we didn't have dinner together. And I would like to have dinner together. It's different now that we're here. We are making a home together. The island was… Something else. It was removed from this. From reality. And here we are. Here we are together. This is our life. Isabella is going to legally be our daughter soon. Dante, I'm happy."

He raised his dark brows. "I'm glad."

"Are you?"

He lifted a shoulder. "I am as I ever am."

"What does that mean?"

"What did you fix?"

She noted he didn't answer, but she went ahead and let him redirect.

"Steak," she said. She waved her hand toward the table.

He cast a glance at it. "Let's eat."

They went over to the table, and Minerva scampered after him, moving to sit across from him. He was being as opaque and maddening as he'd been the night before.

They started to eat in silence. Minerva was feeling frustrated. But, she wasn't going to say anything. She had a feeling that he was doing all of this by design, she just couldn't work out why.

He seemed to enjoy dinner, and when it was done, she served dessert.

Chocolate lava cake.

She held it out to him, and her heart was pounding. It reminded her of that night on the island. When he had offered cake to her. When she had realized that more than the dessert was a temptation when it came to Dante. He didn't seem to remember that. Didn't seem to get the reference that was happening here at all.

Well. She could fix that.

She stood from her seat and unzipped her dress, letting the top fall down, then letting the rest of it fall along with it. Then she walked over to where he was sitting, completely naked except for her high heels.

"There is a second offering for dessert."

He looked up at her, and he pushed the cake into the center of the table. "I think I'll have that now," he said.

"Not yet," she said.

She leaned forward and unbuttoned his shirt, pushing it down his shoulders. He stood, and she began to work at the belt on his pants, pushing them down his legs. And then, she sank to her knees before him.

"Minerva," he said, his voice rough.

But she ignored the warning in his tone. Ignored it completely as she leaned forward and let her tongue dart out, tasting him. Taking him into her mouth.

He groaned, fisting her hair in his hand, holding her steady as she began to pleasure him.

Her position was submissive, to be sure, but he was the one who was shaking beneath her attentions.

It was exhilarating. Doing to him what he'd done to her so many times. But she hadn't been brave enough to do this. Not before. Not because she didn't think she would like it but because she was afraid he would compare with other women and find her wanting. But she finally understood.

Experience didn't matter. Because no other woman

could bring to the table what she did, here and now. It was their connection. And that was why he was afraid.

He was pulling away from her because everything in the two of them was drawing them to each other. There was no denying it. There was no escaping it. No matter what he thought. She curved her hand around his shaft, stroking him in time as she continued to pleasure him with her mouth.

"Minerva," he growled. "Enough." She did not obey. But then, he pulled on her hair, and she had no choice but to go with him.

She was suddenly embarrassed, because what they'd done was in a public part of the house, and while the nanny had been given instructions to stay in the nursery, there was still the possibility they could have been walked in on. Except... They hadn't been. And she found it very difficult to care one way or another.

Dante picked her up, and began to carry her from the room, shucking the rest of his clothing as he went. The trail of clothes would be a clue if nothing else. But again, she couldn't find it in her to care.

He took her into his bedroom, the first time she had been there since they had returned from the island. And he set her in the middle of it, spreading her across the bedspread.

She parted her thighs for him, touching herself as she watched him, looked at his body while he stood there. At his proud masculinity, at the well-defined muscles.

"You're beautiful," she said.

She had nothing to hide. She felt free.

Joyful.

This was sex as it was meant to be. The exchange was more than just bodies. So much more.

He came down on the mattress with her, thrusting inside her body, and she gripped his shoulders.

"I love you," she whispered.

He growled, pulling out and slamming back home. "I love you," she said again, in case he hadn't heard her the first time.

He had heard.

But he was doing his best not to respond, she could tell.

So she said it. Over and over again until it blurred with whimpers of pleasure. Until she lost herself in it. In him.

Until she was certain that the feelings had come straight from her chest and wound themselves around the two of them, that it had joined in with the physical sensation. That it was a real and living entity in the room with them.

Love.

She loved him.

And she wanted him to love her back.

Wanted it, deserved it. Needed it.

If she wasn't ashamed. No. She wasn't ashamed.

And she didn't feel undeserving. She didn't. She deserved it all. Everything.

He flexed against her, his body hitting that sensitive bundle of nerves between her legs, and she cried out, pleasure breaking over her like a wave.

Love echoing in her like a storm.

"I love you," she said, one last time before he shook and shuttered and gave himself over to his release.

And when he pulled away, she knew what he was doing.

She knew already that he was going to try to run from this like he had tried to run before.

But he had been able to get as far as he had only because she hadn't challenged him. But she was going to challenge him now. Yes, she was. She was going to challenge him and she was going to demand what she wanted. Was going to demand everything she deserved.

"I love you," she said again.

"I don't know what you expect me to say to that."

"Well, I would like for you to say that you love me too."

"I can't," he said.

"Can't or won't?"

"It amounts to the same thing in this instance."

"No. It doesn't. Dante, I know that your childhood was difficult. I know that your mother hurt you. But this is different. We are a family. We can be different."

"No," he said, turning away from her. "That's enough, Minerva. I will care for you, I will take care of you and I will be faithful to you, but asking anything more of me is unnecessary."

"No," Minerva said. "It is not unnecessary. It is absolutely and utterly necessary. Because I have spent my entire life asking nothing. Nothing of myself. Nothing of anyone else. I have never demanded that I get everything because I thought for some reason I didn't deserve it. I always felt like the small sparrow in a family filled with glorious peacocks. And I sank down into that role because I was afraid that if I wanted anything more I would be in pain for all of my life. I was afraid that if I asked for something more it would confirm what I believe secretly. That I couldn't have it. That for some reason I wasn't put together in such a way that I deserved it. But I know better now. I want this life, not just for Isabella, but for me. I want love because I deserve it. And so do you. We don't deserve anything less than everything, Dante, and there's no reason we shouldn't have it."

"There is every reason," he said. "Love is a lie. Love is just waiting for other things to come in and prove themselves more powerful. You know what is more powerful than love? Fear. Addiction. Poverty. These things can destroy love. They can defeat it. Trust me, I've seen it. I have no desire to have it again."

"You see examples of love all around you. All around you. There's no reason you shouldn't accept it for yourself. You know that what you're saying is a lie. If all these things exist in the world, why wouldn't you cling to love?"

"I don't want it," he said, turning back around again, grabbing hold of her arms and staring down at her with his fierce dark eyes. "I don't want you. Don't you understand that?"

"You don't... You don't want me?"

"I tried to pull away from you politely over the last few days. But it's become very clear to me that you don't actually understand what's happening between us. I thought that we needed this marriage, but we don't. There is no reason for the two of us to stay together. No reason at all. I don't need your father's money and Carlo is dead."

"It wasn't about me..."

"No. This is over. I will allow the adoption to continue with you and Isabella. I will withdraw my name."

"You're going to abandon Isabella?"

"It is for the best," he said. "I am no kind of father, and she no longer needs my protection."

"What about you? Don't you think she could possibly need you?"

"No. Nobody needs me. I have money, and I have power, and I wield it well. I wielded it to save you, but now that is over. This is done. We are done."

She sat there, utterly and completely devastated. And

he began to collect his clothes. "I'm going back to the office," he said.

"No... Dante..."

"I will arrange for you to go back to San Diego tomorrow."

"I don't want to go back. This is my home."

"No," he said, his voice ragged. "Your home is with your family. And I am not your family."

And with that, he turned and walked out of the room, leaving her there with her heart broken in pieces around her feet.

She had asked for everything. In return, she had lost the biggest, brightest thing she'd ever dared reach for.

And all she could do was curl up in the center of his bed and cry.

CHAPTER FIFTEEN

When Dante returned from his trip into the office, he could hear a soft, plaintive voice. Wailing. He stood in the middle of the room, unsure of what to do.

His eyes were dry and his lungs felt bruised, and he didn't know how he was going to proceed.

With anything.

Minerva had said that she loved him, and there was something about that that had destroyed everything that he built, and told himself he'd built for the last two decades.

How? How had one small woman and a baby utterly and completely taken all that he believed about himself in the world and turned it upside down?

No one should have the power to do that to him, much less her.

And the baby was still crying. Where was she?

Where was Minerva?

Isabella was not his daughter. And she wouldn't be.

He was going to put a stop to the paperwork that would make her his. Because it was the right thing to do. There was no other alternative. She wouldn't want him for a father anyway, and he would be an utterly useless one at that.

He couldn't love.

He couldn't. The baby was crying, and still Minerva wouldn't come. Neither did the nanny. He didn't understand what was happening.

He could go and get her. Wake one of them, as it was three in the morning and it was likely that they were asleep.

But he shouldn't have to.

It was an infant. Surely, he could handle whatever ailed her.

He charged into the room, and he stopped. He gazed down at her little, helpless body in the center of the crib, and everything inside him froze. She was just so… Small. Helpless. And he was brought again back to his childhood.

To the fact that his parents had created him, his mother had given him life, and had just…

He took a step closer to the crib. Slowly, he bent down, taking the tiny form into his arms and holding her close against his chest. He could hear his own breathing, ragged and intense above the sound of the little girl's crying.

He cradled the back of her downy head, and she rubbed her face against him.

"Are you hungry?"

Something about his voice made her startle, then still.

He didn't know how to make a bottle, but he damn sure could figure it out.

And in the kitchen with one arm, that was what he did, while he cradled her close.

He took her back into the nursery, and sat in the rocking chair, looking down at her as he fed her. And he had no idea how he had wound up here.

With an infant.

But she wouldn't be here. Not in his house. Not anymore. Because she and Minerva were leaving.

Something seized in his chest, and then he felt as if everything broke in half. Like a seismic shock had gone through his entire body. This child could destroy him.

As easily as Minerva could.

That became clear in the moment.

This weak, helpless thing held a power over him that he couldn't understand.

She opened her little mouth, one side of her lip lifting higher than the other, and a small growl escaped her tiny body.

His tiger cub.

He was held in thrall just then. He couldn't look away. Couldn't pull away at all.

What was this feeling?

And more important, why did his mother not feel it for him?

Because one thing he knew for sure, feeling this on one side was absolutely the worst fate that could ever befall a man.

Because it didn't matter that his mother had been so distant, it didn't matter that she had hit him for throwing her birthday party. It didn't matter that she had overdosed and died and left him.

He had loved her still.

And no amount of telling himself he shouldn't, no amount of mourning could bring her back. It was pain. Utter, gut-wrenching pain. The kind that you didn't recover from.

And he would be damned if he ever gave anyone that kind of power over him ever again.

He couldn't.

It would be a blessing. That this was done now. Because Isabella would never remember him.

And someday, Minerva would find a man who could give her everything she wanted.

Already that thought hurt too much.

He laid Isabella down in the crib, comforted by the fact that she would have no memory of ever having held him.

But as he walked out of the room, he could still feel the impression of her tiny body cradled in his arms.

And he knew that he would never be able to forget.

CHAPTER SIXTEEN

THANKFULLY, DANTE WAS not around when Minerva, the nanny and Isabella grimly loaded themselves onto his private plane and charted a course for San Diego.

She tried to hold her head high when she arrived at her parents' house, but the minute that she saw her mother she crumpled completely.

Her mother ushered her to sit down, and held her, and didn't say anything.

The entire story poured out of Minerva, all of it. The truth.

"But she will legally be yours?" her mother asked. "Soon?"

"Yes," she said. "Dante had all the paperwork processing. It's all over. But it's been… A nightmare. And we did everything we could to protect her. Everything we thought was right. I'm sorry that I didn't tell you. But…"

"Of course you didn't feel like you could chance anyone knowing," she said.

"I didn't. And it isn't because I didn't trust you…"

"You're her mother," Elizabeth said. "And you would do anything to protect her. Of course you did this. Of course."

Minerva nodded miserably and watched her mother hold Isabella.

"But he broke your heart?" Elizabeth asked.

"Yes," Minerva said. "He broke my heart. I don't know what to do about it. I don't know how I'm going to survive."

"You just will," Elizabeth said. "You will because you have her to live for."

"I just want to sit down and give up."

"But you won't do that either. It's okay to want to do that, as long as you don't."

"I just… I think it would've been fine if I hadn't demanded that he loved me. But I did. I demanded it because I thought… Don't I deserve it? Don't I deserve to have somebody love me?"

"Of course you do," her mother said.

"I know that I'm not beautiful like Violet, or successful. That I'm not magnetic like Maximus, and I'm definitely not a billionaire."

"What does that have to do with anything?"

"I just… They are exceptional."

"Minerva, you are now and always have been exceptionally you. Right down to this whole harebrained situation with the baby. You are utterly and uniquely yourself. And no one has ever been able to convince you to be anything but that. You're strong. And you're stubborn."

"No I'm not. I always just kind of… Go along with things."

"If you think that, then you don't even know yourself all that well."

"Well. Maybe I don't."

"Look at yourself. You stole this baby. You protected her with your life. You roped Dante into everything in spite of the fact that he is a terrifying and powerful man to most everyone else. Very few people would have dared to do what you did."

"I had to."

"Then you married him. Then you demanded that he

love you. Love is not less. It's brave. You're very brave. That isn't something that can be taught. I'm proud of you, Minerva. Not just for everything you did before, not just for what you did with Isabella, but for how you handled Dante."

Minerva felt broken and easily wounded, but she forced a smile, and allowed a moment of happiness in.

"It's going to be all right," Elizabeth said.

"But what if it isn't?"

"Because Dante is a smart man. And you are an exceptional woman. I don't think he's actually going to let you get away."

"And if he does?"

"Then he's not a smart man. But you are still an exceptional woman."

Minerva thought about that all through the rest of the evening and as she laid Isabella down to sleep.

Her mother was trying to help, and she knew that. But in the back of her mind she wondered if fairy tales were for other girls.

For the bright, the exceptional, the beautiful.

Then she looked down at Isabella.

No.

Of course that wasn't true. Of course it wasn't...

It took her breath away how obvious it seemed all of a sudden as she looked down at her own daughter.

What she deserved in life had nothing to do with looks. Or money. Success. It had nothing to do with what a boy at a dance said about her. Had nothing to do with whether or not the kids at school liked her or thought she was pretty.

She had value all on her own.

And so did Minerva.

Whether Dante ever realized it or not.

CHAPTER SEVENTEEN

"WHY IS MY sister back home?"

Dante looked up from his desk to see Maximus standing in his office doorway. No one should be standing in his office doorway. He paid his secretary well to keep that from happening. And Maximus really shouldn't be standing there.

"She missed her family," he said, keeping his expression neutral.

"Why is that?"

He pressed his hands on his desk and stood. "If you didn't know already that we're divorcing, then let me be the first to tell you. But I assume you did already."

"I didn't want to have to kill you, Dante, but I will."

"Maximus, I know you excelled in boxing at school, but I'm a street fighter. You're not going to kill me."

A dark glint shone in his friend's eyes and Dante had the sense that he had gone too far. "Your mistake is always underestimating me, friend. You don't know everything that I could do to you."

"Whether you believe it or not, Minerva was in control of all of this. And her leaving… I asked her to go to protect her."

"My mom told me the whole story. I know Isabella

isn't your baby. I had a hard time believing it in the beginning, I have to admit."

"So, she told you what Minerva did?"

Maximus nodded. "And if my sister wasn't crushed, I wouldn't be here. I would assume that you had done what you did to protect her, and now the deal was done but obviously something happened between the two of you."

Dante lifted a shoulder. "I won't lie to you. She was my wife."

"What happened to your Catholicism?"

"Tell me," Dante said, his temper fraying, "what would be the greatest sin? To divorce your sister or keep her with me for the rest of my life. You know me, Maximus. You know that I'm not…part of your world, not part of the one I came from. Not part of Min's or Isabella's. You know that I don't know how to… I don't know how to be part of a family. Not even yours."

"Your own choice, Dante. We've always wanted you to be part of us."

"And I don't know how to do it," Dante said, frustration eating at him. "Tell me. How should I be a good husband to Min? You don't know how to be a husband. What can you tell me?"

"Nothing about that. Though I had thought that you were a decent human being. My father opened his home to you and I called you brother. Was I wrong to do that?"

Dante had told himself he didn't care about much. But hearing his friend ask him if he was wrong to call him brother made something crumble inside him. The bit of heart, of humanity, he had left.

"If you care about Minerva at all…" Maximus continued.

"I do," he bit out. "I love her."

The words made the back of his neck prickle. Made

sweat bead at his temples. He loved her. It was the thing he feared most because it was the one thing he could not control.

Not ever.

And he'd sworn he would never...

Minerva King.

She had been a girl when he'd first met her. How had she reached around inside him and changed him like this?

How had she become his dearest dream and greatest nightmare all at once?

"Then why are you doing this to the both of you? Go back to her."

His throat was dry. "I... I can't."

Maximus sighed heavily. "Please don't make me talk about feelings."

"*Dio.* Don't."

"You're forcing it. You're forcing me to."

"Can I stop you?"

"Quit being a jackass and go to my sister. Minerva is the kindest and most caring person I know. The kindest and most caring person I have ever known. If she loves you, you've done well for yourself, Dante."

"I never wanted to love another person again," he said.

"Well, what a tragedy. You found someone to love, who loves you very much in return. Some people would call that an unexpected gift. A lot like trying to rob a man at gunpoint only to get offered a chance at a new life. That was brave of you, to take that."

"Desperate," he said. "And I vowed I wouldn't be desperate again."

"Well, here you are I guess," Maximus said, looking around. "In all this glass and chrome. Not desperate at all. But meanwhile, across the country, there is a woman who loves you and a child who needs a father." He turned to go, then stopped. "And you know, the rest of us are fond of you too. My father reached out to you that day. Maybe it's time you reached back, brother."

And without another word, Maximus walked out of his office, as if he hadn't been there at all. And Dante was left with a burning sensation in his chest.

He loved her.

And she was not dead. She was not gone. And he... he had pushed her away because he had no earthly idea what else to do other than...

Accept it.

The idea filled him with dread. The idea of loving her, loving Isabella.

He looked around his office. His glass and chrome. This tower, surrounded by that wall he'd built for himself.

His security.

And suddenly it all meant nothing.

Suddenly it was not a protection, but a barrier. A barrier between himself and Minerva. Brick after brick, built to keep him safe. Built to keep him separate.

It could not endure.

Not anymore.

He loved her.

And it was a gift to a heart that had given up on loving ever again.

But most of all, she might still love him.

Him, a man from nothing. A man who knew nothing of how to love except getting slapped in the face for it.

She had loved him first. Before he knew how to show it or how to admit to himself that he loved her too.

But he couldn't stay safe. He couldn't stay on this side of the wall, not if he wanted her.

Suddenly it all seemed clear.

For love he would.

For Minerva, he had to. His girl, his *woman*. Who loved books and knew that his home had been patterned after *Swiss Family Robinson*. Who understood, somehow, these sharp, strange emotions inside himself that not even he understood.

He was done surviving.

He wanted to live.

CHAPTER EIGHTEEN

IT HAD BEEN a week of feeling like her heart was beating with ground glass inside it, painful and sharp. Minerva was tired of it. Tired of herself. But she was also resolved.

She'd started trying to figure out what she wanted from her life too.

With the help of some of Violet's business consultants she'd begun feeling out what it would take to start job training for single mothers, with special focus on those recovering from addiction, depression, or any woman trying to escape an abusive relationship.

The KatiBella Foundation was on its way to becoming a reality, and Minerva was happy to know that she could honor her friend's memory that way.

And that she could honor her daughter, her inspiration for the foundation in the first place.

But she was still…

She missed him. She loved him. She hated that she did.

She felt utterly, thoroughly grown up. She felt old, in fact. She couldn't believe that just a few months ago she'd come home with Isabella. That only a year ago she'd been in Rome, an innocent university student without a care in the world.

She felt like she had a world of care on her shoulders now.

But she wouldn't change it.

No.

She was…changed. She was in love. And she loved Isabella. She was heartbroken, but she was stronger somehow even in that brokenness. She couldn't explain it, but it was true.

Isabella was asleep, and Minerva hadn't had any luck sleeping at all lately. Instead of even trying, she stole down to the beach and looked out at the waves.

The moon reflected on the water, the sound reverberating around her.

And her heart went tight in her chest.

She missed him.

She wanted to see this with him. To be on the beach with him again. Kiss him again.

She knew what it meant to want someone now. To love them.

She also knew beyond a shadow of a doubt that she hadn't been heartbroken four years ago at her father's party. She'd been wounded, but not heartbroken.

This didn't feel like shame. There was pride mixed in with it. It didn't feel like sadness, because it felt more brittle. More aged. Like it had maybe always been inside her. This sense of what it was like to not have Dante.

She hated him for teaching her this.

But she loved him for teaching her so many other things. Even when he wasn't here.

She put her hand on her stomach and watched the waves crash into shore, the whitecaps visible even in the darkness. He might have given her more than a broken heart, and she really had no idea what she would do if her period didn't start in the next couple of days.

"You'll be okay," she whispered to herself.

Because she would be. She had become the heroine,

over the course of these weeks, these months. And because of that, she knew everything would be all right in the end.

"Min."

The sound of her name rose up above the waves, and she turned, her heart stalling out completely when she saw him standing there. His face looked haggard in the moonlight. The hollows of his cheeks more pronounced, dark circles under his eyes that spoke of the same lack of sleep she had been experiencing.

"Dante."

For some reason, as Dante stood there on the beach staring at Minerva he felt more like that boy he'd been at fourteen, holding a gun he didn't want to use, his hands shaking, than he ever had in the intervening years since.

Perhaps it was because he was only standing there, with a heart pounding heavily in his chest that he didn't want to use.

But he had no choice.

After Maximus had come to see him, he had understood.

He had known beyond a shadow of a doubt that it was already too late to protect him. They had gotten under his skin, these two females who had moved into his home, his life.

Minerva, his tigress, and the tiger cub. Everything was upside down because of them.

Everything destroyed.

He had tried to make it right. He had gone back to work. He had tried to put another brick between himself and his past, but the problem was that the past had crashed through the wall and bled into his future.

It had made him turn Minerva away, and all he could

think of was the incredible pain that had caused him. And then he thought he was going to have to build the wall again. In front of the time he spent with her. The nights making love. In front of those sun-drenched days on the private island.

In front of that night when he'd held Isabella in his arms and understood what it meant to be a father.

And he began to do that. Laying bricks. Over his heart, yet again. But he had realized that he didn't want to stop thinking about them, even if it hurt.

And so he was here. Because he didn't know where else to be.

"What are you doing here?"

"I'm here for you. I'm here to explain."

"It had better be a good explanation," she said, clenching and unclenching her hands into fists.

"I know," he said. "Minerva, it isn't that I don't believe in love. I do. But the problem is that I know what it's like to love someone who can't love you back. I know what it's like to be ill-used and abused and to not be able to let go. To want so badly for another person to care. She couldn't care. No matter how much I wanted my mother to care, she couldn't.

"And it broke me in ways that I can't begin to describe. Except to tell you that I was hollowed out by the time your father met me. I wanted to be ready to shoot him if I needed to get money, to get food. Instead, I found myself accepting his charity. And I thought to myself, *He's offering charity, he might well have disgraceful intentions for me*, and I thought that I could accept that too. I had lost my humanity somewhere in there. I… I lost my soul. Because I quit letting myself love.

"And even when I joined your family, it was the same. I told myself that I was different because I wasn't blood. I held Isabella the other night, and I knew blood had nothing to do with anything. It isn't because of him that I've been distant from your father. It's because of me. Because I never wanted to accept the gift that he offered me. This place in the family. Because I didn't want to need anyone or anything.

"I have been building walls ever since I escaped from Rome. Building walls between myself and the poverty that I had once. Because I thought they would keep me safe. Because I thought they would make it so I couldn't go back. But all they do is keep people out. People that you want. People that you need. And I can't live that way anymore. I can't. Because you showed me a better way. You showed me a better life.

"Minerva, I used to think of you as a mouse, but that isn't true at all. You're a tigress. You are brave and brilliant and you have taught me bravery. I'm sorry that I couldn't stand up and seize hold of it when I needed to. When you asked me to. But I want to do it now.

"Minerva, I am humbled by the gift that is you. You are the most brilliant woman who has ever been. Or ever will be. You are not second, you are first. It's only that my heart was blind. Because that's what it is when you take love away from yourself. You rob yourself of your senses. You make it so that you cannot truly see. But I see now. I see now because of you."

"Me?"

"Yes," he said. "You. You had to become a woman before I could have you, Min. And I... I should have waited until I became the man you deserved before I ever touched you."

"Dante," she said, flinging herself into his arms, wrapping them around his neck. And kissing him.

"That's it?" His voice was rough. "You're not even going to make me work for it?"

"We already worked for it. You already worked for it. And you know what? Even if you hadn't come to your senses, you taught me something. You taught me to demand everything."

"Good. Keep demanding it."

"I will. I will. Dante, you are the most brilliant man I have ever known. And I am really glad that I had to force you to marry me."

"I *want* to marry you again," he said.

"Really?"

"Yes. Not for spectators, not for show. I want to marry you again because I want to."

"Well. I'd like that."

"And then maybe this time your brother and father will want to kill me."

"Well..." she said. "They might."

"Why?"

She twisted her hands in front of her. "There is a small possibility that I might be a pregnant bride."

"What?"

"I'm late. And... We have been doing something that sometimes means..."

"Are you sure?"

"No. I'm not sure. If devastated broken hearts cause missed periods then that could be the problem. It's just that I think more likely it was pregnancy."

"But Isabella is only..."

"I know," she said.

"I'm going to be a father. Two children."

She laughed. "I know," she said. "Isn't that amazing?"

"I..."

His life flashed before his eyes. As if he was dying.

Except he wasn't dying. He was living. And he saw himself, that boy in Rome with the shaking gun, angry and distrustful in private school, starting his first business endeavor, Minerva asking him to protect her. Him demanding she marry him.

All of it had brought him here. To this moment. There were no walls. And he was in no danger of going back. It was impossible. He had been afraid all this time that he might slip back into the slums by accident. But it had never been about the slums. They didn't matter at all. What mattered was this. The people in his life. And he would not lose that. He wouldn't lose them.

And he would never lose the love in his heart.

It had been said that Dante Fiori could condemn a man to any level of hell he chose with just the lift of his brow. That was a fabrication. But what was true was that Minerva King could send him to heaven with just the touch of her lips to his.

"I love you," he said.

"I love you too," she said.

And he knew that he would never be alone again.

He had a family.

Not tied together by blood, but by love.

And that was the most powerful force of all.

EPILOGUE

SHE WAS A pregnant bride. There was no denying that fact. But fortunately, they were technically already married.

Though, that did not stop her father from giving Dante an endless hard time. And it didn't stop her brother, Maximus, from giving him the evil eye, but then, Maximus hadn't stopped that at any point over the last few months.

Minerva wasn't put off by any of it. She was happy. The adoption for Isabella had gone through a couple of months earlier, and she and Dante were legally what they had already been in their hearts: her parents.

She was acting as their flower girl, even though Dante had to carry her down the aisle. And when the wedding was over, since the only guests were family and very close friends, when Minerva threw the bouquet, her sister, Violet, caught it, then stared at it like it was a live cockroach.

"Marriage might be coming for you," Minerva commented.

"Never," Violet said. "Though I like the colors in this bouquet. I could make a very nice makeup palette out of it. Use it as inspiration. I'll call it Minerva's Bouquet. The proceeds can go to KatiBella."

"That is the closest I will ever get to being a mogul," Minerva said.

"You could be one if you wanted to."

She put her hand on her stomach, and she looked at Dante, holding her daughter. "I'm everything that I want to be," she said.

"What's that?" Violet asked.

Minerva looked at her sister, her parents, her brother. Then again at her daughter and her husband.

"Loved."

And she was. For all her days.

* * * * *

COMING SOON!

We really hope you enjoyed reading this book. If you're looking for more romance, be sure to head to the shops when new books are available on

Thursday 20th March

To see which titles are coming soon, please visit

millsandboon.co.uk/nextmonth

MILLS & BOON

Coming next month

A SCANDAL MADE IN LONDON
Lucy King

'Miss Cassidy?' said the concierge a moment later, his voice bouncing off the walls and making her jump. 'Mr Knox will see you now.'

Finally.

'The lift on the right will take you directly to the penthouse.'

'Thank you,' she said, mustering up a quick smile as she got to her feet and headed for said lift on legs that felt like jelly.

The doors closed behind her and she used the smooth ten-second ascent to try and calm her fluttering stomach and slow her heart-rate. It would be fine. She and Theo were both civilised adults. They might be chalk and cheese, but they could handle this. What was the worst that could happen? It wasn't as if she was expecting anything from him. She just had a message to deliver. It would be fine.

But when the lift doors opened and she stepped out, all thoughts of civility and messages shot from her head because all she could focus on was Theo.

He was standing at the far end of the wide hall, with his back to a huge floor to ceiling window, feet apart, arms crossed over his chest. The interminable rain of the morning had stopped and sunshine had broken through the thick cloud. It flooded in through the window, making a silhouette of him, emphasising his imposing height and the powerful breadth of the shoulders. Although clothed in jeans and a white shirt, he looked like some sort of god, in total control, master of all he surveyed, and she couldn't help thinking that if he'd been going for maximum impact, maximum intimidation, he'd nailed it.

Swallowing down the nerves tangling in her throat, Kate started walking towards him, her hand tightening on the strap of her cross-body bag that she wore like a shield. His gaze was on her as she approached, his expression unreadable. He didn't move a muscle. His jaw was set and he exuded chilly distance, which didn't bode well for what was to come, but then nor did the heat suddenly shooting along her veins and the desire surging through her body. That kind of head-scrambling reaction she could do without. She didn't need to remember how he'd made her feel when he'd held her, kissed her, been inside her. She needed to focus.

'Hi,' she said as she drew closer, his irresistible magnetism tugging her forwards even as she wanted to flee.

'What are you doing here?'

The ice cold tone of his voice stopped her in her tracks a couple of feet away, obliterating the heat, and she inwardly flinched. So that was the way this was going to go. No 'how are you, let me take your jacket, would you like a drink'. He wasn't pleased to see her. He wasn't pleased at all.

Okay.

'We need to talk,' she said, beginning to regret her decision to deliver this information in person. With hindsight, maybe an email would have sufficed.

'There's nothing to talk about.'

'I'm afraid there is.'

His dark brows snapped together. 'Your sister?'

'She's fine,' she said. 'Thank you for what you did for her.'

'You're welcome.'

'Did you get my note?' Shortly after he'd fixed her finances she'd sent him a letter of thanks. It had seemed the least she could do. She hadn't had a response.

He gave a brief nod. 'Yes.'

'She loves the flowers.'

'Good.'

'It was thoughtful.'

'It was nothing.'

Right. Beneath the force of his unwavering gaze and impenetrable demeanour Kate quailed for a moment and was summoning up the courage to continue when he spoke.

'Are you in trouble?' he asked sharply.

'That's one way of putting it.'

'What?'

'Sorry, bad joke,' she said with a weak laugh although there was nothing remotely funny about any of this.

'Get to the point, Kate,' he snapped. 'I'm busy.'

Right. Yes. Good plan. She pulled her shoulders back and lifted her chin. 'There's no easy way to say this, Theo,' she said, sounding far calmer than she felt, 'so here goes. There's been a...*consequence*... to our...afternoon together.'

A muscle ticked in his jaw. 'What kind of consequence?'

'The nine-month kind.'

There was a moment of thundering silence, during which Kate's heart hammered while Theo seemed to freeze and pale. 'What exactly are you saying?' he said, his voice tight and low and utterly devoid of expression.

'I'm pregnant.'

Continue reading
A SCANDAL MADE IN LONDON
Lucy King

Available next month
www.millsandboon.co.uk

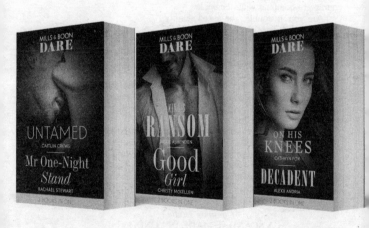

MILLS & BOON

HEROES

At Your Service

Experience all the excitement of a gripping thriller, with an intense romance at its heart. Resourceful, true-to-life women and strong, fearless men face danger and desire - a killer combination!

JOIN US ON SOCIAL MEDIA!

Stay up to date with our latest releases, author news and gossip, special offers and discounts, and all the behind-the-scenes action from Mills & Boon...

 millsandboon

 millsandboonuk

 millsandboon

It might just be true love...

MILLS & BOON

THE HEART OF ROMANCE

A ROMANCE FOR EVERY KIND OF READER

MODERN

Prepare to be swept off your feet by sophisticated, sexy and seductive heroes, in some of the world's most glamourous and romantic locations, where power and passion collide.
8 stories per month.

HISTORICAL

Escape with historical heroes from time gone by. Whether your passion is for wicked Regency Rakes, muscled Vikings or rugged Highlanders, awaken the romance of the past.
6 stories per month.

MEDICAL

Set your pulse racing with dedicated, delectable doctors in the high-pressure world of medicine, where emotions run high and passion, comfort and love are the best medicine.
6 stories per month.

True Love

Celebrate true love with tender stories of heartfelt romance, from the rush of falling in love to the joy a new baby can bring, and a focus on the emotional heart of a relationship.
8 stories per month.

Desire

Indulge in secrets and scandal, intense drama and plenty of sizzli hot action with powerful and passionate heroes who have it all: wealth, status, good looks…everything but the right woman.
6 stories per month.

HEROES

Experience all the excitement of a gripping thriller, with an inten romance at its heart. Resourceful, true-to-life women and strong, fearless men face danger and desire - a killer combination!
8 stories per month.

DARE

Sensual love stories featuring smart, sassy heroines you'd want as a best friend, and compelling intense heroes who are worthy of the
4 stories per month.

To see which titles are coming soon, please visit

millsandboon.co.uk/nextmonth

LET'S TALK

Romance

For exclusive extracts, competitions
and special offers, find us online:

- **f** facebook.com/millsandboon
- **🐦** @MillsandBoon
- **📷** @MillsandBoonUK

Get in touch on 01413 063232

For all the latest titles coming soon, visit
millsandboon.co.uk/nextmonth